THE HUMMINGBIRD HEART

A.G. HOWARD

PROLOGUE

The outskirts of Westminster, London—1891

Mama is a hummingbird.

Willomena watched from the shadows of the empty big top as her mother glided from one trapeze to another—soaring over a net. From up high, she looked as small as the wasp-sized bird Willomena had seen a month earlier sipping nectar from a hollyhock. She had thought it an insect, until Momma bade her listen to the high-pitched song of its wings.

Now the ropes rattled with Mama's movements—playing their own tune—a rhythmic creak. A slant of sunlight filtered in from the open flap, warming the top of Willomena's head while a summer-scented breeze turned through her long curls.

Squatting beneath the benches, Willomena busily gathered her prizes: discarded cigars—she liked those best for the scorched, sweet smell; farthings, crusted brown with mud; red, green, and blue ticket stubs to paste on paper and make pictures.

Everything she found she dropped into a basket with her doll ... a porcelain, cream-skinned beauty with real hair the color of a wheat field.

"See my treasures, Tildey?" Willomena grinned at her doll and scratched her itchy nose, her hands grubby with dirt. Mama wouldn't mind. Dirty hands made the tape grip better. And Willomena's turn to practice came after Mama's. She rubbed her fingers on her leotard when a glistening spatter of crushed stained-glass caught her attention.

"What'd you find there, Dragonfly?"

Willomena patted her papa's shoe fondly before looking up at his face. "A rainbow ... a diamond rainbow." She licked dirt from her lips and smiled.

"Ahhh." Papa crouched next to her, folding his stature to fit beneath the tallest bench. He tweaked her nose. "Be careful. That rainbow will bite."

"Don't discourage the child." A strange man's voice erupted from behind her father.

Papa startled upright, standing in front of Willomena to block her view. She peered between his knees.

The speaker stood in the tent's opening, a black, shadowy giant against the blinding light outside.

"Even at the age of five," the shadowy figure said, "she's already seeking treasure in everything she finds. If that doesn't prove she's fated for him, I don't know what will."

Papa tightened his stance. "You son of a—"

"Now, let's not get personal." Three more men had appeared behind the first one, slapping something that looked like sticks across their palms. "How long did you think it would take him to find you? How long did you think you could keep up the pretense?"

"We have friends here ... they'll not stand by blindly—"

"Blinders can be easily bought. Get the girl."

Willomena sucked in a breath, frozen in place, too scared to know where to run: to Papa or to her hiding place. Grunting, Papa shoved her toward the lowest end of the benches. She ducked to roll under them, her hair catching on the splinters of a seat. As her body completed its turn, the hairs ripped free and she yelped at the pricking in her scalp.

"Run, Willomena! Run and hide!" Her mother's strained voice drifted from the heights, pelting Willomena's ears like hot sand.

"Tildey..." Willomena stretched her arm to fish her doll from the basket. One man snatched her wrist but Papa jumped him from behind and broke his hold. Scrambling out onto the other side with Tildey, Willomena ran for the center ring. Her legs pumped, the dirt beneath her taped feet shifting.

Mama and Papa had practiced this with her over and over. She knew where to go; she knew to fold her body up tight into a space so small no one would think to look for her there.

Yet they never told her Papa would be groaning, that he would gasp with each breath. Willomena's heart pounded, her chest hurt ... maybe Papa's did, too. She glanced across her shoulder, sliding to a stop when she saw him on the ground. One man rubbed Papa's face into the diamond rainbow while another pounded his shoulders with a stick.

"Papa?"

His neck jerked back to expose his face—stained with dirt and oozing blood. "Get..." He coughed and spat out bits of glass slick with red smears. "Get out ... Willomena!"

She started to back away, shaking her head, fingers twisted in Tildey's blue pinafore. Her throat tightened on a sob. She looked up to the trapeze platform to see Mama wrestling with a rope that had bound around her ankle. Another one of the strangers climbed the ladder to get to her.

Papa struggled on the ground. He overpowered one of the men and pushed up to his knees. They screamed at him in that foreign language now ... in the English words only Papa understood.

The second man lifted his stick. A thud sounded when the

blunt end burrowed into Papa's skull. He slumped to the ground and gurgled once. Mama screamed from overhead and Willomena's arms tightened around Tildey.

Tears blurred her view and an ugly silence stitched up her tummy, making it coil tight. "Papa?" Her voice shivered like the leaves on the trees outside.

The two men rushed toward her, clucking their tongues as if she were a frightened puppy. Her legs didn't want to move away from center ring. They wanted to run to Papa ... to wake him. Her gaze darted toward the tent's front flap. Where were all their friends? Why did no one come?

"Run!" Upon hearing Mama's yell above, Willomena dashed toward the back end of the tent. From behind, one of the men caught her elbow, his grip harsh and rough like burlap.

Willomena howled as he tugged her up in midair by one arm. Her legs dangled, her other arm hugging Tildey with all her might. He threw her over his shoulder, knocking the air from her. When she gulped a breath, his tobacco scent sucked through her nose—bitter-sweet like the dark candies Mama liked, and warm like the rum Willomena always smelled on the ring master's clothes. But the stink of the stranger's sweat was stronger, and made her nose burn.

Willomena lifted her head upon hearing Mama's cries. Through a curtain of hair, she watched her dive from the trapeze platform to escape the man on the ladder. She floated toward the net. The abandoned ropes swayed up above her, still creaking as her white leotard flashed like a shimmery cloud descending from the sky.

The fourth man appeared in the shadows beside the net, holding something shiny and silver. With one stroke of his hand, he sliced the anchor lines in the instant Mama stretched out her arms to land.

The mesh net plummeted beneath her, as useless against her weight as a spider's web. A sickening crack broke the air when she hit the ground like a bag of potatoes. The ropes stopped swinging. No more creaking songs. Nothing but stillness.

"Mama!" Willomena's cries shattered in her own ears. Her throat swelled with screams so loud they hurt her lungs. A canvas sack encased her head in blackness. Something inside of her snapped. She screamed again, using Tildey's stiff body to beat the man holding her. When that didn't work, Willomena kicked her legs out like Papa had taught her to do ... like the circus mules that pulled the wagons.

Hot tears drenched her face; her hair clung to the moisture and itched against her cheeks. Shoes crunched over the dirt, walking toward her.

"Fiery little thing," a voice rattled in Italian. Words she understood but didn't want to. "She's going to need that where she's going."

"So, what are our instructions?" The one holding her squeezed tight around her ribs, forcing her to stop struggling.

"First we mark her for the boss." Willomena felt the knife's cold blade raking along her leotard at the small of her back, the fabric catching it with tiny pops. "She belongs to him now. Hell. She always has."

PART I

Not all those who wander are lost.
~J.R.R. Tolkien

ONE

Diurnal assignments for Friday, April 15, 1904:
1. Oil the carousel's cranking rods and ring gear; 2.
Complete design for new ride; 3. Present Lord Desmond
with a written request for funds; 4. Buy a birthday gift for
Emilia in Worthington.

Julian Thornton ceased writing on the assignment page in his log and resituated the pocket-sized leather-bound book in his lap. Leaning his head against the tree trunk behind him, he flipped to the back pages reserved for his inner musings. Fountain pen to paper, he opened his mind, giving voice to the ink.

> *Emilia is sixteen today. My sister—who still occupies my memories as a fine-boned, pink babe swaddled in blankets—is a lady. And I have ne'er felt more inept in our relations. She has sprouted wings and eaten her way out of her cocoon. Now she flies above me, leaving me a mere shadow on the ground. I am an echo fluttering beneath, always a few steps behind or ahead—never in sync.*
>
> *I can no longer talk to her. She's too high to hear me. The only secrets we share are those bequeathed us through our lineage; we were both born of a ghost story, after all. And though most people would consider that impossible, to me, the*

chance of death crossing over into life is more fathomable than the quirks of the fairer sex.

After nineteen years of living alongside ladies, I find that there is an inexplicable pull between the antipoles—male and female—a negative and positive charge that when left uncontained leads to an explosive combustion ... an electron-spin so effulgent it renders anyone in its path blinded by the resulting holocaust.

"Hmm ... so that's how you plan to defeat us, aye?"

The same instant the familiar voice broke into Julian's concentration, two tell-tale drizzles of red syrup oozed down from the branches overhead, landing soundly upon his log's opened pages. The ink melted into sticky purple-black puddles.

Damn. Inhaling the magnolia-spiced morning air, Julian managed to keep the oath beneath his breath. He'd always been taught one shouldn't curse in the presence of a lady ... he supposed it applied even if said lady was in a tree, cozied up in the branches like a narcoleptic monkey.

He drew out his handkerchief and snapped it open to dab the sickly-sweet pools of raspberry ice from his journal's page, hoping to salvage the folded parchment beneath, whereupon he had drawn the designs for his newest amusement ride. "Defeat *whom*, Willow?" He set his book aside along with his pen, regretting the invitation to talk the moment he'd offered it.

"Your mortal enemy, of course. *Women.* You plan on incinerating us with your electron-spin."

Julian's back tensed at her successive snort and his ears grew hot. Having had eleven years to grow up alongside one another, Willow knew how he abhorred anyone reading over his shoulder. He flashed a glare up at her.

"Say, where are your spectacles?" she asked.

Two more sticky droplets fell, this time landing on a snowy magnolia, one of thousands upon the shrubs that surrounded his oak tree like castle walls. Over the past twelve months, Julian had always found solace here in the mornings. However, for the last few weeks his placid kingdom had been stormed by this most formidable foe— quiet as a lizard and clandestine as a cat.

"I've misplaced them," he grumbled in reference to his missing spectacles, turning his head away. He only required them for reading, but often wore them to help people differentiate between himself and his twin brother. "They've been absent for days. Hadn't you noticed?" Hearing a slurp from the leafy canopy which shaded him from the sun, he waited for his intruder's reply.

"*Naturalmente.* I knew something was different. Assumed your head was shrinking or some such. Back to the subject ... best stop your wool gathering. At this rate, you'll never get your finance request ready in time. You have to pitch it this morning so you may leave for Worthington before noon. Emilia will never forgive you if you're not back in time for her birthday dinner tonight."

Julian folded his stained handkerchief and tucked it in his vest pocket. "And pray tell, how am I to make progress with you blotting out my notes like the wrath of God on judgment day, *Willomena*?"

A distinctive plop parted the ankle-high grass beside him where Willow tossed down her raspberry ice from above. Julian winced; he'd not meant to spout off her full name. Although it always snapped her to attention, it also sometimes had the strangest impact on her mood—a saddening effect. As beautiful as the name was, he had no idea why it would sadden her. Just one of Willow's many quirks.

Gnats started to gather on the ice's slushy remains beside him. Julian grinned. Eighteen years old, yet still the woman wouldn't breakfast on a kidney omelet or seed biscuit like the rest of the cultured world. And damned if he didn't find it downright charming.

A rustle of fabric stirred overhead. Even without looking up, he could see her in his mind's eye—a dizzying sequence of grace and agility despite her inelegant pose.

She would be hanging upside down now, her skirts an inverted tumble of plain cotton that mushroomed her upper torso and head. Her chemise would come untucked enough to reveal the prismatic hummingbird tattoo at the small of her lower back—the mysterious marking which she'd never explained—and her lacy pantalets would serve as the only pretense of modesty or whimsy she'd allow herself.

A gust from her movements raked his plaited hair so the shoulder length braid struggled to wrestle free of its leather tie. Still no need to look.

The branches creaked. She was swinging. Back and forth, gaining momentum until her hands could find purchase on a branch sturdy enough to support her slight weight. She grunted, and a sympathetic vibration shuddered in his throat.

He rubbed his fresh-shaved chin. Eyes closed, he pictured her knees releasing, her body a fluid sweep of olive-gold Italian skin as her bare feet drifted to the ground with all the poise of apple blossoms riding a breezy downdraft.

Just as he envisioned her dropping, he felt her standing next to him, radiating warmth from the thrill of descent.

He looked up to meet her gaze and she frowned, the excess of her skirts folded over one arm. Her dark auburn hair draped to her waist, still holding the ravaged crimp of braids not fully brushed out. Tremors skipped through

Julian's fingers—a repressed desire to tame the tousled mess and return it to some semblance of order.

"I know"—he strummed his pen against his leg—"you don't like me using your full name. I will try to respect that. But you must respect my wishes, as well. No more reading over my shoulder."

She bowed to him then—an acrobat acknowledging her captive audience—and the little toe of her right foot wriggled within inches of the collapsed mound of raspberry ice.

He applauded and at last she smiled. He responded with a grin of his own. An effortless response, partly due to the jagged, crimson stain streaked across her lips and the slight gap between her central incisors—the one flaw in her straight white teeth. But the ease with which she made him smile was more than her smudged appearance.

Julian couldn't keep company with any other woman— save his sister, mother, or Aunt Enya—without breaking into an arctic sweat and losing all function of his tongue. Willomena, however, was different. Whatever a lady might do in any given situation, he could rest assured she would do the complete opposite. Which put her, in his mind, in the league of a man. And men he understood.

Willow trounced onto her posterior without any pretense of straightening her skirt. "You've been careless today." Her slender ankles poked out from the billows of dusty fabric and crossed casually. "You missed a cranking gear. And you failed to oil the center beam."

Considering her statement, he noted the oily splotches at her wrists and on her gathered cuffs. "I was in a hurry. Desmond and his wife are to leave sometime this afternoon. Thank you for double-checking the rides."

She shrugged. "I had nothing better to do. You might wish to talk to your brother, though. One of the unicorns is in need of a tail replacement before the guests arrive in June. A squirrel must have nested in it over the winter. I would tell Nick myself, but Lord only knows where he's about this morning."

"A nest, you say?" Julian wasn't surprised. It was the biggest drawback to using real horse hair on the carousel. He scooted over to share the trunk's support with Willow. She propped her back close enough that their shoulders brushed. His nostrils detected raspberries mingled with her unique fragrance—as exotic and intoxicating as jasmine and black opium—and a sudden and sharp pang crimped his gut. His mouth watered. Hunger, he assured himself. He'd eaten very little breakfast. "So, my brother's missing again?" Julian noted the quiver of her black coppery-tipped lashes upon his query.

"I had such a magnificent prank planned for today, what with the maids cleaning the townhouse for Emilia's celebration. Now I've no one to help me execute it." Her frown transformed to a grin of wicked delight that brought to mind a deranged fairy. "It has to do with a box of snails and old Miss Abbot's obsession with clean ceilings. It's a simple enough ruse. I merely need someone tall to boost me on their shoulders so the snails can suction in place. You could help me..."

Julian had his journal on his lap, the parchment with his design and monetary calculations spread out over it, fountain pen in hand. "One might argue that by now we've outgrown such pranks. Besides, I've already too much to do if I'm to make that trip today."

"Well, perhaps I might go along with you to Worthington. My lady's maid is always willing to take a jaunt into town. I could help you choose something for Emilia."

Julian tilted his head in thought. "I've decided to buy her

some of that French stationary she likes to write her poetry upon. Besides, I thought you were chained to the Manor for your banishment from finishing school last month. I don't think you're allowed such an outing at this juncture."

"I suppose." She grimaced, making the dimple in her chin more prominent. "I had to run away. I missed all of you, and all of our jollies. Liverpool gave me the collywobbles."

"The collywobbles? A rather childish locution from a woman so sophisticated she was caught smoking in the school's library on four separate occasions."

"I wasn't actually smoking."

Julian smirked. "So you say."

"Truly. I don't even know how to smoke a cheroot. I was *pretending* to inhale. Besides, it never worked. Headmistress Gribbles kept insisting there was a refined lady hidden within me. She was determined to redeem my thwarted soul."

"Ah. So to punish her for her unwavering faith, you snuck into her chamber wearing a man's top hat and vest, face painted like a clown, and hid within her window seat to give her a *righteous* scare before you absconded and found your way back to us."

Willow snorted—a most unladylike sound, yet somehow dainty when matched with her delicate profile. "You're forgetting; I had on my corset and bloomers. Least I was half-trying to be refined. I'm sure she still wonders to this day how I fit into such a tiny space."

"Yes. Perhaps I should send her an article on hyperlaxity." With a sidelong glance, Julian studied Willow's fine-boned double-jointed frame. That she could bend and knot her body in such pagan poses offered no riddle for a scientific mind. Yet still he'd lain awake more nights than he could count, mystified to physical discomfort by the thought of her lengthy, entangled limbs. "Just six more months." Julian wiped his brow with a sleeve cuff, decidedly too warm in the unseasonal humidity. "Half a year and you could have graduated."

"I would never have survived even another week of fan-flapping and dance lessons. I don't know why Uncle Owen suddenly opted to send me there in the first place. He had no right to expect me to go on his command. It's not as if he's my fath—" her voice cracked on the last word.

Julian nudged her, sensing a pain she would never allow anyone to share. "He only wants what's best for you. You're blessed to have him. And Aunt Enya."

Silent, she stretched her arms behind her head, the fabric molding around her nubile curves as her eyes drifted closed. She'd managed to skip out of the townhouse without a corset again. Julian's mother encouraged such independence, but Aunt Enya was a different story. When Willow had fallen into Enya and Uncle Owen's keep years ago, Enya regressed to the strict sartorial mode of 'loose stays mean loose morals.' It was an argument his mother and aunt often broached but would never quell.

Noticing Willow's beaded nipples beneath the taut fabric, Julian swallowed against his swelling throat. He glanced at the magnolia shrubs for a distraction. "Of a truth, Willow." He resituated his collar in an effort to steady his scratchy voice. "Where would you be had they not taken you in?"

"Always brimming with hypothetical questions aren't you, *il mio piccolo cavolo*?"

Julian smirked. She'd called him her 'little cabbage' since they first met—mostly to annoy him. Over time, it had evolved to a term of endearment. Though English had become Willow's primary language, she still used her native tongue for affect. In fact, she'd taught Julian to decipher and speak Italian so fluently they could have secret conversations around other people. It was the one advantage he had over his brother, Nick. Something she shared only with Julian, and he relished it.

Keeping her eyes shut, Willow returned his smile. "Without my guardians, I would be ... well ... most probably off with the gypsies having an adventure sublime." She smacked her tinted lips for effect. "But I am indebted to your family's generosity. No doubt they saved me from myself, if nothing else."

Opening her eyes, she dropped her arms to pick up a twig. Mesmerized, she held it straight while a lady bug trailed the bumps of wood. In gentle puffs, she blew on the bug, coaxing it to open its wings and flitter away. Her dark eyebrows crimped as she watched its flight, and Julian knew she envied the insect's ability to fly.

He'd spoken to her of the orphanage, yet still he knew so little. Anytime he broached why she'd ended up there after the circus, in hopes to understand why her parents chose to abandon her, she grew quiet and pensive, claiming to have no memory of it. She'd never even shown an interest in finding her family again. So everyone avoided the subject of her past to keep her smiling in the present.

Still, it was obvious a part of her missed her earliest childhood. Being raised as a performer—her mother a trapeze aerialist and contortionist, her father a prop man—a common life must seem very trite.

He suspected that's the reason she left the orphanage yet was happy enough to call the manor home. There was nothing common about a life lived where shops, cafés, billiard halls, ballrooms, and lodging were all at hand within one milieu.

Just as his father had hoped, their home had become a

holiday resort as well-renowned as Bath. There was a sense of grandeur and liberation in every vine-covered arbor, hot spring, and grassy slope. He supposed no one could feel ordinary in such a majestic setting.

Silently, he regarded his companion—so still in her repose. Her lower lip was so full and plump, the upper one seemed thin in comparison. The resulting imbalance formed a perpetual pout. Such a suggestive, sullen frown would appeal to any man, if said man could see past her hoydenish behavior long enough to notice.

Shaking his head, Julian returned to scribbling equations, jaw clamped tight. He'd lied to her earlier, about being too busy to aid in her prank. He always bowed out when she asked him to partake in anything daring or frolicsome.

In all honesty, he'd often imagined what it would be like to tag along as her accomplice. To stand on the brink of her contagious laughter—to feel it rush through his veins. But he feared he could never measure up to his brother for such excursions. Nick had been her consort in pranks and piracy since the day she'd arrived at the Manor of Diversions. They'd run wild like apes from the time she was eight and he was nine—notorious to even the guests for their devilish capers.

Resigned to their differences, Julian touched the nib of his pen to his tongue and tasted ink as he ciphered some figures in his head. With a nod, he jotted down the proper sum. He noticed the absence of warmth on his right side before realizing Willow had stood.

She shook grass from her skirt. "I suppose I'll go visit Leander at the stables since I'm to be imprisoned on the grounds. Perchance he'll let me help carriage train your father's blue roan mare."

"I doubt Leander's at the stables today. This is his honeymoon week, lest you forget."

As Uncle Owen and Aunt Enya's only child, and being only a few months older than Willow, Leander was the closest thing to a brother Willow had. She'd been a part of his wedding three days earlier. But Willow tended to misplace her short-term memory anytime it conflicted with her spontaneity.

Twisting her crimped hair into a knot at her nape and securing it with the ladybug's twig, she scowled. "Honeymoon, bah. What a ridiculous term. At least in Italy, we give it sparkle." She spread out her arms like a butterfly waiting to launch. "*Luna di miele.*"

Her words didn't register. Julian was too busy admiring the graceful turn of her slim, bared neck. With her nape exposed, she looked elegant and refined. Though he'd not dare admit it for fear she'd never wear her hair that way again.

"And on that note"—Willow coiled a loose lock around her finger—"whomever said it had to last more than one night? Consummate the marriage then be done with it. Honeymoon's over. What more is there left to do after that?"

Forcing his attention back to his calculations, Julian mumbled absently while biting on the tip of his pen. "Consummate it again and again ... until you learn every precept and secret of one another's bodies. Until your differences become a natural and necessary extension of your likenesses. Least, that's what I intend to do." A fountain of heat spread through his earlobes upon realization that he'd spoken aloud.

Their gazes met. Willow's eyes sliced through him. The bright, greenish-yellow irises were two toned like stained glass, and with her olive skin deepened to a blush as it was, they stood out even more—appearing to ignite as if the sun streamed from behind them.

"Forgive me," he stammered. "I-I forget sometimes that you're a gir—"

"Oh, that's a fine thing." She cut him off with a mock snarl. "Kick a lady when she's down and out without her partner in crime, why don't you?" Shifting her attention to the magnolia shrubs, she lifted on tiptoe to see over the clusters of snowy white flowers. "I do hope you have that request ready for Desmond. He's on his way over. He seems to be in a hurry ... or a fury. He's beating his fists on his thighs. Have you done something to ruffle him?"

"Not that I could even conceive. I bow to his every whim." Julian scrambled to finish the final equations, smearing ink with the side of his palm. No sooner had he rose than Lord Desmond flapped his way into the shrubs, oblivious to the opening on the other side of the tree. By the time he'd made a hole big enough to climb through, leaves, twigs, and magnolias clung to his clothes and top hat as if he'd sprouted into full bloom.

"You..." Standing a full head shorter, he pointed a gloved finger at Julian and several petals skittered on his sleeve with the breeze. The other hand, bared of any covering, showcased a legion of age spots. "After all these years. I never thought you were capable of such ... such *treachery*."

Willow stepped back to allow the wrinkled, red-faced investor fully within their circle. Her attention alternated between Julian and Desmond.

"Pardon, my lord?" Julian looked down on the little man covered in flowers, feeling a bit like Goliath about to be pummeled by a wood nymph. "To what do you refer?"

"Consider this your reckoning, two-faced knave!"

Willow yelped as Lord Desmond reached up to spank

Julian's cheek with the back of his empty glove then tossed the leather to the ground. A hot, stinging swell raced from the point of impact to Julian's neck and ears, ripening to a full-fledged blush. The ride designs fluttered from his fingers to his feet, covering the investor's glove.

Mouth agape, Willow lifted a fingertip to trace what must have been a flaring red splotch on his face. He brushed her aside and faced the old man, every muscle tensed, poised to react but loathe to lose the funding he so desperately needed. He couldn't afford to be rash. Lord Desmond had been the park's only investor over the past five years.

Willow tucked her palm between Julian's shoulder blades. He relaxed at the touch, bit by bit. The contempt and betrayal on the old man's face was genuine enough. He obviously believed he'd been wronged in some way.

"I demand satisfaction. A pistol duel at sunset." Lord Desmond's voice cracked, as if standing face to face with Julian's chest rattled him. "To think, you with your hand in my pocket, all the while shoving the other one up my wife's skirts!" From the depths of his jacket, he withdrew Julian's missing pair of spectacles and flung them upward into the tree's canopy. Leaves rattled on the wired frame's descent until it landed squarely within the melted raspberry puddle next to Willow's foot.

Willow gasped and stared blankly up at Julian, an odd expression on her face, as if she were the one without spectacles ... as if he were blurred and she couldn't quite bring him into focus.

Julian struggled with Lord Desmond's accusation. In his mind's eye, he pictured the investor's lovely wife in all of her voluptuous glory. She was the same age as Julian and his brother. Nick had often joked about Lady Mina and her decrepit viscount; everyone knew she'd been forced by her parents to marry the old codger for his wealth. Remembering such conversations, a sickening theory took form.

Surely his brother hadn't...

Julian loosened the cravat at his neck. "Sir, there's been some misunderstanding, to be sure."

"My bride admitted everything when I found your spectacles tucked within her décolleté. She's been infatuated by your bookishness since our arrival. Wasn't enough for you to bed her ... now you're calling her a liar?" The old man's face flared to the color of a cranberry. He looked at Willow then back at Julian. "Oh, I see. You don't wish to discourage your newest conquest." He appraised Willow's bared feet, rumpled dress, and smeared lips. "Though it looks like you've already managed to deflower this one, here out in the open under God's own eye."

The rush of heat in Julian's head drained into his chest, hot as flame for the attack on his friend's honor. Her bottom lip had disappeared between her teeth, a sure sign she wrestled a retort of her own. Or worse, she was debating whether or not to physically accost the old man.

Before Julian could stop her, she poked her finger into Lord Desmond's shirt. "Now see here, you pigeon-chested little molligrub!"

Easing her behind him, Julian swept up the old man's glove along with his design and held them out to the investor, jaw clenched. "You will apologize to the lady."

"Lady?" His rival's face crinkled like a dried grape. "I've ne'er heard a *lady* speak with such rancor. Nor have I seen one so proud of her unshod feet. Let her apologize."

Still holding out the design, Julian kept his body planted firmly in front of Willow. "You brought her into this. The apology rests on your shoulders. Then you and I will have a seat beside the tree and get to the bottom of these accusations rationally. We yet have business to discuss."

"Our *business* is heretofore terminated." Lord Desmond jerked away the paper along with his glove and cast them both to the grass. "The only thing left twixt us is a duel. Sunset. In the courtyard." Running a malevolent gaze over Julian, he dusted petals and twigs from his clothes. "Best find yourself a second. Make certain it's someone with a constitution for blood, as I've no intention of missing my mark." Then he retreated through the jagged opening he'd made, leaving Julian sweltering beneath Willow's bewildered stare and the mid-morning sun.

TWO

Cursing her long skirt, Willow tried to keep up with Julian's pace on the way to find his father in the winter garden. It was no easy task. Just when she met him step for step, he'd stall as if to consider something and she'd get ahead. The moment she stepped back, he was already off again.

By the time the greenhouse-style enclosure came into view on the other side of the castle, Willow's breath broke out in pants and beads of sweat dotted her forehead. Sunlight glinted off the garden's glass roof, blinding her. She swiped her sleeve across her brow and slanted her gaze to Julian, his plaited hair shimmering at the nape of his neck much the same as the glass.

He and Nick had their mother's coloring. They both boasted Miss Juliet's dark golden hair and fair complexion. But they had inherited their father, Master Thornton's, features, powerfully sculpted frame, and gray eyes—albeit a lighter version. In fact, Julian's looked like polished silver this morning, offset by the periwinkle vest he wore over his celery green shirt. No matter what his plans, Julian always dressed in vests and cravats to look the part of a gentleman.

"You know your parents will be gardening together." Willow gulped some air. "Do you intend to address your mother as well?"

"No." Julian stopped short and Willow stumbled over her hem to reverse her lead.

Looking up at her companion, she waited to hear his baritone cut the silence. When his full lips trembled like that, they were gathering words from thoughts moving too fast to contain, much like a sky accumulating clouds for a downpour.

"You must distract her." He glanced at the garden and his gold-rimmed spectacles caught the sunlight to illuminate a dried streak of raspberry slush on his lens that he'd missed upon cleaning. "She can't know of Lord Desmond's accusation, most especially of his challenge."

Willow rearranged the twig holding up her heavy hair, drawing down a new strand to wrap around her finger. Julian's mother abhorred pistols, due to his father almost dying years earlier in a duel.

"I'll not stir up old memories," Julian said, confirming Willow's thoughts. "Mother's emotional state is fragile enough. She's still upset over losing grandfather this past winter."

Sensing his sadness, Willow took Julian's right hand. He laced their fingers.

Though the eldest viscount had lived to the ripe old age of sixty-four, it had been hard on all of the Thorntons when he had died. Hardest of all on Julian's mother. Miss Juliet had spent every afternoon with her mentally unbalanced father-in-law in his chamber, caring for him from the day he came to live at the manor until the moment he took his last breath upon his deathbed.

Theirs was a lovely companionship: the blind watchmaker and his caretaker—a deaf milliner that could read lips. But there was much more to Miss Juliet's perception than lip reading. Julian once told Willow that his mother could hear with her heart, capable of a clairaudience beyond normal perception. After getting to know Miss Juliet over the years, Willow believed it. And after watching the eldest viscount interact with his daughter-in-law, Willow realized that though blind, he could see with his very soul.

Being privy to this family's inner-workings had awakened a desire in Willow to change the way she saw and heard things, as well. To be led by something other than the corporeal or visceral, attuned to the spiritual and the introspective. Much like the story of Master Thornton's dead brother.

The twenty-year-old tale revolved around an extraordinary flower and was such a well-kept secret that Uncle Owen and Aunt Enya hadn't even learned the truth until a decade ago. The ghost of Master Thornton's brother had befriended Miss Juliet through a flower in which his spirit resided in every petal, and he had ultimately led her to this manor. Even in her deafness, Juliet could hear the ghost's voice and see his spectral image when no one else could.

Though Willow had never had any such experience with the spirit realm herself, she wished with all her heart she could speak to the dead. She would even give up her auditory faculties in the physical realm, just to hear her parents' voices again. To know they were at peace in the afterlife; to understand why they had to make such a sacrifice for her. Upon that thought, a knot burned and vibrated in her throat as if wasps had taken up residence. She shoved the memory aside, unable to relive it.

Keeping her hand as though he was the one needing an anchor, Julian picked up his stride. It felt as if they'd been walking all morning. Surrounded by a forest on every side, the estate encompassed ninety acres. The front façade alone measured over one-hundred-and-twenty-three meters and was a compilation of a castle, a three-story townhouse, stables, and a winter garden. Willow's adopted family shared the townhouse with Julian's family and a slew of servants.

Willow squeezed Julian's hand, not too tight, merely enough to relish the feel of him. His fingers had calluses where he held a pen or pencil day in and day out, making calculations and drawing designs. Yet his palms were as soft as down. The hands of an inventor, a mathematician, an engineer.

"Thank you for being here. For believing me." Julian squeezed her fingers back without glancing up.

"Of course I believe you. *Sempre.*" Willow didn't dare tell him the truth. That for an instant, when Lord Desmond had first accused him, her secret hope for a future with Julian had almost shattered. Then she remembered who he was, deep inside, and knew that he would never do anything so rash.

Julian had a hyperbolic sense of responsibility and ethics, due mostly to his brother's lack of either. As a result, he always kept himself busy with the upkeep of the manor and intellectual pursuits. But were he ever to change his field of study to more sensual interests, Willow wanted to be the one to assist him. This was the very reason she'd had herself cast out of the finishing school ... so he wouldn't find a lover in her absence.

The beautiful words he had spoken earlier, of his future intentions upon his honeymoon, she had already made each one her own. Tucked them away deep within, a fantasy to hold like oxygen in her chest on nights when she tossed and turned in bed. When the nightmares of her past—the part she had told no one of, not even Julian—climbed her chamber walls like vines of smoke and consumed her with suffocating dread.

With her free hand, Willow rubbed her dress over the hummingbird tattoo on the small of her back, wrestling the fluttery feeling that it was alive, flapping its wings along her spine. A voiceless song, reminding her of things better left forgotten.

Julian's steps slowed and he released his grasp on her fingers. Looking up to follow his line of sight, Willow saw Nick coming out of the castle's front door, his shoulder length hair a mess of unkempt golden waves and his blue button-up shirt half-tucked into his brown trousers. The castle's front door was the only way in or out of the garden— as all of the edifices at the manner were interconnected to the castle by enclosed corridors. Willow had an uneasy intuition that Nick had already visited his parents. But had he told them the truth?

"I'd like a word, Nick." Julian's neck muscles knotted. Besides his blushing ears, it was one of the ways Willow could distinguish him from his twin. When Nick was upset or angry, his eyes hardened to mirrors of slate and his powerful body bristled—a holocaust about to combust. But with Julian, his inner turmoil manifested itself only through the rush of blood to his ears, and in the cords of his jaw and neck. His silvery eyes remained gentle, serene even ... like moonlight on a winter's lake. Nothing seemed to ever rock his steadfast core. Even this, a betrayal by his brother, had not yet broken his calm.

"Willow, allow us some time alone, please." Julian glowered at Nick who returned his brother's stare.

Willow chewed her inner cheek. It was her presence holding Julian to such civility. However, she had a few choice words for his twin before she left. "Nick." His name caught on a growl as she stepped up to him. "You unprincipled slavering *lupo*."

As Nick tilted his chin to look down on her, Willow reconsidered her insult. The smugness in those dark gray eyes cloaked by sooty lashes, his high cheekbones and shapely lips turned on a complacent grin—he looked more like a thief admiring his plunder than a rabid wolf.

"Why hello, Sweeting." He touched the dimple in her chin, the gesture at once tender and duplicitous. "Did I spoil some devious prank in my absence? Are you miffed that you didn't get to rattle the help? Just look at you." His thumb moved to outline her lips. "Eating dessert for breakfast again. So deliciously infantile."

Before Willow could slap Nick's hand away, Julian had grabbed his wrist.

"Let's discuss what you had for breakfast, aye? A romp in the hay with Lady Mina, I'm guessing."

Nick snapped out of his twin's grasp without looking away from Willow.

Smelling alcohol on Nick's breath, she took a step back. "You arrogant, thoughtless inebriate."

Nick licked his lips. "I'm not drunk. Just besotted by your bedraggled beauty." He chuckled—a masculine purr. She'd seen women melt to a puddle of wantonness at the sound. As for her? She despised it.

She harbored no delusions as to what people thought: that due to her and Nick's many escapades together, a romance had blossomed over the years. Even Aunt Enya had pulled her aside once, concerned Willow had been taken in by his seductive talents, but Willow assured her they shared nothing other than feathers in their caps of mischief.

Thankfully, no one was aware of the episode one year ago, when Nick had been alone with her and tried to kiss her. He won a busted lip in the exchange. Willow had refused to be any man's second fiddle, much less his hundredth one.

Nick possessed a fondness for slightly older, cultured women—so long as they had money. Upon his fifteenth birthday, he'd come to see the boundless opportunities allotted him via the manor. He'd honed his skills of seduction on women bred of wealth and loneliness. Much to his parents' utter disappointment and shame, he'd made a career of fornication, earning gifts of fineries and wardrobes by satisfying the lusts of his adulterous lambs. Willow and her pranks had become nothing more than distractions he used to get the ladies away from their husbands long enough to bed them.

In Willow's eyes, Nick would never be the man his brother was. Nick was just a boy with a fail-proof sense of timing and a knack for comedic devilry. Yes, she cared for him, like a rose loves its thorns—an evil necessary for her daily existence. But over the past few years, theirs had devolved to an even lesser symbiotic relationship: she, the remora fish to his shark—feeding off of whatever antics he would allow her to partake in, then cleaning up his messes when he was too drunk or belligerent to care.

Not this time. He'd crossed a line by putting Julian in danger.

She shoved Nick so his shoulder blades slammed against the castle's stone wall. "Couldn't you this once have left your ambition in your pants? The investor's wife of all people? And using Julian's identity! How is he to climb out of this bucket of piss? I abhor what you've become."

Nick straightened his rumpled clothes and met her glare. It amazed Willow how two men could be such perfect images of one another on the outside yet share no likenesses within.

"Truly, Willow." Nick's cocky smile eroded to a frown. He almost appeared wounded. "This side of you is nothing short of peeving. I'm already handling the situation with our father's aid. These are family matters that do not concern our temperamental little ward. So be a good chit and make yourself scarce." He waved her away as if she were a gnat.

"Now wait there," Julian's voice erupted behind her—

husky with the intent to defend. But she held him back. She didn't need protection. Not from Nick. For she knew him within and without. Nick lashed out when he was cornered ... when he knew he was wrong.

Willow's jaw tightened. "Well enough. I'll leave you to your brother. But you can rest assured I'm not finished with you."

Nick shrugged his powerful shoulders. "No matter. I am with you. I've long outgrown your ill-bred pestering." He nudged away from the wall and leaned close enough that Willow winced at the bourbon on his breath. Grasping her elbow, he drew her against him to whisper in her ear so only she could hear. "He's my brother. My *twin.* All it will take is him dabbing it up just once with a lady of refinement. There's nothing sweeter than lying atop the cushion of another man's prosperity. *You've lost him already.*" His hot breath scorched her ear, slipped inside and sparked a reaction.

"Julian would never do that," she hissed back.

"Wouldn't he?" Nick narrowed his gaze.

Julian broke them apart, scowling at his brother. Unwilling to let Nick off so easily, Willow grabbed his open collar, twisting it around his throat. She ignored the feel of Julian's palm on her back, his gentle persuasions to calm down. All she wanted was to hurt Nick the way his words had hurt her ... the way his careless exploitations had hurt Julian.

Nick smirked and swallowed against the clenched fabric. "Just the response I'd expect from a circus urchin."

Willow snapped. Grunting, she rushed against him, manipulating her weight and twisting her body to topple them both to the ground. Before Julian could pull her off, she'd managed to draw blood with a well-aimed cuff to Nick's mouth.

Her toes lifted, her back pressed tight against Julian's solid form. His scent warmed her lungs—amber and musk mingled with a hint of ink. In spite of the comforting elixir, anger burbled to her surface, fed from past memories she despised. She couldn't seem to push it back down. Her insides boiled, as if Nick had unleashed a volcano.

"What the hell, Willow?" Nick glowered at her, swiping a dribble of red from his lip as he stood and dusted himself off. "You almost broke my tooth." He ran his tongue's tip along the perfect upper row of his white teeth.

She strained against Julian's hold, ignoring the stinging stiffness in her knuckles where they'd met Nick's mouth. "Let me be. I want to finish him, blast it..."

Julian looped his arms through hers from behind, holding her spine taut against his chest. "Remember, a proper lady does not act upon impulse." His lips hovered a hair's width from her nape, making her skin ache for want of full contact.

Nick cast her a smug smirk. "Yes, Julian is overtly aware of how ladies in the gentry behave, being as he's my *twin*." He exaggerated the final word—drew it out for her benefit. A reminder only she would grasp.

Willow's mind raced, her blood roared. She growled and kicked out her bare feet, giving it one last attempt.

Julian whirled her around to face him. "*Willomena. Enough.*"

The name startled her back to her senses. She hadn't liked the sound of it ever since the day she lost Mama and Papa. They had screamed it so many times that each syllable reverberated with the terror and hopelessness in their voices. But somehow, when it fell from Julian's lips, the sting soothed away. He put reverence and music in the inflections ... almost as if he were singing a hymn.

"Forgive me," he said. "I didn't know how else to get your attention." The calm in his eyes reached inside her and smothered her flames like a rain of glistening silver sand.

She relaxed as he cradled her throbbing fist in his palm to study her split knuckles. It hadn't been Nick's blood on his chin. It was hers. His teeth must have sliced her skin.

"What did he whisper in your ear to warrant such a tirade?" Julian asked. "What is it that I would 'never do'?"

"Nothing. I'm sorry." Her head bowed. She wasn't sorry for punching Nick, only for Julian having to witness it. Only for making him more upset than he'd already been.

Julian released her and smoothed the wrinkles from her sleeves. "No harm done. Go inside and bid a servant to clean and dress that gash."

Willow flashed a glare over her shoulder at Nick who stood beside the wall a short distance away, working out his jaw and tapping his lips gingerly. She hoped his mouth was as sore as her fist. Their eyes met and she willed him to hold her secret. Of all the foolish things to do. Of all the people she could've chosen as her one confidante. Why had she ever told Nick how she felt about his brother?

Nick stared back with a knowing glint, but wouldn't acknowledge whether or not he planned to betray her confidence.

Fighting a bout of nauseous nerves, Willow turned to Julian again. "I truly am sorry."

"He had it coming." A neck muscle jumped as he glanced his brother's way. "Has more than that coming." Before Willow could respond, Julian escorted her to the castle door. "Find Emilia for me, would you? Keep her occupied until this blows over. She deserves to be blissfully unaware at least on her birthday."

Gripping the latch with her good hand, Willow nodded

then turned and watched from the threshold as Julian gestured for Nick to follow. The brothers headed off in the direction of the wrought iron gates, en route to the amusement rides on the other side of the manor's stony walls. They often went there to fight, out of respect for their mother's sensitivities. Although Miss Juliet knew of their battles, having tended to countless cuts and bruises over the years, she never liked to see them at one another's throats.

Their father had Romani blood and allowed his sons' quarrels to escalate far beyond what most 'civilized' nobles would approve. Boxing and fisticuffs had never satisfied the brothers. They could solve their differences best by short-lived outbursts born of raw testosterone and passion—their methods a mix between bear wrestling and barroom brawls. Master Thornton never allowed things to escalate beyond cuts, nosebleeds and puffed lips, but he attempted to let his boys work out their issues alone. He told his wife that as twins, they needed to push one another in ways no one else would, how else would they become men who could know their own minds and fight for what they believed? How else could they be individuals?

Willow suspected it stemmed from the fact that Master Thornton and his twin had been raised apart their entire childhood. They didn't meet until they were already men with distinctive lifestyles. One, a tortured, love-sick gypsy who could turn a card game to his advantage at the drop of a hat; the other, an angry gambler trapped in a crippled body who drowned his pain in an excess of women and wine.

It was easy enough to surmise what Master Thornton feared: by being raised together his boys would be too dependent upon one another to have their own distinctive personalities, goals, and talents. So he had encouraged each son to branch out into a variety of interests separate from the other. As a result, he'd raised two men who could not be more different, and that shared only one common trait—an overtly critical eye for the other brother's choices.

Opening the castle door, Willow whispered a prayer that if only one twin were to be left standing after today's confrontation, it would be Julian. And that he would be none the wiser to her feelings for him.

THREE

Julian arrived first. His twin hedged through the trees behind him somewhere—the air between them as taut as a whip waiting to snap. Julian had already anticipated his brother's stratagem. Nick would take his time and make him wait in hopes to play on his stress and get the upper hand.

Though his mind was a jumble of questions and accusations, Julian strode through the trellised archway, determined not to lose focus. Sunlight reflected off of the swinging sign where curvaceous pink letters on a black background proclaimed, "*Welcome to a Midsummer's Dream: Decadent Amusements for Lovers of Life and Merriment.*"

Birds sang overhead, sitting high atop poles where parapets flapped at ten-foot intervals along the grounds. The flags, each bearing a white domino or harlequin mask on a pink and black checked backdrop, cast shadows on the ground with their movements. Honeysuckle vines, secured in places with black bows, wound in and out of the eight-foot-high latticework fence which encompassed the half-acreage park. Glistening with morning dew, the blossoms should have provided an aesthetic and olfactory feast for the senses. Any other time than today.

Julian tightened his jaw. It was natural that peace would evade him, knowing what awaited him at sunset ... knowing he was to take a bullet for his brother's latest lascivious exploit. He wouldn't let Nick leave this park until he'd promised a way out of this mess.

Julian sat on the carousel's platform and stroked a red

and white vertical support beam—twisted and glossy like a candy cane. Within the clearing, the rides sat empty and anticipant beneath their canvas canopies of black and pink stripes, waiting to entertain their guests in the summer season. His gaze swept briefly over his two most recent designs. First, the *Ring of Love*—a giant rotating drum that forced participants to tumble into one another. Next was the *Sea of Matrimony*, a large boat formed of laminated wood and suspended with ropes from a gallows-style pole. When rocked back and forth, the seated riders had to cling to one another for support lest they lose their balance. These particular rides had emerged as favorites of the guests, for within them strangers became instant acquaintances and couples had a legitimate excuse to embrace in public.

However, Julian was partial to the simpler, subtler designs of the carousel and Ferris wheel, perhaps because they had been his first additions. Or more likely because they represented a happier time, when he, his brother, and their father had all worked together toward a common goal.

Five years ago, before Nick discovered women, he utilized his gift for carving wood to fashion intricate life-sized fantasy creatures for the carousel: nine stallions—four of them Pegasus and five of them unicorns—along with three stationary chariots hitched to giant butterflies. Father, using his flare for painting, brought each carving to life with gleaming, vivid colors. Julian constructed the inner-workings of the ride, installing bevel gears and offset cranks to give the stallions an up and down motion as they traveled around the mirrored center pole which housed the enchanting tunes of a band organ.

It was a masterpiece, just like the mini-Ferris wheel that the three of them began shortly thereafter. A project Nick lost interest in halfway through, leaving Julian, his Father, and a few servants to finish it. They had been on a deadline, pressed to finish before the summer season, and Willow had stepped in to help, surprising both Julian and his father with her mechanical prowess.

Since then, she always assisted Julian with the upkeep and construction of the rides, which proved to be a great help considering Nick rarely contributed in any way other than the maintenance of his carousel creations.

Casting a glance over his shoulder to check for his absent brother, Julian caught sight of the Ferris wheel. Its bright red gondola-style seats swung slightly with the breeze. He had designed the ride upon the memory of one he'd read about in an article heralding the World's Columbian Exposition in Chicago. In fact, that exposition in May of 1893 had birthed his engineering and mechanical career.

Julian had been only nine at the time, too young to go to Chicago alone, and his father had been busy preparing for the summer season so he couldn't take him. Instead, Father collected any and all articles, periodicals, and photos that highlighted the event so Julian could quench his curiosity. It had helped alleviate the quest for knowledge, although it never fully staunched Julian's desire to cross the cultural bridge and meet scientists and engineers—men of a like mind.

Last year, Father saved enough money to accompany Julian to the National Industrial Exposition in Osaka, Japan. But Grandfather's heart began to fail, and they couldn't leave Mother alone to tend him. The money went instead toward doctor visits, a live-in nurse, and then ultimately funeral arrangements.

To this day, Julian regretted missing that exposition. He'd never voiced his disappointment to anyone in his family out of respect for his grandfather, yet he had told

Willow. She was the one person that understood his need to hob-knob with the technologically and culturally elite ... to debate which of the industry's advancements would carry over into the new century. For Willow shared the same passions.

Julian patted his vest pocket, prompting a crinkle of paper. He lifted out the wrinkled ride design. Willow had been the inspiration for this newest project. *Alice's Adventures in Wonderland* was a favorite book from her youth. While she was learning to read English, Julian had sat with her in the branches of many a tree helping her cipher the words on the pages. Now he wanted to build the *Journey into the Looking Glass* in celebration of the second Lewis Carroll novel—the first book she ever read without his help.

Thoughtful, he studied the rough sketches. As an indoor ride, it would require a large enclosure to house the characters and settings inspired by the pages of the story. Boats shaped like open-faced books, with a row of seats set into the spines, would travel through a long, dark tunnel upon currents propelled by flume pumps. Strings of miniature lights would illuminate the separate showrooms such as the Hatter's Tea Party, the Pool of Tears, and the Queen's Croquet Court. He planned to implement Nick's talent for carving to provide characters for the displays. Father had already agreed to paint everything, including the backgrounds.

Julian had hoped to have at least the enclosure built by the time Willow came home from finishing school for the Christmas holiday so he could surprise her. Nothing made him happier than to see her smile. But now that he had no funding, he had no materials. And it mattered little, for she was here early so he wouldn't be able to keep the secret anyway. Folding the design again, Julian stuffed it in his pocket, trying to staunch an uncomfortable crimp in his chest.

He considered how Willow had defended him earlier to Nick. If she knew that Julian was the one who convinced Uncle Owen to send her to *Ridley's Conservatoire of Manners and Mores* in the first place, she would despise him every bit as much as she did Nick at the moment.

A muscle twitched beneath his collarbone. Is that what Nick had whispered to her earlier? Is that what made her lose composure and strike his twin—that she simply couldn't believe Julian was capable of such betrayal?

"Willomena," he said her name aloud, finding comfort in the inflections of each syllable. "I'm sorry."

"Sorry for what?"

Julian shot to his feet at the intrusion of his brother's voice, turning to face him. "That you called her an urchin."

Nick smirked. "She goaded me into it."

Julian studied Nick's swollen upper lip, tamping the urge to fatten his lower one and give him a matching set. "You started it. What the hell did you say to her to cause such a rampage?"

Nick stepped onto the carousel's platform. He crouched beside a prancing unicorn painted with swirls of iridescent blue and white—like mist draped across a crested mountain top. Inspecting it, he ran his hands along its muscled lines. "Here I thought we were to speak of something pressing, such as Lady Mina's accusation against you." Nick's slate gray eyes baited Julian as he leaned an elbow against a violet and orange butterfly's wing. "What do you fear I told Willow? That it was you who convinced Uncle Owen to send her to that pretentious Hades ... that you made her suffer in that miserable puritanical academy for the lone crime of kissing me?"

"*You* kissed *her*." Julian snatched his spectacles off his face, folded them, then placed them on the chariot beside him while loosening the cravat at his neck. "And from my vantage point, she slapped your mouth for even trying."

Nick grinned. "Ah, from your *voyeur* point, you mean to say. How many months had we been beneath your magnifying glass, Julian? You should've turned it on yourself. Perchance it would have illuminated your motives. You were jealous, why else would you have her sent away?"

Julian's neck throbbed. "She needed to be away from you. From your influence. You would have deflowered her— ruined her. That is the only reason I suggested her hiatus."

Nick's shoulders appeared to grow as he stood. "Harsh, brother. It pains me to know I'm such a deviant you couldn't even trust me with our mutual friend of eleven years."

"Our mutual friend who has blossomed into an alluring young woman—and women are your obsession, along with bourbon and wealth." Julian stepped up onto the platform. A Pegasus's wing stood between him and his twin. Julian traced a finger along the etched barbs, stunned as always by how real the feathers looked. "You proved it this morn by being so drunk you let me take the blame for your affair with my investor's wife. You've lost me my funds for the upkeep and accretion of this park."

Nick's chest expanded beneath his rumpled shirt. "Ah, yes. Your beloved park." He waved at the rides around them. "This hoity-toity dandy-boy meadow of frolics and fun." His gaze suddenly shifted. "What's that in your pocket?"

Before Julian could react, Nick had the ride design opened in his hand.

"*Journey into the Looking Glass*." Nick snorted. "For the building's outer façade," he read Julian's descriptions verbatim, "trees and flowers cut from wood and brightly painted will alternate with geometrically shaped mirrors. A gigantic three-dimensional pocket watch with a round rabbit's face—mimicking the white rabbit from the tale—will wink and pendulate as people board on boats and drift through the tunneled entrance made to resemble a rabbit hole." Nick looked up, his arm held high, thwarting Julian's effort to snag the paper back. "How are you to make the rabbit wink and pendulate?"

Julian's face burned hot under his brother's scrutiny. If only his interest was sincere like it once was. "I've been tooling with gears and motors, utilizing Grandfather's abandoned watch pieces. With what I've learned, I can incorporate movement in the figurines. There will be animated figures inside as well. The caterpillar lifting the hand that holds his hookah ... the Mad Hatter waving to the guests."

Nick simpered. "Oh, that's *precious*. Tell me, this wouldn't be for Willow, would it?"

"It's for our family." Julian grounded out the answer between clenched teeth. "We've made twice the revenue over the past three years due to this park drawing in a younger clientele."

Nick's smile curled like a vine intent on strangling an imposing weed. "It's made you younger in the process. You should be a man by now, brother. Yet you haven't even visited a brothel thanks to this park's consumption of your time."

"Having illicit affairs with prostitutes does not a man make. I'm saving myself, just as Father did for Moth—"

"Spare me the romantic rhetoric. Theirs was a unique situation. Yours is an overblown moral stance. I suggest you lower yourself enough to ravish a whore or two, and soon. Ladies prefer a man with some experience. How else will you know how to please the one you *love*—" his gaze sharpened—

"if you don't work out the foils first with someone who doesn't matter? Or, you could remain a child, dawdling away your days as you always have, playing with toys to curb your primal urges." His expression took on an arrogant slant. "Which, come to think, begs a question that's always haunted me ... what is it you play with at night? I've heard several cats go missing after dark, not to be seen until morning. As your brother, I feel I should enlighten you ... a pussy by any other name, is not the same."

Rage tore through Julian. It scalded his ears then bled into his eyes to color his world red. He rode the wave of crimson, diving across the wing's tip. His head collided with his brother's chest and plowed them both sideways into a mirror on the center pole. The ride designs scattered to the platform beneath their feet.

Julian's spine shuddered upon the crackle of glass raining all around. Heat leaked out of tiny cuts in his scalp then chilled with the late morning breeze. Running his palm along the abrasions, he felt tiny shards prickle his skin.

Wincing, Nick glanced at his own forearm where a spatter of cuts sprouted blood beneath the snags in his shirt. With a chesty growl, he grappled Julian in a bear hug and rammed his back into a Pegasus.

Air shunted out of Julian's lungs at the impact. He tasted the bitter-hot rush on his lips. A jolt of pain shot between his shoulder blades to his neck. Gulping a breath, he used the stallion for leverage and cuffed a knee into his brother's abdomen.

Nick flailed backward, falling against a unicorn's backside. He ended up wedged between its hind legs. Its ratty tail draped like a curtain from the top of his head and around his face.

Before Nick could attempt a counterstrike, Julian clasped

his lapels and straddled his brother's legs, his knees pressed along Nick's thighs. "How the hell am I supposed to get out of this duel? How could you let me take the blame for such an offense? I knew you were a rogue, but I never thought of you as a coward."

Nick's expression shifted from malevolence to shock as he relaxed beneath Julian's restraints. "The old man challenged you to a duel?"

Clenching his jaw, Julian tightened his fingers around his brother's shirt until it pleated like the ripples in a pond. "He's calling me out at sunset. A shame Father doesn't know that detail. Desmond's wife told him I seduced her with my mind. That sickens me most of all. That she thought she was with me the entire time."

Nick clasped Julian's wrists. "No. She knew it was me. She panicked and lied to Desmond to save my hide."

"Why did she have my spectacles then?"

"We had been ... playing games."

"Games? This is my life!" Enraged, Julian shook his brother by his shirt, rocking the carousel's platform. The movement triggered a chirping squeak from within the unicorn and Julian froze at the queer sound. No sooner had Nick shifted his gaze upward than a tiny white nose poked out just over his head from beneath the tail. Julian dragged his brother to his feet an instant before the little squirrel dropped to the platform and stared up at them, quivering. Half-starved and too weak to run, it fluffed out its dingy white fur in an effort to appear intimidating.

"Looks like your park's been invaded." Nick met Julian's gaze.

Julian still ached to scuff his brother's face to a bloody mess. But in that moment, an unspoken treaty passed between them. They both knew, were either of them to continue the fight, the little rodent might get squashed beneath their feet, or escape altogether before they could help it. All three of the Thornton siblings had inherited an acute sympathy for animals from their father. In fact, their family pet had been a wolf from Father's childhood, though it died a week before Emilia's birth.

"Just know ... this isn't over by far." Julian laid out the promise to his brother as he took out his raspberry stained handkerchief and crouched down to scoop the rodent up. "It's in a bad way," he said, captivated by the wiggly ball of fur. "A squirrel should never be so easy to catch." He swaddled it in the cloth to keep it secure, feeling an instant bond. It reminded him of the field mouse he and Nick had once tamed. "Must be an orphan. Looks a bit like Sir Isaac."

Having gathered Julian's ride designs, Nick folded then tucked them into Julian's pocket. Studying the squirrel, he rubbed the gray streak of fur sticking up between its furrowed brow. The rodent screeched a warning. With a melancholy grin, Nick regarded Julian. "Good old Isaac the Newt."

Julian grinned back. The small white mouse had been named after his favorite scientist, Sir Isaac Newton. "What was that ... five years ago? He was the last thing we ever shared."

"Right-ho. Since then, we've been fighting over everything. Especially Willow. I'm not a complete scoundrel, Julian. I know she's unique. Wild and rash. Rare and lovely as a winter rose."

"She's also compassionate, enterprising, scholarly, spontaneous, and witty," Julian added.

"Precisely. She's what we would have been, had we been born a singular man."

Julian almost gave in to a smirk. Nick was right. Willow

was the summation of all of their best characteristics. Yet there was so much more to her. A woman courageous enough to face an untamed horse or climb the highest tree, yet so terrified of the dark she slept with a lantern lit by her bed each night. "We both know she's haunted. Those secrets she keeps. There's a side to her as frangible as a wounded child. And you would only have broken that."

"No. If she'd given me the chance," Nick said, "I would've been faithful. I would've changed my ways for her."

Julian shook his head and nestled the wriggling rodent between his palms to ward off its shivers. "You love the dividends of seduction too much. The fancy accouterments you earn, the gold pocket watches ... the pearl and diamond tie tacks. You'd not give that up for anyone. It is all a game to you."

A deep somberness clouded Nick's eyes. "You're wrong, Brother. And I aim to prove it. I'm leaving the manor today. Taking Mina with me. She's with child. *My* child."

The weight of this confession nearly knocked Julian to his knees. "You're sure it's yours?"

"I'm the only man she's been with besides her husband. And the old fellow was barely able to consummate their marriage. They've only been together that one time seven months ago. She's three months along. You're the mathematician, do the calculations."

Julian always knew his brother's careless philandering would end up hurting some woman, but any aspersions fell stillborn on his tongue. Could it be, that out of this unconscionable situation, his brother was emerging a better man by trying to do the right thing? "When did your affair start?"

Nick perched on a chariot's side rail. "In December, when he first brought her here for the winter season, a month after

Grandfather's death. She was different than any woman I'd ever bedded. Each time she held me in her arms, I felt—" Nick caught himself, as if to admit anything tender might weaken him. "She's very nurturing—surprisingly so for one of her age." He lifted his shoulders then let them fall. "I've heard even strangers can grow to love one another, when a child's involved."

Studying the squirrel's blinking beady eyes, Julian considered a response. He doubted that his brother was capable of such depth of emotion at this point, but he couldn't bring himself to stifle his honorable intentions. "So you're to take her away. Where? And how are you to live?"

"I cannot say where, considering the circumstances. We're keeping that from everyone until the baby is born. As to funds, Father gave me the money he had saved to expand the butterfly garden to a conservatory. It will hold us until I find a job."

Julian swallowed against the knot in his throat. That conservatory was to be Emilia's birthday gift from Mother and Father. "Does Mother know?"

Looking sheepish, Nick shook his head. "She was in the herb garden earlier. I pulled Father aside to speak to him alone. He's to tell her later—after I'm gone."

Julian grimaced, anticipating his mother's reaction. "Emilia. Is she aware that you're going? You know how she adores you. And now you're to leave on her sixteenth birthday and take her gift? She's been writing to that dowager in Ireland, ordering caterpillars and acquiring information on exotic flowers."

Nick shoved hair off his forehead to massage his temple. "Damnit, Julian. Do you not think I've considered all of this? No, I haven't said goodbye to Emilia. I wrote her a note; Father is to deliver it to her later. I can't face her disappointment in me." He paused, deep in thought. "Keep an eye on her, Julian. Our little sister's no longer the naïve child she once was."

Julian pondered this. He'd seen the change already. He suspected that the Countess of Carnlough had something to do with it. The dowager's research and essays on rare species of butterflies came from Ireland far too often and were much too anticipated by Emilia to be purely scientific. For eight months, Willow and Nick both had been privy to readings of her post in the star tower. Julian kept awaiting an invitation, but not receiving one, came to realize that Emilia didn't ask him as she feared he wouldn't approve of the mail's content. He'd been meaning to talk to her about it for some time now.

Truth be known, he doubted his beautiful young sister had ever been naïve. Innocent and untouched? Yes; and she would remain so if he had a say in it. Coddled and spoiled by his father? Without a doubt. But naïve? Never. None of them had ever had such a trait. How could they, growing up in this purlieu for adults?

Father and Mother had done their best to shield them, to maintain a family atmosphere despite the unusual setting. Ever since Julian could remember, Father had opened the manor to guests only twice a year—the summer season of June, July, August, and the winter season of December, January, and February. During spring and fall, the Manor was closed to the public for repairs, and to allot the family time to travel together to Mother and Aunt Enya's hometown of Claringwell, to indulge in quiet nights and lazy mornings. But even in the on-seasons, his parents had always included him and his siblings in the daily upkeep of the manor, so they never lacked for time together.

As for the moral environ, Father went to great lengths to discourage any licentious behavior by the guests. He had the lodging in the castle divided by gender and staffed lady's maids for any unmarried woman that dared come without a chaperone.

In spite of the efforts, one couldn't put chastity belts on those determined to wear only satin sashes, any more than one could put blinders upon a child's inquisitive eyes. Julian and Nick both came to worldly sagacity at an early age through simple observance; and he would be a fool to assume the same didn't stand for Willow and his bright and discerning sister.

"I'll talk to Emilia." Julian said on the cusp of that thought.

Nick narrowed his gaze. "Don't judge her. Just be her brother."

"Of course..."

In silence, they regarded the squirrel. It had given up struggling and now slept in Julian's hands.

"And give her this little fellow, would you?" Nick asked. "Tell her it's my birthday gift. Perchance caring for it will take her mind off of the conservatory until I can repay Father."

Julian tried to ignore the throbbing cuts in his scalp. "It won't take her mind off of your absence. And I was hoping to get your help carving the characters for my new ride. Must you leave today?"

Standing, Nick reached into his trousers' pocket and drew out an envelope. He tapped it against the chariot. "Best we go while Desmond is still reeling from Mina's confession. No doubt, it's more complicated since he's challenged you to a duel. But this could work to our advantage. I'll find him directly. Confess that it was me all along. I'll accept his terms for a duel. He'll be preoccupied today in preparations. Father offered me Grandfather's brougham. As soon as I speak to Desmond, I'll dress as the coachman and sneak

Mina out along the back road from the manor—the one that great Aunt Bitti takes on her caravan runs. At sunset, Desmond will find his bride and me long gone, and you'll be in the clear. Of course he'll want nothing to do with our family thereafter."

"I'll be hard pressed to find another investor soon enough for the renovations to be underway before the summer."

"That's what this is for."

Balancing the drowsing squirrel in one hand, Julian took the envelope offered him. "What is it?"

"A first class ticket to board the *Christine Victoria* in five days. It will take you from Liverpool to New York in six days time. If you catch a train from there, you can be in St. Louis by April twenty-eighth. That gives you two days in a hotel to see the sights before opening day of the World's Fair. I know how you've always talked of the expositions. Just think of the advancements you can experience firsthand, as opposed to reading of them in that *Threshold* magazine you're so fond of. And the place will be crawling with dewy-eyed tycoons from all around the world, salivating for some enterprising means to expand their pockets. Tell them of our manor. Take your park designs, your ideas. With your acumen and charm, you can find new investors for our resort from all around the globe. I'd venture you might even find someone with the carving skills you require."

Julian's head spun. He'd been reading up on the exposition in St. Louis for weeks. A Mr. Willis Carrier was supposed to present his invention there—a system used to control heat and humidity for a publishing company in Brooklyn. Such an apparatus would be the perfect coupe to maintain the temperature in Willow's indoor ride during the summer months. "A transatlantic cruise? Where did you get this?" Excitement warred with concern for his brother's life-altering predicament. It was all too much, too fast.

Nick flinched as he rolled up his shirt sleeve to pick glass particles from his arm. "Mina was planning to leave Desmond. My shallowness precedes me. She didn't think I'd want her once I learned of her condition. She was going to live with her cousins in New York and have the baby there. Now, she no longer needs the ticket. It's yours. You can get a passport in three days' time. There's nothing stopping you." His gaze snagged Julian's, almost pleading. "Watch over everything while I'm gone. The carousel ... repair it as best you can." He smoothed his shirt sleeve back in place.

Julian surveyed the havoc they'd wreaked. Besides the shattered mirror, they had chipped the paint off of several carvings and broke a hoof on the unicorn with the ragged tail. But looking at the furrows along Nick's brow, Julian would have been blind not to read between those lines. Their entire family would be devastated by Nick's leaving, but Emilia and Mother would suffer the most. "I cannot mend what you're leaving broken. I can only hope to suture it temporarily, until you return. The carousel is our responsibility to share—yours and mine together."

Nodding, Nick glanced at his boots. "Then hold it intact until I can join you again. That's all I ask."

Julian tucked the swaddled squirrel in the crook of his arm, trying to stifle the pinch in his chest. Though he and Nick had been at odds for years, they had never been physically parted for any real length of time. "I'll do my best. But don't stay away too long."

When Nick turned to step off the platform, Julian caught his shoulder from behind.

"And Brother, find some measure of happiness."

Keeping his back turned, Nick shook his head, his shoulder tense beneath Julian's grip. "I hardly remember what that is. Here today, gone tomorrow. Just like our childhoods."

Julian released him then, his mind on lost summers rife with fishing trips, water fights in the hot springs at the cusp of winter, explorations deep in the forest on dark autumn nights. A time not so long ago that somehow spanned an eternity between them. "I'm betting there's still some happiness out there to claim."

"Ah." Nick turned to face him as he backed away, a challenge shimmering in his eyes. "You should make that wager, then. Let Willow see to those wounds on your head. I suspect she has the touch of an angel. And something tells me, of the two of us, you're the one she'd give up her halo for." With a nod, he was gone beneath the archway and under the swinging sign.

Julian felt his brother's egress like an ax to a limb—as if an integral part of him was being chopped away, leaving a hollow, seeping ache that would never be cauterized.

He stuffed the ticket into his vest and reached for his spectacles. Though he already knew the Shakespearean verse on the back of the park's sign by heart, he had an overwhelming need to read it. *"If we shadows have offended, think but this and all is mended: that you have but slumbered here, while these visions did appear."*

Cradling Emilia's new pet against his heart, Julian sat down again, dreading the walk to the castle. How he wished life could be as simple to wake from as a dream.

FOUR

After having her gashes seen to, Willow stopped on the castle's ground floor at Aunt Enya and Uncle Owen's linen-draper and hat boutique. She tolerated Aunt Enya's chastisements for her lack of shoes and corset and her raspberry stained face all of five minutes before asking where Emilia was. Once Aunt Enya admitted she hadn't seen her, Willow escaped into the café next door, led by the tantalizing aroma of fresh baked pumpkin tea cake.

She snuck in cautiously, keeping one eye out for Mr. Brewer while tip-toeing toward the marble countertop where his pastries cooled. Hearing the clang of pans from the kitchen off to the left, she soundlessly picked up a knife and lobbed off a generous slab of the cake. Mr. Brewer's snort from the other room made her jump and she dropped the silver blade. It hit the floor with a metallic *thwang*. She dived over the threshold, cake in hand, and scurried up the first flight of stairs, laughing silently at the erratic tickle of her heartbeat. She didn't slow until she heard the crack of billiard balls from the giant game rooms upon the second floor.

Her pulse leveled enough to nibble on the stolen confection, its flavor all the sweeter for the success of her daring escape. She kept to the winding stairs, not even pausing at the third or fourth floors since the ballroom and guest chambers were closed up tight for the off season. By the time she reached the libraries on the fifth flight, her tea cake was half-eaten and her concern for Julian had returned full force on a wave of nausea. She followed the winding staircase past the sixth floor and up into the star tower, hoping Emilia would be in her usual spot.

The ball of anxiety eased when Willow found her there—sitting on a chaise lounge while reading. Weather permitting, Emilia often came here in the mornings with a tray of gooseberry lemonade and her writing appurtenances. Whereas her mother, Miss Juliet, liked to drink steamed chocolate when she worked on her hats, Emilia preferred something chilled and tart, claiming the jolt to her senses shook the cobwebs from her brain.

The eight foot walls gave a sense of privacy, yet sunlight and breezy air poured in through the open roof so one never felt claustrophobic. The tower was magnificent enough at night. In its midst, telescopes and refractors tilted up to offer a view of the stars and celestial skies. But even during the daylight hours, the turret put Willow in mind of some ethereal kingdom. Sunbeams coaxed strands of miniature light bulbs to glitter around pillars and lattices like icicles. The floor, an inlay of black marble, reflected the clouds overhead so one felt as if they were walking in the heavens. Fresh cut sprigs of lavender and mint, tucked within vases, heightened the clean and vigorous atmosphere.

"Have some cake." Willow plopped the treat atop a napkin on Emilia's lemonade tray.

Emilia's head jerked up from her study of the papers in hand. "Why thank you. I'm ravenous." Emilia tucked the papers beneath her thigh and took a healthy bite of the dessert.

Willow shrugged. "Thank *you*. For helping me destroy the evidence."

Emilia gulped down her bite, gaze catching on Willow's bandaged hand. Her dark eyes widened. "He got you, didn't he? Mr. Brewer finally caught you stealing and he struck your hand."

Willow snorted and eased into the lounge next to her friend. "As if that clumsy toad could ever catch me." She twisted the dangling ends of her bandage then let them slowly unwind. "No. This was Nick's doing."

Clucking her tongue, Emilia poured Willow a glass of iced lemonade. "When will you two ever learn? You always get into trouble on your gadabouts." She handed over the drink, then bent to retrieve her writing box. Emilia had inherited her mother's petite, fine-boned frame and nymph-like features, but she had her father's darker coloring—a dewy, olive complexion and a chocolaty sheen to her waist-long locks that matched her thick lashes and shaped brows. In fact, she and Willow looked enough alike with their similar coloring to pass as cousins, so it almost felt as if they truly were family.

The exception was that—like Miss Juliet—Emilia was adored and pampered by Master Thornton. However kind the viscount was to Willow, it wasn't the same as a father's attentions.

Willow tamped the all too familiar surge of envy. She believed, had her own papa lived, he would've treated her much the same way. Not that Uncle Owen wasn't a loving and kind man, but she could never forget her true parents. It's the reason she'd chosen to preserve the titles of *Mama* and *Papa* for them alone, something Uncle Owen and Aunt Enya were gracious enough to respect all these years without question.

Sunlight stroked the mahogany writing box as Emilia lifted it, glinting in yellow streaks off of the bronze hardware. The sharp flash stung Willow's eyes and brought her back to the present. Inside was a secret compartment lined with teal damask. There, a bottle of India ink waited uncorked next to a stylus and nib. Creamy paper, some already adorned with a messy, curvaceous script, fluttered in the breeze just beneath a glass paper weight.

Willow took a sip of her drink, turning her lip at the tartness. Emilia appeared to be following her daily routine, but something was off-kilter. She was dressed in a favorite ivory tea gown of free-flowing lace and muslin. Butterflies, embroidered in copper threads, danced where shimmery leaves of green ivy splayed down both sides of the long bodice's button-up plackets. Wide buttons, covered in brown felt, complimented the brown piping that ran the décolleté.

Granted, just the dress itself meant nothing. Emilia shared her mother's eye for fashion and adored feeling feminine. She always dressed in fine clothes—mostly walking dresses in soft fabrics that caressed her budding curves like a whisper. Nothing too binding or heavy.

It was the hat which gave Willow a sense of an impending outing. Emilia never wore toppers unless she was going out or would be on display.

"I assumed you'd be staying home today, in preparation for tonight's festivities." Willow settled her glass on the roof that served as the floor and indicated Emilia's bonnet.

"Oh, I thought so as well." Emilia rearranged the straw hat to a jaunty slant atop her upswept hair. "But Papa surprised me a moment ago with this. Mama made it for my birthday." She fondled the brim, obviously pleased. The crown was trimmed with a wide silk damask ribbon in variegated shades of brown offset by a dried spray of orange, cornflower blue, and maroon flowers. "Papa bade me put it on and wait here for him. He's driving me and Mama into Worthington to visit the Foxtail Botanical Gardens and then luncheon at Bixby's Tearoom. I suspect he wishes to get ideas for the butterfly conservatory he's soon to build."

Willow cringed within, worried the outing had more to do with Nick's illicit escapades than butterflies. Master Thornton was no doubt doing the same thing as Willow, trying to distract Emilia and her mother long enough that her birthday could be special, because dinner tonight would be awkward at the very least, and that's if there wasn't a duel taking place with one of her brothers in the line of fire.

"So." Emilia beamed at her, unaware and oblivious as she should be. "Papa said it would be a half-hour before they're ready. I've read over Felicity's latest installment this morning. Wait until you hear it." She paused. "Should we look for Nick first?"

Willow poked at the bandage on her palm. "I believe he's otherwise occupied."

Emilia pursed her lips. "Of course. He's napping somewhere, isn't he? You two were sampling bottles in the wine cellar again ... you cut your hand while picking the lock like last time. Is that it?" Her attention stalled on Willow's stained mouth.

"Yes ... you guessed it, proper and true." Slightly guilty, but wholly satisfied, Willow drew up her knees beneath her skirts to hide her dusty, grass-stained feet and cozied into the cushion. "So, your correspondent is no longer the Countess of Carnlough or even her Ladyship. She's Felicity now. Is such familiarity acceptable toward a dowager?"

"She's not some old biddy. She's only twenty-five years my senior—a dowager by circumstance as her deceased husband's property is in her name. Her mind is sharp and her wit is duel-bladed. She *insisted* that I call her Felicity. Seems only fair, as she's been calling me Emily some six months now. Her reputation for magnanimity precedes her."

Willow sucked on her lower lip, savoring the tart residue

of the lemonade she'd sampled. "To say the least. Nick swears she's a libertine."

"No, she's wise. She knows that women are stifled. To the extreme we must stuff piano legs into ruffled pantalets to hide a similarity to the naked female limb. As Felicity says: If we can't find liberty and abandon in literature, where then shall we find it?"

Willow wagged a finger at Emilia. "See? Lusty, libertine thoughts. But rest assured it only makes me like her more."

Rolling her eyes, Emilia grinned. "Libertine or no, once you've shared the brainchild of a story with a fellow author ... well, you're as good as soulmates."

An acquaintance had given Master Thornton the dowager's name when he first sought a caterpillar breeder while drawing up plans for the butterfly conservatory. Emilia and the countess struck up a rapport when Emilia mailed her some questions about what foliage they should plant to satisfy the appetites of specific butterflies.

In short duress, the two realized they shared a love for novels, not only reading them, but writing them. The countess had sent Emilia a few chapters of her work in progress. At first, Emilia struggled to read the older woman's handwriting. It had a very disheveled and strained quality to it. But once Emilia learned how to decipher it, she was awed by the woman's talent for seeing things from the male's perspective per her lifetime of experience.

The two decided to write a romance novel together—a tale of an enchanting maiden who becomes the object of desire and contention between a broken beautiful man and the evil ghost that inhabits his body—under the guise of exchanging butterfly essays and research papers. Emilia was responsible for the chapters in the innocent heroine's point of view, and the countess took the possessed hero's.

"Now..." Emilia slid the papers from under the glass weight, adding the ones she had tucked beneath her thigh, and organized them all in her hands. "Would you like to hear chapter ten of *'The Butterfly's Mistress'*?" She pronounced the title with grand bravado, drawing out each syllable as if it were taffy.

Anticipation sluiced through Willow. She delighted in this tale, in part because the otherworldly premise had obviously been inspired by Emilia's parents' own ghostly experiences. Still, Emilia and the countess managed to make it fresh with their unique setting of a rain forest and rich subplots.

"*Sì, sì,*" Willow answered her friend, trying not to smile. "I want to hear all about the naughty rumpus. Need you ask?"

When she'd lived in the orphanage, Willow had seen her share of naked boys; however indecorous it was, she knew and understood the physical differences between males and females. She'd surmised quite early, with the help of some rather explicit medical tomes with illustrated details on anatomy, how these differences might unite in a spectacular rush of friction and rhythm. Once she came to live at the manor, her theory of the 'naughty rumpus', as she'd coined it, was played out in full color when she stumbled upon a pair of guests in the throes of passion, writhing within the stable's loft. Now she and Emilia had both adopted the term and though they could say it without batting a lash, they rarely managed it without smirking.

Willow leaned her head back against the settee, eyes closed. Soon, Emilia's smooth voice carried her away to a gothic world of forbidden love and passionate yearnings.

Reading such a torrid romance novel aloud was a wicked enough indulgence, one that Emilia's parents might very well frown upon. But were they to know that their proper daughter was writing it alongside a seasoned dowager in lieu of her 'poetry', they would be shocked above half.

Many an evening had been whiled away up here in the star tower, scouring over pages under candlelight. Only Nick and Willow had been invited to such readings when Willow came home for visits from Ridley's. Emilia had never brought Julian into her circle of trust for this particular project, due to his tendency to scold her. He liked to think of Emilia as his sweet, guileless sister who worked in the garden with their father and made hats with their mother.

But Emilia had another side to her, a fire that lapped at the recesses of her soul with seductive imagery and erotic scenes. The flame could only be subdued when turned loose to burn up the empty white spaces of a hungry page. Physically, she remained chaste as any virgin. However, Willow sensed that would change were Emilia ever to find a man who encouraged her defiant spirit and sparked her intellectual muse as this countess had.

"Here's the finest part." Emilia paused in her reading as though breathless, and Willow opened her eyes to find her friend's cheeks flared to an attractive blush beneath her bonnet.

> *"Sitting in the cool of the shade, Benedict and his ghost watched—a voyeur and a doppelganger—caught between darkness and light. Elizabeth stepped deeper into the gleaming pond, holding the bouquet of marigolds against her naked skin. Her breasts peered out from between petals of orange and the pond lapped at her bare ankles. A fine spray from the waterfall coated her long, golden hair in glistening silver down.*

Benedict's need to touch her elicited a groan. His palm covered his mouth and raked his stubbled chin. The demon spirit demanded he take her here and now, savor her flesh, sink into her softness—a slow, warm, descent into suffocating splendor. But the man pleaded that he romance her, persuade her with tenderness and gentle words.

Benedict surrendered to neither calling. Instead, he stayed hidden and watched in dry-mouthed wonder as she indulged in a strange ritual, rubbing the flowers' stamens along her body until fragrant grains of pollen clung in yellow clusters to her dampened flesh. Then, mumbling a rhythmic chant he couldn't quite hear, she tossed the used blossoms to the water so they drifted in lazy succession around her.

Every muscle in Benedict's body tensed, begging permission to act. In the past, it had been the simple things, her daily habits that simmered to desire in his gut. The way her skirt lifted and revealed her shapely calves as she raised an arm to hang clothes on a line; how her curves rose and fell beneath a loose bodice during a swift walk through the forest; or the flame reflected in her vivid lilac eyes just before she blew out a candle for the night. Today, everything had changed. In this moment, she was not exquisite in her normalcy, but remarkable in her madness. She was unbalanced, just like him. His pulse hummed in his ears, a thunderous exultation. Perhaps she could accept him after all—this duplicitous curse be damned.

Just as he stood to make himself known, in the moment it took to slip from his jacket before stepping out, he heard it: the flutter of a thousand tiny wings. They came in droves—black swallowtail butterflies—darkening the mid-day sky with their descent. In a blink, they surrounded Elizabeth, their diminutive curling tongues licking and sipping the nectar from her naked flesh as she held out her arms. She laughed like a child beneath a snowfall.

The throaty sound streaked through Benedict's heart—a raw, ripping sensation. His jaw clenched. Jealousy, green as a meadow and cold as an arctic lake, pumped through his blood. Enraged, he fisted his hands at his sides and allowed the demon spirit to master his will. He would capture and imprison them ... every last butterfly. For they had accomplished in one day what he'd not had the courage to do in all of these seven weeks. They had devoured her; they had tasted of her sweetness and elicited her laughter."

Willow perched at the edge of the settee. "*Maledizione.*" She offered the Italian profanity, wishing she had a fan like the ones at the finishing school, so she might slap a breeze into her face to cool her chest and neck. Instead, she strolled to one of the windows cut into the tower wall which showcased the grounds below and inhaled a clarifying breath of sunlight and trees.

"You see?" Emilia asked. Willow turned to watch her companion tie a string around the pages to bind them. "Felicity has captured the anti-hero's point of view. His needs, his physical responses."

"It is tantalizing." Willow leaned against the chilled, bumpy stones behind her. "But how do we know that's what a man would think and feel without Nick here to offer his insights?" Secretly, Willow doubted that men thought in such a way. Especially not Julian. However, she could certainly see a woman susceptible to that mindset—so captivated by the object of her desire that his everyday mannerisms became a sensual release. She experienced it each time Julian touched a pen to his tongue's tip while considering some mathematical puzzle. A coil of lust unwound within her as she imagined that same tongue tasting the skin on her neck, or trailing her décolleté on a journey to somewhere even darker and hungrier.

"I suppose we shall have to wait and ask Nick's opinion later." Emilia's suggestion broke into Willow's fantasies. "I do wish that Julian could join us. Two men's observances would be better than one. I so often feel like we're excluding him."

A wave of uncomfortable dry heat suffused Willow from head to toe. Just to imagine Julian sitting with them as the carnal scenes unfolded to pictures of the mind—surely he would take one look at her and know she was assigning herself the heroine and he the hero. He could read her better than anyone in the world.

"No," Willow blurted, a bit louder than she'd intended. "You know how aboveboard Julian is. And so protective of you. He'd be aghast."

Emilia grinned as she tucked the pages away in the box's secret compartment. "I am not so sure anymore. Have you seen the latest two rides he's designed? It isn't as if he's an ogre out to commit genocide on the art of making love. He realizes there's a time and place for romance ... for desire."

Willow shook her head. "Julian's the sort of man who will

one day tape his daughter's hands in mittens to prevent her discovery of certain parts of her own anatomy."

At that, Emilia let out a full-fledged giggle, nearly losing the sip of lemonade she'd just taken. She patted her mouth with a linen napkin. "Not so." Stifling a smile, Emilia set aside her glass, straightened her dress, and came to lean against the wall next to Willow. "He would simply tell his daughter that to touch herself would give her leprosy. His is of a scientific mindset, lest you forget."

They both laughed then. A sharp pang of guilt needled Willow for disparaging Julian, even in jest. Deep down, she didn't mean it; but she couldn't have him sitting ringside when her vulnerabilities lay exposed. "Honestly, there's no predicting his reaction to your literary ventures. Better not to chance it."

Shrugging, Emilia sobered. "I suppose you're right. Were I to show him the book, he'd likely have me sent off to Ridley's like he did y—" She slapped a hand over her mouth in midsentence.

Willow stared at her friend, the taste of bile hot on her tongue. "*Julian*? Julian had me imprisoned at the finishing school?" No. Her little cabbage would never betray her like that. He'd held both of her hands on the day she left, listening attentively as she'd fumed. But ... looking back, that could have all been a pretense to sooth his guilty conscience.

"Oh, forgive me, Willow." Emilia's brown eyes were imploring. "Blasted promiscuous tongue. I should tie a band around it until it withers and falls off! Forget I said anything, please." She touched Willow's arm.

Willow jerked away. A surge of blood rushed into her head, making her temples feel as if they would implode. She and Julian had always had an easy companionship. But she'd been sensing tenseness between them before she left for the school the first time. Now she knew why.

Julian, with his straight-laced, list-making, premeditated mentality. It all made sense. It had been only a matter of time until she drove him to madness with her impulsive nature ... her lack of polish and decorum. She offered nothing but turbulence to his standardized life; the one thing that didn't follow his carefully calculated plans. So he'd found someone to train her, to goad her into obedience like a temerarious pet.

She cursed her gullibility. To have thought Julian accepted her as she was, warts and all. Yet upon the first opportunity, he laid her out on a slab—ax in hand—ready to lob off those small protuberances of her individuality that made her so unappealing to him.

A whimper escaped her throat, which further infuriated her—that he could bring out such a sissified reaction. *Il maiale.*

"Well, speak of the Devil dog." Willow clenched her jaw.

Emilia, who'd been standing silent and befuddled throughout Willow's mental breakdown, followed Willow's line of sight through the turret's window down into the courtyard where Julian had just entered the gates. Glancing at the winter garden, he took a swift detour toward the townhouse, stumbling once.

"Whatever is he carrying?" Emilia queried, an obvious distraction tactic.

Still fuming, Willow inched closer to her friend to share the window's view. Emilia's scent of honeysuckle tickled her nose.

"It appears to be a blood-stained handkerchief," Emilia answered her own question as several reddish splotches on the white cloth balled within Julian's palm came into view. He pressed it against his chest and disappeared into the townhouse.

Julian's and Nick's tussles always ended with cuts and bruises, but never a bleeding chest. The image of a pistol duel slammed Willow against the wall, draining her anger away. What if old man Desmond had decided not to wait for sunset? What if Julian had been shot?

She gasped and bounded for the seven flights of stairs, barely aware of Emilia's questioning shouts as her friend gathered her writing box to trail behind.

FIVE

"Julian, hold still."

Julian sat in the drawing room upon a winged back chair—braid taken down and head tilted sideways by his mother's soft hands. Parting his hair, she stood over him, a damp rag draped within her elbow's crook. Tiny red dots speckled the cotton square where she'd been dabbing at his cuts each time she removed a shard from his scalp. Her scent of gardenias overpowered the metallic stench of his blood.

Several candles were lit on tall, barley-twist sconces, though daylight streamed in through picture windows. The sunny heat illuminated the print on the wall's mossy-green damask hangings. Julian studied his mother's face for a distraction. His father often compared her features to that of a fairy queen—delicate, regal, and erudite in one turn. Her hair was still golden and glossy with just a few silver streaks, though she rarely wore it down anymore. And her porcelain skin had aged little in all of Julian's nineteen years. What few wrinkles had formed around her dark-lashed, dove-like eyes merely accentuated the wit and wisdom behind their warmth.

It felt odd to have to look up at her. He and Nick were a head taller than her petite and slender frame the moment they turned thirteen. As grown men, they now towered over her. But that never compromised her ability to influence her sons. What she lacked in stature, she made up for in strength of will, mind, and heart. He cringed as she worked out a jagged piece of mirror from his scalp.

"Julian. Stop moving." She cupped his chin with one hand and pressed the right side of his face against the apron covering her lavender taffeta dressing gown. He could feel the warmth of her through the fabric, absent as it was from any barriers such as layered petticoats. It dawned on him that she and Father both were dressed for an outing.

Julian closed his eyes, fingers clenched to the chair's cushioned arms to counteract the stinging stabs along his scalp. The rhythmic rattle of shattered glass fell into a porcelain bowl—a tinkling accompaniment to the flames popping in the fireplace, almost musical. Times like this, Julian pondered Mother's inability to hear. The fact that she had fallen deaf as a child had made it easier for her to voice coherent streams of words, but it also made him hurt for her even more. For she had once walked in an acoustic world.

He wondered if she ever missed it, though she never claimed to. Perhaps since she'd had the short reprieve from silence twenty years ago, when his uncle's ghost had come to her for help. At times, she spoke of the songs his uncle used to sing that only she could hear. She used to tell Julian and Nick that those very songs lived on through them. But in truth, they were hers alone. For Julian had heard her often throughout his life, humming the Romanian lullabies in perfect tune. It was as if the melodies still lived within her, satisfying any want for that missing sensory element.

Their bond must have been a powerful thing. But it couldn't compare to what she shared with Father. The two could sit in a room, look deep into each others' eyes, and have an entire conversation without moving their lips. It was as if they spoke with their bodies, minds, and hearts.

Mother called Father her 'gypsy prince'. A sweet and tender sobriquet. Julian had to admit, the man did have an air of royalty about him—his face austere with high cheekbones, a full expressive mouth shrouded in a trim black and silvery beard that matched his thick head of hair, and sagely gray eyes which twinkled each time he looked at his family.

And though he had an affinity for vivid, clashing hues in his wardrobe, and even if he was crippled in one foot and used a cane, it had never tainted the distinguished image he presented not only to his family, but to the manor's guests, as well. Eight years Mother's senior, yet still his stature was as tall, straight, and muscular as his sons—due to the upkeep of the grounds and gardens. He wasn't the sort of man to stand by and command his servants. He worked alongside them.

Julian slanted a sidelong glance to the other side of the drawing room where his father knelt in front of the hearth, warming Emilia's new pet. His broad shoulders blocked any view of the squirrel, but Julian could hear its chittering. Father was checking for blood in the ears or nostrils and for any swelling around its head or limbs. He would search for parasites as well.

They'd been through this ritual countless times throughout their lives. Living next to a forest, Julian and his siblings had rescued everything from turtles to chipmunks, even the occasional bat. Their father, with his innate gentleness and understanding of nature, was a master at caring for orphaned and wounded animals.

In an effort to see better, Julian turned his head too far to the left and caused his mother to scratch one of his cuts with a fingernail. A gouging pain radiated across his head. "Ouch!"

She turned his face up to her. "If you don't stop your squirming, I'll have your father tie you to the chair."

At that, Father turned to meet Mother's gaze, pausing to

assure she saw his lips. "Oh, I believe you're perfectly capable of tying him up yourself, my love. Use the Flemish knot I taught you last night." He winked at her.

A blush chased Mother's answering smile and Julian rolled his eyes. He wondered how many other adults had to tolerate their parents behaving like infatuated adolescents.

"Please." Julian glared at his mother. "When I'm one hundred I'll still be too young to be privy to the details of your love play."

His mother feigned being shocked. "Julian Anston Thornton. Your father was referring to our time in the stables before we took our twilit ride on Draba. He taught me how to form a bridle out of rope."

"Huh." Julian held back a smirk. His mother had become something of a legend in their family for fabricating elaborate white lies at the drop of a hat. She never used the ability to whitewash anything important. It was just her way of poking fun when someone was taking life a bit too seriously.

He waited for her to finish dabbing his head with witch hazel. Tensing at the sting, he leaned back enough that she could see his hands. Although she'd read lips since her childhood—at first refusing to learn sign language as she feared to give away her deafness to strangers—she'd long since accepted and embraced that side of herself, and was now proud of who she was. So, she and Father had learned to speak with their hands early in their marriage, passing the ability onto all three of their children as they grew old enough to talk.

Julian often chose this system of communication when he wished to keep their conversation private. *Your evasion might have been convincing, Mother.* His fingers and hands formed the words in place of his mouth. *Had Draba not been twenty-four-years-old, arthritic, and already put out to pasture. There's no riding him.*

Intent on his gestures, she grinned before responding with her own hand motions. *I was speaking of Draba the Second. Leander broke the colt a month before his wedding, remember?* She exchanged a glance with Father and a silent moment passed between them—loving and sensual. He'd been watching the unspoken exchange attentively and either they were both remembering the prior night, or their own nuptials and honeymoon. Father's neck flushed as he returned his attention to the squirrel, positioning it on its back to gently pinch its stomach as the rodent chattered angrily.

Julian knew how rare such marriages were. Society accepted that most husbands kept mistresses to absorb their primitive needs, as wives were meant to be revered as motherly, frail, and inhibited. But his parents had never needed a third in their relationship. They were equals and helpmates in every way. Julian had grown up admiring their devotion, and would settle for nothing less for himself one day.

Wrapping the screeching squirrel in a fresh linen cloth, Father cozied it into a box close enough to the fireplace to warm the creature without overheating. He stood. A concerned wrinkle stitched across his brow as he reached for his brass plated governor's cane.

Mother read his thoughts. "One teaspoon salt, three teaspoons sugar, one quart of warm water. I'll prepare it and bring a dropper."

Father smiled. Gratitude tendered his eyes.

Gathering the bowl filled with bloodied glass, Mother patted Julian's shoulder. "I expect you to find Nick and send him in so I might see to his wounds, also."

Julian squirmed, his chair suddenly uncomfortable and lumpy. He hadn't told her how he'd acquired the cuts, but she always knew. It broke his heart to envision her sweet face later this afternoon when she realized Nick wouldn't be coming at all ... when his father told her of his brother's latest escapade and what it would cost the family as a whole.

She cupped Julian's chin, her grasp gentle. "Are you all right?" she asked.

Julian forced a smile. "Of course. Thanks to your healing touch." He caught her hand and kissed a knuckle.

Her eyes narrowed. Even though his father carried the Romani blood, she was as adept at reading facial expressions as any fortune teller. Thankfully, this once, she didn't press the issue.

After she left the room, Julian placed his spectacles atop his nose, pulled back his hair with a leather tie, and joined his father beside the hearth to regard their tiny house guest. It had managed to wriggle out of the cloth and its fur stuck up in feathery plumes as if it had been struck by lightning. "Bristly little thing, isn't it?"

Father nodded, grinning. "Be a fine sobriquet—Bristles. He seems to think he's intimidating prospective enemies."

"So, you're naming him. That means he's going to live?"

"He's warm to the touch now. But the skin was slow to smooth from the pinch. He's too young to have been fully weaned. I'd say he's missed several feedings. The sugar water should help with that." Father eased into a rusty-orange brocade tailcoat with black satin cuffs that had been hung on the divan next to the fireplace. The split-swallow tail fluttered into place behind him at the bends of his knees. Such long tails had gone out of fashion after the mid nineteenth century. But then, Father didn't follow conventions any more than Mother did. "The little fellow has a chance," he took up the conversation again. "Given a quiet place to rest. We'll need to be diligent in keeping the cats away. And the next few hours will be crucial."

Julian considered their past experiences with nursing animals back to health. Squirrels—one of the most fragile and demanding as babies—weren't even capable of eliminating their own waste in the beginning. They had to be taught to relieve themselves using strategically placed pressure with a handkerchief every four hours or so. It was akin to waking up with a newborn for changes and feedings. Julian regarded his father's teal vest and black trousers. "You're dressed for an outing. Why not let me look after Bristles until you return?"

"Thank you." His father appeared soothed by the suggestion. He placed a palm against the fireplace's bricks as he propped his bad foot on the hearth and stirred the flames with an iron poker. "I plan to take your mother and Emilia to Worthington. They're having a puppet show at the botanical gardens. I hoped an afternoon of drollery might soften the blow of Nick's confession. I intend to tell them over lunch." His jaw twitched as he set the glowing hot poker in its stand. "Of course, your mother already senses something. She asked me earlier why Desmond seemed so angry. I made up an excuse. It's the first time in twenty years deception has darkened either of our hearts." He sighed. "Nick told me everything. About his plan ... about you being mistaken for him in all of this. I'm assuming that's why you fought."

"We made our peace." Julian tamped down the urge to tell his father the omitted detail ... that his brother practically placed him in the sites of Desmond's pistol. But on his way to the townhouse from the amusement park, Julian saw Nick speaking to Desmond outside the stables.

Nick's plan was in motion now; no need to bring anymore worry to his parents. "Nick wanted Emilia to have the squirrel for a pet. So she would have a birthday present in the absence of her conservatory."

His father's shoulders slumped forward, an elbow resting on his knee. "I wanted so much more for that boy than a loveless pairing started out on the run. I blame myself. He knew your mother and I disapproved of his lifestyle ... yet we didn't physically reprimand him, or send him away."

Julian's ear tips tingled. It infuriated him that his father would feel responsible. He had never laid a hand on any of his children due to the history of abuse in his family. Instead, he taught them right from wrong through gentle gestures and a shining example. No lectures or punishments could ever have matched up to that. "It has nothing to do with you, Father. Nick has justified his choices based on his own warped rules of conduct. Now he'll have to live or die by them."

Father lifted his foot down, set aside the poker, and cast a glance over his shoulder, watching for Mother. Even though—as long as Julian and he stood with their backs to the door—everything they said would be unreadable to her, his father didn't approve of isolating her in such a way. He'd always insisted no one disrespect her by 'speaking behind her eyes' when she was in the room. They were either to use sign language, or assure she was facing them with good lighting.

"I saw Nick take out the brougham earlier," Father finally said, assured she was still in the kitchen. "He and Lady Mina must be gone by now. I hope he'll contact us soon. Keep us apprised of the baby's welfare." He locked his pensive gaze on Julian's wounded head. "You said you made peace with him. But I'm sensing that's not wholly true."

Julian frowned, wondering if the feelings of resentment were so plainly drawn upon his face. "Have you thought of what this could mean for the manor? I can possibly find new investors, but what of patron attendance? Lord Desmond could ruin us with just a word."

His father's calm expression didn't change. "I don't believe he can ... or will. It would shame him every bit as much as us. Besides, I'm more worried for Nick at the moment."

"No need for that. He's as pithy as always. He called Willow a circus urchin earlier without any regard to her feelings about her past."

Raking a hand through his beard, Father frowned. "There's no excuse for such insensitivity."

"And I suspect he told her I had her sent away to finishing school the first time. She'll never forgive me if she knows. I could lose my dearest friend over all this."

His father's profile—glazed by flickering firelight—softened to a knowing smile. "Dearest friend, aye? That's all there is to it?"

Nick's angel comment from earlier danced in Julian's mind, taunting him with thoughts of Willow surrendering her halo. Was it possible, that her feelings were deeper than friendship? Would that not explain her attempts to be with him each and every moment ... how she blushed beneath his gaze at times ... how she trembled at an accidental graze of shoulders or thighs when they were working side by side on the park's rides? Perhaps she'd been feeling every bit as confused as him about their standing of late.

Julian lifted the poker to stir the flames again, though they needed no stoking. "We are so different from one another," he considered aloud, not sure if he wanted his father's input or just to hear himself reason it out. "I'm studious, she's frivolous. I'm a planner, she's impulsive. And she's so private about some things ... about her past." The ash sifted and the wood crackled as if in protest. Julian put the tool away.

"Ah yes, a woman who's mysterious ... she can captivate and hold you for all eternity." Father's eyes had that far-away glaze. He shook his head, as if to wake himself, then tickled the now sleeping squirrel curled up in the box's corner. "Did you notice the resemblance in this little fellow?"

Julian, relieved for the change of subject, assumed he referred to Bristle's likenesses to Isaac the mouse. "Yes. Nick and I discussed that earlier."

Utilizing his cane, Father walked to the window and looked out at the trees. The silver highlights in his thick hair glistened as the sun stretched its spindly fingers across him. "Aunt Bitti has brought so many things to this manor throughout her nomadic sojourns; some that have changed our lives forever. For the better, I'd say. Wouldn't you?" He didn't turn. Simply let the silence stretch between them, waiting for his son to answer.

His enigmatic reticence made Julian uneasy. "Are you speaking of Willow again? Of the way she came to us?"

After a pause, Father raised his cane to tap the window. "I never would have thought those domesticated white squirrels would breed with the local wild grays."

"Oh." Julian smiled and looked down at Bristle's sleeping form. "The trained ones Aunt Bitti stole from the traveling carnival and loosed here last summer. I hadn't made that connection to this little fellow."

Father turned, looped his cane over his elbow, and braced his hips against the window seat. Drawing out dress gloves from his pocket, he slapped them across his palm. "Bristles is white with a characteristic grey stripe. There must be interbreeding taking place. Who would've thought two such different orders could come together so beautifully?" A grin played at the corners of his lips. "I would venture, once we get to know Emilia's new pet, that we'll see their offspring hails the best of them both. The gray squirrel's spunk and the white squirrel's cunning."

Feeling a rush of heat in his neck, Julian drew back from the fire, annoyed he'd fallen into his father's trap so easily. "Do we not have more important things to discuss than my and Willow's relationship?"

Slipping into his gloves, his father shrugged. "I just want you to be honest with yourself. Owen plans to send Willow back to Ridley's within a week. He made peace with the head governess by offering the school a very generous donation. You mightn't be seeing her again until December break. And if all goes as planned, she'll graduate and be ready to come out on the marriage mart by the following Season. If you have something to tell her, now would be a good time."

Julian suppressed an anxious twinge behind his sternum at the thought of Willow being presented to perspective suitors. The fact that she was being sent back to finishing school could actually work to his advantage. He'd been concerned for Willow's reaction when he went to the convention in St. Louis without her. If she was settled at Liverpool before he left, she needn't even know he was going. He'd be home by mid-May, prior to her winter visit. Perhaps, while they were apart, he could work out how he truly felt about her. About everything.

"No. Now is not the time," he finally answered, tugging the envelope from his vest. He held it up to the sunlight to reveal the writing through the parchment. "This ticket belonged to Mina, but she no longer needs it. Before Nick left, he gave it to me. In five days, I'm boarding a transatlantic liner. I'm going to St. Louis to attend the World's Fair in search of investors."

"You're going to St. Louis?" Emilia's question came out on a gasp.

Julian turned his attention to the doorway where a trio of females stalled with gaping mouths.

"To the World's Fair ..." Willow repeated, her hands clutched to both sides of the doorframe.

Julian swallowed hard. Her hair was down and disheveled, face flushed as if she'd run the entire way from the castle, the curved top of one small bosom peeking out from the thwarted neckline of her dress—looking so improper and bewildered he lost all faculty of speech. His gaze held painfully, as if crucified to hers.

"And whatever do you mean that Nick has left, too?" Emilia peered over Willow's shoulder, rippling the tension with all the proficiency of a pebble in a quiet stream.

Mother nudged between both girls, leading with the kettle of sugar water. Having seen enough words to piece together the gist of the conversation, she met Father's guilt-ridden gaze. "What have you been keeping from me?" Her voice tightened, as if frost coated her vocal cords to make them rigid. "How long have you known our sons were leaving us?"

SIX

Misero e brullo. The sun hid beneath a drapery of thick clouds—peering out sporadically to cast the world in a watery green haze. It was just the sort of sopping, stagnant weather Willow would have expected to underscore her portage back to Ridley's: the realm of conduct and manners.

Half-dressed and waiting for Aunt Enya to return and help her with her corset and stays—being as she was 'expected to dress properly for once'—Willow watched the rain streak the windows in her attic room. Drizzling silhouettes crawled across the cheery cream-colored walls and the elegant but simple chandelier that hung above her bed from unpainted wooden rafters. The crystal tiers glistened and dulled with the storm, as though shadow and light were trapped within each prism, forced to fight for dominance.

Other than the glass fixture, only the bed covering—a warm, muslin quilt boasting embroidered mauve roses and green ivy paired with a dust ruffle and pillow shams the color of soft summer sage—and the lace curtains added a touch of delicacy and color to the otherwise sparse attic room.

Willow had chosen this room herself, for its privacy and isolated safety. When she first came to live at the manor, the long glass windows had already replaced the door that once led to the grounds. The adjoining outdoor stairway had been torn down, leaving the room high and unreachable, like a castle's turret. Now the only exit led to Emilia's turquoise room inside the townhouse, via a passage in the wall, the entrance of which was covered by a portrait of Master Thornton's Romani mother, Gitana.

Before Willow's arrival, the attic room had belonged to Master Thornton's Aunt Bitti and was windowless, cold, and smelled of rich spices and the scent of wolf. It was the way Bitti preferred it, being a nomad. In time, Master Thornton had convinced his roving aunt to allow him to spruce up the surroundings, to make it more livable, perhaps in hopes to persuade her to stay for longer spells, though it never worked—luckily for Willow.

Chilled by the overcast sky and the resulting shadows, Willow turned her attention to the trunk at the end of the bed. She ran a fingertip along the crackling white paint, nostalgic for the scent still ingrained in the lining no matter how many years passed: exotic perfumes, candle wax, and spiced candies. Not only had the wooden box been her transport into the Thorntons' lives, she'd folded her body up and hidden inside throughout the years since, each time she felt overwhelmed by memories too violent and confusing to escape.

Right now, she ached to crawl in once more; her muscles and joints twitched with the want of it. *Escape.* Since she'd learned of Julian's betrayal, Willow had begun to rethink leaving the orphanage all those years ago. Where would she be had she stayed there? Was it so bad really, aside from the poverty ... the confinement?

She remembered the place vividly: the three-story farmhouse with caving walls and leaking roof, set on the outskirts of Manchester. Willow knew after hearing of Master Thornton's childhood that there were worse fates for the innocent and defenseless. She couldn't help but be grateful to the old farmer, his wife, and their in-laws for never once laying a hand on the children. But sometimes, a child *wants* to be patted or held. And as they were considered tantamount to the oxen and donkeys—brought into the fold to help lighten the workload—they received the essentials, nothing more. Having no sense of home anymore, her heart began to feel cold and numb. She envisioned it formed of crystal in the shape of an hourglass, with every emotion slipping through like sands—moment by moment. Once the bottom was filled and the top left empty, she knew she'd have no more feelings at all.

In place of affection and companionship, Willow had sought intellectual fodder to occupy any spare time each day. Able to read only Italian words, she had searched inside the farmhouse for picture books of any kind. After she'd exhausted all of the illustrations and diagrams in the dusty medical, technical, and agricultural tomes strewn about, she developed a routine of secretly following the farmer and his brothers-in-law upon their ventures into the equipment outbuilding. She refined her English and learned the inner workings of motors by hiding like a bat in the loft's rafters and watching the men tinker with plough engines and farm machinery.

She used to pretend to be a part of their small group; a part of their jokes and bantering; a part of something ... anything. In the beginning, her only real companion was her doll, Tildey. In time, she made one other true friend: Vadette—a girl two years older than her, though similar in size.

They rarely had time to play with one another. The farmer assigned typical daily chores to the other orphans: feeding chickens, cutting hay, mucking out the stables. But Willow had other assignments. Strange assignments. The farmer's wife drilled her on the acrobatics and contortionist acts she'd learned during her time with the circus—something the other children considered play. Due to this, most of the orphans snubbed Willow for being their keepers' favorite. But Vadette never judged her. Instead, she would come to watch the acrobatics when her chores were finished.

In spite of their poverty, the farmer managed to refurbish an old silo with trapezes, tightropes, spinning wires, and nets to accommodate Willow's skills. When Willow advanced enough to practice in solitude, Vadette started to visit more often. She wanted to learn for herself, and Willow readily accepted the companionship, showing her friend how to swing from the trapezes and spin wires, how to bend her body into ungodly poses, and even teaching her to speak Italian.

Willow felt safe during her training, up high where no one could touch her. But birthdays and Christmas were unsettling. She would always receive gifts from an anonymous sender—wrapped in crisp parchment with rainbow colored bows. Each time, she threw the presents away unopened, for the scent radiating from them reminded her of the man that had held her as she watched her mother fall: a foreign tobacco rife with murder. Even at her young age, she came to understand the link, that whomever had killed her parents so heartlessly had put her in the orphanage so they could watch her from a distance. This made her desperate to escape.

An opportunity allotted itself just a few weeks after Willow's seventh birthday.

The farmer and his wife had rounded up the sixteen children and carried them into Manchester for a 'new' wardrobe. *Camp Field Clothing Resellers* had the best bargains on used garments. Clothes and hats were to be shared by all, altered to fit by belted waists and rolled-up sleeves and hems. Their keepers only invested in white shirts, straw hats, and brown or black breeches—as they could be worn by either sex and lent themselves to physical labor.

While digging through a pile of tattered clothing, Willow had spotted a gypsy caravan peddling on the other end of the cobbled street. The wagons were painted in bright colors, and the sun reflected off of them to stain the pupil. Each time she blinked, the image reappeared on the back of her lids. There were palm readers along with sellers of baskets, fruit, chairs, and fiddles. To lure spectators, a musical troupe comprised of an oboe, violin, pan flute, and tambourine stationed themselves next to the main thoroughfare.

Mouthwatering scents drifted across to Willow's nose, murmuring of unfamiliar delicacies, sweat born of open-ended travels, and the waxy-warm incense of pagan rituals. The dramatic costumes embodied a sense of freedom and entertainment she had been missing. In her young mind, these nomads with their reclusive sophistication reminded her of circus performers. They *felt* like family ... like home. Or the closest thing she could remember of it.

Unlike Julian, Vadette had been a loyal friend that day. She proved it, playing Willow's doppelganger. They swapped hats and Willow broke away from the group of orphans, unnoticed, to weave through the mesmerized crowds. Staying to the shaded edges of shops, she found one brightly painted wagon far removed from the others. Opening the back door, she eased within unseen. Toward the front was a trunk three fourths full of scarves, rolls of canvas, stubby half-used candles, fur-trimmed shawls, and strings of beads. Sinking inside, she folded her body into a rectangle and drew the contents over herself as if immersing in water—a baptism of sorts. For she knew, when next she emerged, she would be reborn.

Careful to tuck a fur collar over the edge to allow for ventilation and a slit of light, Willow eased the lid down. A strange calm engulfed her and she began to make up her own words to a muffled gypsy aria playing in the streets.

"I am a wanderer; my heart is filled with sand. I travel all around the world, and conquer foreign lands."

She fell asleep to the sound of her own voice. When she awoke, she felt her surroundings jostling. The wagon had belonged to Bitti Faa, Master Thornton's nomadic aunt. The old woman parted off from the rest of the caravan upon their passage through Worthington and rode into the manor's gates. Imagine Bitti's surprise, and everyone else's, when she opened her treasure chest to hand out gifts to the family, only to find a frightened yet eager stowaway.

The Thorntons had managed to give her heart life again—to stop the sands from running out on her emotions—for they had offered her a home filled with love, affectionate hugs and kisses, and kindness. Still, although she came to adore them as her own, she could never share the tragic scope of her childhood. How she got into the trunk was the sole part of her past she'd admit to. As to her parents' whereabouts, or why she ended up in an orphan workhouse to begin with, no one knew. They all assumed her hummingbird tattoo signified her time in the circus. Better that way. Willow didn't want to weigh them down with the mystery of her parents' violent murders.

Yet there was a part of her, now that she was older and wiser, that craved answers for herself. That wanted to know why any of it had happened at all. A hunger for revenge had awakened—a sickening sweet desire that nurtured her hatred like the black rotting flowers which Master Thornton used in the gardens for mulch.

A chill skimmed Willow's spine—the breathy purr of

phantom wings inked along her lower back beneath her chemise.

It was doubtful she would ever have the chance to explore her past, to seek out who or what was behind her parents' deaths. As of now, the sole purpose of her existence was to play the part of a debutante bride. No lofty elitist would allow his wife to go gallivanting about in search of answers to a shady past.

A pang of self-reproach shuddered through her. Here she had the opportunity for a pretentious education which would land her a wealthy husband, yet she wasn't even grateful. Perhaps she was no better a friend than Julian. She'd left Vadette at the orphanage without a thought.

The final thing Willow had said to her was not thank you or I'll miss you ... it was a request that Vadette take care of Tildey, her inanimate toy who had been left behind at the orphanage.

What had become of poor Vadette? Was she poverty stricken? Sad and broken? Alone?

Willow's thoughts burst into fragments as she heard Aunt Enya's even, plodding steps ascending the stairs in the secret passage. She had hoped Emilia might've succeeded in their plan—to convince Enya to allow Emilia's assistance with dressing Willow so they might have one last impromptu, and *improper*, chapter reading, but it appeared Aunt Enya held firm on her wishes to have Willow to herself.

Cheeks warm, Willow turned to face the door the moment it creaked open, revealing her guardian. Enya's forty-nine years of age had refined her lovely features to a deeper reflection of stern intelligence. She had fine lines along her forehead and around her eyes, and two silver streaks forming in her red hair, one above each temple. The effect, when she wrapped her hair about her crown and tightened it to a bun, highlighted her face like a halo of moonbeams—the only part of her appearance that lent itself to softness or whimsy.

"I have some things. For your time away." Aunt Enya pulled out a bottle of perfume from the basket dangling on her wrist. "The first one is from me."

Willow unplugged the cork and sniffed. Crinkling her nose, she frowned. "What is it?"

"Expensive. And French. Sophisticated enough to help you fit the role so perhaps you won't run this time."

Sighing, Willow laid the bottle on her bedspread, biting her tongue to keep from speaking the truth: that it smelled like something a bee would vomit.

"Also, Leander wanted you to have this. From him and Sarah." Aunt Enya handed off an Italian carved cameo on a black velvet ribbon to be worn as a choker. Leander's wife had a cousin who lived in Venice and she often received gifts she considered far too extravagant for a stableman's wife. Sarah was always generous to share them with Willow, in tribute to her Italian heritage.

"And Emilia sent this up." Aunt Enya shook her head in a scolding gesture. "She said it's to keep you company, until you may come home and capture fireflies in a jar again."

Willow opened the scalloped-edged handkerchief and ran the satiny rectangle across her palm. The cloth was dyed the color of midnight and embroidered with glittering silver fireflies—an obvious consolation prize from Emilia for her unhappy return to Ridley's. "It's beautiful." She smiled. "However, nothing can take the place of magical summer nights in the forest."

"Magic." It was Aunt Enya's turn to crinkle her freckled nose. "There's no direction in such frivolous pursuits. I didn't capture an upper middleclass husband with magic. It took work. Give it a chance, and Ridley's can iron these youthful follies out of you. Help you see that with manners and grace you can experience more *mature* rewards."

Willow wanted to argue that grace and manners would play no role in getting the only mature rewards she was interested in after reading Emilia's novel—but she stopped her tongue cold. She would never betray Emilia like that, even to give her aunt a well-deserved shock.

Speaking of shocks, the last gift her guardian drew from the basket made Willow's jaw drop: the delicate mother of pearl watch pin Uncle Owen had given her during her first term. She'd left it at Ridley's when she'd escaped so swiftly, and was heartbroken to think she'd lost it through her carelessness. Biting the inside of her cheek, she took it gently from Aunt Enya's hand. "Uncle Owen found it? How?"

Her guardian's green eyes softened. "Before he handed over his donation to the school, he insisted they find it. Had them look on every floor, in every wardrobe, and beneath every bed. He refused to send any money without it."

Willow held the chilled metal fisted tight until it warmed. It was her good luck charm, having both her father and mother's imprint upon it. She flipped it to the back where Uncle had her full name engraved: *Willomena Antoniette.* With a trembling fingertip, she traced the etchings. A poignant smile tugged her lips in remembrance, a counterbalance to the pinch in her heart.

When she had first ended up here, the only things about her parents she could remember, other than their unbidden deaths, were their first names: her father's—Antony, and her mother's—Mariette. Her parents had been so secretive, always changing their identities, she couldn't remember their true surname. In respect for her lack of memory, and to honor her parentage, Uncle Owen had combined their first names into one. Now, *Antoniette* held a sentimental value no other designation could ever match.

A few years ago, Uncle Owen and Aunt Enya had offered to adopt Willow, to give her their name, but she could never betray her parent's memory in such a way. She adored both of her guardians for respecting her wishes.

Her eyes watered. "Thank you, Aunt Enya. For everything." She hoped her perceptive guardian would grasp the full scope of her gratitude.

Enya squeezed her shoulder in a rare display of affection. "Be sure to stop in and say goodbye to him once more before you go. You know he'd come up here himself to give you this if he could. But the stairs ..."

Willow nodded. Though age and a bad back had crippled Uncle Owen, and he spent every moment of every day in his wicker wheelchair, he stood taller to Willow than most any man. He had raised her with fatherly tenderness and compassion, treating her just as he did Leander, as if they were brother and sister in truth.

She understood his need to protect her future ... to aspire to see her married to wealth and comfort. If only she could make *him* understand that she wanted—no, needed—so much more than that.

"Now." Aunt Enya gathered everything into a pile. "Let's pack these away and get you dressed. Next time, you'll come home with Ridley's approval and you will be a new woman. A marriable one."

After hugging Uncle Owen and all the rest of her family goodbye, Willow had come out to sit in the carriage, wanting time alone before being carted off once again.

"*Marriable*. Is that even a word?" she mumbled to herself, taking comfort in a derisive snort. Her eyes felt heavy, ancient from lack of sleep. Over the last few nights, she'd stayed awake to bridge the hours, to stretch them out long enough she might find some way to avoid her pampered prison. But today had come upon her swift and unmerciful as any bird of prey, and she'd failed to come up with a plan.

She licked her lips. The sweet taste of the hot elder wine she'd sampled behind Aunt Enya's back before stepping out into the dreary day still tingled on her tongue. She supposed a part of her was glad to be going, free from the raw emotions and wounded sensitivities weighing upon that townhouse. Every chamber had an air of gloom about it in Nick's absence. In spite of his annoying selfish habits and insatiable appetites, she had started to miss him. Hard to believe the man who called her an urchin and merited a punch in the face turned out to be the one twin who accepted her as she was.

Perhaps it originated from her being the keeper of his confidences. She was the only one Nick had ever told about a visit he made to a brothel at age sixteen. He'd seen a young, beautiful courtesan being skewered through the chest with a knife, and he'd engaged her attacker in a fight. To this day, he didn't know what had become of the courtesan; he assumed she had died, having himself been dragged off by some friends he was with. But it proved that there was courage and compassion deep within him. Both of which Julian seemed to be sorely lacking in.

Adjusting her lacy, flounced walking dress of chiné floral silk—revoltingly feminine with its apricot rosette and green leaf print—Willow glanced out the window past the streaks of rain. Trunks and bags were being brought out onto the porch by the footmen ... her entire identity reduced to nothing more than a few parcels of luggage.

She trailed her gaze upward. Above the weeping scenery, the sky mirrored the same faded lilac hue painted along the carriage's trim and axels. It was an odd color for a sky ... almost as if blue would be too buoyant, or gray too composed, so heaven chose something in between—dreary enough to match her mood.

Master Thornton had insisted she take his canary yellow berline, as the thoroughbrace suspension made for swift travel. Not to mention the separate hooded rear seat which would keep the tiger, Abrams, reasonably dry while he sipped brandy to keep warm in the damp chill and guided the strawberry roan through muddied roadways.

At first she'd been flattered that the viscount should wish to send her off in such style. Until she found out who would be accompanying her to Liverpool en route to his sea-quest venture. To share the two-hour trip with Julian would be interminable. She had earlier confronted him for his traitorous contribution to her send off to Ridley's, but he stammered and stumbled over any reasonable explanation. Ever since then, they'd hardly said a word to one another. Now all they had left was goodbye—finality wrapped in a grudge and beribboned with stubbornness.

Keeping her gaze on the goings-on outside the carriage window, she brought her *pingat* up to her chin, covering her arms, chest, and abdomen in the lacy woolen cape. The fringe of apricot-glazed beads clacked together as she tucked it behind her shoulders and resituated her hands in her lap beneath the wool.

Willow's brain stung from thinking too much. The carriage's interior had been scrubbed and polished for the journey. Oil of turpentine smothered the more pleasant aroma of bayberry candles lit within two glass hurricane-style candelabras and mounted on either side of the window at her right. The scent anesthetized her, made her eyes heavier.

Her attention perked as Julian stepped out of the townhouse. The lilac curtains on the carriage's side windows and navy pin-striped paper on the interior walls reminded her of his outfitting—polished navy tweed pants, a lilac silk puff tie, and an embroidered vest in a marriage of both hues. He lifted his face, his mouth opening to taste the rain. He'd worn his thick hair unbraided today, a cascade of golden light falling to his shoulders. The vision sent echoes of lust into her very core. Why did he have to be so bloody handsome? Her anger would be easier to maintain if he had the face of some bulging aquatic creature and a wide-gaped mouth which only emitted harmless bubbles when it opened.

Regardless, she would not forgive him. He didn't even merit a goodbye, since he didn't have the decency to apologize. Obviously, their friendship meant nothing to him at all.

Master Thornton stepped out and put his arm around his son's shoulder, going over some last minute instructions. She flushed, remembering what had taken place between Master Thornton and Miss Juliet over the past few days, wishing Julian could be more like his father.

Miss Juliet had blamed Master Thornton for lack of closure, insisting that had he told her about Nick's leaving when he first found out, she would have had the opportunity to say goodbye. Whereas most husbands of nobility would've bought their offended wives jewelry or a new gown to smooth their surface feathers, Master Thornton had reached into Miss Juliet's very soul—to heal her from the inside out.

On the first day, he'd gathered a bouquet of flowers for her from the winter garden, painting each of the petals with chocolate—Miss Juliet's favorite flavor. On day two, he gave his wife a black and white sketch he'd drawn of an open palm holding both halves of a ruptured heart, and an eye dripping tears the color of blood. At the bottom, he'd scripted the simple words: *Forgive me.*

In the woods on the third day, Willow abandoned all propriety to spy from a treetop upon the viscount and his wife in their gazebo. Master Thornton had lined the floor with magnolias so thick they looked like snow. The couple stood in the center, face to face, holding one another. First, Master Thornton took down his wife's hair, removing the pins. When it shimmered like a fine satin curtain, his hands skimmed its length to her waist. Without a word spoken aloud, their lips moved in synchrony. Willow—having heard about their winter wedding in that very gazebo years ago—had no doubt they renewed their vows.

Willow hiccupped and wriggled in the carriage seat. Be it the residual effect of the wine or the image of Master Thornton and Miss Juliet's sensual kiss following their silent ceremony—a whorl of warmth descended to Willow's lower abdomen. Her hand skated involuntarily beneath her cape, as if an invisible string tied her fingers to the hot, prickly sensation all along the tight curve of her stomach.

Provocative shadows swirled in her mind and stitched her eyes closed. She leaned back and allowed herself to relax, drifted away from the thumping rain, popping candles, and the voices of the footmen outside. In the tableaux of her dreamscape, she became the bride while Julian played the role of the groom. Entranced, Willow gave herself to this man she knew so well beneath their gazebo—his lips and hands unfamiliar in their masterful possession of her. And as he guided her to lie upon a cushion of magnolias and peeled away her clothes, Julian ceased being the traitor, and became her lover.

SEVEN

Vaguely, Willow heard the soft clack of beads ... felt the *pingat* slip from around her shoulders and catch on the rise of her breasts. Then, the hazy spread of heat at her forehead roused her enough to realize the carriage was moving.

When she opened her eyes, she found Julian perched over her, his opened lips mere inches from her brow, intense in his concentration on his fingers where they fidgeted on either side of her shoulders, trying to catch the beaded cape. His right knee was propped beside her left hip and his golden hair swung on either side of his face with the carriage's rough motions.

Her body grew warmer, flushed from his kisses and caresses in the gazebo of her dream. Was she still sleeping?

"Julian...?"

Meeting her gaze, Julian jerked his arms behind him at the same moment the berline took a curve much too fast. He and Willow both toppled to the floor with her landing on top of him. Loose papers shuffled from one end of Julian's empty seat to the other. The jolt in Willow's elbows when they hit the wooden planks on either side of Julian shattered any illusion of sleep.

"Blast it, Abrams, slow down!" Julian banged his fist against the carriage's wall.

Sprawled over him in the small space, Willow felt every ripple of her companion's muscles when he moved—even through her corset, pantalets, and petticoats. One of his thighs ended up trapped between the squab and Willow's hip. His other thigh was wedged between both of hers, cradling her against his groin. Their chests—in perfect symmetry—rubbed to torturous friction as Julian knocked on the wall again. His jaw angled back and his neck muscles corded as he strained to look out the window, as if in some way it would make the tiger hear him.

Obviously, Julian hadn't noticed yet that their pose was highly indecent ... not to mention *intimate*. Willow became dizzy, his amber and inky essence weighing in the air all around her.

"Abrams!" Julian yelled again.

"*Stop. Moving.*" Willow managed on a trembling breath, her palms flat against the vibrating floor on either side of his head.

"Oh, sorry." Julian propped his head against the wall and trained his gaze on her through the spectacles at the tip of his nose. "Are you hurt?"

"A bit light-headed," she whispered, disarmed by the depth of his eyes from this shadowy angle. Soft yellow light flickered from the candles on the opposite wall, but too high up to reach the floor.

With Julian's help, Willow tried to push to her knees, but the carriage turned another sharp corner and she ended up wedged even tighter against him.

In one blink, his shadowed irises no longer looked pewter. They were night-clouds swallowing the moon. His body language changed along with his eyes. His palms cupped her sides where her waist curved into her ribs, far too languid in their stasis to be incidental. Every nerve ending in Willow's body smoldered.

Strands of hair had escaped her chignon and tangled with the long drop curls Aunt Enya had formed at her temples. The frizzy mess hung over her mouth and fluttered with her breath, drawing Julian's attention to it. He stroked the hair away, as intent upon her face as she'd ever seen him with his calculations.

"Willomena," he mumbled.

He was the only person in the world who could make her name sound like poetry. Her body threatened to turn to liquid, all of her righteous indignation—once coiled like a skittish viper ready to strike—dissolving to sinuous desire. Desperate to gain control, she dragged herself awkwardly into her seat in the rattling enclosure, nearly tripping over her petticoats.

"Careful." Julian's command was husky. He caught her elbows and eased her back into her squab from a crouched position. As she smoothed her dress, he took his opposing seat and covered his lap with some papers, refusing to look at her.

The carriage ride at last leveled out to a smooth roll. The wet landscape passed through the windows at a reasonable rate—no longer disorienting in its blinding blur.

"What were you doing?" Willow asked, her heart quaking as if still caught in the carriage's earlier momentum.

"I ... was checking to see if you had any ... busted ribs." Several strands of his hair had tangled around the left earpiece of his spectacles and stuck out in a fan-like fray. She considered reaching across to free them, but any such contact would weaken her resolve.

Willow prodded her own fallen strands back into her chignon and repositioned two pins to capture it. "Before that." She paused, awaiting his attention. When he forced his eyes up, she motioned to her cape, draped like a beaded waterfall half-on and half-off of the squab. "Why were you taking it off of me?"

"No, no." He swallowed, tucking back his hair behind a

reddened ear. "I was trying to place it back on your shoulders. Abram's erratic driving caused it to slip. I suspect the old man has too much brandy on his empty stomach. He should have eaten breakfast this morn when father offered it." Julian's lips formed a grim line as concentrated on his papers again. "You'd been sleeping for over an hour with the most placid smile on your face. I didn't wish you to get chilled and awaken prematurely."

Willow bit her tongue. Of course, he was mollycoddling her like a mother hen. For her to have believed for one moment that Julian—of all men—would be led by some carnal fantasy to touch her when he had work to do? How preposterous.

She glared at his papers, wishing she could ignite them with her gaze. She was sure they were the designs to the new ride he had yet to tell her of—the one he'd been so secretive about. In all of their years together, he'd never once shut her out of his plans for the park. Now she had lost that part of him, too.

She sucked on her lower lip, wondering why he had to keep touching his tongue with that blasted pen.

"Willow," he mumbled, pushing his spectacles in place on the bridge of his nose. "Is there something you need?" He peered at her over his lenses, the papers rattling in his hands.

Willow tightened her mouth against an answer.

"You know I can't concentrate under someone's stare. We've almost an hour left. Find some way to amuse yourself, hmm?"

Biting back the snarl rising in her throat, Willow began to dig through her gilt-framed silken handbag, hoping to find something to throw at him.

She pushed aside the perfume, velvet choker, and

scalloped-edged handkerchief, stopping at the pocket watch. Sighing, she traced the cold face. The gilded hands told her they indeed had over a half hour before they reached Liverpool. She refused to dally away her final minutes of freedom submitting to Julian's annoying seclusion. Putting everything back in her bag, she cleared her throat. "Might I borrow a piece of parchment?"

Without looking up at her, Julian rifled through the pages, slid out a blank one, and handed it across to her. He then returned to his work, curling the paper's upper end so she couldn't see his scribblings.

Chin set, Willow tore a tiny piece from the paper and crumpled it up—quietly. She followed suit with the rest until she had a small pile of rolled up wads on the squab beside her thigh. She'd managed to throw six of them into Julian's hair before he even realized it.

"Blast it, Willow." He finally glanced up at her, his face the color of a cranberry as he dragged the balls out of his hair.

She shrugged. "You said to amuse myself."

Jaw spasming, Julian tossed the wads to the floor then tucked his work away inside his journal. "Could you, just for today, act the part of a lady?"

Her hands clenched together on her lap so tight her fingernails pitted her skin without her even realizing it. "Oh, but you're seeing to that. It's the whole reason for this ride, is it not?"

"Come now, Willow. You know I didn't mean it that way. Can we please get past this?" Julian leaned forward and tugged on her hands, trying to loosen her clasp. "I cannot stand to see you in such turmoil."

"Because you know it is you who should be in turmoil. You're the one who wants me to become someone I'm not."

His hands released hers and gripped his legs, wrinkling the tweed which encased his muscular thighs. "Not so."

"You never gave me any reason why you had me sent away. So, I must assume that not only am I lacking as a lady in your eyes, but as a friend, as well."

"You couldn't be more wrong." His chin stiffened upon the statement, an expression of somber chastisement. The sort of look she envisioned him bestowing upon his child one day.

Her stomach fluttered as she fantasized being the mother of said child—an old habit she couldn't seem to break. "*Assurdità.* I'm not even worthy of helping you with your park plans anymore." She waved a hand toward his journal and the papers folded within. "You are hiding them from me."

"What then? Because I have something I wish to keep private, for whatever reason, that means we are no longer friends?"

"Friends don't hide things from one another."

"But you've been hiding things about your past for years."

The tattoo on Willow's back grew warm and fluttery. "It is not hiding something if you can't remember it. That's not the same as keeping intentional secrets. Secrets can ruin friendships." She spat the words, ignoring the bitter flavor of hypocrisy in each syllable and vowel.

Julian's expression changed. His eyes sharpened beneath his reflective lenses—a keen inquiry of her features—as if preparing to measure her reaction to his next statement. "Well, then we haven't been friends for some months now. For you've been intentionally withholding my sister's faculty for writing romance."

Willow's mouth gaped as her accusation backfired. She'd never considered he might know. But it made sense. Julian and Emilia had been inseparable over the last several days.

Emilia had wept bitterly the day of Nick's leaving, not for the postponement of her conservatory, but for his failure to say goodbye in person. His note did little to comfort her, even if he did promise to write as regularly as possible. Had Julian not stepped up to distract her, Emilia might never have swept aside her grief and moved on to other things. Together, the siblings had stayed up into the wee hours of that first night, nursing Bristles and recapturing lost conversations. That must be when she told him of the novel.

"So, you know about Emilia's alliance with the dowager." Willow answered, her pinky twisting the curl at her left temple.

Julian watched her finger's movements. "In fact, she's given me the first twelve chapters to review on my trip. I've already read through five, and am quite impressed by her talent."

Willow had to admit, it shocked her that Julian didn't seem the least bit ruffled by his sister's hobby. It was almost as if he had suspected all along. Could it be he had never bought into Emilia's explanation of caterpillar research and essays being the sole reason for her affiliation with the Countess? Was it possible he was more perceptive about human nature than she'd given him credit? That he saw more of the world around him than Willow thought ... less absorbed in his amusement park and intellectual meanderings than she had once believed?

"I must say, though." His velvety baritone centered her attention on him. "I would rather have sat with the three of you in the star tower and read it together."

Guilt stomped upon Willow's conscience. What a hateful and underhanded tactic—separating sibling hearts, just to protect her own selfish one. Moisture burned behind her eyelids. "I'm so sorry. I never meant for you to feel excluded."

He shrugged. "I understand. I know I come off as a prude at times." Leaning forward again, he removed his spectacles, tucked them in his pocket, and stared deep into Willow's eyes, an atypical rakish smile stirring his lips. "But I vow to you, I'll never tape mittens on my daughters' hands simply to keep them pure. A threat of oozing boils should suffice."

Willow's tears retreated back, absorbed into her body to douse the sudden flame of mortification in her gut. "Emilia told you *that*?"

He laughed, and the sincere levity of the sound rushed like cool, refreshing water through Willow's veins.

"You aren't angry then?" she asked, taking his hand.

Still grinning, he clasped their fingers. "Not in the least. Sisters are notorious for saying such things about their brothers. Why should Emilia be any different?"

A relieved sigh burst from Willow's lips. Of course Emilia hadn't exposed her. She'd always been a faithful friend. She must have used Willow's joke as her own, to cast some frivolity on an otherwise hurtful and uncomfortable conversation with her wounded brother.

Willow looked down at their entwined hands, admiring Julian's rough fingertips in contrast to his smooth palms. "Have we irrevocably damaged our friendship through our secrets?"

He paused to consider the answer. "Our relationship has been changing for sometime. But the shift wasn't due to any prevarications. Rather, I believe the change came upon us first, and caused the secrecy."

Willow met his gaze. "What sort of change?"

Julian hesitated and smacked his tongue, as if it were swollen in his mouth. His free hand wiped his forehead where tiny beads of sweat had broken out, though the cab remained chilly. "Well, for my part, when I'm with you of late … even when I simply think of you … I am left"—he gulped—"unmoored." His fingers tightened around hers. "You wish to know why I had you sent away? It was because … because of my confusion over you."

Willow's breath hitched. Had she heard him right? Was he at last seeing her as a prospective female? *Prospective female* … she almost laughed thinking what Emilia the writer would say of such a warped turn of phrase.

But this was not a time for giddiness. This was a time for astonished ruminations, for Julian had brought her hand closer so he could rub the back of her wrist with his thumb. Of its own accord, her palm flipped to curl around the fingertip and hold it.

His jaw muscle bunched in reaction to her forwardness. Their eyes locked. "And what of you, Willow? How do feel about me?"

She sensed a strain of uncertainty in his voice, as if he feared the answer. "Unmoored," she whispered the borrowed delineation, just loud enough to be audible. The rest she left unsaid: *Adrift without anchor—no lighthouse, no compass, no sun, moon, or stars. Nothing to guide me but inconsistent waves of passion and fury. The sweet calm of platonic companionship forever lost at sea.* She had waited so long for him to share those feelings. Now, to realize he combated a similar disequilibrium, she found herself at once terrified and thrilled.

She watched the vulnerability shadowing his face and at last understood why he'd let his defenses down today. Julian had lost Nick who was a part of his own soul, being his twin. Now, he was on his way to a foreign land, leaving all of his family behind. He must feel so lonely. But he didn't have to be alone; if only she could convince him of that.

They both started as the carriage came to a halt.

Outside the rain-soaked window, Ridley's groundskeeper opened the wrought-iron gates. On the other side of the nine-foot fence, the four-story rusticated stone building stood out blood red against the late afternoon's brooding sky. All eighteen shuttered windows stared back from their segmental arches like the stultifying, vapid eyes of some all-seeing monster. The gabled roof made of white verge-boarding, which was intended be charming with its gingerbread effect, appeared more to Willow like gnashing teeth.

Every time she faced this school anew, she had the sense she was to be consumed—chewed up and swallowed—never to be seen again. Surely, now that Julian had confessed having some confusion over their standing, she could convince him that they needed time together to sort things out … that she needn't be left behind to be eaten alive.

"Do you know what they serve here for breakfast each day, Julian?" She watched the groundskeeper step out of the carriage's path. "Rice blancmange. A dish of rice molded into a gelatinous mound and served with raisin compote—an oozing sauce of which the prime ingredient appears to be overfed ticks. *Blancmange.* It even sounds like a parasitic infestation."

Julian laughed as the berline lurched to a start and eased through the gates. She laughed, too, while still cradling his thumb in her fist.

He coaxed her hand up, opened her fingertips, and pressed his cheek to her palm on a soft rush of heat as he whispered, "Lord, I'm going to miss your laughter. I'm going to miss *you.*"

The confession slid between her life lines and reached into her heart, surrounding the organ in an icy vise. "But you don't have to miss me. Don't you see? Take me with you. Remember how we used to read Huckleberry Finn? How you helped me with the hard words? It is only fitting that we see the Mississippi in one another's company. Wade through the mud, chase frogs, ride a steamer. Together it would be so much more jolly."

He laid her hand gently back in her lap. "It would. No doubting it. But you must stay here and graduate. Uncle has already paid for your education and then some. Besides, you haven't the necessary papers, and propriety forbids an unmarried lady to travel with a man."

Willow fought the urge to scream. To have made such headway and then to have the old, fastidious, righteous Julian reappear to level it all to dust. "Yet here I am with you in the berline, without an escort."

"You know that's different. We've only travelled a few dozen miles. And we have Abrams as a chaperone."

Willow rolled her eyes. "That drunken pandanoodle couldn't chaperone a rock."

"This time apart," Julian continued unscathed, "will help us make sense of what we're feeling. A lot has happened to overturn our lives the past few days. We need to assure we're not simply reacting. We must understand our inner selfhoods before we commit to anything prematurely. Neither of us are even accomplished yet. A person has to reach their full potential as an individual before they can give themselves over to another."

Of course. Back to him wanting her to be a courtly, well-behaved lady; to prove herself worthy of his affection by graduating from a finishing school. Willow itched to strangle him.

Accomplished. Full potential. That's why she was here. So she could master the lardy-dardy art of winning a man.

Easing her fingers into her crocheted gloves, she settled her ivory touring hat atop her head and adjusted the broad brim to a slant. The lacey netting along with an arrangement of apricot feathers dangled down the back of her neck and tickled.

"You're right as always, Julian." With dramatic flair, she flung her *pingat* across her shoulders, daring him to try to help her. As if reading her hostility, he flattened his hands on the seat beside him.

A raucous clamber shook the roof as Abrams scrambled down from the outer seat to lower the steps for them.

Willow arranged her drop curls so each one hung in front of an ear lobe the way Aunt Enya had instructed. She glared at her fellow passenger. "I'll certainly be able to embrace my inner self though needlework, etiquette, and dancing. Such an environ is so much more fertile to the soul and mind than say ... philosophizing with scientists and inventors at a World's Fair in a foreign land rich with heterogeneous traditions and folklore. I can become so much more accomplished by knitting a doily with my own two hands than by viewing the inner-workings of a sewing machine at the Singer Manufacturing Company exhibit, yes?"

"You've been reading my brochures."

She gathered her handbag, casting a sneer his way. "Your own fault for strewing them about the townhouse in effigy to my miserable destination."

The door flung open and a cold wind burst inside, smelling of rain and stale defeat. Willow's curls flapped about her head. She tucked them behind her ears, delighting just a little in her rebellion against Aunt Enya's desires.

Julian, having managed during her tirade to put on his own gloves and hat, climbed out first to help Abrams rub down the horse's legs after its earlier run. Willow waited in the carriage. She wished to hold off stepping onto the accursed grounds until the last possible moment.

After giving the strawberry roan some water, Julian sent Abrams ahead with Willow's luggage. "And get some coffee upon delivering the bags within," he commanded the retreating tiger. "I expect my ride to the docks to be smoother than our journey here."

Julian held an upturned palm to help Willow down.

She gritted her teeth and accepted his assistance. A soft patter of mist coated the trees and her face. While he checked the luggage rack to assure the drunken tiger had taken the proper bags, she shivered and gawked at the house.

The monster grimaced back at her. Tearing her gaze from its ugly façade, she caught sight of movement along the side path woven through the rhododendron shrubs which surrounded the school. Abrams' small frame was tottering toward the back of the house, no doubt to take a piss in the gardens before carrying her luggage inside. He looked as indiscriminate as a smudge against the dreary landscape in his black cape, a scarf that covered all of his face except his eyes, and a black wide-brimmed hat which devoured his head. He tripped once as he rounded the corner. He'd end up passed out under some bush before all was said and done. He probably wouldn't even be discovered until the next day when the groundskeeper did his weeding and pruning.

Until the next day ... after Julian's ship had sailed.

A wicked grin teased Willow's lips. "I am a wanderer, a wanderer I am." The song from her childhood curled her tongue on a melodious murmur.

Julian appeared at her side. "What were you looking at just now?"

Willow turned her back to him. "Simply admiring my prison."

"But I heard you mumble something ... something about being a wanderer."

"I was singing a harmless ditty."

Grasping her elbow, he whirled her around to face him. "Don't even think about it."

"Think about what?" Smug, she watched the condensation transform his concerned expression to a showcase of glorious, glittering skin.

"Running away. I want your word, Willow." The muscle in his throat throbbed while the ends of his hair flailed beneath his hat. "No." He took off his glove. "Better yet, I want you to shake on it."

"On what?" She feigned innocence, batting her eyes as tiny droplets gathered on her lashes.

"That you will be here upon my return from St. Louis. I want you to promise I'll see you again without having to search the corners of the world for you ... we still have much to discuss of our future."

Our future. She did like the sound of that. But what was this future contingent upon? And could she trust him to come back from *her* dream destination unfettered—the same man he'd been when he left?

He planned to read chapters from Emilia's book. Willow had walked through those pages ... an awakening of a most sensuous kind awaited him. And he would be on an ocean liner filled with sophisticated women—the same ilk as Nick's many conquests.

Nick's warning nibbled at her psyche: *"He's my brother. My twin. All it will take is him dabbing it up just once with a lady of refinement." Twin ... twin ... twin.*

No. Julian wouldn't find someone else. Wouldn't vanish from her life like her parents had. She wouldn't allow it.

"Promise me, Willow." Julian held out his bared hand.

She paused, her face hot in spite of the gelid wind. "*Naturalmente, il mio piccolo cavolo.* I promise you'll see me again without having to go to the ends of the earth." Pasting on her most angelic smile, she peeled off a glove and spit into her palm. The saliva sat on her flesh in a lukewarm spray, a reminder of such pacts they'd made in their youth.

Julian stared at her hand. The beads on her cape rattled, stirred by the wind.

"If you want to shake on it," she prompted, "we should do it up right. As you know, a spit pact is irrevocable."

His jaw clenched. He spat into his hand. Upon grasping hers, he dragged her behind the carriage—out of eyeshot of the school. Then he drew her close until she was on her tiptoes, their palms pressed together between their chests. His free fingers molded her nape beneath the hat's netting and tilted her head up. She felt them weave into her hair, tasted his breath as he spoke.

"We're adults now, Willow. High time we change our bargaining tactics."

Willow's pulse danced in her neck. She inhaled a thin strip of air.

As if tied to her breath, Julian's mouth moved in to skim hers. A gentle, chaste peck, slick with rain—but more exacting in its dominion over her than any impassioned kiss she'd ever experienced in her wildest fantasies. Her legs weakened, and had he not been holding her up, she surely would have melted into the earth.

When Julian broke the soft, warm contact, he kept their foreheads pressed together, eyes closed. With marked reluctance, he freed his fingers from her hair then drew back, leaving her lips—her entire body—aching for more of him.

He squeezed their joined hands one last time. A feverish

light shone in his gaze. "Now a double pact has been made. There'll be no breaking it."

Entranced, Willow nodded. The once tepid wetness between their palms grew hot—an element as binding as glue.

Their clasps released in unison. He pulled his glove back on without wiping his hand.

She followed suit, struggling to stand against a torrent of vertigo, pondering how his lips had tasted of ink and rain, as if she'd savored the very essence of his soul: prolific and pure.

Taking advantage of her thoughtful silence, Julian cupped her elbow and escorted her around the carriage and across the grounds. Then he climbed the veranda stairs alongside her and stepped over the threshold to deposit them both within the monster's gaping mouth.

PART II

There is something ... sets the gypsy blood astir.
We must rise and follow her;
When from every hill of flame,
she calls and calls each vagabond by name."
~William Bliss Carman

EIGHT

Diurnal assignments for Thursday, April 21, 1904:
1. Get a haircut and a shave; 2. Acquaint the captain and
acquire a passenger manifest; 3. Befriend any and all
tycoons onboard; 4. Learn how to properly kiss a lady...

Julian sat up in his canopied bed, his back propped on pillows. He nudged the spectacles where they pinched the bridge of his nose and glanced over his journal once more. Dawn funneled through the ship's portholes—rosy, cylindrical waves of light. The bed's azure curtains filtered the glow, bluing the pages on his lap and causing the script to appear to dance. Upon closing the book, Julian shoved off his covers and parted the canopy.

The room felt chilly but the sun warmed his shoulders, molding around his muscles to ease out the knots. He swung his legs over the side of the bed then stretched while appraising his first class surroundings. The color scheme—bed clothes of deep blue against a wall and rugs of rich cinnamon hues—reminded him of the fall season at the manor, when the burnt orange and saffron leaves fluttered against a penetrating autumn sky.

He wondered what the other first class interiors looked like here in the men's quarters. One thing they all shared, according to the steward who had helped him transport and unpack his luggage, was their floor plan. Each private stateroom bragged a sitting parlor, a separate sleeping quarter, large portholes, electricity, and a bathing room with a hip bath and private water closet. Julian had taken full advantage of the bath last night ... washed up with the complimentary lavender and mint soap. Though his skin still retained the calming scent, the tactic had failed to produce a good night's sleep.

Here in the sleeping quarter, with the entrance to his parlor closed, he felt boxed in. Cinnamon velvet, cushioned like quilts, covered the back of the door and the walls from floor to ceiling. Luxury stretched around him on a landscape of pillows. Every piece of furniture—the bed, wardrobe, and nightstand in the bedroom along with the winged back chairs and table in the parlor—was nailed to the floor. Should the waters get rough, one could simply affix themselves like a barnacle and hold on for dear life.

But from his perspective, the cushioned walls seemed more like a padded cell. And if he continued on these lunatic meanderings, he would be acquainting himself with such accommodations long after their liner docked in five days. He was going mad dissecting every thought and action of those last moments with Willow.

He had sensed the wanderlust in her. A desire for freedom. He'd seen it in Great Aunt Bitti enough to recognize it. By kissing Willow, he'd hoped to stifle that nomadic stir in her heart. To give her a reason to be patient and wait.

But to perform as if he were smooching the muzzle of a pet ... closed-mouthed and juvenile ... no doubt she thought him a bluenose puritan.

Little did she know his thoughts had been anything but pure from the moment she'd straddled him in that berline's cab. She'd awoken every attribute that marked him a man. The mere thought of her soft curves flush against him, her pelvis shifting across his thigh—

That is what had truly inspired that kiss, not the threat of her running. And even such a small sampling had been tantalizing. Her lips were sweet and creamy smooth. She tasted of honey, salt, and heat.

He wondered what it would have been like, had he followed the impulse to intrude upon her further. To pin her against the carriage, to explore her mouth's warm recesses with his tongue. But he didn't know the first thing about braving such an expedition. He'd read of such oscular feats in Emilia's novel ... seen them played out between couples on the manor. He knew they existed, yet knew nothing of enacting them.

Julian pressed two fingers against his lips, warming them with his breath. It appeared his worldly brother had been right all along. Julian lacked practice. Romancing a woman of higher carnal aptitude than him once or twice would've honed his wooing capabilities. He wanted to sweep Willow off her feet. Not trip her over his blatant lack of sophistication.

He stood. The engines hummed beneath his bare soles—a soothing rhythm that caused his nightshirt's hem to sway gently beneath his knees. Despite his drowsiness and confusion, he needed to get out and about. He had much to do on this first full day aboard the *Christine Victoria,* all of which he'd need to accomplish before the masquerade ball being held in the first class music room tonight.

He strode to the wardrobe and opened the hinged mahogany doors. Cedar chips and pine needles—stuffed in cheesecloth and tucked into his shoes by the steward—greeted his nostrils with an invigorating freshness. Considering his choices, he took down his burgundy frock coat and black pinstriped trousers. He opted for a tombstone shirt with a beige silk vest and puff black tie. Then, to top off the ensemble, a derby hat of pecan felt. Once he'd spread his trappings out on the bed, he set his spectacles on his nightstand and brushed his hair to draw it back into a queue.

As he shrugged into his shirt, he noticed his limbs felt dated and dense, as if moss had grown over his cartilage and bones throughout his sleep. He'd tossed and turned the moment his head hit the pillows last night, worrying if he'd made the right decision in sharing his perplexed emotions with Willow.

What if Willow decided she didn't care for him after time to think it over? What if he was too boring for her?

He could address that on this trip: step outside of his comfort zone, stop being dull as dishwater and find some adventure. Were he to have some grand tale to tell her upon his return, she'd view him in a different light. She'd view him as a man like Nick. A fearless swashbuckler ... a man worthy of a lady's affections and admiration.

Julian filled his lungs and smoothed the high-notched lapels of his vest where they expanded with the movement. Then, dropping the derby atop his head, he gazed one last time at the cheval mirror against the back wall and smiled. Here it was breakfast, and he had a sudden craving for some raspberry ice.

He headed for the parlor to search for his gloves. No sooner had he opened the bedroom's door than he heard a commotion in the corridor outside his stateroom. It appeared the actual purpose for the cushioned sleep chamber walls was to insulate against sound.

Grabbing his gloves from the parlor table, Julian stepped out the main door and locked it.

Standing in the corridor three doors down, a powerfully built passenger in a brown pinstriped Birmingham suit growled at a steward. *"Un fantasma!"* The aristocratic man pointed to the room behind him, his bass voice booming. *"Un fantasma nella mia stanza!"*

The bewildered steward clutched his uniform cap in front of his waist. No more than fifteen-years-old and covered in freckles, he began to wilt like a flower. "I'm sorry, Mr. Sala. Please, I-I don't know what you're sayin'..."

The man's Italian complexion deepened as he shook a fist. *"Richiedo una stanza differente!"*

Several doors cracked open throughout the hall to reveal other men in nightshirts, men with periodicals in their hands, men straightening button plackets or ties—all of them either curious or annoyed by the uproar.

Compassion for the young steward drove Julian into the heart of the confrontation as he pulled on his gloves. First, he tipped his hat to Mr. Sala, then to the befuddled crew member. "Might I be of some assistance? I'm familiar with his language."

The steward, who looked a bit like an owl with wide yellow eyes, tufted brows, and a round face, nodded so hard Julian feared his head would bounce off and roll across the carpeted floor. "Thank you. Thank you, Sir." He shoved his sailor's cap over his cropped red hair.

Julian turned to the Italian and offered his hand along with an introduction. The man's many rings nearly crushed his fingers. Mr. Sala's chiseled features—a good twenty years older than Julian's—became animated as Julian listened intently to his complaints. The man ended his spiel by yanking off his Borsalino hat and spinning on his heel to reveal the back of his head.

"Hmm." Julian turned back to the steward. "Well, it appears someone cut off Mr. Sala's braid while he slept last night. He said it used to go down past his waist." Both Julian and the steward regarded the jagged remains of the Italian man's hair. He still had the ends secured at his nape, so short they stuck out from the edge of the leather band like a bobcat's tail. "Apparently, he sleeps with it plaited and someone snipped it off at the first winding."

The steward glanced across Mr. Sala's broad shoulders at the half-opened door. "Someone broke into his room, you say?"

With that, all of the peeping spectators shut their doors to a concert of clicking locks.

Julian met the Italian man's gaze. It struck him how dark his irises were—like glistening onyx stones.

"*Un fantasma*," Mr. Sala said. His thick lashes flickered as his voice softened to a plea. "*Dirgli, per favore.*"

Julian cleared his throat against a lump of skepticism. "He's convinced a phantom did it. He said he woke up in the night to see the braid floating through midair. He went back to sleep, thinking he was dreaming. Then he awoke this morning to find his hair gone. He wants another room. One that isn't ... *haunted.*"

The steward's face flushed to a red so flaming, his freckles disappeared. "B-b-b-but..." he stammered. "There ain't no more rooms in the men's quarters. And the cap'n won't allow an unmarried man to lodge on the couples' end or the ladies' deck. It's again' regulations."

"*Ho veduto altre singolarità.*" Mr. Sala stomped his tasseled shoe, nearly in tears. "*Richiedo una stanza differente!*"

Julian laced his hands behind him. "He claims to have seen other oddities. He insists you move him."

Beads of sweat appeared on the steward's upper lip. "W-what kind of oddnesses?"

Julian relayed the question. Upon Mr. Sala's answer, Julian studied the Italian man, trying to weigh his sincerity. A shame Mother wasn't here. She would know just by looking if he was lying or possibly demented.

Hesitant, Julian removed his gloves—his hands growing uncomfortably warm. He redirected his attention to the crew member. "There are places in the room as frigid as the arctic. And when Mr. Sala walks through them, the hairs on his arms stand up ... as if an electric shock passes through him. Sometimes, puddles appear upon the floor out of nowhere. And," Julian glanced at the man who nodded him onward, "and he smells things."

The steward appeared almost relieved. "Well that I can fix. I'll get a scullery maid in right this minute. She'll take care of any stenches or leaks."

Julian tucked his gloves away. "You misunderstand. These things are otherworldly, according to your patron. The puddles appear and disappear without any warning. And the smells move from one part of the room to another, as if wafting on a breeze. There's the scent of stagnant water then a woman's perfume. And there's one last thing." Julian paused, trying to frame Mr. Sala's concerns carefully to keep the man from sounding like a lunatic. "There's a pair of antique shoes he found in his room when he awoke. They were sitting in the midst of his parlor. When he tried to pick them up, they clomped around on their own to escape him."

"Aw, c'mon. Surely he's funnin'?"

Julian regarded Mr. Sala's pinched mouth, noting the worried tremble. "Looks serious enough to me. He wants the shoes thrown overboard."

Several rooms had eased open again throughout the course of the conversation, curiosity getting the better of their occupants. At this point, enough ears had heard the predicament that by afternoon, everyone on the ship would know about the haunting.

The steward thrust a gaze over his shoulder. "This is wicked horrid. Wicked I say. This will be bandied about until no one will take the room. Aww..." He ran his hand across his forehead in an absent gesture, knocking his cap off again. "Cap'n will have my stockings to hang. I'll be barefoot and jobless, you'll see." His adolescent voice took on a nasal quality escalated by his distress. "I should ne'er have discussed it out here in the open. But I couldn't get Mr. Sala back in his room, right? He wouldn't go in."

"I'll trade him rooms," Julian blurted before thinking it through. And it was the most unusual sensation, letting his tongue off its leash in such a manner. It was ... liberating. Is this what spontaneity felt like? No wonder Willow liked it so much. One side of his mouth tweaked on a smile as he bent to pick up the steward's cap, dusted it off, and handed it back.

Both Mr. Sala and the boy stared blankly at him.

"You'll take the room?" the steward asked, returning his cap to his head. "You ain't afraid of the specter?"

Short of telling the crew member and their multi-eared audience his family history, Julian couldn't very well explain his neutrality toward ghosts. Though he'd never seen one himself, he believed they existed. And if this room had one, well, what better way to have an adventure than to befriend a ghost? Not to mention, he would be in the good graces of this Italian man who was obviously wealthy, judging by his attire and expensive finger jewelry. Perhaps he'd be so grateful he'd invest in Julian's park plans.

"I'll take the room on the condition you leave the shoes with me." Julian tagged on the caveat, remembering from his uncle's story that spirits were often tied to objects. "And I'll help you pack up Mr. Sala's things and move them to my cabin, so he'll have no need to go in again." Julian glanced at the multitude of inquisitive gazes all along the corridor. "Unless one of you should like to volunteer your occupancy?"

His offer was met with doors slamming, coughs, and nervous mumbles.

Mr. Sala's exotically handsome face smoothed with relief. He took Julian's hand and pumped it. "*Grazie.*"

Julian managed a smile himself. "You're welcome." Then he looked down at the steward. "Let's get to it then, shall we? I have much to accomplish today, and I'm getting a late start."

⌒ᴐ•ᴄ⌒

Inside the wheel house, Captain Everett offered Julian a cup of coffee.

Julian held it beneath his nose, letting the pungent, nutty steam fill his nostrils and warm his lungs before taking a sip.

"I believe I can help you, Master Thornton. Aye, and help you I will. Least I can do for a hero. Mr. Sala holds a lot of clout in the shipping industry ... he could've ruined my liner's stellar reputation had things gone differently." The captain smoothed the brownish-gray beard along his chin as he shuffled through some papers next to the navigation panels. "Now where is that passenger manifest?"

The captain had already given Julian a tour of the wheel house. He'd explained the gauges and monitors: a variety of magnetic compasses, an indicator that showed at what angle the rudder was set, a clinometer which registered the degree of roll the ship was experiencing ... most helpful in rough weather.

Normally, Julian would have been thrilled to glut his mechanical appetite on the shiny brass and silver gadgets. But he was still wrestling with an image he'd seen earlier—an adolescent immigrant boy that he'd passed in a crowd of people while coming up to the promenade. Though the lad had held his head down, a large-brimmed hat blocking his face, something about his chin rang familiar.

Julian couldn't put his finger on it. But he would.

"Ah, here it is." The captain recaptured Julian's attention. He scratched his beard and glanced through three sheets of paper. "Well, Mr. Sala, as you know, is one of the wealthiest men on board. Then there is a Judge Victor Arlington from St. Louis. Aye. He ate at my table last night at dinner. Spoke in some length of the hotel and sea-water bathing business he owned in Liverpool. He was in London to sell the properties ... hopes to meet some enterprising young minds at the World's Fair to invest in."

Julian set aside his coffee. Though inspired by the news, he had noticed the two-way telegraph radio at his left. "Might I send a wire while I'm here?" He had an urge to check on Willow ... to tell his family to keep him posted on how she was fairing at Ridley's.

Captain Everett called over one of his crewmen. "Hymie will take care of you Master Thornton. Hope to see you this eve at the masquerade." With that, the captain tipped his uniform cap and left the wheel house.

After sending his telegraph, Julian headed downstairs to the barber shop.

He took a seat, third in a long row of chairs against the wall. He had brought his *Threshold* magazine and laid it open on his lap. This issue outlined the exhibits being offered at the St. Louis' World's Fair, and last night before he retired to bed Julian had circled five he wished to visit. But at the moment, reading was the furthest thing from his mind.

Instead, he was captivated by the gleaming barber pole in the salon's center. The red and white peppermint swirl brought to mind his carousel at home and the tiny white squirrel now in his sister's care. The snip-snip of scissors and glassy rattle of tonic bottles provided an almost hypnotic backdrop to his musings, lulling him deeper into thought.

Julian wondered upon his family: Emilia, Mother and Father. How must they be faring in that lonely townhouse? Although he wasn't there to suffer Nick's absence daily, Julian felt the hollowed emptiness even in this foreign place. Yet at the same time, some good had come of his brother's impromptu flight. For Julian had never felt closer to Emilia.

They'd spent that first night of Nick's departure together in the drawing room, nursing little Bristles to health. Over the next few days, the squirrel became their binding tie. Once the tiny white rodent got his bearings, he showcased a most charming and comical personality. He'd won everyone over and had become an established member of the family before Julian and Willow had left. In fact, upon their departure, Bristles sat on Emilia's shoulder, nesting within her dark hair as she waved goodbye to the retreating carriage. Julian had no doubt the little fellow would keep his sister occupied and happy until his return.

"So ... did you get a gander at the phantom shoes?" An American accent startled Julian from his thoughts.

Julian refocused on the magazine in his lap. "Pardon?" He tucked the magazine between his leg and the seat as he shifted his glance to the American man just ahead of him in line for a shave.

The heavy man resituated in his chair, rolling from one hip to the other until satisfied with his progress. "I'm Judge Victor Arlington, from St. Louis."

Hanging his spectacles over his vest's placket, Julian took the hand offered him. He couldn't believe his luck. Now, if he could just hit it off with the man, he might have a prospective investor. "Julian Thornton. Nice to meet you, sir." The shake was firm but not crushing. Julian's father had taught him that much could be said of a man's character through a handshake.

Straightening the navy blue vest which barely contained his bulges, Judge Arlington grinned. His greenish-blue irises nearly vanished with the effort, as if invisible threads had been sutured through his puffed cheeks and eyebrows then cinched tight over his eyes.

"Sorry for intruding upon your introspections." His tanned skin glowed in places with a rosy sheen, especially his nose and cheeks. Paired with his greyish-white hair and the long moustache waxed to curl up at the edges, he had a jolly appearance. "You're the talk of the promenade at the moment. Everyone knows of the haunted room. I was just curious what the infamous shoes look like."

Julian leaned back in his chair, soothed by the ethers of hair tonic and cologne surrounding them. "Ah. Well, I assure you, they're unique. I know a bit about trends, having a mother and sister invested in ladies' fashion. I'd venture the shoes are from the eighteen hundreds, judging by the embroidered fabric and inward-curved heels. The toes are pointed beyond what could possibly be comfortable, but they're immaculately preserved. And the color is most unusual..." Julian paused as he noticed the men on both sides of him were listening with their mouths agape. He tamped the urge to laugh out loud. To think, here he was in a barber shop, entertaining men with talk of ladies' fashions.

"Go on," Judge Arlington urged, oblivious or uncaring as to their audience.

"Um ... they're yellow. Rather like buttercups at the cusp of spring. And then there's the sparkling buckles." With this, Julian stopped short. As nice as the judge seemed, diamond studded shoe buckles could awaken a surge of greed in any man. Julian surmised that the one reason Mr. Sala hadn't tried to take them was due to his own superstitions.

Julian had considered selling the shoes himself so he'd have no need for any investors. But in good conscience, they weren't his to sell. Not to mention that something about them called to him ... as if they were capable of affecting emotion. They felt frail, in need of protection. This determination to keep them safe had prompted him to find a hiding place for them during his absence from the room.

"Buckles, aye? Some kind of jewels, maybe?" the judge asked.

"Nothing of value," Julian answered without pause. "Glass gems were all the rage back in the eighteen hundreds, you know."

"Of course." Judge Arlington's plump expression folded to a sheepish smirk. "I know nothing of the sort, actually. But I believe you're trustworthy, lad. You have a good handshake."

Julian returned his smile, feeling a bit chagrinned for his lie, but warmed by the shared sentiment. "So ... you say you're from St. Louis? Are you on your way home then?"

"I am. And just in time to attend the World's Fair with my family."

"I'm attending as well."

"I suspected such." The judge tipped his head to indicate the magazine beneath Julian's thigh. "Might I have a gander? I collect *Threshold*, but haven't seen this month's issue yet."

"Of course." Julian tugged it out and handed it over. He decided this was the perfect segue into a discussion on investments. "Do you have any specific reasons for attending?"

Opening the magazine, the judge nodded. "Actually, yes. I'm seeking—"

"Have you made contact with the specter yet?" A blonde man in the barber's chair interrupted the judge. The customer gawked at Julian from the mirror's reflection. One shoe tapped against the chrome foot rest as if impatient for the answer.

"Um. No." Despite the man's rudeness and ill-timing, Julian had no choice but to answer now that the seven other customers and the barber were staring at him. "I've seen some puddles of water, but when I bend down to mop them up, they vanish."

Several men caught their breaths.

"But no ghost, as yet?" The blonde man was a persistent inquisitor.

Julian considered telling them about the one strange episode he'd experienced. His wardrobe had flung open and a jacket slipped off its hanger to swirl around the room as if someone wore it. Someone invisible.

Looking at the men's enraptured expressions, he decided against sharing. Were he to divulge such details, he'd have a line of hopeful spectators at his stateroom door within the hour. "No. I've seen no ghost. I was only in the cabin long enough to unpack my things. And the steward was with me most of the time. Perchance the phantom's shy."

Everyone but the silver haired barber guffawed at Julian's joke.

The barber slathered foam on his patron's face with a brush. "You'd do well to take it serious and sleep in a nightcap," he mumbled, "lest you end up scalped like that Italian hoodlum."

"Hoodlum?" Julian shifted in his chair, the wrinkles of his trousers cutting into his thighs.

The short man next to him snickered, swinging feet that almost failed to touch the floor. "Have you not heard?

Carmelo Sala is rumored to be a don for the Cosa Nostra."

"*The Italian mafia?*" Julian's blood curdled. "He invited me to lunch later today." This was a bit more adventure than he'd planned on. "Surely it's not true."

"True enough that I won't be displaying my most recent purchase." The barber set aside a moustache cup filled with shaving cream. He opened a drawer beneath his marbled countertop then fished out a glossy black braid. "I bought it from an immigrant runt this morn. Just after dawn. I'd no idea what had taken place in the night ... no idea it was Mr. Sala's. It's not worth my neck, though."

Julian's interest perked. Could it be that Mr. Sala had dreamt the hair-floating incident after all? That in fact, someone had snuck into his room and snatched it off his head as he slept? But how could a child have broken into the cabin unnoticed? He'd checked the lock himself upon taking the room. There were no scratches on the latch indicative of someone picking it. Besides, how would any of this explain the self-propelled shoes? "You say a child sold you that?"

"Aye. Quiet little lad, no bigger than a pup." The barber coiled the braid back into the drawer then pointed to a laundry line strung from one corner to another against the back wall. Instead of towels or rags, differing colors and textures of hair hung from it like hirsute flags. "Those urchins are always selling hair to me for my wigs. I never ask where it comes from. Might be changing *that* policy now."

Morning light filtered through the portals to shimmer on the display. One in particular caught Julian's eye. Not yet formed into a wig, it was a deep auburn cluster of ringlets, the same shade as Willow's hair—though it was far curlier than hers. Julian's mind wandered. What must she be doing at the moment? Music lessons or something equally stimulating. He grinned, envisioning her plunking away at

A.G. HOWARD

the piano, composing a song so flat and off key it would sour the cream in the head governess's tea.

"You're right to laugh." The judge flipped a few pages in the magazine, recapturing Julian's attention. "For heaven's sake. It's like being in a roomful of tittle-tattling dowagers. A *don*. Just because he's Italian and enigmatic." He snorted.

The short man leaned forward to see around Julian. He narrowed his eyes at the judge. "If it not be true, then explain the four exotic beauties he boarded with. They haven't the look of prudential about them. They're prostitutes, to be sure. He's here to recruit some of your American fare for his ring, no doubt."

"Nonsense." The judge grimaced. "Those women are rumored to be his daughters."

The little man huffed. "No doubt they think they be. His kind ain't above stealing little girls then raising them for their own uses."

Judge Arlington absently flipped through some more pages as he looked his antagonist in the eye. "It is my understanding that they are a family of traveling thespians. In fact, they're to perform a snippet from a play tonight at the masquerade. They're taking a side trip from their bookings. Mr. Sala's chaperoning them to the World's Fair so they might see the exhibits."

"More likely so they can *provide* some exhibits. Of their nether regions." The short fellow laughed so hard he nearly tottered off his chair.

Several other men muttered obscenities and chuckled.

Anticipation of his imminent afternoon with Mr. Sala settled over Julian like a dark fog. "Perhaps I should reconsider our luncheon."

Judge Arlington closed the magazine. "No. I say you keep that appointment with him. Find out who he is so you can silence all of this foolish hearsay. Poor man. Can't speak a word of English to defend himself. You're his one opportunity for a fair shake, boy."

Julian nodded. "He did have a kind smile. And he seemed to need a friend."

"That's the spirit." The judge winked. "And if by some chance he turns out to be a notorious criminal, at least you'll be on his good side. One, you saved him from a ghost, and two, you'll have saved him from eating alone. Nobody likes to dine alone."

Julian smiled, liking the judge more by the minute.

As Judge Arlington stood for his turn in the barber chair, Julian rose beside him, leaving his magazine on the chair to hold his spot. He stepped around men's outstretched legs to make his way over to the hanging wigs. Unfolding his spectacles, he slid the earpieces in place. "You say the child brought Mr. Sala's braid early this morn?"

The barber draped a sheet over the judge's wide form. "Aye. He brought that, too." He gestured with his foam-filled brush to the hair that looked like Willow's. "And that's highest quality. It was soft waves when I first laid hands on it. Now look at it. Takes a pin-curl easy as you please. No telling how far that little thief had to wander to steal such a mane. The lady must have been a beauty."

Wander. Thief. Beauty. Unease simmered within Julian's chest as he reached to pull down the cluster of hair. He nestled his nose in the curls. A familiar exotic scent gripped his lungs like a fist. The tune Willow sang while staring at her school uncurled within him, sultry and ethereal: *I am a wanderer, a wanderer I am.*

Perception, edged with dread, heated the tips of his ears. He'd caught her watching Abrams as the driver stumbled into the gardens. Then, shortly after they'd stepped into the school together, Willow disappeared from Julian's view. He'd been besieged by a flock of governesses clucking like hens as they led him into the kitchen where they coaxed him to stay for coffee and fruit tarts.

When time came to leave, his hostesses forbade him to go upstairs to the girl's quarters in search of Willow. He was forced to go without saying goodbye. If not for seeing Abrams—a blur of black in his cloak, scarf-covered face, and large brimmed hat—sitting rigid and sturdy in the driver's seat, Julian might have turned back for the school and demanded to see Willow once more, just to ensure her resolve to stay. But he took Abrams' sudden equanimity and sobriety as a good omen, that all was well in the world.

In one blinding flash of reason, Julian saw the flaw in his logic. No cup of coffee, no matter how black and potent, could have sobered the driver in that forty-five minute interim. With his body type being so small, a woman could easily have filled Abrams' concealing clothes.

Julian squeezed the hair in his hand. How could he have overlooked such obvious facts yesterday? Then again ... he *had* been distracted by Willow's kiss.

"Oh, hell." Julian turned to face the barber. "Whereabouts would one find this little boy?"

Scraping foam and whiskers off his razor into a bowl positioned beneath the judge's rolled chin, the barber shrugged. "Steerage, no doubt. All the immigrants bunk down there. But there's hundreds of them. You'll never turn out one little thief ... especially one of that size." He proceeded to put more shaving cream on the judge's cheeks, avoiding his moustache.

"We'll see about that." Julian headed for the door.

"Wait! That's my hair!"

Julian paused, one hand on the door latch, the other

tangled in the silken strands. He glanced over his shoulder. Two men stood up from their chairs, prepared to pounce on him.

Turning full around, he met the barber's eyes. "I think I know who this belonged to. I will bring it back."

"Absolutely not! It's pin-curled to perfection. You'll ruin it."

The two men grappled Julian's elbows and tried to drag him toward the barber. Julian considered pounding them both. Lord knew he'd been in enough scuffs with his brother to better these two city nobles. Instead, he dug his heels into the floor and didn't budge. The men dropped their arms and backed up, as if surprised by his strength.

"What say," Julian began, "should I bring the hair back damaged I give you the phantom shoes in exchange?"

The judge, with shaving froth dripping from his right cheek down to his jaw, studied Julian's determined expression in the mirror's reflection then glanced at the barber standing over him. "An ideal trade. Better than a trade, even. People will pay just to get a look at those shoes. You'll make ten times what you could with that wig. And you have us all as witnesses to the bargain."

Julian's neck throbbed, awaiting the barber's decision.

As he wiped his razor on a towel, the barber nodded. "All right. We have an accord."

"Thank you." Julian directed the words to the barber, but his gaze appointed his gratitude to the judge. It appeared he'd made a persuasive ally today. An ally he would find again later to talk over some business. Victor Arlington was a man Julian would enjoy working with.

"Don't be expecting me to hold your place in line for a shave," the barber called out as Julian rushed into the corridor.

Cradling the soft curls in his palms, Julian strode toward the service stairway. If his suspicions about Willow were true, a scruffy chin was the least of his worries.

NINE

Willow scooted her chair against the outer wall of the wheel house where the captain and several officers sat within, navigating the *Christine Victoria*. She turned her back to the windows. She disliked being so close to any crewmembers, but it was the most secluded place on the crowded promenade deck. And being noticed by the crew paled in comparison to what would happen should Julian see her. He would hold her captive then send her right back to Liverpool the moment they docked in New York.

She had to stay out of his sight at least until they boarded the train to St. Louis. Once there, he would have no choice but to let her join him on the tour of the World's Fair. She'd waited her whole life for an opportunity like this ... and she had every intention of seeing it through.

A canopy above Willow's head shaded the row of chairs that lined the walls of the ship's superstructure. Blankets hung across the whicker backs, waiting to accommodate lounging passengers, of which thankfully there were none at the moment. This location offered a bird's eye view of everyone. Those who strolled the bright openness of the walkway to fill their lungs with salty air; those who stood at the rail and watched the sea breathe and billow as it spread all the way to the horizon in a gurgling and glistening swath of blues and grays.

Willow tugged her cap low on her forehead and propped an elbow on the chair's arm, tapping the dimple in her chin. Ankles crossed, she moved her feet in time with her pulse, clunking the men's boots she'd borrowed together. She enacted the boyish slump she'd been practicing for the last several hours and contemplated her clothes: the broadcloth jacket—scratchy and masculine, the tweed pants—liberating and roomy in spite of their itchy discomfort. She'd had to discard Abram's cloak and hat lest Julian recognize them. These replacements, though suitable for her charade as Wilson—an immigrant man-child—offered little protection against the morning chill. Her pantalets and chemise underneath didn't help much either. What she wouldn't give for a soft, fleecy union suit. Such a men's undergarment would insulate her from the wrists to the ankles.

Still, her gratitude toward her new companions, the Helget family, would not be stifled by this minor discomfort. They'd given her all they could upon her impromptu appearance in steerage after she climbed out of the trunk she'd stowed away in on the wharf. Being German immigrants, the parents had limited knowledge of the English language. Their children, Engleberta and Christoff— were taught to speak English by their schoolmarm in Germany and had been Willow's translator. The family had little money or possessions. Heavens. The dear children were even shaved bald, having succumbed to a plague of lice on their way to England. Yet everything they could spare had been rationed out to Willow—a man's hat, clothes, boots. She had wanted to pay them back.

Willow opened her lapel to glance at the one article she'd brought with her for luck, having left the others behind at Ridley's. The mother of pearl watch-pin from Uncle Owen might have been a fair trade, but she could never part with it so callously. The sentimentality held too strong a bind around her heart. So Willow had sold the only thing she could—cutting off the braid she had rolled up and tucked beneath Abram's hat—and gave the proceeds to the Helget family.

A soft gust of wind licked her neck where her cropped hair stopped just beneath the brim of her cap. Despite the bright sun, the air had a bite to it. Goose bumps rose on her nape, the skin vulnerable without her long locks to cover it. Closing her jacket again, she reached up and rubbed the soft bareness, the ache of detachment bristling her palm.

It unnerved her, this reaction. She'd never thought of herself as vanity-stricken. But then, she'd never realized her hair was such an integral piece of her identity. Precious memories had been tangled within that mane. Perhaps that's why she used to wind it around her fingers, so she could feel tied to lost moments of her past.

In her earliest childhood, her mother used to brush out Willow's long hair and braid it each night as her papa played at nursery rhymes. He'd touch Willow's right eye, then her left, his fingertips grazing her mouth and ending with a tender pinch on her tiny nose. Slumping lower in her chair, Willow mimed the song he would sing during the ritual in his deep Italian brogue. "This is the beautiful eye and this is its brother; this is the little church and this is its door bell." Although it never rhymed, or even made sense for that matter, it had been one of her favorite nursery songs.

Beneath the shaded canopy, she fought the moisture welling in her eyes as her nose twitched in remembrance of his and Mama's tenderness.

She refused to cry. Instead, she thought upon happier memories tied within her hair. At the Manor, Aunt Enya used to set Willow's auburn locks in pin-curls as together they recited sonnets by Lord Byron—their beloved English poet. Appreciation of his work was the only thing the two ever held in common.

Then there was Julian. Throughout their youth, each time he'd find her atop a tall tree, he'd tease her from below: "Rapunzel, Rapunzel, let down your hair." And Willow would toss a handful of leaves or unripe fruit into his face—depending upon her mood.

Now, Julian was no longer her childhood playmate. He was a man, and she couldn't forget how his fingers had wrapped within her hair yesterday afternoon when he kissed her. How the sense of him, intertwined with some living part of her, had been more stimulating than any scene she'd read in Emilia's novel. What would Julian think of her now ... sheared like a sheep as she was? He wanted her to become *more* of a lady, not less of one.

A birdlike whistle rippled Willow's depths of self-pity. Looking up, she caught sight of six-year-old Newton. The tiny boy had sidled into a group of unsuspecting aristocratic men packed like cattle at the ship's bow. Most of them were married. One could tell not only by their wedding bands, but by the fervor with which they smoked their cigars and clung to every boisterous joke as if these things were the last remaining lifelines to their manhood.

Newton's black, round eyes flashed in Willow's direction. He gestured with his chin toward a lanky, balding man in the midst of the crowd. Willow nodded. Upon her response, Newton ducked between men's legs and into the depths of the group unnoticed. She bit her lip. If he was caught pickpocketing, she would take the blame. It was her desire to attend the Greek gods and goddesses masquerade ball tonight. All so she could be close to Julian ... to spy upon him from behind a mask.

She could not endure the torture of knowing they were both on this ship yet a world away from one another. She couldn't have Julian attending the gala without her, dancing with beautiful women, possibly kissing some wanton trollop with those soft, sensual lips of his.

Willow pressed her fingers to her mouth.

Luce del cielo. How could a man who'd never kissed a woman be so blasted good at it? He'd barely grazed her lips yesterday. But just thinking on the sensation, on the promise behind that gentle restraint and simmering heat, left her eager to discover what that mouth and tongue would be capable of given the proper nudge. She couldn't allow some other woman to unlock that side of him.

The party was for upper class passengers, being held in the first-class music room. The only way she could have access to an appropriate costume would be to steal one along with some ribbons, scarves, and lace from the ship's tailor, then alter it enough to warrant it unrecognizable by this evening. She planned to return the costume tomorrow morning, so it was actually more like borrowing.

Willow and Newton had peered into the tailor's boutique windows earlier. They spotted three goddess costumes upon the wall—Hera, Medusa, and Aphrodite—complete with masks and wigs. Since they needed no petticoats or crinoline beneath the form-hugging gowns, any of them would suffice. The sign upon the boutique's door had pledged the tailor's return at eleven sharp. That gave them one hour. Seeing as he was preoccupied up here for the moment, all they needed were his keys.

Willow held her breath and studied her watch again. Newton popped out from the crowd. He wore a nefarious grin—strangely out of place on such a cherubic face. He glanced her way and patted his jacket pocket, his small legs strolling briskly toward the staircase.

Pulse jumping, Willow scanned the men. None of them seemed the wiser. The tailor was still tied to his conversation with the overweight fellow next to him. Willow stood, and attempting a masculine stride in her heavy boots, followed in the footsteps of her accomplice toward the second deck where the stores and barber salon were located.

Willow clasped Newton's small hand in hers. Because of their height difference, his wide-brimmed hat scraped her waist from time to time with their shared steps. They wound through the quiet corridor of the men's quarters, both keeping their heads down when they passed anyone.

By looking down and resisting eye contact, they gave the impression of being on an errand. At one point, they were stopped and questioned by an elegant Englishman leaving his cabin, but Willow spoke deep from her chest—in hopes to sound like an adolescent male—and used Italian. The befuddled man finally gave up, assuming Willow and Newton were lost. He shrugged them off like fleas and went on his way, too busy to care what became of the two impoverished boys.

Tucking the stolen costume deeper within her buttoned jacket, Willow gulped against a sandy throat. How she longed for a raspberry ice to moisten her tongue. She didn't want to be here in the men's hall. It was too risky. But she took solace in the fact that Julian would already be out and about for the day, marking off errands in his journal as he accomplished each one.

Due to Newton's inability to speak, Willow had no idea why they were here or what they were after. But when he asked her to follow with erratic hand gestures, Willow acquiesced. She owed him for all he'd done for her since they'd met. First, he had taken her clipped hair to the barber and sold it to keep her identity secret, then he'd lifted keys off the tailor and stood watch at the shop's door as she stole a costume. They were partners in crime now, without question.

The mask slipped out from beneath the hem of Willow's jacket when she and Newton rounded the last stretch of the men's quarters. She wedged the disguise higher between her breasts.

Without any warning, Newton came to an abrupt halt in front of one of the staterooms. He glanced up at Willow then hammered the brass knocker. As if echoing the rhythm, Willow's heart slammed into the satin mask pressed against her sternum. What was he leading her into? Who did he know here?

The lock clicked. Newton shoved the door and it swayed open to reveal a lush sitting parlor complete with oriental rugs, wood floor, and mahogany walls.

Willow forced herself to step over the threshold alongside her companion, greeted by the faint scent of brackish water and a woman's perfume. Freezing air rushed over her then vanished, as if she'd walked through an invisible wall of ice. The hairs on her body lifted in response. She glanced to the other side of the door and struggled to make sense of it. There appeared to be no one else in the room, only Newton ushering the door shut behind them.

The Helget children had known Newton for a week before she met them all, and they jabbered to her constantly about his many magic tricks. She hadn't believed them. Children were notorious for rapid flights of imaginings, especially in the poverty sect where lack of toys and books left them bored. But what else could explain his power to unlock the door without a key?

Already light-headed over her lack of breakfast and the

morning's excitement, Willow dropped into a high-backed chair lined with heavy cut velvet. "Newton ... how did you do that?"

The boy lifted a finger to his mouth, shushing her. He stood stiff in his tattered suit and cap, looking every bit the serious, miniature man; such an endearing pose, she would have smiled had the situation not been so queer.

His rustling clothes became the only sound besides the purr of the ship's motor. Willow watched in silent wonderment as the child proceeded to spin in a slow circle, his expressive eyes touring the parlor ... searching.

She had a passing suspicion that he might have come to steal a map or two. Christoff had told her of Newton's obsession with any sort of geographical chart or topographical depiction, of his tendency to sneak into first-class rooms and steal maps to foreign lands. He had quite a collection already. She supposed he liked to imagine travelling to such places.

Willow's musings ceased as she heard it: a soft knock drifting from the bedchamber. Newton heard it as well, for with a start, he sprinted through the opened adjoining door. Willow jumped to her feet and followed. Upon her arrival, she found the boy digging through drawers in the black oak wardrobe.

Willow waited next to him, mesmerized by the faint tap. "Whatever is making that sound?"

Furrowing his tiny forehead, Newton paused, up to his elbows in folded squares of men's under things. Willow wasn't sure why, but seeing the intimate articles made her stomach and throat flutter, as if blind moths butted her from within, trying to find their way out.

Newton dragged one arm free to point at his booted feet.

Willow frowned. "What ... *shoes*?" That made no sense.

How could shoes be making such a sound? Newton must have misunderstood her question. "You mean to say we came in here for shoes? What's wrong with the ones you already have, little widget?"

He scrunched his face at her in obvious annoyance. His thick lashes shifted down and he plowed through some union suits. Their backside flaps unfolded to hang out of the drawer like fleecy tongues. Willow considered getting a pair of the long underwear for herself, but decided she'd have nowhere to stash it for the walk back to steerage.

She reached up to twist her hair around her finger, meeting only skin. Her nerves jittered. If they didn't make haste, someone was sure to catch them here. She could tell by the determined set to her accomplice's jaw that he would not leave without his prize.

Willow flung open the wardrobe doors to help him look. A shot of nervous energy skittered through her as she recognized the clothes hanging on the rod. No mistaking them ... she'd seen each and every vest, jacket, and trouser donning Julian's flawless physique at one time or another.

When her hand passed across the vest he'd worn yesterday, her mind spun out of control.

She wanted to drag it from the hanger ... to imagine his body filling the fabric again. To smell his scent still warm upon the lining. But it wasn't his scent that teased her nostrils; it was the woman's perfume again. The lingering floral aroma took on an entirely new connotation knowing who this room belonged to.

It couldn't be the perfume of a scullery maid; the fragrance was expensive and ambrosial—gardenia with wispy notes of sweet black licorice. It appeared Julian had been entertaining a lady. His first night on board, and already he'd fallen beneath some rich debutante's spell just like Nick had warned. A surge of righteous indignation flamed through her. She would plump Julian's peepers the next time she saw him. Give him two black eyes to match his black heart.

She caught Newton's arm, disgusted by the moisture gathering along her lower lashes. "We must leave."

The boy shook his head, insistent. Pointing to his feet, he silently begged for more time.

Before Willow could respond, two voices broke outside in the corridor. She winced, slapping at her tears. "Hurry and find the shoes," she said to Newton. "I can't be seen by the unfaithful sot that bides here."

Willow's trousers rubbed between her thighs as she rushed into the parlor and pressed her ear to the door.

A woman's timbre rose, rich and throaty, from the other side. "Has he any idea how they got here, in his room no less?" A practiced trace of seduction softened the edges of every word.

"No," another woman's voice answered in a younger, lighter tone. "But he said they didn't even appear to be damaged by the water. They must be invincible. Just like the story said."

The older woman *tsked*. "Invincible, ha! I guarantee those latchets are removable and priceless. I cannot believe he simply left them there. At the very least he should've snapped them off, after all she went through."

"He said he tried. He insists they ran from him."

"He's delusional. Superstitious," the first one answered.

"Have some compassion ... he was weeping when he told me. You of all people should understand. You know what she meant to him. What they both meant..."

Willow shivered and drew back from the door as a chill drifted over her. Then, feeling a contrast of warmth, she glanced down. Newton held a wooden box in his hands. A shuffling sound came from within the container. In a matter of seconds, the shuffles grew to loud thumps.

Frozen in disbelief, Willow mouthed, "Quiet," to her accomplice, thinking he must be causing the raucous.

Newton lifted the lid. His lips mimed unheard words, soundlessly scolding the contents. Catching a glimpse of yellow shoes moving within like a captured rodent, Willow grabbed her collar, nauseous.

She must have fallen asleep on the promenade deck. This was all a nightmare. Most likely she would wake up within the brig, arrested for stowing away on the ship. She took solace in the thought. Better that, than to admit she'd lost her mind.

She continued to watch her companion in disbelief. In spite of his efforts to tame them, the shoes would not still.

"I hear something." The provocative woman's voice broke from the other side of the door, closer now, as if she spoke against the wood. "Are you sure the occupant is out for the day?"

"Yes. I saw him leave the barber's salon," the youthful voice answered. "He went off in the direction of the service quarters."

"But I hear something—"

"The maids are coming," the second woman interrupted. "We must go."

Willow pressed an ear to the door, listening as their footsteps faded away down the corridor.

She turned to Newton, determined to make a run for steerage before the maid arrived. He had dropped the box and held the shoes in his hands. Seeing them displayed in the light, the glistening latches caught Willow's eye ... mesmerized her. They moved across her vision like dancing stars. A strange feeling overtook, a yearning to wear them ... to feel the shoes alive against her skin.

Unable to fight the impulse, Willow leaned against the wall, worked off her cumbersome boots, and snatched the embroidered accessories away. She slipped them onto her naked feet.

When she looked up from admiring the latchets, a semi-transparent woman stood beside Newton in her undergarments—an outdated chemise, stays, and petticoat—all the same buttercup shade as the antique shoes. The stranger was dripping wet, making puddles on the floor. Yet she hovered in place without casting a shadow from the sunlight behind her. Willow propped herself against the wall, her breath a heavy stone caught in her lungs.

"About time you notice me, you beef-witted dandy."

Mouth agape, Willow regarded the woman from her long, dripping hair to her bare heels that were lifted several inches from the floor, as if she still wore the shoes. Water drizzled from her toes. "Who are you?" Watching Newton reach up and hug the woman, making contact enough to wrinkle her petticoat and leave wet spots on his clothes, Willow flung out a hand. She stared in disbelief as her fingers skimmed through the woman as if she were smoke. "*What* are you?"

The woman raised a well-arched eyebrow and flapped her hands so her elbow-length sleeves ruffled, flinging water droplets that dissipated in thin air. "I'm a bird-of-paradise. Can't you tell?" She simpered. "Boo!" Willow yelped and the woman laughed until her translucent face appeared flushed.

Speechless, Willow tried to calm her heartbeat. She dragged a shoe's toe through one of the puddles beneath the woman, only to have it dry up instantly, as if absorbed into the floor. If Willow hadn't heard the story of Julian's uncle ... had she not known about the ghost-flower and come to believe in it, she might have fainted dead away. Here she'd longed for years to speak with her deceased parents. Now instead, she was face to face with a dead, soggy, debutante, judging by the stylish lace petticoat and the extravagant shoes upon Willow's feet.

Something about the woman's features comforted Willow. The delicate nose, the softly pointed chin. By the way Newton held the ghost's hand and smiled, it was obvious he felt quite comfortable around her. He acted as if he'd seen and touched her countless times before. Not only that, he *liked* her.

The cloying scent of perfume became overpowering. This was all getting to be too much. Willow's knees nearly buckled. "I don't feel well."

"If you're going to wretch, aim away from the shoes." The ghostly woman scowled at her. "I don't wish you to be soiling them. And don't be thinking you're going to whisk me off anywhere. You, too, Newt." She frowned down at the boy, quite uppity for someone who was eternally half-dressed. "I've decided I'm to stay here until we dock. This room has a new occupant and he's …" A winsome expression crossed her face. "He's all that is amiable. So put the shoes back in the box and leave them."

Newton shook his head vehemently. He pointed to the ghost, then to himself, then laced his hands together over his heart.

"I love you, too." The woman's voice softened. "But it's nice here. I'm weary of chasing that Italian adulterine. I've found a new playmate."

The clouds of skepticism cleared enough for Willow to realize the playmate the woman referred to was Julian. "Has … has this room's occupant seen you, by any chance?"

The opaque woman laughed. "Of course not. His feet are

too big to fit in my shoes. And he has no chance of seeing or hearing me any other way."

"But Newton ... he does. He can even touch you. And he's not wearing your shoes."

The little boy glanced from Willow to the ghostly woman, an unspoken acknowledgement of Willow's observation.

"Ah. And therein is the rub, aye?" The ghost laughed again—a sound as harsh and disorienting as hail hitting a tin roof.

In spite of the ghost's annoying reaction, a rush of relief chased away Willlow's earlier anger at Julian. He hadn't brought a woman to his room after all. Least not a live one, and not intentionally. But why would he have within his possession such shoes?

A knock busted on the stateroom door, startling Willow. She teetered in the tall, curved heels on her feet. In her haste to right herself, she toppled a small table and a pewter vase filled with peonies clanked to the wooden floor.

"Master Thornton? I've come to tend your room." A scullery maid's voice echoed from the other side of the door.

"Come back later," Willow managed to croak the words in a deepened voice. "Not feeling well." She thrust out a few hoarse coughs for good measure.

"As ye wish, Sir."

The sound of the door across the hall opening and closing prompted Willow to peek outside. From one end to the next, the corridor was empty. Ghost or no ghost, they had to leave before Julian returned.

"Let us go, Newton." Willow tried to step into the hall, only to find that the shoes felt weighted, as if bags of sand were tied to the heels. She turned around to see the hovering woman glaring at her, arms crossed.

"As I said. I'll not be accompanying you." The spirit's eyes glimmered with an otherworldly light. "I'm hoping the new occupant might bathe tonight and give me at peep at what's under his dappers. He's fine as fivepence, that one."

Willow glowered. "If you think I'm to leave you here with my..."

"Your what?"

"My dear friend. If you think that, you're nothing but a pea-goose in petticoats." Willow tugged at the shoes but they grew snug, tightening around her feet as if someone squeezed them.

The phantom smirked. "You're not taking those off *or* leaving this room."

Newton made a grunting sound in the back of his throat then bent down and yanked the shoes off of Willow effortlessly. The floating image vanished in mid-retort. As Willow worked the men's boots back on, she glanced at Newton. "Thank you, Newton. We have to get back to steerage."

The boy's eyes filled with tears. His tiny hands clasped over his chest again.

"Oh, don't you worry," she grumbled. "She's coming with us whether she wishes it or not." She had no inkling what the relationship between Newton and this quarrelsome scantily-clad phantom might be, but it was obvious he needed her.

Willow stuffed the stolen costume into the box, padding the shoes so they couldn't move. Snapping the lid in place, she took Newton's hand. The container started to shake and tremble, trying to escape her hold. Willow secured it against her chest as they rushed down the corridor. She breathed a sigh of relief, glancing over her shoulder once to watch Julian's room fade around the corner.

The instant she turned back around, she plowed into a man as big as a bear and knocked him to his knees.

TEN

Julian sat in the bustling first-class dining room, reluctantly waiting for his luncheon companion. It seemed such a waste of time. He had more pressing issues to pursue. He'd only kept this luncheon appointment in the hopes that Mr. Sala might offer some insight into the boy who had stolen his hair. If he did, Julian might finally have a clue as to Willow's whereabouts.

Upon hearing Judge Arlington's chuckle from across the room, Julian swiveled in his cushioned chair. Seeing one another, they both waved. Julian restrained the impulse to go over and talk to the judge. He would need to be mentally settled when he broached the subject of his amusement park.

For the moment, business was as far from his mind as eating. Even the smell of fresh baked apples and veal cutlets drifting from the table a few feet away failed to stir his appetite. He couldn't stop wondering if Willow might be suffering from lack of sustenance.

The beauty of the room was lost on him. Small oval-shaped windows, their sheer curtains drawn back with sapphire tassels, reflected sunlight off of the white linen tablecloths all around, illumining them like patches of snow. The centerpieces—glass vases filled with transparent marbles and vividly dyed feathers—glistened. Julian averted his eyes from the glare.

However, the formality of the tablecloth that draped the entirety of the circular table did serve one purpose: it made it easier for him to hide Willow's hair. He patted the auburn curls, hung over his lap like some boneless pet. Having been tucked in his vest for a time, they were more waves now ... limp and frizzy and nearly reaching the floor. No matter. He'd already decided to trade the barber the phantom shoes, as soon as he had a chance to retrieve them from the stateroom. He didn't care a whit about the diamond crusted buckles. Not when Willow might be aboard, being forced to sleep in steerage where men and women were crammed together with little privacy and even less jurisprudence. The thought of some uncultured swine touching her...

With a start, Julian's eyes snapped open as he realized his fingers clenched the hair, much less gentle than they had when he'd kissed her. He eased free from the tangles.

His exploration of steerage had never taken place. He'd run into Captain Everett and asked for a look at the loading manifest. There had been an abundance of trunks and boxes brought on board, any of which could've provided the ideal haven for a limber circus performer. By the time Julian finished looking over the list, he was due for lunch with Mr. Sala.

So many questions tormented him now. Had someone scalped Willow of her hair? Had she sold it of her own accord so she wouldn't have to sell other, more precious parts of her selfhood? The thought that Willow might be somewhere on the ship getting into trouble right at this very moment twisted his stomach like a knotted rope. He would get any information from Mr. Sala he could then head straight to steerage, post haste. He needed to find her ... to talk to her ... to *shake* her.

"*Ciao.*"

Julian's head snapped up at Mr. Sala's greeting. He levered out of his chair just enough to pump the Italian's hand once while still keeping his lap draped by the tablecloth. "*Ciao.*"

Mr. Sala took off his wide-brimmed hat. He wore a strange expression on his face—a look of disquiet, rather like the one he'd been sporting earlier today in front of his room. He had cut his hair since Julian had last seen him—cropped off the back so it clung close to his neck and just below his ears.

Mr. Sala apologized for being late, not offering any reason, then took the seat opposite Julian. From all around them, the chink of silver against china played an almost rhythmic cadence. Julian borrowed the tempo to ease his mind, to gather his thoughts.

Bad enough the rumors that surrounded this man. Combined with Julian's unrelenting concern for Willow, it was bound to be a disastrous scouting venture. Julian's chest burned with the effort to hold in the battery of questions he wanted to ask. He had to be tactful, else he might raise suspicions and endanger Willow if she was indeed a stowaway.

"Might I take your order?" A waiter in a lavender vest and pale yellow shirt filled their goblets with red wine. The crewmember's wiry frame shaded the sun from Julian's face. Julian proceeded to translate for Mr. Sala, ordering them each a portion of mutton in caper sauce along with some fried cucumbers.

Upon the waiter's retreat to the kitchen, Julian met Mr. Sala's intense black gaze, at a loss to start the conversation.

The Italian's lips trembled in the midst of his olive skin. "Why is for the wig? You wear for costume ... tonight?"

Mr. Sala's knowledge of the hair in his lap bewildered him until he looked down to find a long, glimmering lock had twisted around his ankle where the tablecloth failed to meet the floor. But even more startling than the sighting was the man's use of the English tongue. Julian sat rigid against his cushioned chair. "You speak English."

The man attempted a smile, his lips pulling the cleft in his chin until it disappeared. "*Sì.*" The smile faded instantly as his gaze turned downward toward Julian's lap, as if trying to see the hair through the tablecloth.

Julian balled up Willow's curls and tucked them within his vest. "Why the pretense earlier? Everyone on board believes you're incapable of having a conversation. This morning, all of the confusion ... it could've been solved without my help."

Mr. Sala's attention returned to Julian's face. "Foreignness is measuring pole."

Julian crinkled his forehead, trying to make sense of the words. "Measuring pole?"

"*Sì.* You make to communicate. Defend me with nothing to gain. So I know you as honorable. How I measure you ... your worthing."

Julian realized the man had meant to say measuring stick. "Ah."

With an arch of the brow, Mr. Sala glanced around the room. "I stay quiet from others, better for to be ... how you say ... protection? Some people want only to know my purse. They are no friend to me." He grimaced and flung out his hand. "If I can speak no but Italian, they stay liberated of my pockets. Better. I no want to be put upon by fairly weathered fiends."

Julian chewed his inner cheek to stifle a grin. "You mean, fair-weathered friends?"

The man's dark eyebrows slanted down, thoughtful. "Do I speak it wrong?"

Julian lifted his wine and held it up in the sun, shamed by

his own earlier motives—coming to the man's assistance mostly to gain an investment. A ray of light refracted through the liquid and cast a spread of pinkish dots on the white table cloth. "On the contrary. You speak the sentiment perfectly, sir." It appeared Judge Arlington had been right. Mr. Sala needed kindness, and Julian would offer that. He'd get his capital elsewhere.

"You keep secret for me, then?" Mr. Sala raised his wine goblet. "So I might be private."

"I don't see any harm in such a ruse. You have my word." Julian clinked their glasses and took a sip of the warm wine.

Mr. Sala indicated the lump in Julian's vest. "The wig—" He clamped his mouth shut as the waiter brought their meals.

Plates of food and warm, crusty bread filled the once empty table. The waiter bowed his head then left them to eat. Julian glanced through the aromatic steam at his companion. "I saw this hair today in the barber salon. The color reminds me of someone. So I acquired it to keep her memory fresh while I'm away from home. Away from her." There. As close to the truth as he was willing to hedge. Mr. Sala appeared sincere, but Julian didn't know or trust him enough to share his concerns about Willow.

The Italian's lips set to a firm line. "This someone must be *molto* beautiful. Hair of such color ... is rare. People pay high price for it." Mr. Sala's lashes turned down as he pulled free a slice of bread, his many rings glimmering in a strand of sunlight.

Julian started to look closer at them, but lost his train of thought when the Italian man barked a new question.

"She is your wife?"

A slight tickle shuddered Julian's throat and he decided to concentrate on slicing his mutton. "My wife?" The knives provided by the restaurant were dull and barely made a dent. "No. Perhaps my sweetheart one day." The memory of their chaste kiss stung him like a slap in the face. He finally tore off a small chunk of meat with his fork and savored the gravy as he chewed.

"Ah. *Seduzione.* You take adventure ... to learn art of love."

It was the most coherent thing Mr. Sala had spoken thus far, not to mention the most humiliating. "What makes you think I'm lacking in such training?"

"I see bristles in you, each time a lady does pass."

Fighting a surge of embarrassment, Julian frowned. "Well, it's not as if anyone offers instructional manuals on the subject."

Biting the edge off of a salted fried cucumber, Mr. Sala smiled and pointed his fork at Julian. "You meet my troupe. The girls answer all such questions. Much more than brilliant *ingénues*, are they. You keep company with us this evening after their performance. You will attend the gala, yes?"

Julian nodded. Did this confirm what the men in the barber salon suggested? That the girls were only fronting as thespians ... that they were less than savory—working on the fringe of morals? "Are these girls your daughters?"

Chewing thoughtfully, Mr. Sala became somber. "No family have I. Though I once had..." He waved his hand, as if to banish the slant in conversation. Julian was shocked to see the man's eyes had misted.

"These girls ... good girls," Mr. Sala mumbled. "Care for me. Respect me. I consider them family, in that. Is why I take them to World's Fair. Is competition on opening night—an acting guild. Champions go on around and around."

Julian remembered reading about the talent contest in

his *Threshold* magazine. There was a rehearsal being held for the actors and actresses on the eve before the fair opened to the public. The winning thespian troupe would be paid to perform at all of the best playhouses around the States during the upcoming year. At least this explained why Sala was taking the girls to St. Louis. It was more than just a pleasure trip, after all.

Julian's fingers played nervously with the bright-colored napkin that had earlier been fanned within his goblet like a peacock's tail. Unfolding it, he wiped his mouth and the fabric snagged on his unshaved chin. "So tell me of your troupe's acting experiences." He tucked the napkin behind his cravat and tugged a piece of bread from the loaf. "What playhouses have you booked in recently?"

Taking a drink of wine, Mr. Sala met his gaze with intuitive perception. "Three months past. At the Britannia ... in Hoxton. The girls perform a restoration comedy."

Julian had read of this particular theater in a fine arts magazine once. "I thought the Britannia was home to a permanent acting company run by the Lane family. How did you, an outsider, manage a booking there?"

The Italian tried to cut a sliver of meat with the inadequate knife at his place setting, frowned, and dug around in his jacket pocket. He surprised Julian by drawing out a stunning silver scabbard about the length of his hand from wrist to fingertip. He slid out a dagger knife with a four inch blade, the sparkling handle accented with what appeared to be garnets. "Four years ago, the company parted their strays." Mr. Sala said, ignoring Julian's stunned stare as he proceeded to carve his meat with the meticulousness of a surgeon.

"They parted *ways*?" Julian asked, intrigued by the knife but refusing to be distracted from his original objective.

"Ah..." Mr. Sala chuckled at his tongue slip. "*Sì*. Parted ways. Now they bid for outside talent most often." He inspected the tidbit of mutton on his fork before sliding his lips over it and chewing thoughtfully.

Julian tore his gaze from the dagger. "What was the comedy your troupe performed there?"

"*The Feigned Courtesans*." Mr. Sala's eyes met and held Julian's, as if awaiting a reaction.

Nearly coughing up his bite of cucumber, Julian smiled. Having heard of the play's premise—in which the innocent heroines pose as famous courtesans to escape arranged marriages and the expectations of a suffocating society—he understood the irony. "You caught me."

"I hear nonsense speak." Mr. Sala wiped his mouth. "It is untruth. Are sweet, my girls. For to be stunning and talented is a crime, no?"

"It shouldn't be. Any more so than being foreign and wealthy." Julian cut off a sliver of mutton, then gestured to Mr. Sala's dagger knife. "Beautiful workmanship. Did you make it?"

The man studied it thoughtfully, and a sentimental wrinkle formed above his brow. "No. I am ... collector. Of things old and mystical. With enough magic in hand, one can right wrongs in past, yes?"

Julian listened intently as Mr. Sala proceeded to share the dagger's intriguing history. According to rumor, a kind and peaceful pauper had once been accused of killing a king that had two sons. The eldest prince had a wizard beneath his thumb, and had once ordered a spell cast upon his dagger's handle so it blazed to red hot flame when anyone else tried to hold it, rendering it usable to only himself. Once the younger prince proved the dagger as the weapon, there was no question that his brother had killed the king to steal the throne. Thus the pauper's life and good name were restored.

Silence wreathed them as Julian let the story sink in. Moved by the fable, he wiped his mouth with a napkin and cleared his throat. "What say I do everything in my power to see that the rumors of your reputation are silenced while upon this ship?"

"*Grazie.*" Mr. Sala raked the remaining gravy from his plate with a crust then scooped it into his mouth, grinning. "And I do everything in my power to see you be an *esperto paramour.*"

"An expert of romance, aye?" Julian grinned. "That's going to take some doing." He gulped down one more bite of mutton before deciding he was full. "Mr. Sala ... might I ask you one last question?" He laid down his silverware with a soft clatter and reached into his pocket, putting on his spectacles.

"*Naturalmente.*" Mr. Sala pushed his own empty plate aside. He wiped off his dagger's blade, sheathed it, and upon returning it to his pocket, drew out a plump cigar, offering one to Julian. After Julian refused graciously, the man lit up and puffed the smoke from the side of his mouth. The scent drifted across the table—a mix both sweet and pungent.

Julian leaned back in his chair. "Is there someone on this ship that might have a vendetta against you? An immigrant, perchance, or even someone posing as one?"

The expression that passed over Mr. Sala's face should have been one of surprise, not one of guilt. "Why for you ask such?" He slapped smoke away from between them.

Julian played with his fork. "It has been rumored a young immigrant might have snipped off your hair last night as you slept." He couldn't divulge any other details without betraying the barber's confidence.

Mr. Sala held his cigar off to the side and guzzled down

his remaining wine. He returned his goblet to the table none too gently. "No. No. It was phantom. *Un fantasma* ... as I say. You no to believe my own sight? These," he pointed to his eyes, "infightable."

Infallible. "I see. So, why would this phantom choose you to haunt?"

Mr. Sala's face darkened and he waved his hands as if swatting gnats, causing smoke to billow all around them. "No wish to discuss. The happening ... is finished. Phantoms everywhere on ship. Shoes run away. Phantoms no haunt me now." His chin clenched as he placed the cigar back in his mouth. "Is finished, my part. Is finished forever." His eyes watered, and Julian debated if it was from the smoke or from something deeper-seated.

Silence overtook as the waiter reappeared to present an ornamental box of French plums laid upon a glass dish garnished with brightly colored sweet meats. He took away the men's plates, dumping the remaining bread crusts and pieces into a basket looped around his arm before he left. Julian had seen servers do the same at other tables, and absently wondered what they did with the leftover, gnawed-on bread.

Not the least bit hungry for dessert, Julian forced himself to take out a sugared plum from the box and popped it into his mouth—an excuse not to speak. He didn't know what to make of Mr. Sala's queer reaction to his question. To be fearful was one thing. But this was more. The man seemed downright defensive ... even sad. It appeared ghosts had been tormenting Mr. Sala for much longer than Julian had originally assumed.

The lines in Mr. Sala's forehead smoothed when he motioned over the quartet of beauties from his troupe. Julian, realizing he was about to be introduced to all of them, stood to leave, but too late. Suddenly, he was surrounded by the ladies and choking in a dense fog of foreign perfume and estrogen. His throat grew tight and his palms clammy as he kissed each one's hand.

The most voluptuous one of the bunch didn't release him upon the gesture. "So, Master Thornton. What in particular do you do?"

He forced a tight smile. "I ... give rides to ladies." The words tripped over his lips like a discordant melody. "That is to say, I'm part of an amusement park." Wincing, he bit his tongue for its blatant disobedience.

The lady squeezed his hand. She glanced at her companions who each took turns raking his body with approving gazes.

"Is that so?" Another one of the beauties spouted. "You must be quite the popular attraction."

They all giggled.

Julian felt as if he were drowning. After Mr. Sala graciously turned the conversation to the ship's cuisine, Julian dismissed himself on the grounds his food hadn't set well—which wasn't far from the truth. On top of feeling like a bloody fool, he was still worried sick about Willow.

When he stepped into the corridor, a scullery maid approached him, her mop cap puffed atop her head like a gray mushroom. "Master Thornton, I thought ye should know. I saw some scallywag immigrants roaming your hall earlier. When I checked your stateroom, the door was ajar. Let the Cap'n know if anything's gone missing."

Julian thanked the woman and took a detour to his cabin, his pulse hammering. There was only one thing he had worth stealing, although they didn't belong to him at all. His footsteps hastened as he wondered if the shoes would still be there.

Pinching her nose, Willow sipped her lukewarm, lumpy soup and studied the dim surroundings of steerage. Her right shoulder ached from its collision with the Italian nobleman in the men's corridor. He had been a sturdy one. Though Newton had quickly absconded without being seen, the man had looked her right in the face. His hat had been knocked off kilter, and his brim shaded most of his features so she didn't get a good look back, but her ears still stung from his vocalizations as he scrambled to his feet and backed away from her.

Un fantasma. He'd repeated it at least four times before turning about and stumbling the opposite direction, obviously shaken. As she'd picked up the costume and shoes that had fallen from the box, Willow couldn't help but wonder how he could have known about the ghost tied to them.

Drinking another sip of soup, she put the episode from her mind. It didn't matter at the moment. All that mattered was that she had managed to get back to steerage without seeing Julian.

Sighing, she pressed her back against the wall, sitting cross-legged on her hammock-style bunk—one in a line of a hundred others like it that stretched along the walls across rows of iron tubing. In the bunk above her, a man muttered something in his sleep and turned over, his bulk weighing down the canvas so it crushed the top of Willow's head. Making a fist, Willow whacked at his backside. "Get off, you nodcock!" With a snort, the man rolled again until the weight lifted from her head then resumed his deep breaths.

This was the main reason Willow had opted to dress as a boy. There was no privacy here in steerage ... no division between the sexes. Unmarried women quartered among men and were offered no more respect than if they lived promiscuously. Better off to *be* a man, or at least a reasonable facsimile thereof.

Here in the ship's belly, devoid of any portals, steerage had an air of stuffiness and gloom about it. Lanterns hung in distant intervals upon the wall to cast hazy yellow clouds that reached barely two feet from their origins. This left the entire midsection— where trunks, luggage, and cargo formed a tribute to society and commerce—a breeding ground for ominous shadows.

Ever since she was little and a sack swallowed her head to blind her while a man etched a tattoo on her back, Willow had required light to help her relax enough to sleep soundly. Whereas most people preferred the black of night to shutter their thoughts and settle their inner meanderings, for Willow, such blackness formed an easel whereupon disturbing memories and imposing fears played out in a spectrum of vivid color. Light chased away these images ... obscured her past, sheltered her soul. So without her own lantern by her bed last evening, her sleep had been restless.

And now, though it was merely afternoon, several of the bunks held sleeping bodies that snored, grunted, or coughed. The unusual symphony acted as a contagion and tugged at Willow's eyelids. She fought their weight. Tired as she was, she wouldn't give in for risk of oversleeping and missing the masquerade in a few hours.

To keep herself awake, Willow slurped some more soup and shifted her attention to the sounds of the Helget children and Newton playing seek and find amongst the shadowy luggage and trunks. They had finished their paltry lunch of barley and bread crust porridge. Re-energized, they busied themselves with the frivolities of childhood. Something she envied.

Most of the other children and adults that usually occupied steerage had retreated upstairs to the third-class promenade deck to partake of the sunlight and fresh air. Willow had stood in line with Newton and the Helget family earlier when the stewards brought down the huge kettles to dole out the swill—provided for one farthing per dinner pail. With so many different cultures present, miscommunication bred chaos, and the stronger pushed and crowded so that the weaker were left with lesser portions. Rumor held that here on the *Christine Victoria*, the lower class's meals were concocted of the leftovers from the first class dining room. Not that it mattered. The balmy, pestilential air from sweat-ridden bodies and unsanitary toilet conditions made for an ill-faired dining experience anyway.

Now, done with eating, Willow carried her pail to where the others were stacked so they would be ready for collection by the stewards when they brought dinner later. Then, remembering she wouldn't be here for dinner, she wove her way to Newton's bunk on the opposite wall and, after moving aside his collection of maps, sat down. Leaning over, she drew out the shoe box from beneath the canvas hammock.

Upon their arrival to steerage, Willow had kept her costume stuffed in the box to prevent the shoes from having space to move, fearing someone might hear them and make off with Newton's treasure.

Willow had tried to speak to Newton earlier, to understand his connection with the ghostly woman. With each question she asked, Newton would glance up as if the specter were standing right beside him, distracting him from listening. He enacted that odd way of hand gestures and moving his lips with nothing issuing forth—the same way he had communicated with the ghost while in Julian's stateroom. It was unlike any sign language Willow had ever seen, and she'd learned signing aplenty, living with Miss Juliet on the manor. Willow had tried to have the child write out their mysterious conversations on a piece of paper. But it appeared the only thing Newton had ever learned to scribble was his name.

So ... cloaked here in this isolated darkness—with Engleberta, Christoff, and Newton whiling away the afternoon in play as Mr. and Mrs. Helget slept soundly in their bunks—Willow decided to converse with the ghost on her own.

Scrunched close to the wall, Willow shoved the costume to one side of the box and slipped the antique shoes on, wiggling her toes to savor the slickness of the satin lining. She tossed Newton's blanket across her legs so no one would see her feet should they pass by. There was a flash of cold air then a hint of perfume when the ghost appeared. She stood in front of Willow, squeezing excess water from her long, dark hair.

As if just realizing she had company, she grimaced. "Oh botheration! Could you not have left well enough alone? To go from a stateroom to this swivel. Have you any idea how I abhor it here?"

Willow started to bid the woman to speak quieter, then remembered no one else could hear her. "*You* abhor it?" Willow whispered. "How do you think the rest of us feel? We're the ones trudging through the filth. Least you're..." Willow clamped her mouth.

"Dead? Deceased and half-dressed? Eternally indecorous?" The ghost rolled her eyes. "Ah yes, that is a lovely consolation." She shook the lace of her petticoats.

"Um, sorry. It must be ... difficult."

"To say the least. An eternity of the gapes." With that, she yawned loudly and plopped down on an empty bunk nearby.

The canvas sunk and a wet spot darkened the weave.

Intrigued by the netherworld's odd rules, Willow attempted her first question. "Might I ask why you're half-dressed and wet?"

"No, you may not."

Biting back her annoyance, Willow tried again. "Your name then?"

Shoulder blades propped against the wall behind her, the ghost smiled and studied her shaped and buffed fingernails. "I've always been partial to Nadia. What say we go with that?"

Willow tamped the scowl that wanted to break. "All right, *Nadia*. I'd like to know of your relation to Newton."

"And why do you wish to know?" Nadia's voice held a bite of defensiveness.

"Because he's my friend. I've been taking care of him, and he of me, since we met."

"Yes, I've been watching you. You appear to be a sufficient companion." Nadia's mouth curled on a snarl, as if it pained her to admit such.

Willow tucked Newton's blanket around her thighs. "It is as I suspected, then. You can see him, and he you, even when your shoes are in the box?"

"Only if the shoes are in the same vicinity as Newton can I see him, or vice versa. Otherwise, it's a bit more difficult. I'm tied to the shoes, and cannot be away from them. If there is distance between Newton and the shoes, or anything solid between us such as doors or walls, then we can only hear one another's thoughts."

"So that's how you knew it was Newton outside the stateroom door when he knocked? You read his mind and knew to open it?"

Nadia held up a finger in a scolding gesture. "Ah. But I

didn't open it. I merely unlocked it. I might be able to trigger a few gears in a lock's mechanism, but I haven't the corporeal presence to open a door."

Willow glanced again at Nadia's indented bunk, wondering as to the canvas's reaction to the ghost. "I'm confused."

Nadia laughed. "As am I."

"You can interact with the physical world somewhat, though?"

"I can affect some things mentally. But I'm most powerful if my shoes are out of the box; one of my favorite tricks is flouncing around in people's clothing to make them think they are having delusions." She laughed. "I've found it's easier not to question the rules of nature as they apply to me now. What was your name again? *Wilson*?" The ghost laid all the way down, her left arm flung over the canvas bunk's edge. Her hammock started to sway. "You're quite a curious little fancy boy."

"I'm not a boy." Willow forgot to whisper. Mrs. Helget's interrupted snoring a few bunks away stiffened her muscles. Only when the German woman shuffled to a more comfortable position and returned to sleep did Willow relax again.

"Of course I know you're not *physically* a boy." Nadia's softly glowing eyes ran along Willow's frame. "But the clothes a person chooses to wear often speaks volumes of their true identity."

Willow's cheeks flamed. Her palm cupped the short hair fringing her nape, far too conscious of her loss of femininity over the past two days. She never would've thought such a thing would bother her. She was beginning to wonder if she'd ever known herself at all. "Fine then. Judging by your sparse attire, I would say you are at least a century old and you've given up style for comfort. So, you must be Newton's," Willow counted on her fingers for effect, "great, great, great, great grandmother. Am I safe in that assumption?" She wasn't about to admit that the woman looked very close to her own age.

Nadia swung her legs over the hammock and sat rigidly, frowning. She thrust out her nubile cleavage. "I am no one's century-old grandmother. Do I look like a frumpy, warted old hag to you?"

Willow smiled at Nadia's reaction. It appeared the ghost's vanity superseded her acrimony. Perhaps all Willow needed was a few well-placed honeyed words to get on her good side. "I was trying to make a point, that's all. You are quite lovely and fashionable, even with your lack of clothing. But you must have a connection to Newton. To be able to touch him. To communicate."

Nadia settled her hands primly in her lap. "I am his half-sister." Her gaze flitted to the open staircase at the other end of steerage where Newton and his friends had moved.

The children played around the bottom step in splashes of yellow light that filtered in from the upper deck. Engleberta and Christoff's pale, bald heads reflected the glare like the marble gazing-globes in Master Thornton's winter garden. Willow felt a twinge of home-sickness at the thought.

Nadia stretched out her legs. "I never knew my mum. But Newton's mum died during his birth. Newton had hemophilia and we almost lost him as well, had he not had a blood transfusion. I was the only family member available, since our unfaithful sot of a father was on one of his 'business trips'. It was me that saved Newt. My blood flows in his veins. That is why he can touch me, even now. We share the same life essence."

Willow nodded. "So ... where is Newton's father now?"

Nadia scowled. "I took my brother from him. Stole him clean away."

Willow's shoulders tensed; this hit too close to her own tragic loss of family. "You took him from the only parent he has? Even if the man is not perfect ... do you not understand the bond ... the connection between a child and their parents?"

Nadia shoved her hammock so it would swing faster. "You know nothing of our father. He would have corrupted Newt." A shudder blurred the ghost's image, as if she shook with rage at the memory. "He was rarely home anyway. I'm the closest thing that little boy has ever had to a parent. I'm the one he bonded to. I taught him to draw pictures so he could speak his mind despite his still tongue. I taught him to understand English, and to write his name. I'd meant to teach him how to write and read other words, too, until I..."

Willow sensed sadness in the ghost's broken explanation. "So your father never found you or Newton before your demise?"

In a flash of greenish light, Nadia's gaze regained its earlier haughty demeanor. "Our father thinks we are dead. Both of us. He has thought us dead for well on a year now."

Willow's jaw dropped. She couldn't frame any response.

"The fall that killed me nearly killed my brother," Nadia offered. "'Tis why he's terrified of heights. He doesn't like water much, either. You should see how I have to bribe him to board ships."

Willow pondered this. Did this mean little Newton had been in the care of no one other than a ghost for all these months? The accident he experienced, it explained some quirks she'd noticed: the way Newton gripped the stair railings until his knuckles were white as he ascended or descended to differing levels of the ship; the way he refused to climb the luggage piles with Engleberta and Christoff, and how he stayed far away from the railings on the promenade deck when the other children fought over who got to look at the ocean lapping the ship's hull. It also came close to explaining why Nadia appeared to be perpetually wet. Perhaps they'd fallen off a bridge.

Willow drew the cover up to her chin, shivering. Poor Newton. Experiences on the brink of death, whether personal or of a close loved one, could have a very negative effect on a child's psyche.

Her focus trained on the stairwell where Newton and his friends had ventured behind the partition, out of sight. The Helget children's voices carried over, barely discernable for the loud hum of the ship's motors. Worry draped like an icy cloud over Willow's heart, and she considered if she should check on the children, until Nadia interrupted her musings.

"It is a tragedy that tied me to those shoes," Nadia resumed her spiel. "But it's mine and Newton's shared blood that enables him to keep me here between earth and heaven." An odd expression crossed her opaque face—one of regret or deep sadness. She almost looked tired, if that were possible for a ghost.

Willow wiggled her toes within the shoes. "You mean to say, Newton is holding you here against your will? You're not here by choice?"

"Is your garret empty, gapeseed? I'm a half-naked spirit tied to an object. Do you think I wish to be in such limbo? I cannot find peace until Newton releases me." She held her hands in front of her so the chemise's sleeves draped like wings from her arms. "Until then, we are bound together; and to keep from going mad, he helps me with my pranks. Entertainment, as it were."

Something Willow herself could relate to. Hard to believe she shared any characteristics with a ghost. "Pranks. Does this have anything to do with Newton stealing and selling that wealthy man's hair?"

Nadia's mouth clamped shut.

Willow dropped the covers and stood. The blanket pooled over her feet. "*Arresto dell'OH!* Don't you play the innocent lamb. I was wondering how he could possibly have managed it without stealing the key or picking the lock. You helped him get in while the man slept. Have you any idea how much trouble he could get into? Have you heard the rumors about Mr. Sala?"

The phantom snorted. "Mafia..."

"Yes. The mafia. What do you know of Sala? Why did you pick him?"

"I know enough to assure you he is—" before she completed her answer, Nadia glanced up at Mr. and Mrs. Helget who had both been awakened by Willow's raised voice.

Knowing they couldn't have understood her without their children translating, Willow forced a smile and nodded at them. Then the sound of nervous chatter turned her to the trio of children scampering in her direction.

"A man!" Panting, Engleberta bounced into the hammock where Nadia sat, the force of her realness rippling the ghost's image like a reflection in a puddle. Willow was surprised to see the canvas had already dried.

"We met ... a man," Engleberta said—breathless. "Looking for you, Wilson." Excitement thickened her German accent.

"The nerve!" Nadia's form reappeared standing behind the breathless Newton. "Regardless that these children are immigrant brats ... someone should teach them some manners! I was sitting there first."

166

Willow cast Nadia a scalding glare then turned again to Engleberta. "What man?"

"He had your hair in his pocket!" Christoff chimed in, his prepubescent voice cracking.

"Asked if we knew who it matched to..."

The Helget parents blinked, their expressions still fuzzy with sleep. Willow knelt down beside Engleberta, the blanket pooling across her feet. "And what did this man look like?"

"A real gentlemen. Fine clothes ... hair the color of sunshine." Engleberta smirked dreamily.

"He needs a shave," Christoff was quick to add. The boy wiped his chin with a filthy hand, leaving a smear of black. They'd been playing in the soot pile again.

"Still, he's pretty as a painting. And you've a smudge on your face, Chris*toad*."

"Men ain't pretty, *Berta*," Christoff chided as he wiped his chin, making the smear worse. "But he's smart. Has spectacles to prove it." The youth curled his forefingers and thumbs over his eyes in demonstration. When he drew them back, he favored a raccoon.

Julian. Pulse tapping like a woodpecker in her neck, Willow fell back on her hips, sitting full onto the filthy floor. How could he have come to suspect her presence? If he was whiskered, he must not have been to the barber shop yet for a shave; so how had he stumbled upon her hair? "What did you tell him?"

Christoff grinned. "Since you said you was hiding from someone on board, I told him the hair was Berta's. That our mum and da selled our hair so we could eat."

In response, Engleberta rubbed her bald head, marring it with a sooty print. "That tied his tongue good, it did. He even gave us a handful of farthings. Think he felt sad for us."

Engleberta held out the coins. "I'd say he has lots to spare. Asked if we'd seen a pair of shoes gone missing from his cabin—"

"That's not the best part," Christoff interrupted. "He's gonna give one of us lowlies his first-class stateroom and free meals in trade for them. He's off to draw a picture. Gonna pass it around steerage for to spread the word."

The brother and sister laughed but sobered as their parents slipped from their bunks, barking out German as they wiped the children clean with handkerchiefs and took the coins from their hands, obviously seeking details about the money.

"Aren't you a narcissistic little chit?" Nadia's voice pulled Willow's attention away from the boisterous family. "Thinking you're the only one our Julian was looking for. He's looking for me, as well. And seems quite desperate to find me. Now that he's put a reward to it, come nightfall, there'll be no hiding place down here safe enough for those." She gestured to Willow's hidden feet.

Willow gnawed on her fingernail. This would put a definite crimp in her plans. She turned her back to the Helgets to assure they couldn't see her speaking to the ghost. "That nubkin. He's always been too smart for his own good."

"Well, I find intelligence to be a very appealing quality in a man." Nadia smirked. "Good to know, since it appears I'll be rooming with your 'dear friend', after all."

On his sister's snide remark, Newton regarded the blanket over Willow's feet, sadness etched into his face.

"You're a heartless wretch. Do you know that?" Willow glared at the ghost. "Can you not see how your apathy hurts your brother?"

Nadia frowned. "I'm not meaning to wound you, Newt. I wish just a little fun … it's the least you can do, keeping me here so long."

Newton shrugged without looking up.

Sitting in her hammock again, Willow dragged the blanket up across her thighs. She glanced around at the other bunks, thankful most everyone still slept. If what Nadia said was true, it was only a matter of hours until a stampede of immigrants would burst down the stairs in search of the shoes. No bunk, trunk, or box would be left unturned in the effort to win a key to luxury.

As Willow considered her options, Newton's soulful gaze tightened around her heart with the precision of a noose. She understood his desperation not to be separated from his sister again. She knew all too well the pain of living without a family. Uncle Owen, Aunt Enya, and Leander had been a wonderful substitute. But she still had moments when the void of shared blood overwhelmed her with an ache that could not be staunched.

"Rest easy, little widget," she whispered to the boy as he helped her slide the shoes off beneath the blanket and ease them into the box. Over the past day and a half, Willow had become quite adept at changing clothes beneath a blanket. "I'll not let anyone take your sister from you." Willow kept her gaze locked on Nadia as the ghost disappeared with a disgruntled sneer.

Willow and the boy settled together on the hammock with the shoes between them, covering themselves and the box with the blanket. She curled her arm around Newton's sparse frame and drew him close, nuzzling her nose in his dust-scented brown waves. "You and Nadia shall accompany me to the first class deck when I attend the gala tonight."

Drawing back, he looked up at her, his expression a mask of questions.

"No worries." Willow squeezed his shoulders. "I know the perfect place to hide you both."

ELEVEN

"A husband's an insect, a drone, a dormouse…"

"A foolish matrimonial lump…"

"A cuckoo in winter…"

"An opiate for love…"

Julian stood against the back wall in the first-class music room, gazing over the heads of the crowd seated in plush chairs around the dimly lit main floor. The audience members—garbed in costumes and masks—sat laughing, captivated by a duo of Mr. Sala's troupe as they performed on stage amidst a glow of brightly burning candles in tall brass sconces. Sporadic flutters of light and shadow upon the actresses' powdered wigs and heavy makeup cast an air of foreboding about them, a contradiction to the frivolous piece they performed. Mr. Sala had chosen a scene from Act four of *The Virtuoso*—a satire by a seventeenth century playwright named Shadwell. Though well-rehearsed, the beautiful and talented actresses, one dressed as a man and the other more curvaceous one as a lady, failed to retain Julian's attention.

The missing phantom shoes held him captive. How could those boys have entered his room? He hadn't lost his key … and there was no sign of his lock being broken or forced open.

Be it a result of the sea air, or backlash from his and Willow's kiss, he now wrestled a side of himself he'd never encountered. Skepticism—of a strange and foreign breed—had him second guessing every cerebral instinct since he'd boarded this ship. It was as if the whispers of his heart, the murmurs of his emotions, had become boisterous shouts, far overpowering his once indomitable sense of reasoning.

He couldn't stop picturing the pair of shoes breaking free from their box and clomping away on their own—enabled by the same unseen entity that had danced in his jacket earlier this morn. Ridiculous, but it seemed the most obvious explanation, considering the lack of evidence that would point to a break in.

If Willow were here, he could discuss it with her. She would thrill to engage in such speculation. But she wasn't. When he'd finally made it to steerage he found that the hair had belonged to a little immigrant girl. All along he'd imagined Willow's scent on the wig, imagined her taking Abrams' place as the carriage driver on the way to the dock.

He rubbed his whiskered chin. Pity the little bald children.

Though laughter bubbled all around in response to the animated thespians on stage, Julian's frown deepened. To think that all of these upper-class passengers had earlier indulged in a hearty meal of fish and oyster pie, baked artichokes, and brandied strawberries for dessert. He doubted those poor immigrant children ever got dessert. That in mind, he decided to purchase a few boxes of chocolates from the confection shop and take it to steerage tomorrow for the little ones. Although it would seem a much more solemn sojourn than earlier, without any chance of running into Willow.

This disappointment that she wasn't on board befuddled him. No doubt by tomorrow he'd get a response to his telegraph confirming she was settled in at school. Such news should make him happy considering Willow had made a spit pact—*a double pact*—promising to do just that. Yet he missed her; and he couldn't think of any excuse as to why, other than the fact that he cared deeper than he wished to admit.

"An excuse." The actress playing the male role barked the line as if reading Julian's thoughts. Resituating the domino mask over the top half of his face, he focused again on the stage.

"A necessary thing..." The femininely attired ingénue took her cue.

"Good for nothing but to cover shame, pay debts, and own children for his wife." The cross-dressed actress tipped her hat in a masculine manner and wriggled her fake moustache, prompting the audience to laugh.

The other actress smoothed the décolleté of her dress and opened her fan wide, fluttering a breeze over her face as she simpered demurely. "In short, a husband is a husband, and there's an end of him. But a lover is—"

"Not to be expressed but in action." Taking her hand, the mustachioed actress led the other toward the curtain behind the stage. "I'll show you what a lover is with a vengeance, madam. Come along."

They slipped through the slit in the curtains and the audience rose to offer a standing ovation.

As everyone clapped, the chandeliers hanging from the ornate domed ceiling blinked on to brighten the entire music hall. An exquisite crystal fountain with sculpted glassy birds glistened and gurgled in the room's midst. The figurines reminded Julian of Willow's hummingbird tattoo ... the most exquisite and mysterious part of her, least of what he'd seen thus far. So many nights he'd imagined tracing that colorful outline of feathers with his fingertips, following the wings that nestled along the curve of her lower back at the brink of two lovely dimples. Heartbeat spiking at the thought, he pushed himself from the wall and wove through the chairs toward the spray of water, his bare feet skimming across the cool, polished parquet floor.

Crew members sprung to life around him—some scooting the seats against the room's walls to open up the area for dancing and others carrying in trays of long-stemmed goblets filled with sangria wine.

An orchestra came out from the stage curtains to set up their instruments.

"So, what did you think?"

Distracted from his study of the glass birds, Julian turned at the familiar voice, his toga hem brushing just beneath his kneecaps. He had hoped he might see Judge Victor Arlington tonight.

Julian smiled, struggling to drag his thoughts away from envisioning Willow's nude body. "I think it was a ripping good show. And you?"

"A spectacular presentation." The judge's jiggly, bared arm waved a server over, taking two glasses of wine from the tray. He handed one to Julian and held out his own, merry eyes twinkling beneath his half mask. "So, do we drink to your new friend's success? I'd say Mr. Sala has proven false those misconceptions of his girls beyond a doubt's shadow. No one can refute that they are thespians now."

"Agreed. *Salud*." Julian clinked their goblets and took a sip of the warm liquid. Its oaked flavor evaporated on his tongue, leaving behind a bitter aftertaste. "Though I did learn they aren't his daughters. He's escorting them to the World's Fair so they might take part in that talent competition on opening night. They certainly have a chance at winning. The ladies are indeed accomplished in their art."

"That they are. I read about the opening night festivities in your *Threshold*. You left it behind in the barber's shop today, by the way. It's in my cabin. I'll return it to you tomorrow." The Judge licked his wine-stained lips. "Say, did you find the owner of the hair?"

Julian swallowed another sip of wine, grateful once more for the judge's support earlier in the barber shop. "Yes. A sad story that. Some German children had to sell their hair so their family could eat. They were as bald as baby sparrows."

"Pity. It's a harsh life for the newcomers. But America has much to offer them, if they're diligent enough to work hard. There's jobs aplenty."

"This particular family is headed to Chicago, from what the children said."

The judge stepped aside as a couple passed arm in arm. "They must be going to the Hull House. It's a settlement home. They'll give aid to the immigrants until they can gain footing. Wise choice, since they have children to care for. I hope they find happiness in the States."

Julian grinned, pleased by his companion's compassionate nature. "I'm glad to see you attended, Victor. Who are you then ... Zeus, perchance?" He regarded the man's rotund form filling the full length robe. A peach and green shoulder drape hemmed with gold cording completed the outfit.

"Me and about twenty other rascals that were taken in by that enterprising tailor. Have you seen how many men are running around in this very costume? Down to the laurel leaf head piece." He tapped the copper circle on his head. "How did you manage to find an Adonis?"

Julian, having taken another swallow of wine, nearly strangled. "Adonis! That's a generous misconception. Since I was late arriving for my fitting, I was fortunate enough to get one made from scratch. From a sheet no less." Julian held out his bare arms and laughed, feeling ridiculous in the rather short costume. He was unused to having his calves and shins on full display. "By the time he finished, it looked like a circus tent. I'm grateful he tacked on the gold rope belt at no extra cost."

"Maybe you should have worn your haunted shoes, to complete the outfit." Grinning, the judge sipped his wine, leaving his moustache fringed with burgundy droplets.

"Huh. Grand idea ... had they not gone missing from my room."

"Ah, no! When?"

"A scullery maid saw two immigrant boys wandering the upper decks this morn. One a child, the other an adolescent. I've no doubt they're behind it." Julian chose not to mention his suspicions that the shoes might have meandered off on their own.

The judge resituated his mask, as his glass had knocked against the lower edge, slanting it. "Any ideas how you're to find two immigrant boys among the multitude?"

"I've enacted a plan in hopes to bring the shoes to me. We'll have to see if it comes to fruition. Needless to say, I'm avoiding the barber tonight. I ruined the wig ... and now I've no eighteenth century latchets to cinch my side of the bargain."

The musicians started to warm their instruments, forcing the judge to raise his voice. "Well, with a mind such as yours, you'll figure something out." His free hand clapped Julian's shoulder. "And I'm glad to offer any assistance in haggling with the barber. We had a fine chat earlier during my shave. He's a fairly equitable fellow, once you get past his stinginess."

Joining his companion in another sip of wine, Julian ran a gambit of the room, peering over his glass's rim. "Well look there. It appears Medusa has arrived. Over by the doorway, watching us. Could it be she's interested in the king of the gods?"

The judge glanced across his shoulder through the milling crowd of costumes. "Ahem. No. Surely you've heard tales of my wife, Hera. She's known for her formidable jealous temper. Besides, I believe our Medusa has vested interest in the god of vegetation. That would be you, Adonis." He glanced back at Julian. "Unfathomable. Wearing only a bed sheet, yet you still manage to outshine the rest of us. Ah, to reclaim the muscles and carriage of youth. She can't tear her eyes away."

Julian studied the delicate framed woman. Standing alone, she wore a form-hugging dress of billowy, sheer green fabric. Her snake headpiece—made of shimmering wired ribbons and leaves—covered all of her hair, leaving her slender neck exposed. So elegant.

Returning Julian's appraising gaze, she held a feathered mask up by its handle so it covered the top half of her face, exposing pretty, rouged lips. Her pink tongue eased out to break the seam of her mouth. A rush of heat simmered in Julian's gut at the sensual affectation.

"Maybe you should take the initiative and ask her to dance?" The judge said.

Julian's throat tightened. "Um ... no. No, I don't believe I will."

"Aw, come now. Adonis wouldn't leave a beauty like that to the wilds. The wolves will no doubt be sniffing at her naked heels by the time the first song ends."

Julian grinned, admiring Medusa's slim ankles. It was a rare sight indeed, to be privy to the exposed feet of a lady in such a public venue. Willow would've loved such a privilege. Like several of the men at the masquerade, some women wore no shoes. It seemed being on board this floating palace insulated them from some of the strictures of outside society. "Wolves, aye? Surely she can fend for herself. One would think venomous hair could trump a simple canine."

The judge chortled. "Oh-ho. Spoken like a man who has a lady at home."

"I've a lady in mind." Julian gnawed his tongue.

"You're just a young pup, still. Are you sure you want to waste a once in a lifetime opportunity?"

Julian shrugged, trying to appear nonchalant. "An opportunity to dance with a lady doesn't seem so extraordinary. I've had such occasions before, and I'm sure I will again."

The judge grinned. "You've obviously spent too much of your life with your head in books, lad. As they say in the States: you have to sow a few wild oats before you can feed that prized mare. This," he gestured toward Medusa, "is fortuity incarnate. I've heard being at sea can act as an aphrodisiac to some women. It's the sensation of being in a bubble ... impenetrable by the outside world. They drop their inhibitions. Go on. At least talk to her."

Julian's tongue started to swell and his hands felt clammy. "I-I wouldn't know the first thing to say."

"Bah!" The judge snatched away Julian's empty goblet and handed it off to a passing server. "Just ask her to dance. And you'd better hurry; you might have competition from one of my doppelgangers."

Julian had noticed the other Zeus as well. He kept looking from Julian to Medusa from behind his full face mask. Upon catching Julian watching him, the small man stepped into a corner, his cobalt hair so dark it blended into the shadows around him.

"He can have her," Julian at last answered the judge. "I'm not putting myself in the game." He motioned to the chairs against the wall, waiting to accommodate those who didn't wish to dance. "Let's you and I sit. I have some business I'd like to discuss with you."

"Business? I'm intrigued." The judge shifted his goblet to the other hand. He walked with Julian but glanced again at Medusa as she gave a piece of paper to a crew member and turned to leave the music hall. "Aww. She's leaving. You'd rather speak of business than pursue a golden opportunity towards carnal education?"

"This is more important. It's the very reason I boarded this ship. The reason I'm going to St. Louis." Julian settled his foot on a chair, lifting his costume's hem to expose a small leather pouch cinched just above his left knee. From within, he drew out some of his past ride designs. "I am an engineer. I design amusements ... in the form of mechanical rides. And I've a proposition for you."

He'd snagged the judge's attention. His companion lifted his mask off his face and settled it atop his head, taking a seat. He ran his palm down his moustache, smoothing the white hairs as he looked over the papers Julian handed him. "These are incredible. And you've had success with them?"

Before Julian could respond, a crew member approached him.

"The lady in green wished me to give you this, Sir." He handed off the missive to Julian, tipped his uniform cap, and left.

At a loss for words, Julian gawked down at the judge.

"Well open it, boy." The man's contagious grin sparked Julian to unfold the parchment. Everyone around them had fallen into dancing alongside the instruments.

Fingers crinkling the paper, Julian read the script silently: *Adonis—I offer you a dance in the moonlight and then a kiss at midnight. Meet me on the promenade deck where our only audience will be the stars. I anxiously await our rendezvous, Lady Medusa.*

Gulping against his prickly throat, Julian crumpled the paper inside a fist. "She wishes to meet in private."

The judge stared at him in wide-eyed reverence. "I told you. Lucky bastard."

Julian dropped the wadded missive on a passing steward's tray.

Judge Arlington folded the ride designs. "I'm retiring to my stateroom. I will take your designs with me. We'll talk business tomorrow. But tonight, you can't let opportunity pass you by." His tone was resolved, if not a tad envious.

Julian struggled with the decision. "I wonder if she might be one of Mr. Sala's ingénues that I met at lunch today."

"Go to her and find out. Were I twenty years younger and unmarried..." Patting his bulging stomach, the judge sighed. "Oh who am I kidding? I would never have had a chance with such a woman. Go on. Let me live vicariously through you."

Trying to hold his pulse in check, Julian took a deep breath. Perhaps this *was* a once in a lifetime opportunity. When else could he pretend to be another man entirely? There was much bravery to be forged from behind a domino mask. Guilt tapped at his conscience, but he pushed it aside. He had no intention of practicing anything more than kissing. As the man, it was his duty to know how to give a competent kiss.

"Perhaps I might have a few wild oats yet to be sown."

"I'll say." The judge whistled.

"But I'm only sowing one of them tonight..." Julian made a point to assure his companion. Or was it he that needed assurance?

"Of course." The judge smiled, holding up his goblet in a toasting gesture. "I've found that famous last words go down easier with a swallow of wine." Twirling the glass in a taunting manner, he gulped down the last of his drink then stood and nudged Julian toward the door. "Now, be on your way, before our goddess changes her mind."

She stood at the bow—looking every inch the goddess. The gossamer fabric of her gown appeared even more transparent in the dim light, leaving almost nothing to the imagination. Every nuance of shadow where her body curved, every dainty line of her bone structure, everything that marked her a woman, was on full display. Julian strode toward her slowly, letting the cool night air whip the fallen strands of his hair around his temples, letting it chill his bared arms, wishing it could distract him from the animal lust starting to brew beneath his skin.

Scanning the deck, it appeared that he and the lady had the promenade to themselves. Whether that was a good thing or not, he couldn't decide.

He still wore his half-mask, and she'd tied hers in place using a ribbon from her head piece to free her hands. They were strangers, for all intents and purposes. Soon to be intimate strangers, if the insinuations in her missive held any sway.

His hand trailed the cold metal railing as his footsteps ate up the short distance between them. The inky sea hugged the ship on all sides—as possessive and ominous as a nest of storm clouds—indiscernible from the night sky but for the stars. Julian resisted looking at the foamy rivulets being parted by the ship's intrusive bow, hyper-aware of the sensual innuendos all around him tonight ... of things he'd never taken the time to notice before.

He tipped his head as he approached his companion. She returned the half nod. Then he propped his elbows on the railing, studying her while a fine sweat beaded his brow.

The moonlight on her flesh was a scintillating spectacle, as if tiny prisms of light twinkled from her every pore, and the breeze carried over her scent—a dark floral temptation. Swiping the moisture from his forehead, Julian quashed another stab of guilt. Only a kiss, and then he'd call it a night.

"Do you hear the music?" Medusa murmured over the quiet lapping of the ocean, her voice so soft he couldn't place if she was one of Mr. Sala's girls.

His mind rattled … searching for an appropriate response. *Music.* What the hell was she talking about? The first class music hall was too well insulated for any of the instruments to reach them up here.

His teeth clenched. He should answer as Nick would. Say something imaginative … charming.

"I hear it," he untangled his thick tongue to extract the words.

She looked out at the water—offered him nothing but a profile, indistinct with the mask veiling the true form of her face.

"I hear the breath of the sea," he continued. "The sighs of the stars. The music of the night. Is that to what you refer?"

At this she turned to him, her dress rustling against her flesh. "Yes. Oh, yes." One side of her mouth lifted, pleased by his response.

He was surprised at himself. For a man who struggled to form even one coherent stream of words in a woman's presence, he had managed a fine poetic epigram. It appeared all those hours spent reading his sister's chapters had unearthed an unmined skill. Bolstered by the accomplishment, he pushed off the rail. "Well, as we have our musical accompaniment, would you honor me with a dance?"

She faced him. "A waltz beneath the heavens with Adonis," she said softly. Her smile deepened as she offered her gloved hands. "How could I refuse?"

He placed his palms against hers and gestured to her hairpiece. "I do ask that you keep your snakes at bay." He almost cringed as he said it, feeling more like Nick by the minute.

His flirtatious innuendo had the desired effect, for she giggled and entwined their fingers. "Rest assured. I won't ask the same of you."

His hands squeezed hers—a nervous reflex. His tongue stuck to the roof of his mouth again. He managed to begin the dance despite his weighted feet.

"So ... you're a bard and a jester?" she asked, glancing up into his face.

He had to lean in to hear her over the water.

"An amateur at both, I assure you." He led her footsteps in a pattern of rhythmic squares. The sea's wavelets provided the perfect cadence and they floated on the deck, a breeze stirring their costumes. The cool wood slid beneath his bare feet, gritty in places from dirt that had fallen off of people's shoes.

"But you are no amateur dancer." His partner's breathless observance flattered him.

He studied her glittering eyes, finally comfortable in his skin for the first time since he'd arrived on the deck. His sweating had subsided, and his tongue shrunk to its normal size. He felt at home when he danced. He felt in control—like himself.

Having grown up on a holiday resort, he'd attended his share of galas; waltzed with his sister and Willow countless times to allow them to partake in the festivities while maintaining their pristine reputations. All of the Thornton children knew how to spin their heels.

Julian still remembered the first time he'd danced with Willow. He had been fourteen and she thirteen. Even then, there'd been taut threads of tension between them at the proximity. He'd always assumed it simply because they so often argued and challenged one another ... but now he realized that it had been so much more complex than that.

Deep in thoughts of Willow, Julian twirled his partner along the deck. A mist settled over them, cutting the moonlight considerably. The bottom half of her face blurred in the shadows, and the mask of feathers and satin became his focal point lest his thoughts wander to her flimsy gown and the delicacies hidden beneath. Delicacies he kept at arm's length, so as not to tempt either of them.

As if sensing the direction of his thoughts, his companion stopped mid-step. Julian had to compensate for her sudden change of direction and nearly tripped over her bare feet. Their toes brushed and Julian couldn't ignore the titillating tingle that passed between them at the contact.

She stared up at him, swathed in mist, expectant. They were close enough, that if he bent his neck just so, their lips would touch. Her slender, gloved fingers reached up to trace his chin. The crackle of silk catching on his whiskers launched a pulse of white heat from his neck to his chest.

Vaguely, behind them, Julian thought he heard something—a thump outside the wheel house. He turned to look but could see nothing for the darkness and fog.

His partner cupped his chin and steadied his gaze on her. "Accompany me to my stateroom."

Julian balked. He had no intention of going to her room. "Did Mr. Sala send you?" He relied on his caution to calm his body's uproar.

"No one sent me. I came of my own accord."

"But you are one of his troupe, yes?"

"If you wish to know my secrets ... we should retire to a more intimate setting."

"What say you show me what's under your mask first? Here, I'll lead by example." He lifted off his covering and settled it atop his head.

She sighed approvingly. "Just as lovely as I imagined Adonis would be."

"Now your mask," he insisted, refusing to be captivated by the pretty words.

Hands joined to his again, she drew Julian toward her as she backed up to brace herself against the rail. "Do you not read mythology? You'll turn to stone should you look upon me."

Julian's ear tips burned. Time to channel Nick once more. "Ah, but am I not a statue already? Inanimate until I feel your skin on mine? In your missive, you promised me a kiss."

She sucked in a breath, as if his sensual poeticism pierced her lungs. "Is it yet midnight?" From beneath her glove, she eased out a pin-watch. "We still have an hour. Perhaps I could tantalize you with just one taste."

Lifting up on her toes, she skimmed velvety lips over his chin. Her mask's forehead brushed against his nose. The surge of her warm breath acted as a rope, pulling Julian closer. Fighting the instinct to embrace her, he gripped the rail on either side, their bodies pressing together gently. He swallowed hard, ready to become her pupil—to embrace the tutelage she was so willing to give. His eyes closed as her fingers worked into the plaited hair at his nape.

An instant before their lips met, something hard struck the back of his head, biting his scalp. A metallic *thunk* sounded and his companion yelped as the offending item clattered to the ground. Julian released the rails, looking down at his feet where a copper Zeus headpiece gleamed in the soft light.

Rubbing his pounding head, Julian bent to retrieve it.

"Your head is bleeding—"

"Shush..." Julian pressed a finger to his lips. "Listen." Panting breaths broke from behind the wicker chairs surrounding the wheel house—barely audible over the lapping water. "We're being spied upon." He made the announcement loud enough to be heard by the intruder.

With a burst of speed, Julian sprinted toward the darkness.

Flushed out, the raven-haired Zeus bolted from behind a chair where he'd been hiding beneath a blanket. The underarm seam of his robe caught on the wicker weave and he struggled to get free, still draped in shadow. He'd just managed to rip the costume loose at the expense of the seam when Julian—from a few feet away—leapt to tackle him. "Got you!"

They crashed to the ground. The youth was a wildcat, gouging fingers into Julian's biceps, grunting and writhing his legs with such fervor Julian couldn't get him pinned down. Medusa stayed linked to the rails, clear of their struggle, rooting for Julian over the short distance.

He finally managed to pin the wiry Zeus' belly to the deck and secured his arms behind his back, crouching over him.

"Get me a crewman," Julian bade Medusa, his body aching all over from the encounter. "I'll hold him here until you return."

"No ... no please ... no crewmen," Julian's captive whispered on muffled gasps, his masked face pressed into the ground.

Julian leaned closer. "Why shouldn't I turn you over to them, after such an affront upon our persons? You could have put the lady's eye out had I moved but an inch."

Medusa had come to stand beside them now. Her body eclipsed what little moonlight filtered through the mist to illumine the scene. As if spurred by the renewed darkness, Julian's captive started to writhe again. To regain control, Julian straddled the young man's hips—which come to think of it, where rather shapely for a man...

"Should I bid the captain?" Medusa asked.

Her question shook Julian from the assessment of his captive's body. He tightened his grip on the youth's wrists. "Yes, yes I think that would be best. Perchance this lad needs to spend tonight in the brig, until he sobers up."

"I'm not drunk, you dog," Julian's captive sputtered in a hoarse voice.

"What else could possibly explain your unfounded malevolence? Go get the captain, please."

"What is that all over your arms?" Medusa touched the smudge of black on Julian's wrist.

Curious, Julian noted the smears along both of his forearms. The same color—black as his captive's hair—was also on his bedsheet costume in several places, as if it had come off during their wrestling episode. "Ah. I believe we have an imposter here."

"An imposter?" Medusa's query hung in the air.

Julian smiled. He'd been right earlier. This had to be the immigrant lad that had stolen his shoes. "Get the captain. This boy has some explaining to do."

Julian's captive stiffened between his thighs and mumbled beneath his mask. "Wait, *il mio piccolo cavolo* ... wait."

The words drained the blood from Julian's face. He

shoved his own mask—having fallen around his neck in the chaos—back to the top of his head. "Oh Lord."

"What is it?" Medusa asked. "What did he say? I couldn't hear him..."

Holding his captive's wrists with one hand, Julian used his free elbow to nudge Medusa out of the line of moonlight. He drew open the tear in the robe's side seam, shoving aside the fabric just enough to expose his captive's lower back and the cinched waist of a pair of pantlets. *Ladies' lingerie.* Inching the waist down, Julian found half a feathered wing staring up at him—a tattoo where those shapely hips curved in perfect female geometry.

"Blast it." He gritted his teeth on the words.

"Whatever is that?" Medusa inched closer to study the exposed skin.

Julian covered up Willow's back, adrift between fury and elation. "A ... bruise. He must've been hurt in our tussle." He could feel Willow's panting breath where his knees braced her ribs, and lessened the pressure between them. He cursed himself for not realizing sooner ... for being so rough with her. His mind scrambled for some way to get rid of Medusa so he could check her wounds.

He carefully eased off, helping Willow up, all the while holding her costume's torn seam closed to maintain the charade of her identity. "Perhaps I should take the lad to my cabin. He appears to be docile enough now. I'll send a steward for a physician and the captain. Forgive me for cutting our time short. Can you find your way back to your stateroom?"

Eyes narrowed beneath her mask, Medusa checked the pin-watch in her glove again. She appeared annoyed, but nodded. Julian held his breath until she vanished down the stairwell.

Willow glared at him, a fire raging from behind the crooked mask's eyeholes.

"Are you hurt?" Julian reached to straighten the mask.

She slapped his hand aside before he even made contact. "Only my pride."

He winced, remembering how he'd been dancing and romancing Medusa... how close he came to kissing another woman.

In front of Willow. *Damn.*

Voices drifted from below as passengers headed back to their staterooms. The masquerade gala was ending.

"Stay close to me." Julian grasped Willow's elbow against her reluctance to comply. He led her to the stairs. "And don't speak a word until we reach my cabin."

TWELVE

"It wasn't what it seemed." Julian shut his stateroom's door behind him.

"Oh?" Willow chunked her mask to the floor and spun to face him in the midst of the parlor, her olive complexion gilded with the lamp's soft yellow glow. "You weren't sneaking around hugger-mugger with that painted lily so you could pluck her petals? How presumptuous of me." The black smudges where color had drifted from her hair to her forehead and cheeks accentuated her scowl.

Julian tamped the urge to wipe away the smears. "What did you put in your hair?"

"Soot."

"Ah. You are the resourceful one, aren't you?"

"And you are a disloyal pig-snout. *Come la sfida voi bacia un'altra donna!*" Her hands waved in the air to accentuate her words.

Julian fought a smile. Despite her flaring temper and sullied appearance, she was a sight for sore eyes—standing there in a torn toga with cropped hair the color of coal—which come to think only made her lashes appear darker and accentuated the greenish-gold glimmer of her irises. "Now, that is not wholly true. I didn't actually kiss her ... as you well know."

Willow tsked. "Aw, poor deprived statue of stone. To think, tonight you could've become a real living man. Had I not been there to—"

Julian lifted a finger. "Ah-ha! Had you not been *there*. As

189

in here. As in what in heaven's name are you doing on this ship after swearing to me you'd stay put?"

"Ugh!" Willow flopped to the floor and proceeded to peel her pantalets off while holding the robe strategically in place at her thighs. "I swore no such thing. I simply vowed that you would see me again, without having to look all over the world for me. Ergo, I held true to my end of the bargain."

Julian gaped in wide-eyed wonder at her profile. What was she doing? Undressing? How the hell was he supposed to concentrate on winning this argument with her long legs exposed?

Visions of her contortionist poses rattled through his frazzled mind—teasing him with all the things that toned, limber body could do. He struggled to rein in the lewd fantasies, but there seemed to be no strong enough incentive. Not now that they were at last alone together: on a ship, in an isolated room ... no chaperones, no chance of interruption. No one with any idea what they were doing in this moment. Not even their family.

Family.

That managed to halt his rampant musings.

"Uncle Owen and Aunt Enya." He cleared his throat upon hearing how ragged his voice sounded. "Just think of the panic your absence will cause back home. We must apprise them of your safety. That's our most pressing concern."

"No, I believe the most *pressing* one is why your body was *pressed* to Miss Queen of Vipers up there."

Dumfounded again, Julian watched Willow stand so the robe's hem fell back in place to cover her legs. She then carried the discarded pantalets across the room. Something glimmered at the waist and he recognized the pin-watch his Uncle Owen had given her.

"You brought the watch with you?" Julian said, trying to

connect all the puzzle pieces in the midst of battling his screaming libido. "Why didn't you sell it instead of your hair?"

"You *would* ask that. Always so logical ... so analytical. Ever heard of sentimental value? I will never part with my watch, you insensitive clot. It enriches my life and brings me luck. Least it did in the past." Glaring at him, Willow shook her pantalets waist-side down over the table where he'd left his spectacles. Two cloth napkins tumbled out, formed into airtight bags which were secured shut by the pantalets' drawstring. Untying the string, Willow exposed the contents of each makeshift bag to reveal the crushed remains of the restaurant's main supper entree—fish and oyster pie. "Dinner's ruined, thanks to you and your faithlessness."

Julian wrinkled his nose, catching a whiff of the seafood while she smoothed each napkin open.

"*We must understand our inner selfhoods before we commit to anything prematurely.*" Willow bobbed her head as she jabbed at the crumbles of crust and fish with a rigid finger. "*A person must reach their full potential as an individual before they can give themselves over to another.*"

Before Julian could respond to her blatant mockery of his earlier sentiments, Willow scooped a handful of food and flung it at him. The cold, crusty bomb slammed his forehead and disbursed like a slushy snowball around his bare feet. Pungent gravy oozed along his brow and crumbs clung to the fine hairs at his temples.

"Damnit! Must you always throw things at me?" Growling, he scraped away the mess from his stinging forehead, gravy squishing between his fingers. He wiped his hands on his toga. "Have you lost your mind?"

Edging away from the table, she propped her shoulder blades against the wall, her expression as ravaged and broken as the damaged fare which now spotted the floor and rug. "Possibly. But I have an even better question. Have you reached your full potential yet? Or is waking up in a strange woman's bed to be the pinnacle of your selfhood? You're more like your brother than I ever deemed possible."

The hackles on his neck raised. Scraping muck from his brow, he strode over to her. He stopped long enough pick up his spectacles. He glanced at the mirror on the wall over the table, erasing his brother's image by placing the wired frames on his face. "Take that back."

He read her intentions, saw her shoulder tense to send her hand to the table for more ammunition. Julian got to the food first, raking it off into the floor behind him. A flaming heat suffused his entire neck. "I said take it back."

Smug, she braced her shoulders and lifted her chin. "I wish I could; I wish I didn't believe it. Men are all the same. It is always about the beauty and money, isn't it? Well, I'll never have money. And I haven't a chance to win you ... especially now that I ..." Her fingers absently reached up to her shoulder to find a strand of hair to twist, meeting nothing but skin.

"Now that you what?" Julian prompted, looming over her small frame.

"Look like a man—" Her voice broke, her hands covering her face.

Julian froze as she began to weep—her body a heaving mass of emotion. Had the wall not been behind her and him in front, she would have crumpled to the floor.

Was this the same woman who had lashed out at him two seconds earlier with her lukewarm leftovers? Was this the same girl that used to stock crickets in the coffee bin at the manor, just to watch the maids skitter atop the table and expose their bloomers at breakfast? Or was this the broken child she never let him see?

He had no idea what levels of poverty and degradation she'd witnessed over the past hours to bring her to this place, what sort of desperation she'd felt. She'd had to have been at wit's end to cut off her locks and pawn them for a measly handful of farthings.

Julian started to reach for her then paused, afraid she might come out swinging. He wasn't sure how he should dredge the depths of this new, vulnerable Willow. He wanted to take her in his arms and calm her tears ... assure her that he'd keep her safe.

The old Willow would slap him senseless should he infer she needed his protection. What would this new one do?

Hesitant, Julian tugged her wrists away to reveal puffy eyes and streaks of black where tears had mixed with the soot on her face and trailed down to her chin. He bent his knees so he'd be level with her red nose. "Come on, now. It's not so bad as all that, is it?"

She tried to jerk her hands away and cover herself again. "I couldn't ... e-even get a lady's costume. I look so ... *mannish* ..."

Julian straightened his stance. "No. No." Braving pulling her to him, he folded his chin over her head and stroked her hair where it hugged her ear. "You look nothing like a man. Perhaps a fine-boned young boy, but not a man."

He realized he'd said the wrong thing when her sobs escalated.

"Willow. Ah, Willow." His lips grazed her sooty hair. She seemed so fragile with her arms wedged between their bodies, curled up between her breasts—with her naked feet touching his. "You could don men's suits and be bald like those little German children," he murmured against her scalp, "and you'd still be the most feminine, fascinating woman alive."

An echo of breath heated his chest where her nose and mouth nestled. "Perfect. Now I'm a sissy."

Julian smoothed her hair again as if she were a flustered child. "Lord, woman. You're too masculine; you're too feminine. Make up your mind."

"I can't." Willow sniffled, snuggling deeper into him. Her tears dampened his robe. "I am ... discombobulated."

"I can see that."

She pushed back and frowned up at him—wet cheeks catching glints of light. "This is all due to Ridley's. It altered me. You sent me there to assuage your confusion, but it only caused me more."

Julian's jaw tightened. It was time she learned the truth about the real reason he wanted her there. "I wasn't completely honest about that ... I saw Nick kiss you a year ago. I didn't want to lose you to him, but hadn't the fortitude to admit it. Even to myself. Sending you away for a time was the easiest solution to a timid man's problem."

After a few strained moments, she licked her lips. "Had you but told me, I could have explained the kiss. That it meant nothing. That it was just your brother being a rapscallion. I never fell for it. We could've avoided all of this, could've already worked all our confusion out. You hid your feelings so well..."

He'd expected fury, but instead, her features saddened, affecting him like a knife to the gut. "Yes. I am nothing if not accomplished in my stupidity. Do you think you can forgive me?"

Glancing at her feet, Willow didn't answer. Julian stared at the top of her head and considered dropping to his knees to plead for another chance.

Thankfully, she glanced up before he could. "I suppose I must forgive you." Her fingers clenched his toga, wrinkling it at his chest. "I'm out of things to throw at you."

Julian braved a grin. He drew her into another embrace, relishing the feel of her in his arms. He couldn't remember a time he'd hugged her like this, and couldn't imagine why it had taken this long to try. "Do you feel better now?"

Her hands eased out from between them and circled his waist, squeezing him back—a delightful pressure. She turned her head, flattening her cheek to his chest. "I'm not sure. I am starting to think I don't know myself at all. As if I can no longer stand on my own two feet. I feel lost."

Julian nuzzled her head. "Then I'll carry you. I shall help you find your way. Fair enough?"

"Are you sure you can? You admitted to being stupid."

Smiling against her hair, he shrugged. "I have a great capacity for learning."

"Ah. So that's what drove you to pursue another woman tonight. So you could *learn*." The accusation stretched out and vibrated against his sternum, as tense as a plucked harp string.

Willow hedged back. He released her, but rested his hands on the excess fabric around her waist to keep her from wandering too far. Now that he had her here with him, he didn't want any more rash feats of escape.

"You'd never kissed anyone before me," she pressed, her thumb swiping at what must be glaring black smudges along his nose and chin where they'd burrowed in her hair.

A lump settled at the base of his throat. He couldn't bring himself to respond. It didn't matter; she could read the answer on his face.

"So ... Medusa was to be your tutor for kissing?"

Chagrinned at how foolish the plan sounded upon hearing it aloud, he nodded. "But nothing more, I promise."

Willow punched his chest. "Pollywoppus. We can practice

all those things together, you know. That is as it should be."

"I didn't want you to think me inexperienced. Or boring."

"I find your inexperience to be quite stimulating."

"But I'm an intellectual, premeditating clod."

"A what?"

"Nick told me that women—"

Her finger sealed his lips. "Aha. There's where you went wrong. Listening to your unscrupulous brother. Personally, I've always found the bookish side of you to be most erotic. And spontaneity is highly overrated."

"Is it?" Julian held her wrist and eased his tongue around her finger, licking off a coating of crumbs and sauce. "Are you sure about that?"

A flush colored her cheeks. She inclined against the wall, catching a breath. "You've been studying Emilia's novel, page for page."

Julian cringed. "In the future, could you not bring my sister into our interludes? It tends to have a dampening effect on things."

"Sorry." Her voice trembled.

Julian nodded. His leap at spontaneity had distracted her, just as he hoped … replaced her anger with something much more manageable: awe and wonderment.

"Now." Julian banked his palms on the wall at either side of her temples. "What are we to do about you? You've soot in your hair and you need a bath." He watched her expression in the soft light, saw her struggle to be in control.

"Well, you have soot on your face and you need a shave."

The both huffed a laugh.

Her lashes fluttered shyly. "I apologize for pelting you with pie. Oh, and the copper headpiece. How's the noddle?" She raked her fingers through his braid, loosening the plaits to caress his throbbing scalp.

He leaned into her touch. "Nothing but a scratch. I'm sorry I pounced on you."

She shrugged. "It was a fun frolic actually. Seeing as I thoroughly trumped you."

"Huh. That's not the way I remember it." He leaned closer. Her seductive scent intoxicated him with all the potency of opium. He brushed his lips across her brow and cheek. A sound—like a kitten's mewl—slipped from her mouth. Then, like a cat leaping on its prey, she bounced to her tiptoes so their mouths met awkwardly, bumping their teeth with a loud clack.

Julian rubbed his lips with his thumb. "If you would just have waited a moment..." He was surprised he managed to speak without a lisp.

Willow scowled as her tongue ran across her front teeth as if checking for cracks. "You were taking too long. It has to be timed just right or it loses its potency."

"How would you know that?" He had to temper the jealousy raging within. "How many men have kissed you?"

"Other than your brother's brazen attempt ... none." Her eyes turned up at him with a sheepish slant. "But I've seen it done aplenty."

"As have I. But seeing and doing are two completely different things, as I'm learning. Now hold still." Before she could argue with him, he caught her chin and planted his lips firmly on hers, swallowing her surprised gasp.

He knew he'd won when her fingers clasped his nape; when her lips, so soft, drew him deeper. He framed her face in his palms and tipped out his tongue—tentative—to sample the honey he'd been craving ever since that first taste. A whimper shuddered in her throat. Bolstered by her reaction, he broke her lips' seal so their tongues could touch and twine. After savoring her flavor, he drew back and gauged her reaction through his spectacle's steamy lenses.

"Oh..." she murmured breathlessly, her eyelids heavy.

Grinning, Julian touched the lovely dimple in her chin. "See? Now I know we did it proper. You're blushing."

Clapping a hand over her lips, Willow muffled a snort. "How can you tell?" she asked from beneath her fingers. "Your spectacles are fogged."

Julian laughed and pushed her hand aside, kissing her again. She laughed with him until something in her movements—in the way her stomach grated against his groin—quelled all levity. The instant their bodies made full contact, they both froze.

"Not so funny anymore," he mumbled.

She tensed. "Not so at all."

"Should we stop?" he asked, hoping he could—not wanting to.

"Speak my name."

"Willow."

"No. My full name."

Tasting the corner of her mouth, Julian grinned. *"Willomena."*

"More," she whispered against his lips.

"More of your name?"

"More of you..."

"Mmmm." Julian edged his kisses down her neck. His teeth nibbled, tasted, feasting on her soot and tear-streaked skin. When he reached her throat, she held him there and said something indecipherable—a plaintive plea that hummed under his mouth and drove him to the edge of madness.

Time seemed to blur around them, no longer holding them in its wake. Any inhibitions, any insecurities shattered as Julian surrendered to raw excitement. Why had he feared something so natural ... so bone-deep compulsory?

He secured her ribcage and lifted her as she tightened her grasp around his neck. Pinning her between him and the wall so they were eye level, he stormed her mouth again, enacting a slow and consuming swathe with his tongue. She opened to him, receptive and wet and warm. Her teeth were smooth, the roof of her mouth bumpy and tickling—a glorious contradiction. When her tongue met his, a flourish of electricity shot through him.

Their bodies aligned in perfect symmetry, a reminder that she had nothing on underneath the robe. He eased one of her nimble legs around his waist, fingertips drifting over her naked calf. They gasped in unison, sharing bursts of staccato breaths.

Overwhelmed by the urge to carry her to his bed ... to enact all of the fantasies he'd been suppressing for years, he became brazen. His hand found the tear in her toga, slipping within to stroke her silken flesh along her waist, searching for her tattoo. When his fingertips reached the bend at her lower back—stroked the dimples that bordered the mark— her skin trembled at the contact.

"Wait..."

Julian jammed his teeth together, his mind thick and fuzzy. Unsure if he'd heard her voice or someone else's, he dragged his perceptions to the surface, refocusing. Forehead pressed to hers, he opened his eyes.

THIRTEEN

"Please, wait ..." Willow mumbled the reluctant request once more, although it wasn't at all what she wanted.

Julian's gaze met hers. She tilted her head to lick the corner of his lips, tasting salt and a stray crumb from the fish pie. He grew still to appease her curiosity. But the instant his hand shifted toward her hip again, she tensed. "Julian, we must stop."

"Oh, right." His voice was gruff and gritty, affecting the same raw tingle through her blood as his whiskers along her skin.

She touched her chin, remembering the abrasive friction as he helped her unwrap her leg from his waist.

"I-I don't know what got into me. I acted like a beast." He let her slide down his body, grounding her bare soles halfway on his warm feet and half on the cool floor. Her robe's hem fell into place and grazed her ankles.

You acted like a man with desires. She was too dazzled to say it aloud. Instead, she held his arms around her and snuggled into his sculpted frame—seeking that intimate solidness against her abdomen that she'd only read about in biology tomes, undeniable proof that he desired her as much as she did him.

"I have no excuse," he mumbled. "Other than I've wanted to be close to you like this for longer than I dared admit to myself." His confession rushed along the top of her head, stirring her hair.

This was not what she'd expected when he'd captured her

on the promenade deck. No. This was so much more resplendent than anything she could've ever anticipated. She inhaled deeply, luxuriating in his scent.

She hadn't dreamt it this time. The beautiful words he'd spoken, the tenderness of his touch. And to think, he'd battled his attraction to her for a year ... perhaps more. She would have been furious that he'd hidden such feelings, had she not been so elated to hear him acknowledge them tonight.

Now his body was here, standing before her, blatantly declaring its need for her. And the kiss ... *cieli dolci* ... the kiss. It was just as she'd imagined—an all-encompassing barrage of sensation. To think they had only skimmed the surface.

Tensing, Julian pulled away. Willow felt the separation like ropes snapping free, leaving her unbalanced, tottering. She relied upon the wall's strength to sturdy her while she tried to recover.

Julian's face was flushed, his spectacles smeared and crooked, his hair out of its braid and tousled. She'd never seen him look so disheveled. She assigned the stunning image to memory—this masterpiece of unguarded emotion and vulnerability that she had painted with her hands, her lips, her body.

"Please, say something. If I frightened you by moving too fast, I won't forgive myself." He took off his spectacles which he then cleaned with a leg of her pantlets draped at the table's edge. His eyes softened. "I'll never intentionally hurt you. You know this?"

Willow smiled and nodded. *Always the gentleman.* He was going to be a wonderful lover. Thoughtful and tender. "You misunderstand." She straightened her robe, wishing they were rolling around as they had on the upper deck. Only this time, without the cumbrance of clothes. "I stopped you because we are not alone." She gestured to the pulverized dinner strewn about the floor. "I brought that back for him."

"*Him*?" Julian had returned his spectacles to the bridge of his nose. "Him who?"

Willow smiled. Was that jealousy in his tone? "Come with me." She laced her fingers through his.

Shaking his head, he fell into step beside her, avoiding spatters of food on the floor. "And where are we going?"

"To the bedchamber, of course."

His steps slowed but he continued to follow, a befuddled expression on his face. As Willow reached for the door latch, Julian halted her wrist.

"Wait, I don't remember shutting my bedroom before I left for the gala."

Willow's palm flattened against the wooden surface and she chewed her inner cheek. "That was my doing. I tucked him into bed and closed it so he'd feel safe."

"Tucked him ...? Wait, you've been in my stateroom before this?" Julian's eyes widened. "*You* were one of the immigrant boys slinking around in the corridor earlier!"

She attempted a charming bow. "I go by the name of Wilson."

Julian did not look amused. "So, it was you who stole the shoes, just like you did the costume—"

"I brought them back. They're here now, so it's all right."

"It is never all right to steal. What in hell is going on, Willow?"

Willow watched the blush darken his complexion, no longer a sensual rush of heat but a threatening combustion. "I decided, since you sent everyone in steerage on a scavenger hunt, that the safest place for the shoes would be the one place no one would look. Here."

"Why should you give a fig for the shoes?"

"You'll get your answers. First, I need to check on him. Please keep your voice down. He's sleeping."

"No one can hear a thing in that bedroom. It's insulated."

Willow shushed him again.

Julian stepped between her and the door, blocking the knob. "I want an explanation, and I want it now. How did you get into my stateroom?"

Feeling every bit the fish in a frying pan, Willow wished she could flop around to alleviate the heat. "She unlocked it for me."

"*She?*" He raked his hand through his hair, smearing remnants of pie through the strands. The effort made it even messier. "I thought you said 'he'. How many guests are you harboring in that bedchamber?"

"Only one. Sort of. It's complicated."

Julian rolled his eyes. "Always is with you. Just open the damn door."

Willow crinkled her nose as she pushed around him. "You needn't be so cross."

"I needn't be so—?"

"Shhh..." Willow pressed a finger to her lips and eased the chamber door open, ignoring Julian's reddening ears.

The creaking hinges fell silent, suffocated by the room's cushioned luxury. Darkness greeted Willow, soft and eerily serene. As she opened the door all the way, the light from the parlor slanted across the canopy's opened curtains, revealing a small lump in the middle of the bed beneath the covers.

She took a step onto the plush carpet. The nap expanded between her toes as if she were sinking in sand. Julian hedged in behind her, his hand rested on her lower back— enticing, or perhaps chafing. Willow couldn't decide.

"And what was your plan?" Julian whispered next to her ear. "Were you to be here when I returned? Were you to reveal your presence to me tonight?"

"No." Willow answered on a threaded breath. "I was to gather up everything and be gone before you got back. By watching you, I would know when you were about to leave the party."

"Brilliant."

Willow didn't have to see him to hear the sarcasm. Nor did she comment on it. Something seemed out of place here, and that uneasy apprehension held her distracted. "Newton?" She spoke his name aloud, hoping for some reaction from the inanimate lump in the bed's midst.

Seeing no movement, Willow rushed in, losing the warmth of Julian's palm on her back. Propping a knee on the bed's edge, she willed her nervous stomach to stop pitching, then reached out to nudge the lump, hand sinking into the plushness of a pillow. Her breath left in a *whoosh*, as if a leech burrowed into her lungs—sucking out her oxygen.

"Newton!" Ripping the covers aside revealed nothing but bed clothes. Even the shoes the child had been snuggled up to were gone. "*Signore dell'OH*. He's missing!"

Julian switched on the lamp, illuming the scene in amber light. "Willow, calm down. Tell me who this Newton is."

Willow dropped to the floor, lifting up the bed covers to look beneath the frame. Nothing—not even a dust ball. "A tiny lad. Yay high." She stood and held her trembling hand level with her waist. "He can't talk." She spun in a circle, scoping out the room. "He's an orphan. I'm responsible for him, Julian! He's dependent upon me..." Highlights of her own abduction burst like bright light in her mind. Her helplessness, her terror.

The familiar flutters awakened along her spine where her

tattoo splayed its wings. "Someone took him!"

"All right, now, sit down. You're as pale as rice pudding." Julian caught her wrist.

She wrestled against him, her experience muddling her sensibilities. "I have to find him now!"

Julian lifted her against her struggles and carried her to the bed. Propping her to sit, he knelt in front of her, hands on her knees. "Calm down. Stop jumping to conclusions. Let's think this through, logically. Would he have gone back to steerage without you?"

Willow couldn't stop her mind from racing. "I-I don't think so." She nibbled her fingertips. "No. He was so excited to be here. To sleep in a real bed. And he couldn't wait to taste the first class fare. No. Something happened. It had to have!"

The room blurred through a film of unwelcome tears. The blue bedclothes and cinnamon cushioned walls and carpets swirled to a sickening hue of brownish-green. She jumped up and started for the door, nearly bowling Julian over. "I have to find him!" She slapped moisture from her lashes.

"Oh, no you don't." Julian lunged and caught her around the waist. "You're not even properly dressed underneath that costume, remember?"

Willow tried to pry his arms away, to wrestle free. "I haven't time! He needs me."

Julian forced her to face him. Compassion merged with resolve in his steadfast gaze. "I can't imagine you leaving such a small fellow all alone, feeling this fiercely for his protection."

"Of course I didn't leave him alone. I'm not a beefwit. He had Nadia."

"Nadia. The one who let you into my room, I presume? Is she a scullery maid?"

"No." Breaking out of Julian's hold, Willow moaned. "Ugh. We're wasting time with this. That wretch must have talked him into leaving. Though I cannot imagine why she would, as determined as she was to see you in your skivvies."

"See me in my...?" Julian's skin flushed. "But I don't know any Nadia."

Willow considered if it was worth the explanation. Her musings fell stillborn upon a sniffling sound from inside the wardrobe. Julian heard it as well. He'd made the distance and thrown open the doors before Willow even arrived to glance around his shoulder. A pair of soulful black eyes—wet and glistening like pebbles in a creek—peered out from behind the wall of jackets, trousers, and vests. The child looked nothing less than terrified.

"Is this your little mouse?" Julian looked over his shoulder at Willow.

Willow dropped to her knees with arms outstretched, unable to stop the tears of relief. "Oh, Newton! Were you frightened, widget? Did you have a bad dream?"

The child launched himself into her, nearly knocking her over.

"Whoa there." Julian stepped behind Willow, his legs supporting her back.

She held the boy's warm body, snuggling him as he cried. Newton kept pointing to his feet between sobs.

"Do you know what he's trying to say?" Julian ruffled the child's hair.

Willow met Julian's gaze, sickened by the answer. "Someone broke in while we were at the gala. Newton managed to hide in the wardrobe. But they took Nadia ... they stole the shoes."

Standing in his parlor, Julian pressed an ear against the bedchamber door. He thought he'd heard some movement on the other side. No doubt wishful thinking. Any sound would be muffled by the room's cushion.

When would they wake up already? They must still think it nighttime. It didn't help that the sun was enmeshed in storm clouds.

Julian's night had been long and restless. He still couldn't believe he'd managed to last the hours without sneaking in to stare at Willow. It had been no easy feat, to attempt sleep in a chair in the parlor, seeing the soft light filter from beneath the bedchamber door; all the while thinking of her body dewy from a bath and encased in his long underwear ... sharing the bed with someone else.

Nothing more humiliating than being envious of a six-year-old child.

Julian shoved away from the door and flopped back into the chair that had been his bed last night, attempting to write his tasks for the day in his journal. He needed to return Willow's hair to the barber and pay the man for any damage to it. He needed to find the shoes. And to that end, he needed to question Mr. Sala and his girls, for he still suspected Medusa was one of the thespians from the troupe.

However, the words wouldn't slide off his pen. The only goal he wanted to write was: *Make love to Willomena*, and that would never do. He had a responsibility to see her safely home and unblemished. He couldn't toy with her innocence so blithely. Though he wouldn't mind exploring her body in other ways. Growing somber on that thought, he finally settled for two words: *Love Willomena*.

He'd never considered how deeply interwoven his mind, heart, and libido could be. He'd foolishly thought they could all be kept in separate compartments—giving one precedence and dominion as the other two waited patiently in the background. Until he realized that this particular woman, the one he'd grown up alongside ... who he laughed with and fought with throughout his youth, touched every part of him.

He considered it a blessing no one had seen through Willow's disguise thus far—else he would've had a man or two to kill. The unfamiliar prick of possessiveness stabbed at his heart—a venom so potent it scalded his veins with every pump of blood. The thought of another man touching her, hurting her, was worse than unbearable. Yet in some warped, twisted way, it brought him to a place of utter clarity. To know that he could feel so deeply, that such intense emotions could flourish in the wilds of a stoic, straight-laced heart ... well, it gave his entire future new vision.

Taking off his spectacles and laying them aside, he pinched the bridge of his nose and strode to the misty window. He pressed his forehead against the chilled glass, his thoughts bouncing like the frothy waves. When he'd first stepped onto the promenade deck just before dawn in search of the captain, he'd been surprised to hear the thunder, to find the skies gray and swollen. Now they seemed to be getting thicker ... darker.

The captain had accepted Julian's story. That his brothers had managed to sneak onboard. That he would pay their fare if need be, and keep them locked within his stateroom unless escorted by him. Then Julian sent a telegraph home—a bit cryptic since he had to rely on a crewman to send it—but it fit his lie enough, yet at the same time got the point across. He told his family not to worry about anyone gone missing from home, for they were indeed here on the ship and being cared for. He bade they not answer back, for things were better left in his hands. To please trust him to be responsible. He hoped they would honor the request, and not break the elaborate web he'd woven.

Lost to his thoughts, Julian barely heard the bedchamber door creak open. He turned to find Newton looking up at him, wearing a judgmental scowl along with one of Julian's dress shirts as a bed gown. The sleeves were rolled up to the elbows so they would graze the boy's wrists; the hem fluttered just above his ankles.

Unnerved by the child's severe scrutiny, Julian thought upon Willow's strange tale of the ghost tied to the shoes: how the deceased Nadia was a part of Newton and his past—that the boy and ghost had worked together as a team to relieve Mr. Sala of his hair, though Willow had no inkling why.

Staring at the little thief before him, Julian wondered if Newton could read more than just his dead sister's thoughts. Perhaps he could read the thoughts of the living, as well, and he'd heard Julian's inner grousing about his presence in the bedchamber. Perhaps Newton intended to cut Julian's hair next.

Julian flashed a glance to the bedchamber door to find it closed again. Willow must be dressing. He would be forced to make nice with the mouse on his own. Having not been around many children throughout his life, Julian found them almost as enigmatic and puzzling as ladies.

Straightening his cravat, he fought his swelling tongue. "Good morning, Newton."

The boy's expressive eyes narrowed to slits—so deep brown and fathomless, they appeared almost black. It reminded Julian of Mr. Sala's penetrating gaze, birthing a wild theory that would require further introspection. With the lad scrubbed clean, he definitely appeared to be of foreign descent, considering his dusky skin tone and the color of his damp hair. Perchance he couldn't even understand English. Though he seemed to understand Willow well enough.

"Um. All right then. Did you rest peacefully?" Julian attempted again, biting back his envy for the tot's sleeping arrangements.

Not even attempting communication, the lad ambled over to the chair and climbed astride. There he sat, a miniature prince on his throne, ready to crush Julian beneath his royal thumb. The expression upon his face was not one of confusion. It was intelligent disdain. He understood every word Julian said, but simply refused to respond.

Julian could sympathize with the boy being unable to speak. But why the obvious malignity? At least with Willow, Newton made an effort to gesture and pantomime his needs and thoughts.

Determined to forge an alliance, Julian strode to the table to retrieve a steel dome-lidded tray he had filled with delicacies from the first class café not twenty minutes earlier: buttered eggs; toasted Gloucester cheese over sizzling, ripe tomatoes; and almond-iced sweet rolls.

"I understand you want to sample some first-class fare. Would you like to start with breakfast?" Tilting the lid, Julian loomed over the lad, just close enough that the aromatic steam swirled in a cloud around them both. Julian ignored his growling stomach. He had to wait for some sort of response before dishing out the food.

Newton lifted his chin, his tiny nostrils quivering. Still, he didn't budge.

Stubborn. "Aren't you hungry, mouse? The bread and cheese last night ... that's nothing to the savory delights on this tray. These sweet rolls, mmm. The icing melts on your tongue like sugared snow."

The boy smacked his lips, the ire behind his eyes softening an almost indiscernible degree.

Julian checked the grin that wanted to break over his lips. He returned the boy's silence, along with his stare. Balancing the tray on his palm, he took off the lid and dropped it to the floor. The clang reverberated through his teeth. Sweet roll in hand, Julian lifted it to his mouth. He took a bite, holding the child's gaze as he chewed. "Mmm, mmm. *Spectacular*. Should you want some for yourself"—he swallowed—"all you need do is nod. A simple nod, yes or no."

Newton's chin set. He clambered to his knees in the chair. Without any warning, he gripped the tray, nearly managing to steal it from Julian's hold. Julian had to drop his sweet roll to secure the opposite end.

Glaring at one another, the two engaged in a tug-of-war.

"All I'm asking," Julian said through clenched teeth, "is a bit of civility."

Newton tightened his hold.

Giving it one last attempt, Julian clamped his fingers over the tray so hard the metal edge bit into his fingers. He leaned back slightly, using his body for leverage yet careful not to totter Newton from his perch. "A wink. I'll take a blasted wink. Simply show a little effort."

The boy smiled like the Devil himself and released the tray.

Julian crashed backward to the floor, sizzling eggs and seedy tomatoes slapping against his chest. Grease and hot yolk seeped through his thin shirt to scald his skin.

Cursing, Julian raked the mess off with a clatter of silver. Newton snickered, an imp in a cherub's form.

The burn on Julian's chest fired his temper. He scrambled to his feet. Before the lad could jump down from his perch, Julian secured his elbows, pinning them to

Newton's sides as he held him on the chair at arm's length. Newton's legs bucked out, one at a time, but Julian managed to deflect the kicks.

"Calm down, would you?" Julian snarled.

Butting out a knee, Newton almost guffed Julian in the ribs. Julian lifted him up to eye level. The boy's feet dangled in midair as he struggled to get free. "If you'll but show a *little* remorse, just a trifle, we can work together and clean this mess."

Newton let out a screech as piercing as a hawk's cry.

The bedchamber door flung open. "Put him down!" Willow stood on the threshold, fresh and breathtaking in Julian's lavender shirt with her treasured watch pinned to the lapel. Straight-legged trousers hugged her hips—the hems rolled to cuffs and the waist held up by suspenders which skimmed the outside of her breasts and pulled the shirt's fabric taut. Julian almost forgot the squirming captive in his grip.

Her hair had been brushed smooth. She'd fastened the long bangs behind her ears with the pins she'd used the night before to hold her Zeus's headpiece in place. With it back to its natural color, the hairstyle showcased her incredible eyes and thick lashes even more than last night.

Julian wanted to tell her she looked ravishing. Instead, his throat dried and expanded, as if he were gulping down an entire desert. "You will have to wear a hat and jacket if you're to leave this room at all." After realizing what he'd blurted out, Julian could've kicked himself. Instead, Newton managed to do it for him, clipping Julian in the stomach.

Disgusted with the entire situation, Julian seated the little thief back in the chair. Newton screeched again as Julian held the boy in place by his shoulders. The sound sliced his eardrums. "Any child that can make this much hullabaloo can certainly find a way to communicate and be civil."

Gaping at the display—the room's mess, Julian's hold on Newton—Willow shook her head in disbelief. "Whatever are you doing?" Her voice held the same anxious inflection as it had the night before when she'd convinced herself the boy had been kidnapped. "Let. Him. Go."

The instant Julian liberated Newton's shoulders, the tot's bare feet dropped to the floor and he ambled toward Willow. He threw his arms around her, burrowing his face into her abdomen.

Julian scowled. "Unbelievable. No doubt my chest is sprouting puss-filled blisters as we speak. I'm the one that suffered the brunt of the encounter, yet you're not showing the least concern for me."

Willow frowned as she led Newton back to the chair. "You're the one reputed to be an adult." She settled the tray on Newton's lap and offered a sweet roll, waiting for Newton to start munching on his breakfast. She patted his head. "Do you have a map?"

Julian gaped, dumbfounded, realizing the question was directed at him. "A map? Whatever for?"

"He likes to look at maps. It is what he does to entertain himself. I want to occupy him so I might address you. In *private*."

Julian turned to his desk and dug through the drawer where he kept his ride designs and paper work. "I don't have a map, but the former occupant left a copy of the ground plans for the World's Fair in his haste to abscond this room *with half his hair gone*." Julian shot an accusatory glance over at Newton. The boy continued to fill his cheeks with sweet roll, seemingly oblivious to the inference. "I need to return it, but you may look at it for now." Julian held the diagram out to Newton.

The boy refused to touch it until Willow took it and gave it to him. Then, satisfied by his interest in the topographical markings, she motioned for Julian to follow her into the bedchamber.

He eased the door shut behind him, leaving it cracked enough to hear the sporadic rattle of the ground plans and clang of silverware. He threw a winsome gaze at the unmade bed. A flood of torrid fantasies—each of them entailing Willow's naked body twined around his like a snake on a pagan statue—slammed through his brain. When he met her reproachful glare, he felt smaller than the specks of dust floating in the air between them.

"Never do that to him again," she said.

"Do what? Try to induce him to attempt an interchange with me? I wasn't bloody asking him to speak, Willow. Just to connect in some way. He was staring at me as if I were pig's slop—purposely ignoring my every effort. And I've done nothing to merit such disrespect. I gave him my bed, after all. The bed you were sleeping in. By the by, you wouldn't have needed to burn that blasted lantern all night, had I been holding you in my arms."

Her cheeks flushed, making her eyes even more vivid. Lord, he wanted to kiss her; but the way she looked at him … as if unsure who he was … unsettled him.

"He blames you." Willow's eyebrows furrowed. "For Nadia's absence. For the stolen shoes."

"What? Why? I had nothing to do with—oh." Newton must have eavesdropped last night and overheard Willow suggest Medusa was sent by someone to distract Julian while her accomplice ransacked the stateroom. Willow conjectured it was tied to the first time she and Newton had been here and stolen the shoes—how she overheard two women outside Julian's door planning to come in for something. Combined with the fact that Julian instigated a steerage-wide search for the shoes amongst the immigrants, it was no small wonder that the mouse blamed him. In Newton's eyes, Julian had endangered the boy's dead sister ... however ludicrous such a concern seemed.

The egg yolk on Julian's chest started to dry—tightening to any itchy crust. He loosened his cravat and scratched absently. "Well, he could have stuck his tongue out or brandished a kidney punch. I just don't like being ignored."

"And he doesn't like being held up high like that. He's afraid of heights."

Julian felt like nothing less than a bully. "I - I had no idea."

Willow's finger fumbled along her bared neck for a tendril to twist. She finally settled for clenching her fingers through the tuft of hair at her nape. "Yes. You've no idea ... no idea how terrifying it is for a child to be held captive in such a way ... to feel helpless to escape. To be powerless against an adult."

Julian narrowed his gaze. They were no longer speaking of Newton at all. "But you do, don't you? You do know what it's like—firsthand."

Regarding her bare feet, Willow made her way to the bed and perched on the edge with her knees drawn to her chest. Her arms wrapped around her legs until her hunched frame appeared as frail as a paper sculpture. As if she might blow away with the slightest breeze. As if she wished to.

Julian came to sit beside her, easing onto the cushions, in hopes to anchor her. "Forgive me. I would never wish to frighten any child. Even unintentionally. I'll work to be more patient. Children ... well, they're a whole new animal to me. But I'll honor Newton's eccentricities. I'll give him all the time he needs, from this point on." She didn't look at him.

Instead, her signature pout curved her bottom lip, and Julian ached to find the key that would loosen the tumblers of her locked-up secrets. "Please, Willow. Trust in me. Let me help you carry this burden. I've waited over a decade to understand."

Soft light from outside reflected off the bedclothes and draped her flawless complexion in echoes of blue. "I-I've already told you. I can't remember any—"

"A lie. If we're to broach a new future together, we must break down the walls of your past. *Together.*" His arm circled her waist.

After an excruciating pause while she fondled the watch at her lapel, she leaned into his shoulder—warm, soft, and fragrant. "I'm not lying." Her voice quavered. "I *can't* remember. Not that I haven't the ability, or the memory ... just that I am too much a coward. To remember it ... to speak of it ... will make it real. And I cannot relive the reality."

The sun slid completely beneath a cloud and the room darkened around them, as if the sinister confession had prompted a cosmic reaction. An acidic dread ate into Julian's gut. Willow had told him once that she'd had her tattoo since she was five. He'd always wondered how anyone could justify burning a brand on a child's tender flesh. However beautiful the hummingbird, he couldn't even fathom the pain she must have endured upon its etching.

"Did your parents hurt you?"

Her face buried deeper into his shoulder. "No. No. They tried so hard to stop those men. We traveled with an obscure circus from Italy all the way to London to escape them. Mama and Papa tried so hard—" He didn't have to see her face to know that her eyes were pinched shut; that her expression was more turbulent than the sky outside. "I watched them die trying."

Julian took off his spectacles and tossed them toward the pillows at the head of the bed so he could nuzzle the top of Willow's head. Through wayward strands of hair, he gawked at the shadows playing on the wall. *She'd watched them die?* His insides felt gutted, scraped raw of any words. But his over-analyzing mind wanted answers: What men? Why did they want her? Or was it her parents they were after and she was simply in the line of fire?

When the tears came, Julian pulled her full onto his lap so her head snuggled under his chin. He situated her legs to hang over his thigh. Then, rocking, he held her warm, soft body tight to quell the questions in his mind. She needed a rock, not an inquisitor.

She wept quietly, hardly moving—the only proof of her grief the hot wetness glazing his neck. While he cradled her, rage and helplessness warred within him. *Men.* She'd said men. Despite his best efforts, one question begged asking.

His nose nudged within the silken waves at her crown. "Did the men ... violate you?" Saying it aloud gored his insides—a deep-gutted purge of black rot from his soul. If they had, he would find them. No matter how long it took. No matter whom they were. He would find each individual involved and watch them die the vilest deaths imaginable.

Between sniffles, Willow wiped her face with her cuff and tried to gather her composure. "No. Not in the way you think."

"Thank God." Julian hugged her. "Can you tell me, then?"

Nodding, she took a deep, shuddering breath. "The strangers came one afternoon ... when Mama and I were practicing our trapeze act." Her hands clutched his lapels. "Papa was there, too. Had I not gone back for Tildey, had I not hesitated, they would never have been murd—" A sob caught in her throat, squeezing off the final word.

Julian couldn't stand the conviction in her voice, as if she truly believed she'd caused the tragedy. "Who was Tildey?"

"My doll. My parents died because I went back for my doll instead of running."

"You were a child. You were thinking like a child. That's a natural reaction."

"Not for me. I knew what to do. They'd rehearsed that moment over and again. As if they'd expected it..."

Julian kissed her head, trying to calm her. This answered one of his questions. These men had been after Willow from the beginning. "Do you know why they wanted you?"

She shook her head and sniffed. "And I don't remember their faces at all. They put a sack over my head, but I could feel the roll of the carriage when they took me away. I could hear the creaking of the suspension and the horses nickering. It was so dark." Her fingers tightened, catching the fine hairs on Julian's chest, pinching the already tender flesh where he'd been burned. He embraced the sting. It grounded him, kept him from exploding into a thousand pieces.

"I held Tildey so tight. She was all I had left. And I started chanting over and again: 'Mama is a hummingbird, Mama is a hummingbird'... to forget her fall ... for if she was a bird ... she could fly, you see." Willow's voice became small and wispy like a child's and the words started to gush out faster, as if she were a well overflowing. "I chanted it for the entire trip—what felt like hours. The men tried to shush me, but they never hit me or touched me, as if they'd received instructions not to. When the carriage stopped, they took me somewhere inside, still bagged and blindfolded. I smelled a fire and antiseptic—" Her voice broke again. She cleared her throat to gain control. "They chose a hummingbird to mark me as punishment for my nervous rantings. All these years,

I've never looked at it. Not once." Her jaw moved against Julian's neck, and he sensed she must be sucking on her lower lip. "The men left me at the orphanage after that." She tensed in his arms. "Do you think it's a sin to hate someone, Julian? To want to kill them with all your heart and soul?"

Fighting his own battle with hatred at the moment, Julian couldn't answer.

Taking a deep breath, Willow shivered. "I've tried to forget them, to forget it all. But I could never forget the mark was there. Even after it no longer hurt. The other children told me what it was, teased me about it. And sometimes ... sometimes even now it feels as if it's alive, swishing its wings across my back to mock me. A taunting song only I can hear."

A bout of nausea overtook Julian. No wonder she'd left the orphanage. She'd wanted to escape anything tied to her parents' death. But she could never escape her own flesh.

He held her tighter, as if he could be a shield to the anguish battering her. He felt so impotent. He should've been prepared for such a possibility, familiar with his father's tortured youth. Yet to hear this repulsive tale from Willow, to envision her as an inquisitive and vibrant little girl in braids, witnessing the death of two parents that loved her ... it left Julian's innards rocking. A turbulence more unsettling than the looming question mark that had once shaded her past.

"I'm so sorry." A pale benefaction of sympathy that could never vindicate her shattered innocence and childhood. Her weight on his lap shifted as he stroked her skin, dried the tears from the cheek faced away from him. Then his fingers nestled into the hair at her nape and his lips hovered at her ear. "No one will ever leave you powerless again. I'll see to that."

"I know you will. It is why I never left the manor."

He kissed her temple, overwhelmed by her faith in him. "I'm glad you left the orphanage, though. I'm glad you found us."

She leaned back to meet his gaze—eyes dewy and soft, nose the color of a ripened berry. He couldn't help himself ... he kissed the tip of it.

The action brought an unexpected reaction; her lips sought his mouth, searing him with salt and sweetness. He ran his hands through her hair and twined their tongues with a nobler intent than the night before. This was not about satisfying his urges. This was an exchange of comfort and support, so much more intimate for the starkness of their frayed emotions.

"Willomena," he spoke against her cheek, fingertips running the length of her spine. "I'm here now. Let me help you banish the memory."

FOURTEEN

A soft patter of rain hit the windows—a rhythmic lull. The room darkened to a purple haze and Willow drew back slightly to watch the color of Julian's eyes change with the shadows. The silver surrendered to a glimmering gray, as hypnotic as the innermost cinders of a dying fire.

This is why she loved him. Gentle, steadfast, and protective Julian. Even as a youth, he'd been her guardian. He not only helped her learn to read English, he'd taught her how to swim as he feared she might fall into one of the many ponds at the manor and drown; he'd shown her how to ride a horse—how to tame a colt with a slice of apple and a gentle voice so she need never fear the wildness in its gaze. And now, in this moment, when her ravaged past lay raw and writhing at his feet, he stepped over it and held out his hand to be the bridge she'd never had, so she might leave it all behind.

She remembered when she had first started wanted to tell him. On her twelfth birthday, when they sat in a tree together, reading *Alice's Adventures in Wonderland*. She'd watched Julian's mouth as he recited Alice's shock upon eating some cakes that caused her to shrink: "'*But it's no use now,' thought poor Alice, 'to pretend to be two people! Why, there's hardly enough of me left to make ONE respectable person!*'"

Willow had wished to admit that very day that she was two people herself. The impulsive young girl he knew, and the damaged child that had shrunk away after watching her parents die. But she could never bring herself to say it aloud.

Until now.

"Tell me," he murmured, still cradling her in his lap. "Tell me what I can do."

Hearing a rattle of paper in the parlor where Newton was still preoccupied, Willow took Julian's hand. "Mend my heart." She pressed his palm between her breasts. "It hurts inside my heart." Her eyes blurred with tears again.

He held her gaze as she moved his fingers to massage her sternum over her shirt. Ripples of linen squeezed her breasts. His focus shifted, taking note of her body's outline beneath the fabric. Slowly, he slid his hand down, raking his thumb beneath the heavy swell of one breast.

Riding the sensation, Willow exhaled a trembling breath as his arms eased around her hips, securing her tighter on his lap. He bent to skim his mouth along her collar bone, his breath hot and rapid. She buried her face in the silky hair at his nape, smelling the faint scent of lavender from his bath the night before. As she twined her fingers through his braid, he moved his lips lower, across her sternum—soft, gentle kisses. The crisp linen shirt caught on his whiskers with tiny popping sounds.

She wanted to feel that bur against every inch of her bare skin; but she couldn't forget they had company in the other room. "Newton ..."

Julian's lips glided upward, stopping at her neck. "We could lock the bedchamber door," he whispered against her throat as he followed her racing pulse to find her mouth once more.

She met the lingering press of his soft lips—matched it with her own intensity before breaking away. "We shouldn't leave him unattended..."

"You're the one who needs attending." Julian's hand

drifted down to sculpt her breast—the faintest palpitation, as if he hesitated to cross those boundaries. The careful ministrations unfurled a dark, hot yearning ... a demand for more. She whimpered.

Julian looked into her eyes, his own dark with passion.

The rattle of silver sounded in the parlor, followed by a drawer opening. Newton was exploring. Soon enough, he'd find his way to them.

Julian sighed and pressed his forehead to Willow's chin, his thumb stopping over her covered nipple in mid stroke, leaving her aching for more. A soft rumble shook his voice box. "You're right. I promised to be a responsible guardian."

Trying to ground her senses, Willow measured his words for bitterness but found none. Julian understood her connection to Newton in a way few others could. The boy was alone in the world, just as she had been at his age, and needed someone to watch over him as the Thorntons had her.

"We should get the day started then." Julian extricated himself from Willow's embrace, helped her off his lap onto the mattress, then kissed her wrist as he began to stand.

She caught his hand and tugged him to sit again. "What are your plans?"

He paused, palms rested on his knees. "First, I'm to apologize to your mouse for earlier. Then I'm going to take him with me to the barber while I get a shave. He needs a haircut. And he's returning all of the farthings the barber gave him for that stolen hair. The child must learn some morals." His gaze shot around the room. "Say, where did I put my spectacles?"

"You dropped them by the pillows."

Julian crawled across the bed, sinking into the cushioned mass of covers on his way across to retrieve the glasses. "I suppose after that, I should take Newton to the tailor. Get him a suit made. He should look the part of a viscount's son, after all."

Rolling to her side, Willow smiled. "So the captain believed we're your brothers? That we stowed away without your knowledge?"

"He did ... *Wilson.*" Julian winked, pausing mid-crawl to dig for his spectacles. "And he's not even making me pay for your occupancy, so long as I keep you both out of trouble." He grinned. "Come to think, it might have been easier just to dole out the coinage."

"Oh, ha." Willow twined her body into a tight ball and flipped over to position herself between Julian's hands and knees before stretching out beneath him on her back.

"Now there's a fine trick." Julian smirked. Behind the levity of expression lurked a baseborn hunger that sent a tremor of excitement through Willow's body, just to see how much he wanted her.

Her fingertip trailed his mouth, captivated by the fullness. "We're keeping Newton, then?"

Julian settled his body atop hers, supporting his weight in his arms. Sensual heat swirled through Willow's abdomen as his hardened planes and angles effected a sweet invasion into her curves and hollows.

"The lad's not an orphaned squirrel, Willow." His voice lowered to a husky rasp, as if he, too, was rocked by the mock joining of their bodies. "I'll try to help him feel at home with us for now. But it's imperative we find his father. I might know who he is. He's on this ship. And he needs to be apprised that his child is alive after all."

"Who?" Willow asked, already intuiting the answer.

"Mr. Sala. They have the same eyes. No mistaking it. I believe the lad is following him."

Willow's muscles stiffened. She and Julian had discussed Mr. Sala last night, and came to the realization that he was the Italian nobleman she and Newton had run into in the men's corridor the day before. Willow had to agree it was a possibility he was Newton's father, after watching how the child reacted to the man—how quickly he had struggled to get on his feet and escape. "If that is true, there must be a reason Newton hasn't revealed himself. Nadia said their father would corrupt him. And Mr. Sala might very well be behind the abduction of the shoes from your room. That unsettles me."

"Yet you admitted you're not sure you believe anything Nadia says." Julian tapped one of the pins in her hair, causing part of her bangs to slide loose. He played with the glistening strand. "And we could be wrong about Mr. Sala's involvement with the shoes. Perhaps Nadia turned Newton against their father to appease some personal grudge she harbors."

"Please. Don't act on this until we have more information. Newton's safety is our priority, above all else."

Julian's jaw clenched. "I don't feel right about keeping this quiet. The man seemed very sad when he spoke of having no children. I believe he misses his son greatly."

Pulling her hair from Julian's fingers, Willow scowled. "Can you just this once take the lower road? Lie to Mr. Sala until I can speak to Nadia again. I must question her further."

"That's impossible, seeing as we don't have the shoes. Unless Newton can tell you where she is."

"Only if Nadia knows where she's been taken. So far, he has told me she only sees darkness around her. She must still be in the box. She's removed from the physical world when she is in that box unless Newton is in close proximity. So unless someone takes the shoes out and Nadia gets a look around, she can't tell Newton where she is. She can only make him more fearful through her own worry and helplessness."

Julian sighed. "Damnit, Willow. This is against my better judgment."

"Why must you always surmise that your judgment is better?" In an effort to get out from under him, Willow tried to spin her body around, popping Julian in the cheek with her elbow.

He cursed.

"Oh, *il mio piccolo cavolo*. I'm sorry." Wincing, she reached for the red spot that was sure to make a bruise.

Julian started to pull away, but winced and let her touch him instead. "First you trop me in the noddle with a headpiece. Then you slap me with food. Now this." He caught her hand and molded it to his cheek. "You're not a lady to be loved with kid gloves, are you? Boxing gloves are more apropos."

"Did you say … *love?*" Willow asked. The sun came out at that moment, highlighting the same expression of shock on his face that she felt sure she wore.

Julian's ears turned a fiery red, matching the mark on his cheek. He struggled to speak, as if his tongue had been nailed to the roof of his mouth, until Newton shoved the door open and sauntered inside. He held up the ground plans.

"Well, there you are!" Julian rolled off of Willow, avoiding her gaze and sounding far too relieved to see Newton, much to her annoyance. Julian stood, smoothing his grease laden clothes. "Let's you and I get cleaned up, mouse. I'm going to treat you to a tour of the first-class deck. What say?"

Diurnal assignments for Friday, April 22, 1904:
1. Love Willomena...

Lounging on the floor, Willow read the journal entry once more, taking full advantage of having the stateroom to herself in Julian and Newton's absence. They'd been gone for an hour on their errands. Banking on Julian's reluctant promise that he would practice caution and wouldn't let Mr. Sala see Newton, she had relaxed enough to take a nap and clean up the breakfast mess. She'd just started to fold the fairgrounds' map when Julian's journal beckoned to her from the parlor table's drawer. In spite of how angry he'd be for her nosiness, she read his diurnal assignment over and again. Now she could even see it with her eyes shut tight. *Love Willomena.*

Did he? Her heart danced on a lyrical pulsation, clamoring against her ribs like chimes on the wind. His tender concern when she shared her past, his tentative yet passionate exploration of her body while they shared the bed, they had all testified to the emotion.

Still, only when she heard it from his own mouth would she know it was true.

She realized he'd been taken off guard earlier; that a man as staid and analytical as Julian would be hard pressed to admit something so abstract, something which would render him defenseless to her own response. But she wondered if his hesitance to admit such might be because she had a wicked nature, and his sense of right and wrong made him reluctant to consider her worthy of commitment.

He'd seen the many pranks she'd pulled with Nick over the years without remorse. How the two used to combine their skills to pilfer bottles of wine from the cellar, or to lift trinkets of lesser value from guests, such as appliquéd handkerchiefs or jeweled buttons—all for the mere thrill of the lift. They had always returned the wine and curios: the wine bottle showing up in the kitchen, lighter by a few swallows; the buttons or kerchiefs appearing beneath the patron's beds or pillows, none the worse for wear.

However, if Julian knew the exhilaration she'd experienced upon stealing the costume from the tailor or the electrifying rush of life that thrilled her upon each lesson in pick-pocketing offered by Newton and the Helget children, he would never think her "marriable."

Even she wondered about herself ... about this absence of contrition. From her experience, certain circumstances lent themselves to thievery—in fact condoned it. Sometimes people had to steal to survive: to feed the crying children they loved—to put a roof over their heads and quilts on their beds in the dead of winter.

The thought of poverty-stricken families brought to mind the Helgets, and Willow had an overwhelming urge to venture down to steerage and visit them. Julian had bought four boxes of chocolates early this morning to take to the immigrant children. He intended to deliver them later today. Willow couldn't understand what harm there would be in taking them herself. Everyone in steerage already believed her to be a boy, after all.

There was one complication: Julian had made her promise not to wander about the ship without him. And if she expected him to uphold his promise to hide Newton, then she had to uphold hers, as well. But she knew where steerage was. Truth be told, there would be no *wandering* to it. Only a straight jaunt down the corridor to the stairwell ... much like her prior vow to him, it was all in the wording.

Her conscience pricked. No. He'd be furious.

She had to find something to occupy herself here. Julian

had suggested she read Emilia's novel in his absence. Standing to tuck the journal back into the parlor drawer, Willow held the fair's ground plans up to the window so the watery daylight glazed the back of the parchment.

The light pierced through a spattering of tack holes at the lower midst of the map. The perforations marked the Japanese Pavilion exhibit where the thespian competition was to be held. This was the reason Newton had shuffled into the bedchamber to burst her and Julian's intimate bubble earlier. In some way, that location was personal to the widget. Willow only hoped this wasn't further proof that Mr. Sala was his father.

Newton's family or no, something about the man made her nervous, though she couldn't quite put her finger on it. Even if she didn't get a good look at his face during their collision in the corridor, she still couldn't shake the sense that he was only wearing a nobleman's mask. That there was more to him behind the disguise.

Folding the parchment, she slipped it into the drawer with the journal then poured a cup of tea. The steam warmed her cheeks and wound her senses in maple and vanilla. The ship's engines hummed beneath her bare feet on her stroll to the bedchamber.

After setting the cup and saucer on the table by the bed, Willow found Emilia's manuscript laid out on mattress, already open to a passage. She didn't bother sorting through to find where she'd left off. Instead, the words drew her in, and she settled amongst the covers to read.

> *Easing inside the stone shed, Elizabeth closed the door behind her. The damp scent of mildew and soil banked within her nostrils. A soft flutter stroked her ears ... a familiar sound, yet distant in her memory. Something she'd been missing.*

She took another step, feeling her way through the darkness with the soles of her bared feet, afraid to light the lantern. What would her punishment be, should Benedict find she'd lifted the key from the pants he'd flung upon the bed during their lovemaking? How would his darker side react, should he learn that after he'd given her body such rapturous pleasure, she'd waited for him to fall into slumber so she could slip out from the sheets and venture into the forbidden garden to storm the shed in its midst?

Dirt rolled beneath Elizabeth's bare feet. The flutters seemed to accelerate with her approach to the back wall. No longer able to resist her curiosity, she lit the lantern and grew nauseous at the sight that greeted her.

Black swallowtail butterflies —thousands upon thousands of them—butted against their glass prisons. Along the bottom of the cases, other butterflies crawled one upon another, resembling moving mounds of black and white speckled leaves. These had given up their will to fly, their spirits crushed.

Rage and revulsion crept over Elizabeth like shadows born of the lantern's flickers. So this was why she had been bereft of her precious butterflies? Benedict had been capturing them and chaining their freedom to boxes of glass.

He had sworn his love and devotion. He said he only wanted what was best for her—wanted to heal her. Why then would he take the one thing that gave her spirit delectation and light, and hide it away here, imprisoned by darkness?

Willow stopped reading to sip her tea. Swishing the mild flavors through her teeth, she felt every bit the caged butterfly herself.

Regole senza senso. Men and their unreasonable prohibitions. What right did Benedict have to forbid Elizabeth from visiting the gardens ... to keep her from her beloved pets? What right did Julian have to run about the ship all day and frolic with Newton, when he wouldn't even allow Willow to visit her friends? She doubted he'd even let her accompany him to steerage later. She had a sinking feeling he expected her to stay in this claustrophobic stateroom until they docked in four days.

How absurd. She had already proven convincing as Wilson. Jaw clenched, she swung her legs over the bed's edge and smoothed the wrinkles from her trousers. Her friends needed to know she and Newton were safe. She refused to have them worry all morning until Julian got around to carrying the chocolates to them. If she didn't apprise Christoff and Engleberta of her and Newton's whereabouts, they might get into some sort of mischief this morning trying to find them. Willow wouldn't allow that.

Resolute, she rearranged Emilia's pages, tied them together, and placed them in the wardrobe. She put on some boots and pulled one of Julian's hats low over her head, tucking her cropped hair beneath it. Then she adjusted her suspenders and shrugged into a frock coat. She had to roll-up the cuffs so her gloved hands could grasp the boxes of chocolates.

Stepping into the corridor, she tweaked her hat at a nobleman who returned the gesture without pause. The scent of lemon verbena wreathed her on his passing. There was her proof. Now that she looked the part of an upper class lad, no one would question her presence here. Julian had no need to worry or be angry. Besides, she would be back long before he even knew she left.

FIFTEEN

Julian adjusted his spectacles to regard a hanging assortment of ready-made gowns while the tailor, Mr. Higgly, measured Newton for a suit. Willow would be in steerage by now. Julian had no doubt of it. Asking that woman to stay put was like asking the wind not to blow.

Had Sir Isaac Newton ever met Willow, he would not have coined his laws of motion, for she would've disproved every one ... least as they pertained to the forces acting on a body and the motion of said body. And speaking of bodies, as alluring as Willow's was, most especially when the light shimmered along her skin just so, and her amazing eyes showcased that ravenous desire shaded by the uncertainty of virtue ... she could entice the blasted planets into her orbit and they'd have no choice but to drop down and follow.

Julian himself was a testament to that—hopelessly helpless to resist her pull, and often duped by her schemes. But this once, he felt sure he'd bettered her. He'd left the chocolates out in broad sight to tempt her. He'd left the manuscript turned to the perfect passage in hopes to light her inner fire.

With or without his prompts, he knew she wouldn't stay in that cabin. Oh, she would try. Possibly clean up their breakfast mess ... perchance even take a nap. But in the end, her nomadic tickles would get the better of her, and she'd soon be gallivanting all about the ship in search of the haunted shoes.

Thus the genius of his plan: give her something else to do.

Something that would take her directly to steerage and back to the stateroom without any detours in between. For she would be arrogant enough to think Julian wouldn't suspect a thing so long as she returned before he finished his errands.

He rubbed his shaved chin, smirking at how she would react when he confronted her about the missing chocolates. She wouldn't make any excuse. She would be straightforward and unapologetic. One of many things he admired about her.

Julian lost track of his thoughts as across the room Newton wriggled upon his stool, a disgusted scowl upon his face.

Julian couldn't blame the mouse, especially in such gloomy surroundings. Devoid of any windows other than the glass door, the shop relied upon electricity for illumination. The yellowish lights dimmed in popping intervals, evoking an aura of melancholy. The bolts of fabric and hanging tools offered the only form of décor. This place was not nearly as inviting as his mother and uncle's shop at home—full of natural light and beribboned with laces and feminine splendor. A few vases of fresh flowers could do wonders for the musty smell here, as well.

Newton rubbed his nose, as if cued by Julian's thoughts. With the new haircut, Newton's resemblance to Mr. Sala was uncanny. They even shared some of the same mannerisms. Julian would abide by his vow to Willow the rest of the day. But come tonight, he intended to find Sala and speak to him. Man to man.

Newton blew some air out of his nostrils, sounding like a disgruntled pony. Grumbling, the tailor resituated him, forcing his arms out straight then over his head and around as if the lad were a windmill.

Trailing his finger along a lush velvet trim, Julian

admired the pre-made gowns once more. He wondered which one Willow would like. He had every intention of restoring her wounded sense of femininity; even if it meant spending the last of the extra money his father had given him. The finances would work out. If Judge Arlington conceded to a partnership, Julian would ask for a good-faith deposit ... enough money for return train fare and the ship ride home. If the judge resigned interest ... well, Julian might have to sell his own hair.

Julian glanced up as the tailor pursed his mouth so tight his face resembled an albino prune. Though Julian couldn't read lips like his mother, it took no such talent to know that Mr. Higgly was annoyed with Newton's energy. He clenched the child's elbow to spin him on the stool and stooped, trailing the measuring tape from Newton's hip to his ankle.

The child faked a sneeze across the tailor's balding head. Mr. Higgly dropped the measuring tape and growled as he dabbed the top of his scalp with a handkerchief.

Julian grinned. He understood Willow's strong attachment to Newton in such a short time, especially considering her broken past. Julian's gut twisted to think she would soon be hurting again ... that he would be the cause of her heartbreak when he reunited Mr. Sala with his son.

This new maternal side of Willow was quite surprising. Julian had never thought of her as a mother; she didn't even like to play with dolls as a youth. But after learning of Tildey—how Willow blamed her parents' deaths on her concern for the toy—he finally understood that quirk.

Movement in his peripheral returned his attention to the tailor shaking his finger at Newton. Julian's shoulders tensed. As much as Mr. Higgly obviously disliked children, it was better he didn't know that Newton had helped steal a costume. Julian had brought the robe and headpiece in on his own, claiming to have found it outside the door. At first he'd felt ashamed of the lie, but now, he could see the wisdom in it.

Julian took off his spectacles and dropped them into his pocket. Then, singling out the fitted gown he'd chosen, he freed it from its hanger. He cleared his throat and strode in their direction, stopping the tailor in mid-snarl.

"Mr. Higgly, surely you're done with the lad. He appears every bit as weary of the measurements as you are." Brown paper patterns, tacked to the wall, rustled upon Julian's passing—generic silhouettes of shirts, bodices, skirts and breeches which were to be draped over the body and pinned to the appropriate size before cutting fabric replicas. He stopped at the sewing table. "I'd like to purchase this and be on our way. We'll return for his suit later … say, tomorrow afternoon."

Upon seeing the expensive dress draped over Julian's arm, the tailor's choleric scowl morphed into an illustrious smile—complete with crooked white teeth. "Yes, Master Thornton. Tomorrow should suffice." He jotted some measurements then dragged Newton down from the stool, hedging him toward the sewing table.

Upon their arrival, Julian placed a hand on Newton's shoulder in a show of support, surprised and pleased when the boy didn't tense beneath him or jerk away. After laying out his money, Julian spread the gown over the table's scarred surface, imagining Willow's curves sheathed in the coppery satin. He prayed it would fit. It looked to be the right size. Should it need any alterations, his mother and Aunt Enya could fix it at home. He leaned down to whisper to Newton. "What do you think, mouse? Will she like it?"

The boy nodded, his little fingers running along the slick fabric, as if he'd never touched anything quite like it.

"Splendid choice for your lady back home, Master Thornton. You have a fine eye for fashion." Mr. Higgly's spidery-veined hand brushed Newton aside. "Don't wish to soil it, young sir."

Julian drew Newton against his thigh and rubbed his head reassuringly. They both watched in silence as the tailor proceeded to tuck the black chiffon sleeves inward, making a straight line of the side seams.

"The buttons down the back can be tricky. And this beaded fringe requires extra care. It is French-jet and mercury glass. And the pleated chiffon train should be removed and cleaned separately." With a master's precision, he folded the gown into a crisp square. "There is a pair of ruffled gossamer mitts that accompany this ensemble. I'll wrap them along with the gown in some paper for you."

The instant the tailor disappeared into the store room in back, the bell on the front door tingled. Julian turned to see Judge Arlington step across the threshold.

"There you are." The judge yanked off his hat on the way in, shaking raindrops from the brim. "Been looking for you on the upper deck. Quite a drizzle up there. Ran into the captain. He told me about ... ah, this must be one of your brothers."

Julian tamped the tangle of nerves rising in his throat. "Yes, this is the youngest one. Newton."

The judge wobbled over, crouched down, and looked Newton in the eye as he shook his hand. "You're a dapper young lad, aye? Going to be as handsome as your brother, I see."

Newton wrinkled his nose and snorted.

"Not so sure he takes that as a compliment." Julian laughed, trying to curb the nervous edge to his voice.

The judge arched his eyebrows. A merry smile danced

beneath his white moustache. "So, how old are you then?"

Newton stunned Julian by holding up six fingers. He hadn't expected the boy to respond at all; but then again, after being treated like a recalcitrant puppy by the tailor, Julian supposed Newton was thrilled to find any nobleman who would treat him as an equal.

"Six years." The judge returned his hat to his head. "Ah. I remember when my youngest boy was six. He had the best time riding a ferry along the Mississippi. Are you going to visit the river?"

Gazing up at Julian, Newton shrugged.

"Hmm." Judge Arlington balanced his hands on his lumpy knees. "Haven't planned that far yet? Maybe you'll be going straight to the fair to ride the Ferris wheel. I hear tell it's two-hundred-and-sixty-five feet high. Doesn't that sound grand? Think of how far you'll be able to see."

Newton's face paled. He shook his head, backing away from the judge until he hit Julian's thigh.

Julian kneaded the boy's tense shoulder. "He's not too fond of heights. He won't be riding any Ferris wheel."

The judge struggled against his weight to stand. Julian ended up cupping his elbow to help him.

Judge Arlington nodded his gratitude, smoothing out his brown suit. "I'm sorry. I assumed, seeing as you design rides, that this little tripper must be the one to test them out."

"That would be my *other* brother. Wilson. He works with me on the rides." Julian noted how sweet lies were starting to taste on his tongue, so long as they were honeyed with a hint of truth and a generous dollop of justification.

The judge adjusted his navy-colored tapestry vest, flicking droplets of water from the weave. His gaze caught on Julian's cheek. "Fine bruise there. Who gave you that?"

"Ah, Wilson again. We had a ... disagreement."

"Well, seeing as I plan to join you in this amusement venture, I should like to see your family stay intact for the business. Do you suppose the two of you could make up with one another, keep it civil for the duration of our trip?"

Though elated that the judge wanted to invest, Julian mentally stumbled over a fantasy of what making up with Willow might entail. "Of course."

"Might I meet the daring Wilson and hear his take on the park?"

An onslaught of mixed emotions rocked Julian's innards: desire to secure the funding, but fear that his new associate would see through Willow's disguise. "We could go back and wait for him at the stateroom ... I believe he's out on an errand at the moment."

Newton cast a puzzled frown up at Julian. The concern in his dark eyes screamed louder than his earlier rampage over breakfast. Julian attempted a distraction. "Say, Newton, I left your new hat on the floor beside the gowns. Could you go fetch it, please?"

The boy gripped Julian's fingers, hard, an obvious demand they go find Willow—*now.* Julian patted Newton with his free hand. "We will stay and talk with the judge until Mr. Higgly brings our package. Wilson will join us at the cabin soon. I am sure of it."

Grimacing, Newton broke his grip and stomped over to the dress rod.

"Doesn't talk much," the judge said. Less a question than an observance.

"Not a day of his life." Julian clipped his answer, confident the judge would understand his bid for privacy.

The judge's kind eyes narrowed at him. "Rather new at this, aren't you?"

"New ... at what?" *At lying? Yes.*

The judge nodded in Newton's direction. "Taking care of your brothers. I'd surmise you're busy at home with your park and don't spend much time with them. This will be a good experience for you. You should see what your parents do day in and day out for them. A man needs to know such things. Especially one who has a lady at home he wishes to court. You'll be thinking of a family of your own one day soon, no doubt."

Julian's lips tightened to a wry grin. "No doubt." His attention shifted to watch Newton kick his hat beneath the line of long gowns in a fit of annoyance. "All right, mouse. Now you'll have to crawl on your belly like a worm to find it."

Newton made a face, looking again like a disgruntled cherub. Dropping to his hands and knees, he dived beneath the line of hems in search of the hat. The dresses dragged his body, swaying in and out with his movements as if they breathed. Dust puffed up from beneath to fleck the skirts with powdery stains.

Julian rolled his eyes. "Stupendous. This will give Mr. Higgly a full-blown paroxysm."

Judge Arlington's hearty laugh echoed in the small room—as rich and robust as the gongs of a church bell. The movement of his belly bobbing up and down caused the edge of a rolled magazine to peek out from his vest.

"Is that my *Threshold*?" Julian asked.

Still flushed from his chortle, the judge glanced down at his chest. "Ah, yes. And your impressive ride designs." He drew out the magazine with the papers tucked inside.

When Julian secured them in his pocket, Judge Arlington pulled out another magazine from his vest. This one he opened, flitting through the pages. "There's something I wish to show you. Did I mention that I collect these magazines?"

"You did." Julian put on his spectacles and moved closer, making a conscious effort to ignore the slapping of Newton's palms on the wooden floor beneath the gowns.

"Well, when you described the shoes to me yesterday morn, they sounded familiar. I wasn't sure why, until I got back to my stateroom and remembered reading an article about a theft at a museum in Spain little over a year ago ... a theft that involved a pair of eighteenth century latchets. Ah-ha." He held up the open magazine, pointing to a black and white drawing—an exact replica of Nadia's shoes.

"Well I'll be dam—"

Coming up from behind, Newton nearly knocked Julian over trying to get a glimpse. He now looked like a pastry, coated in white dust as he was, but at least he'd managed to retrieve his hat.

"Are these your missing shoes?" The judge pressed, still holding up the magazine.

"Yes." Julian avoided Newton's accusatory glare ... felt it burning into his neck. "Is there any history behind them?"

The judge clucked his tongue. "Not many details here. Seemed they belonged to a Spanish princess or some such. When she died, they were donated to the museum. Not sure what the story is. Oh, but those buckles you thought were inlaid with glass? They're diamonds. You were holding a fortune in your hands, and didn't even realize it."

"You don't say."

So intent on his study of the sketch, Judge Arlington apparently missed the lack of astonishment in Julian's response. "What I find truly intriguing," the judge continued, "was how they ended up in Mr. Sala's stateroom. The circumstances surrounding the theft are quite unusual. It says here the shoes disappeared from the museum in the night. No one ever found any indication of a break-in. All of the locks and window panes were intact. People speculated that they simply walked out on their own, right past the night guards posted at each door. The crime was never solved."

Newton fidgeted, as if nervous, and Julian wondered if he knew something. Had Sala been behind the theft of the shoes, after all? That would explain how they ended up in his room ... and that could be what Nadia had meant about Newton being corrupted by his father.

Perhaps Willow had been right all along about waiting to hand the boy over.

"The shoes are apparently haunted, in truth," the judge said.

Julian peered over his lenses at him. *You don't know the half of it.*

"Or rather, there is a curse on them." Julian and Judge Arlington's heads jerked up as the tailor's nasally voice interrupted. He stepped into their circle, holding Julian's wrapped package. Without missing a beat, Mr. Higgly snatched the magazine out of the judge's hand. "I had no idea these were the shoes everyone was going on about yesterday. There is a dress tied to this theft. A Fontianna masterpiece ... pastel yellow with floral brocade. Décolletage wide, mutton sleeves with contrasting white lace. Fitted bodice with a stomacher." The tailor flushed with reverence as he described the gown. "Yes ... I remember hearing of this in the fashion circles. It was a great loss to the industry, being the first Fontianna custom design. It even had a handmade brooch that kept time, which affixed to the décolleté. The Fontianna brand was engraved upon the back." Focus slipping down to Newton, the tailor paused as if puzzled by the boy's grubby state. "What have you been into—"

"The curse, Mr. Higgly." Julian slipped a palm through

the package's ribbons and released it from the tailor's hand, letting it dangle from his fingers as he nudged Newton behind him. "You mentioned a curse."

Judge Arlington took back his magazine as well, jolting the tailor from his study of Newton.

"Right-right." Mr. Higgly sniffed, winding his empty hands together. "The gown and shoes belonged to the illegitimate daughter of a Spaniard princess and a gypsy man. Apparently, the princesses' royal husband had raised the child all the way to womanhood, thinking she was his. When he learned of his wife's affair, he ordered their daughter burned at the stake. But the gypsy grandmother, she put a spell on the shoes and gown, and they wouldn't burn. Unfortunately, her magic couldn't save the girl. She writhed and screamed until the flames—"

"That's enough of a description, thank you." Julian glanced down at Newton's eyes, wide and round like glossy chocolates in the midst of his powdered face. Julian doubted the gruesome tale was appropriate for one of such a tender age. If the boy had nightmares tonight, Willow would have Julian's head on a platter.

Mr. Higgly's attention fell to Newton again. He reached out, skating a line through the thick film on Newton's sleeve. He rubbed the white dust between his finger and thumb, thoughtful. "It is said that the royal husband went mad with guilt after that. In every corridor of the castle, he would hear the flapping of the gown's sleeves ... the clomping of the shoes. And when he would turn around, there they would be—the gown strewn over a chair or a stair rail ... the shoes lying on the floor beneath. To escape the haunting, the man took his own life with a noose. After the tragedy, his wife donated the articles to a museum. She claimed the spirit had served its purpose and should be left to rest."

Julian turned this information over in his mind. Perhaps Nadia had been dead much longer than she told Willow. Perhaps she was lying about being Newton's sister. Could it be possible *she* was the princess's daughter's ghost? Still, none of this explained why she was sopping wet. The illegitimate daughter had burned to ash, after all.

Lifting his fingertip to his nostrils, the tailor sniffed the dust he'd raked from Newton's clothes. Then his gaze swept the room and landed on the rod filled with smudged gowns. A series of high-pitched, whistling whimpers burst from his nose. Casting a frown in Julian and Newton's direction, he stomped into the back room, sputtering something about cleaning solvent.

"That's our cue." Julian clenched the package and guided Newton to the door. Behind them, the judge followed, chortling again.

Julian had just gripped the latch when it tugged out of his hand, opening from the opposite side. The bell jingled wildly as he bumped into Willow. The shock of the encounter caused him to drop the package to his feet. For a moment, they just stared at one another—her skin coated in black soot, her head uncovered, hair unkempt. The mortified expression she wore could have chilled the sun to an arctic orb. With a trembling hand, she withdrew a doll from beneath her jacket.

Her bewildered eyes held Julian's as she whispered, "Tildey. I found ... Tildey." The toy tumbled to the ground as Willow threw herself into his arms.

PART III

Wandering between two worlds;
One dead, the other powerless to be born.
~Matthew Arnold

SIXTEEN

Rain slapped the portals, tinted a soft yellow by intermittent flashes of sunlight through the clouds. Droplets streamed the glass like spilled champagne.

Drawing the bedcovers over her head, Willow hid her eyes. Still, the image remained: Christoff and Engleberta leading her to the pile of luggage in the shadowy midst of steerage.

"See what we found." Engleberta had hardly been able to control her glee at their success in picking the antique trunk's lock. Willow had thought to scold them for violating a stranger's belongings ... yet she didn't.

"A wrinkled old man owns it. He's hunched with a bump on his back." Christoff demonstrated, walking with a curled spine.

"And he's skinnier than Chris*toad*." Engleberta giggled.

Christoff glared at her. "He comes down sometimes at night from the upper deck and digs through it. Has some queer things inside." The boy lifted the lid.

Willow groaned on the memory. Why had she knelt down? Why had she looked within? Had she no conscience? That small still voice other people were equipped with always seemed to cow to the villainous curiosity which fired her being.

Perchance God was finally punishing her for that. That's why she'd met with such an ominous awakening. For there in the old man's trunk, beneath an avalanche of oddities— ballet shoes, leather harnesses much too small for any horse, coiled ropes of all shaped and sizes, rings and rings of tingling keys, and cylindrical tubes for holding maps and charts—Willow had unearthed Tildey. The doll's rosy cheeks were worn and faded, her wheat-colored hair a tangled, dingy shadow of its former glory. But there was no mistaking. She would know Tildey anywhere.

In a warped coincidence, Willow was trapped on an ocean liner with the very past she'd tried so hard to outrun.

She drew the covers tighter over her face. Her stilted breaths sucked the blanket in and out. A balmy heat enveloped her nose and cheeks on every exhalation. Feeling suffocated, she slapped the covers off and sat up just in time to see Julian peek his head in the door. The scent of roasted duck and buttered truffles slipped by him, titillating her nostrils.

"Are you hungry? I can make a plate and bring it in."

The memory of his tenderness when they first came back to the stateroom—drawing a lavender scented hip bath for her, coaxing her into bed when she was little more than an unresponsive bag of bones—suffused her with comfort and gratitude. But now, seeing the concern in those gray eyes that knew her within and without, stirred vulnerable whispers in her heart, butterfly tremors that shook her chest and made her want to cry like the little girl she once was.

She refused to give in ... to be weak in front of him again. Looking toward the wardrobe where the doll waited within a locked drawer, along with Julian's gift from the tailor she had yet to open, Willow shook her head. "No. I couldn't possibly eat."

"You need sustenance." He eased inside with a glance over his shoulder before closing the door and latching the lock. "I'm worried for you. Newton's worried. He's been begging to come in and see you. I think he wants to see the doll as well ... he seemed captivated by it earlier."

Willow hesitated, running a palm along her bared nape. "Is the judge still here?"

Julian nodded. "He's eating with Newton in the parlor. I asked him to keep the mouse occupied so I might have some time with you. But he'll not be leaving our cabin until you're properly introduced. Until he sees for himself you're all right."

Willow slumped. "I am such a flummet. To expose my identity to your acquaintance. I-I just was so stunned ... and, I had to see you. I needed your arms around me."

"Shhh." Julian came to sit on the bed's edge, smoothing the bangs off her face to kiss her forehead. His lips stayed there, a warm press as he spoke. "It doesn't matter a whit. He would've found out in due time since he's investing." Julian drew back, leaving his palms at her temples. "He'll be coming to the manor for the summer season. Better he find out now. We can trust him, Willow. He won't say a word. As far as the rest of the passengers and crew on this ship are concerned, you're still Wilson."

Catching Julian's hand, Willow held it against her cheek. "Thank God for your cleverness ... putting your hat on my head and spinning me out the door like you did. I don't think the tailor would have been quite so compliant as the judge was."

A tender smile turned Julian's lips. "No. But he didn't see you. And since no one was in the corridor, we've nothing to fret over."

"But we *do* have something to fret over."

Nudging their foreheads together, Julian sighed. His hands rubbed her arms, sliding the soft fleece of his union suit across her flesh. He'd insisted she change into it earlier, to help alleviate her shivers. "Are you sure that it's Tildey?

After so many years ... and other little girls had to have had a similar make of doll."

Breathing in his scent of amber, trying to balance in the vortex of emotion which captured her courage and lifted it out of reach like a withered autumn leaf, Willow gestured to the wardrobe. "Bring her here. I want to show you something."

Julian frowned, as if considering the wisdom of such an action, but then complied. As the bed sunk again with his returning weight, Willow slid into the indention so their thighs touched, needing the contact.

She took the doll. Hands shaking, she turned it over and lifted the ragged pinafore—little more than strands of faded blue thread. Then she tugged down the bloomers with her index finger to expose the doll's lower back. Etched within the porcelain was a crude rendition of Willow's tattoo.

Just as she remembered.

The sight of it drew her insides tight and pierced them—as if a barbed noose had cinched around her lungs. She couldn't gauge Julian's reaction by his expression. Instead, she allowed the hitch in his breath to be her cue to continue. "At the workhouse, one of the boys once took Tildey from me long enough to carve this with a knife. To tease me."

The blush of his ears reached his neck. "Had I known you then ... had I been there ... I would have—"

Willow stroked his smooth jaw. "I know."

"What does this mean? That one of the children at the orphanage took it for themselves in your absence, and in some twist of fate they are here on this liner?"

"I did have a friend. Her name was Vadette. I gave the doll to her. If she's here ... oh, I would be delighted to see her again."

Julian shook his head tentatively. "You said the children mentioned the owner of the trunk being a skinny, old man."

"Perhaps her adoptive father?"

"Perhaps your *kidnapper*. What if he went looking for you at the orphanage after your escape? What if that farmer and his wife had nothing to give him but your doll?"

Willow drew her knees to her chest, pulling free the covers from the other side of the bed with her movement. Even wrapped within the bedclothes, she still felt exposed. She had considered that possibility already, and the thought of the old man being responsible for her shattered childhood left her teetering between terror and righteous indignation. After all this time, the chance for answers and sweet revenge might be just beyond the threshold of this stateroom.

"How can this be," Julian said, "that you would end up in the same place as him so many years hence?"

"I was fated to meet him. To face him."

"Hell no. No you were not. This is all my doing." Neck muscle twitching, Julian stood and paced to the window.

"What? Why?"

"I set the stage. Left Emilia's manuscript at just the right page to tease you. Left out the chocolates to lure you."

"That is a load of cobblers, Julian. You knew I would go exploring regardless what I promised. You knew I would find some way to justify leaving this room. So you tried to send me on the safest route possible. Stop blaming yourself."

"This has become far too coincidental for my liking." His fingers gripped his braid, as if seeking stability. "You're not to leave this room again. For the duration of the trip. You're not to poke your head into the hall ... you're not even to slide a finger through the crack beneath the door. Understood?"

Having anticipated this reaction, Willow struggled to remain calm. "So you'd lock me away. Leave me powerless, just as when I was a girl."

"That's not fair." As he faced her, his hands formed fists.

His half-buttoned shirt gaped at the movement, exposing the slight furring of blonde hair across his sternum. "I am trying to protect you. Would you leave me powerless to do that?"

"I need to know. I need to know *why* ... to make sense of who I am. Who I was." Her eyes burned. She blinked hard to contain the tears. "To understand why Mama and Pa—" Her voice quavered despite best efforts. "Why they had to die for me."

Julian turned to look out the window again, his broad back stiff. His shirt drew taut, outlining his corded muscles. In their years together, she'd watched him grow from a gangly preteen to this substantial and vigorous man who could protect her; who could be a wall between her and the world. But at this moment, she needed him to be her buttress, not her barrier. "I have the opportunity to close my past forever. To open my future. A future with no more storms looming over me."

"*If* the trunk's owner is responsible for your tragedy. And *if* we can find him before he finds you." Julian propped his arm over the portal's upper curve, his forehead against the glass. "There are far too many *ifs* floating around. I deal in absolutes ... math and analytics. Facts that can be proved. Equations that have immutable answers. I don't like uncertainty. Not when it involves the welfare of someone I—" He cut his words short, refused to look at her.

Willow twisted out of the bedclothes and eased to the floor—the carpet springing beneath her bare feet. The rub of her footfalls sounded loud to her, as if it meant to out-sing the rain pelting the window. "If he *is* responsible, he is but an old man now. Age is immutable. Which in turn makes it a fact that he's as harmless to me as a moth to a wasp. I need no longer fear him. He should fear *me*." She spoke the words as though emboldened by them. Her quivering stomach belied her ruse, but only to herself.

When she reached Julian, she hugged him from behind and buried her nose between his shoulder blades to feel his sturdiness and breathe him in.

He tensed.

"*Fidar del mio cuore,*" she soothed. Her palms glided upward along the hardened planes of his abdomen. She stopped at the heat of his skin where the shirt lay open. His heartbeat jumped against her as she found his sternum and tangled her fingers in his chest hair.

He gripped her hands in place, pulled her closer against his back so her abdomen was forced to suck in slightly to accommodate his firm buttocks. Her breasts were flush with the middle of his back, absorbing his warmth.

"I do trust in you, Willow." The thrum of his voice tickled her temple where her face rested between his shoulder blades. "It's the means with which they took you that worries me. Do you forget your abductor had henchman? It is plausible—*likely*—he has a younger crop working for him now. Were he to realize you're here—"

"But it might not be him at all. It still could be Vadette. The old man could be her chaperone. An uncle ... a grandfather."

Coaxing her arms loose, Julian turned and drew her into his embrace. He cupped the back of her neck, holding her face to his chest. The fine hairs brushed her cheek and she snuggled closer.

"I'll inquire amongst the crew as to this man's identity." He spoke into her hair, hot tufts of air cushioning each word. "I'll speak to the captain tomorrow. Surely there's a note of who owns the trunk on the manifest. Allow me this, please. I"— he paused—"am responsible for you. Uncle Owen would never forgive me were I to let you endanger yourself heedlessly."

Willow bit back a disconcerted sigh. He wanted to be her knight in shining armor. Yet he still couldn't bring himself to attribute a title to the depth of his feelings. "If I agree, then I'll be a prisoner here in this tepid room for the duration."

"Should you bide my request, your stay in this room will be anything but tepid." Lifting her face, Julian watched his fingertips run a sweeping caress along her cheeks and the line of her jaw.

To be the object of such scrutiny—more fervent than he ever attributed his ride designs—sent a tingle all the way to Willow's core.

"I have plans to romance you during your imprisonment," he said, a telling flush in his ears.

"Such as?"

"Well, not tangible, concrete plans as yet ... but I expect to have a stunning epiphany at any moment. Once I have a diagram drawn up, I'll get right to it." He grinned sheepishly.

His shy honesty was more sensual than any pretty promises could have been, and so charming she couldn't help but smile back.

He traced her lips. "But for now, we should get you into some clothes and introduce you to the judge."

"*We*? Does that mean you're to help me dress?" Suppressing a teasing grin, Willow batted her lashes.

"You need help, do you?" Julian arched a brow. Outside, the rain pelted harder on the portals, a thumping rhythm which darkened the room and echoed in Willow's pulse— primitive and earthy.

Willow caught his wrists and pulled them behind her, guiding his palms on a slow slide from her lower back to her hips. Once his fingers curved around her bottom, drawing her closer, she wound her arms around his neck and quivered in pleasure. "Getting out of this union suit. The buttons ... they are ... difficult."

A rapt somberness enveloped his handsome features, and Willow knew she'd succeeded in seducing him out of his worry, however temporarily.

"Well, I do have a knack for buttons." His long lashed gaze held hers.

"*Pushing* them, in any case." She rebutted.

Grinning, he shifted his hands to her waist, as if to hold her in place, though she had neither the inclination nor the strength to escape. His mouth found hers, raking across her hungry lips, almost brutal ... not the delicate, nurturing kiss of earlier when she told him of her childhood. This kiss burned heavy and firm—a branding—as if to assure her that he was the man capable of protecting her from all the dangers at door, either perceived or corporeal. Following his lead, she opened her mouth. He met her with an ardent union, his tongue filling her.

He'd had some wine while she'd rested ... she could taste it within the warm recesses of his mouth, and her own tongue wrapped his, seeking more of the tart sweetness. A groan drifted from her throat.

Hearing the clang of silver from a tureen in the parlor, she broke the kiss.

"Newton and the judge are busy with lunch," Julian assured, as though reading her mind. His lips moved down her neck in a balmy trail. "Perchance their new camaraderie can win us some privacy over the next few days ... what I wouldn't give for two hours alone with you." His hands caressed her breasts, no hesitation this time.

Basking in sensation, Willow rocked on her heels as he shifted her around to pin her between him and the padded wall. His knee wedged between her legs to lift her—leveling their faces. The pillowed upholstery molded to her back in stark contrast to him, stiff and unyielding.

She gasped at their perfect alignment—desire spiraling into liquid flame—his thigh a stimulating resistance. Dizzy, she leaned her head back while Julian pressed kisses at her collarbone, his fingers working between them, opening the button placket to liberate her breasts. His breath grew shallow, tortured, as if he couldn't get to her fast enough. He moaned softly when the buttons finally started to give way, one by one, leaning in to christen each minute revelation of skin with his mouth.

When at last one breast came free, a chilly release to the open air, he stopped. His jaw twitched as he drew back in keen appreciation. He skimmed the outside of her nipple with his fingertip without making full contact.

His unhurried exploration was pure torture. Willow clasped his braid, arching against him, an urgent plea.

He resisted by locking his neck rigid, bewilderment gathering behind his eyes. His breath broke in trembling intervals. She'd seen this reaction only one other time. Their first gala together at the manor when Willow was thirteen. Aunt Enya had allowed her to attend, but only with Julian as her escort. He'd taken her hand to lead her in a waltz, stiffening when he'd touched her. It had perturbed her back then. She'd thought he was disgusted by her. Now she knew the body language for what it was. He had been nervous ... teetering between astonishment and terror.

The same way he felt at this very moment.

"Julian, touch me."

"One moment. I've never looked upon anything so glorious. Allow me pause."

Willow groaned as his finger took another leisurely stroll beneath the lower fullness, grazing the tip of a rib.

"I know you've seen breasts," she grumbled. "You've lived at the manor just like me."

"Oh, but I've never seen one that begged for my touch, and mine alone." His eyes flashed up to hers for an instant, a possessive fire glimmering in their darkening depths.

"*Toccarlo, per favore...*" She felt almost at the edge of sanity, in a heady battle between tears and laughter.

Sighing, he tipped his head to taste her, at first tender and reverent, as if he sampled the fragile petals of some candied flower. Then he became lost in her, taking her fully into his hot mouth with an intensity that spurred by a growl deep in his throat and produced a stinging hum high in her sternum. A drunken thrill buzzed inside her brain, knowing they were not alone, but still so very isolated in their little corner of the ship. Two vagabond hearts committing sin within the shadows.

She whimpered, needing to cry out for the intense pleasure, yet worried they would be caught. Her face buried in Julian's hair to muffle her reaction.

They both froze as Judge Arlington's muffled voice reached through from the other side. "I say Julian, the lad's getting a bit restless out here. He's asking to see Miss Willow."

Julian released her and a cold rush of air tightened her nipple to a painful peak.

"We'll be right there," he said loud enough for the judge to hear through the door. Then he whispered, "I need ... a moment. Go get dressed in the bathing room." Kissing her forehead, he lowered her to the floor and resituated the union suit across her breast. The fleece clung to her and he traced the bump over the fabric. "We'll continue this later. I promise."

Holding his gaze, Willow took his hand and raked her

tongue along his palm in a warm swath. His left eyebrow raised. She held up her hand, urging him to lick hers. With a puzzled smirk, he followed her lead then she matched their wet palms and laced their fingers together.

"Spit pact." She grinned.

Julian tightened his grasp for an instant. "Unbreakable."

Once their fingers released, she backed up. "You have four days to make good on that promise."

～ ೨•ೕ ～

*Diurnal assignments for Monday, April 26, 1904:
1. Visit Mr. Sala and look for shoes; 2. Speak to the captain about the trunk; 3. Romance or nurture Willomena, pending her physical state...*

Julian had not made good on his promise. They had run into a storm of ill proportions—three days of angry skies, crashing thunder, and riding the rise and fall of a ship as the waves pounded the hull. Newton was panicked in the beginning, until Julian lured him away from the portal windows and distracted the child's mind. Drawing, and also playing with Willow's doll, kept him occupied enough to make him forget the water slapping at the glass.

As for Willow, it hadn't been such a chore for her to stay in the stateroom after all, for she'd been bedridden. Over half of the passengers were laid up in their cabins, either seasick or tending loved ones or acquaintances that were. Even Mr. Sala ended up sealed within his room, so wracked with tremors and nausea his girls had to take turns sitting with him.

Julian's bedchamber smelled intermittently of vomit and ammonia as the scullery maids hopped back and forth from cabin to cabin trying to stay abreast of the stenches and bed changes. The corridors were empty, the dining halls and shopping venues all but abandoned. No one dared step onto the promenade deck for fear of falling overboard.

Judge Arlington came by twice a day bearing food, else Newton would have had to resort to stealing again, as Julian refused to leave Willow alone in her state. He had to be available to give her sips of water or the wayfaring stick of crystallized ginger provided by the ship's physician. Julian had spent most of his time sponging her face and hair with a cool washcloth and smoothing balm over her lips to keep them from drying out and cracking.

Not to say the woman demanded such care. She made a valiant effort to reclaim control over her stricken body. Several times over the three-day span, Julian caught her wobbling into the parlor to see to Newton, only to end up flat on the floor, woozy and heaving into the bucket she had wisely hooked around her arm. Julian would then carry her back to the bed and scold her, all the while astonished by her sheer determination to care for this child who wasn't even her own.

Seeing his cabin mate so concerned and attentive for another human while within the clutches of such a debilitating illness had plunged him even deeper into the depths of wistful admiration. He was now so far within those depths, he feared he might drown in them.

This morning, Julian hadn't yet heard a peep from her, though he'd checked on her several times to assure she hadn't managed to suffocate herself with her bedclothes. She'd been sleeping peacefully for twelve hours straight, the first time in seventy-some hours she'd managed to rest at all, and he was thankful for still waters and sunny skies. A fair omen, he hoped.

Perhaps things were about to come together, and he could glean the answers to Willow's doll and the phantom shoes. Julian had sent a missive via a steward, asking Judge Arlington to come so he might run some errands to that end. The judge sent back an affirmation and would be arriving at any minute.

Closing his journal, Julian stood and stretched his legs. Newton lay in the parlor floor on his belly, feet in the air and ankles crossed, studying a grouping of maps the judge had brought by to entertain him the day before. Julian had to admit, the mouse had been an ideal companion over the interminable interlude, sitting with Willow and keeping the cabin picked up and clutter free so Julian could concentrate on her care. He'd managed to wiggle his way into Julian's affections in the process. The two had even worked out their own form of communication.

The breakthrough came on the first night of Willow's illness, when Julian had just finished sponging her off and putting her in fresh clothes. After seeing her naked, he had to think up some distraction, so he pulled out his ride designs and began to sketch. Newton came to stand beside him and watched him draw with such intense fascination that Julian offered the boy a slip of paper and a quill of his own. He was a fine little artist, and proceeded to sketch out his thoughts and worries in caricatures—as plain as if he had spoken them aloud. It was obvious someone had taught him to communicate in such a way long before.

Throughout Willow's illness, Julian and the boy had 'spoken' at every opportunity. He'd even asked Newton if Sala was his father, though the child chose not to answer that. Which was as good as a yes, in Julian's opinion.

Placing his journal in his pocket, Julian opened the desk drawer and thumbed through the pictures little Newton had drawn thus far. He sought one in particular. It was a near perfect rendition of Willow's birthmark. The lad had drawn it on Friday in an attempt to ask to play with the doll. Up to that point, Julian had kept the toy locked in the drawer in the bedchamber and Newton hadn't had access to it. In fact, when Julian couldn't decipher the drawing's underlying message, Newton ended up having to lead Julian to the drawer to make him understand his desire to see it.

What baffled Julian was that the only time Newton had seen the doll was when Willow carried it back from steerage. There was no way he could have known of the etching on the doll's back since Willow had to lift away the doll's clothes in order to show it Julian.

A soft knock on the door jolted him from his thoughts. He put away the sketch and shut the drawer. Newton leapt up to open the door before Julian even had a chance to turn around.

Judge Arlington's plump, cheerful face greeted them. "Ahoy there, young lad. Looks as if you survived the storm."

Newton pointed to his calves encased in the finest hosiery and a new pair of knee high breeches.

"He's showing you his sea legs," offered Julian.

"Ah. Well earned, no doubt." Judge Arlington chortled and patted Newton's head with his free hand, balancing a covered tray in the other. Steam curled from the edges, rich with the tones of vanilla, cinnamon, and warm bread.

"You brought breakfast." Julian grinned, taking the tray and setting it on the desk top. He'd barely had time to lift the lid before Newton snatched a bowl of custard and a spoon then settled in his usual place in the winged chair to shovel food into his mouth.

"It looks as if I'm none too soon." The judge grinned.

"Yes. We were about to start noshing on ink and paper."

Julian returned his smile then guided him to the desk so they could each claim a plate and a honey-glazed roll. "What have you heard ... in the way of our reaching port?"

The judge drizzled some honey on his bread and licked his fingertip. "The storm has set us back only by a day. We should reach harbor by tomorrow morning."

"Good. Then we can still make it with one day to spare before the opening festivities, granted the train has no delays."

"Have you told Miss Willow yet?"

Julian noticed Newton's head pop up at the question. "No. Not yet. Would've been the coward's way to tell her when she was only half-conscious." Noting Newton's ever-growing interest in their discussion, Julian pressed a finger to his mouth to stifle any further questions on the subject of the fair.

Casting a sidelong glance at Newton, perception crept across the judge's face and he led the way to a divan in the room's center. "How is she today?" he asked as he sat down.

"She's been asleep since early last eve." Having taken a seat beside his friend, Julian sunk his teeth into the sweet, yeasty breakfast roll. "Surprises me that it hit her so hard," he said between chews. "She's an acrobat ... used to swing from a trapeze on a daily basis. One would think her stomach could tolerate such motion."

The judge gulped down his own chunk of bread. "Interesting. You say she was an acrobat?"

"Grew up in a circus."

"Huh."

"What?"

Judge Arlington smacked his mouth, as if the honey had stitched his moustache to his lower lip. "Just a coincidence, I suppose. In the barber shop, the day after the masquerade, a man was boasting about his liaison with one of Mr. Sala's girls after the party—I believe he said it was the jolly, voluptuous one. Anyway, the man claimed..." The judge glanced over at Newton who had made his way back to the other side of the room for more food. Judge Arlington lowered his voice and leaned toward Julian. "He claimed the woman was a wild lover. That her limbs were flexible as flower stems. Like a contortionist. Doesn't that talent bode with acrobats and their ilk?"

Julian fought a crimp in his gut. He'd had quite enough of all these coincidences. This one had to be explicable. "I'm sure those women have had many experiences performing. They are trained and well-travelled actresses, after all. Perchance that particular woman toured with a circus herself, before Sala pulled her into his troupe. That's plausible, wouldn't you think?"

"Of course." The judge ate a chunk of bread glistening with honey. "Just think it's interesting."

Julian frowned as he stood to take his plate to the desk. He drew his spectacles from his pocket and secured them upon his nose and behind his ears. "I should be going. You'll be alright here, with them?"

Newton had already taken Julian's place on the divan. He had a map in hand, eager to show the judge some great discovery.

Judge Arlington smiled and took the other side of the map offered him. "We'll be fine. See to your business. I'm sure your lady will be awake by the time you return."

SEVENTEEN

"All I ask is five minutes of his time." Julian tightened his stance in the corridor to keep his shoe wedged over the threshold as the actress tried to close the door against him. He wasn't leaving until he searched every corner of Mr. Sala's stateroom for Newton's sister and her ghostly footwear.

"He is too ill for visitors, Master Thornton. He's only just getting over the seasickness." The lady scowled.

Something in the turn of her chin reminded Julian of the night on the promenade. Come to think of it, her lips were very familiar as well. The looked like the lips he almost kissed. He couldn't let on that he suspected her of distracting him that night—of being an accomplice in the theft of the shoes. He had to be smart ... play the part of the besotted suitor.

He drew his spectacles down and peered over the lenses. "Ah. But surely you wouldn't have me stand here and turn to stone as I wait." It surprised him how at ease he felt. His tongue no longer swelled, his flesh no longer clammy with sweat.

He had nothing to fear of women anymore. He knew how to use his mouth to draw a purr from a woman's throat ... how to caress her until her bones melted to putty beneath his fingertips. It was an unforeseen boon of his and Willow's blossoming relationship. One which he'd have to thank her for later.

"Stone?" A chagrinned expression met Julian as he

focused again on the woman wedged in the doorway. "Spoken like a man who's made acquaintance with Medusa." She almost smiled.

He took his cue. "Yes, but I've lost all faith in mythology, I fear. Seeing as you look upon your fellow actresses every day, the rules state they should be naught but statues at this point, yet from what I understand, they're flexible as any *contortionist*." He propped his arm on the door frame, awaiting her reaction.

Her gaze disappeared behind long, blonde lashes as she studied his tasseled shoe crammed within the door jamb. "Contortionist." She almost choked on the word. "Why would you make such a comparison?"

"You know, you never gave me the kiss you promised ... or even your name." He looked deep into her crystal blue eyes, noting that she was older than he had first assumed. At least a good six years older than him.

"My name is Louisa."

"Miss Louisa. Please, I've been seeking you everywhere on this ship since that night. Don't disappoint me again. Give me my faith back. At the very least, invite me in for a cup of tea so we might discuss these lapse rules of mythology. Perhaps even rewrite our own."

She sucked in a breath. "A *quiet* cup of tea. My chaperone is on the other side of this stateroom, you see."

"The noise level will be entirely up to you." Julian kept his gaze on hers—words flowing from his tongue like honey-tipped rain.

Flushed, she pressed a hand to her chest, eased the door open, and ushered him in. Her blonde hair shimmered, parted in the middle and coiled against the back of her nape with tiny white flowers tucked into the seams. As she led him to the sitting area, her dressing gown swooshed across her ankles and the train dragged behind her—an exquisite beaded and embroidered ensemble of lavender chiffon over ivory lace.

Due to his sister and mother's appreciation of fine clothes, he was well aware of the expense tacked onto such hand-woven artistry. Most travelling thespians didn't make enough money to indulge in such fineries. This lady, as well as the others—judging from their attire the day he met them in the first-class dining room—were well paid for whatever their services to Mr. Sala might be. Services, which with each new day, became more and more suspicious.

Julian cast a glance around the room. Louisa seemed to be the only one here with Sala for now. The closed bedchamber indicated that the burly man was sleeping, hopefully as soundly as Willow. If Julian could rid himself of the self-appointed nursemaid, he could rummage through the stateroom and bedchamber without anyone being the wiser.

"Might I tempt you with a pastry, *Adonis*? They're famed for offering vigor and stamina." Brow arched, Louisa held out a plate piled high with panettones and strudels. The sugary crusts glistened as they passed through the sunlight which streamed from the portal windows. Julian's nose tickled upon the fruited scent.

He took one, a plan formulating in his mind.

"The cook sent them over." Louisa explained. "Mr. Sala won't start his day without his sweets. I doubt he'll feel up to indulging this morn, so we have them to spare."

A glossy filling rich with crimson berries oozed from the edges of Julian's strudel. He placed it upon the napkin offered him. "Thank you."

With a nod, Louisa set a cup of steaming tea upon the table beside his chair. "So ... how is the lad?"

Julian's first thought was of Newton, and he almost strangled on his piping sip of tea. Did Sala know about his son? "Lad?"

Her white teeth coaxed a dainty nibble off of the edge of a panettone. "The one you wrestled with on deck. Did you press charges?"

Julian flipped through the possibilities in his mind. With the proper response, he could turn this around—measure her guilt or innocence. "I turned the sot loose. I suppose he's back with the immigrants. But I should've kept a closer eye on him. Bloody little thief stole the phantom shoes. I intended to speak to your employer of the loss. I thought he should know, since he feared the shoes as he did. He might be relieved to hear they're gone from the men's quarters."

Louisa went pale and settled her tea cup on her saucer with a clink, leaning forward in her chair. "The *lad* stole them? On the night of the masquerade?"

Her shock appeared sincere enough. Or was she simply acting? Julian would leave nothing to chance. "Yes. I brought him back to my room and tended to his wounds. He insisted he needed no physician, so I let him go. It was only after he absconded that I realized the shoes were gone."

"I see." Sipping her tea, Louisa narrowed her eyes much the way she had when she kept regarding her pin-watch on the night of their dance. "And here I thought you were coming to return Mr. Sala's property."

"The shoes?"

Her brows twitched. "No. You have something else that belongs to him. Something far more personal and consequential than a pair of women's shoes."

Unease quavered in Julian's gut. She *did* know about Newton.

He took a healthy bite of the strudel, forming words

around the tart berry and citrus filling. "Perchance you might be a little less vague."

The pulse in her neck throbbed beneath a ray of sunlight. "The ground plans for the World's Fair. Those weren't easy for him to come by. He left them behind when you switched rooms. We need them back. *He* ... he needs them."

Julian swiped a napkin across his mouth. "Whatever for? Everyone knows where the tournament of thespians is taking place. Or do you have something else planned for that night?"

Her lips tightened to a line.

Tiring of their cat and mouse, Julian caught a breath, locked it within until he felt veins protruding in his neck. He clutched his hands around his throat, gasping for air.

"What..." He wheezed. "Is in..." He hacked. "This pastry?" He bent at the waist, gasping. His spectacles slid from his face and clunked to the floor.

Louisa leapt to her feet so she could slap his back. "Why it's ... it's barberry chutney is all!"

"All-erg-ic ..." Julian clenched his throat tighter so his eyes bulged, his body rocking with the violence of her pounding palm between his shoulder blades. "Can't—breathe!" He flopped to the floor in a gasping heap—all for effect.

"I'll get the physician!" She was out the door in an instant, her skirts rustling as she raced down the hall.

Julian replaced his spectacles as he stood. This would be an amusing tale to share with Nick one day, how the unpracticed, intellectual clod tricked and out-performed a grand actress. The thought of his brother sent a painful twang through his chest. He dusted off his clothes, shut the door, and locked the latch with a click.

He had less than ten minutes to search for the shoes before Louisa returned with help.

"You're sure you're up for this, Miss Willow? You've been quite ill—"

"Shhh." Willow shushed the judge over her shoulder as they took the first steps down the empty stairwell toward steerage. "It's *Wilson*." She tightened her gloved fingers through Newton's, an attempt to ease the child's fear of the steep incline. "We must get a manifest number off the trunk. How else is Julian to ask the captain of its owner?"

"I am sure Julian could seek the number for himself," the judge interjected between rasping breaths.

"He's no idea which trunk it is, has he?"

The judge grew silent, aside from his panting. The descent was obviously difficult for one of such stoutness.

Willow, on the other hand, felt invigorated by the exercise. Ever since she'd awakened, bathed, and dressed, she'd felt buoyant and charged. Three days laid up in a bed had left her bones and muscles twitching for some form of active stimulation. Winding her legs around Julian and kissing him breathless would have been her first choice for expending such energy, but he had already left when she awoke.

After eating a boiled egg—one of the first times she could remember ever craving something other than sweets for breakfast—she talked the judge into letting her take this little jaunt. Truth be told, she actually didn't talk him into it so much as insisting he let her go. Then he, in turn, insisted he follow.

She'd withheld the real reason for this sojourn. During her twelve-hour doze, her subconscious had replayed her visit to that trunk in a vertigo-induced circus nightmare.

In the dream, she was a child again. With each barefooted

step around the stacks of baggage in steerage, she found them taking on new shapes: pyramids of clowns, bears, horses and feathered performers, all balanced atop one another. She was back at the circus, albeit a much hazier and dimmer rendition than she remembered. She skipped along the center ring, excited to be home at last. Grit and discarded trash snagged between her little toes. A spotlight clicked on to illuminate a trunk. From within came a thumping sound, and girlish giggles. "Tildey!" Willow cried out, racing across the distance to find her doll, her pigtails slapping her face and neck upon each bounding step. The creak of abandoned trapezes swung overhead, cutting intermittently through a thick cloud of fog. Yet it wasn't fog. It was tobacco—a stench that seeped into her leotard, her tights, her very pores, until she could taste it coating her tongue like bile. The spotlight shifted from the trunk to a trapeze just above her where a shape took form in the light: a graceful silhouette in a shimmery leotard and glistening tutu. "Mama?" Willow whispered in the dream, forgetting Tildey for the chance to see her mother perform once more. The trapeze vanished into thin air but the aerialist continued a controlled descent toward her, held in place by harnesses attached to the center pole. A face came into view, painted white like a clown, with bloody eyes and a hollow of a mouth—stretched wide on a perpetual scream. Willow yelped and squeezed her lashes shut, willing away the creature ... for it was not Mama. When she opened them again, the freakish performer exploded into a flock of hummingbirds made of ink. They skittered around Willow, buzzing wings scraping her skin and hair, imprinting tattoos everywhere they touched. She screamed and stumbled backwards, bumping into the trunk which was then somehow right behind her. A tinkly, off-key lullaby drifted from inside the giant box. The lid shook and shuddered, as if something wanted out. Whimpering, Willow had tried to back away, but her feet grew heavy. She looked down and ballet shoes, covered in steel spikes, swallowed them up. The empty harness that had held the ghastly aerialist slithered toward her like a snake, coiling itself around her legs and arms to hold her in place. On the final haunting strains of music, the trunk's lid popped open, and out from the midst rose a hunched old man, holding Nadia's haunted shoes upside down. Blood and water gushed out of them—a stench of copper and stagnancy—and the man laughed with a voice that gnawed into her bones like a thousand snarling wolves.

Newton's fingers squeezed Willow's, bringing her back to the present. She shook off the memory of that nightmare, though was left with the same suffocating sense of dread that had coated her, along with a fine sheen of sweat, upon first waking from it hours ago.

She proceeded to descend the stairway, needing to see the contents of the trunk again in reality. She had to know if it was a clarified memory, or simply a feverish dream. Finding Tildey had caused everything else within that luggage to fade into the background. But now that her subconscious had had time to replay what she'd seen, she *knew* what the harnesses and spiked shoes were used for. She'd used such items herself while practicing aerial stunts with her mother as a child.

If she was right, and she hadn't imagined those items, it was proof that whoever owned that trunk wasn't Vadetta ... that they were someone far more dangerous, someone tied to her life—and her parents' deaths— in the circus.

Willow stalled on the last quarter of the steps as Engleberta came bounding toward the stairs to greet them— her bald head as round and blue in the dimness as a full moon. "Wilson! Newton! You're back!"

"Good morn, Berta." Willow adjusted Julian's jacket over her shoulders to assure the lapels covered her chest. Her fingers paused on her pin-watch, prompting a concern for the time. They needed to hurry before Julian found them missing from the cabin. He would not be so understanding this time, were he to find her gone.

Engleberta stared at the judge and Willow gestured toward him. "This is our new friend, Judge Victor Arlington."

Engleberta offered a hearty hello and the judge did his best to reciprocate, despite his worried and winded state.

Newton tugged at Willow's hand and nodded toward the empty stairs behind their German friend as she hopped her way up to them.

Catching his inference, Willow asked the girl, "Where is your brother?" Though they fought constantly, they were never more than two steps away from one another.

"Oh." The girl snorted as they began descending the stairs again. "He ate two whole boxes of those chocolates you brunged before the storm hit. Had his head in a bucket for three days. Stinky wart. Serves him right for not sharing."

Willow grinned. She'd missed the ongoing rivalry between the two children. She almost envied it, having never had such a sibling relationship. Leander had been a wonderful brother, but he lacked feistiness. Every time Willow had tried to start a fight with him, he'd surrendered, led by his submissive nature. She used to imagine a brother who could give back what she gave. Nick and Julian were both prone to squabble with her. Perhaps that's why she'd spent so much of her youth gallivanting with the twins instead of her surrogate sibling.

Engleberta skipped around Willow and Newton as they took the last step. "Christoad is abed still. Wants me to play cards with him all day to pass the time. So boring! Newt, can you come visit?"

Willow gave the boy's hand a squeeze. "Go on then. The

judge will accompany me. We'll come find you on our way back up."

Judge Arlington nearly stumbled trying to manipulate his round body down the final drop while holding the railing. Willow reached out to support his elbow and he nodded his gratitude, though his white moustache wiggled in a nervous manner. His voice raised to be heard over the engines' roars. "We shouldn't stay long."

Willow nodded. "Engleberta, I wish to look at the trunk again. Is it still in the same place?"

"It's moved to the portmanteau maze." The girl offered the information over her shoulder as she tugged Newton toward her family's bunks.

Willow turned the opposite direction and grabbed a lamp from a hook on one of the walls. She followed the dangling light, shortening her steps to keep pace with the judge. As some of the other immigrants watched from the bunk-lined walls, she repositioned the hat on her head. She had forgotten how loud and claustrophobic steerage was. The stench was worse than she remembered, humid and weighted with the smell of stale vomit. These poor people hadn't the added benefit of scullery maids and ammonia; she doubted if any of them had had ginger either, to ease their nausea.

"I'm appalled that you stayed down here alone." The judge glanced sideways at her. His jolly face folded to lines and puckers where shadows raked across him as they ventured out of the reach of the lamps.

Willow tempered her unease of the darkening surroundings. "I could never have talked Julian into letting me accompany him on this ship. Not until I was already on board and we'd set out to sea."

"He said you had to beg, steal, and borrow. Must have

been difficult, to lower yourself to such a level."

Willow shrugged. "I rather didn't mind the stealing—" She bit her lip, annoyed that she'd let that slip. The judge was so friendly and magnanimous, she found herself speaking her mind much more often than she meant to. "I mean, I didn't mind as much as I *should* have." Her shoulders tensed. "Perhaps it's better you don't tell Julian that?"

The judge assured her he wouldn't with a kind smile. They walked alongside one another in companionable silence for a moment. "So, you stowed away just to go to St. Louis. You want that badly to see the World's Fair?"

Willow clenched her jaw, not answering. She tried to concentrate on the whisk of the tweed trousers rubbing between her thighs, though it was muted beneath the engines.

"Ah." The judge's long moustache curled around his smile. "It was never about the fair. It was about the company. The man that designs the rides."

Willow felt her face heat as if the sun were beaming down on her, even though they were entrenched in darkness. "You can't appreciate his brilliance until you've seen the park."

"Oh, I'm already convinced, just by his drawings." The judge's labored respirations had finally returned to normal. "I understand you're brilliant as well. That you had a hand in the mechanics. An impressive talent for a lady."

Willow shrugged. "I'm good with motors and such; but Julian has the gift of vision. He can see a ride in his mind and draw it out on paper then map out the measurements and materials required to complete it. His ability with math is inspiring. In any case, I appreciate your discretion in the matter of my gender. I can't even imagine the scandal it would cause. It could destroy the manor."

"Well, we can't have that. I've vested interest in it now."

The mountainous maze of luggage came into view, its black silhouette towering over them like a great yawning mouth. Willow stepped across a tattered portmanteaux. The toe of her heavy boot caught on the bag and she nearly tottered over.

This time, the judge grabbed her elbow. "You know, if you're still concerned for appearances, I could amend the matter of your being unmarried. Though I have no lawful jurisdiction until we get to St. Louis, it could suffice for a good faith gesture. I've no doubt Julian reciprocates your affections. I've never seen a man care for a sick woman yet still hold the look of desire in his eyes."

Desire. Willow struggled to silence her erratic heartbeat as they picked out a path through the luggage. At the mere memory of how Julian had cared for her so tenderly during her illness, she could have flitted to the top of the luggage pile on wings.

Yet the man still couldn't admit his feelings aloud.

No. There would be no impromptu nuptials in her future. Though she was ready to make her vows today, Julian's premeditated mentality would stretch their blossoming romance into months or years of lengthy consideration. "I believe your taciturnity will be enough, Judge Arlington. We can uphold the masquerade for the duration ... from here to the train to St. Louis and back again, even."

The judge cleared his throat, as though bothered by all the secrecy.

Willow eyed him suspiciously. "You don't disapprove, do you? Surely otherwise you would have already had me taken before the captain. Or had me imprisoned in the ladies' quarters."

He waved his plump hand to ease her anxiety. "No. No. I'm not one to judge."

Willow met his gaze and they shared a smile over his pun.

Together, they ducked into a passage where the tall stacks of luggage, crates, and trunks tangled up to resemble winding walls on either side of them. Willow would have to weave her way through the labyrinth to find the trunk, and the entrance whittled to such a tight space that the portly judge would have to wait at the entrance. "I'll return shortly."

He tugged his palm from his moustache to his chin, a gesture Willow now recognized as a nervous tick. "I'll hold watch here."

Nodding, she twisted sideways and easily skimmed through while holding up the lantern to suppress her unease of being alone. She wouldn't let her nightmare dissuade her from this mission.

After winding through three different mazes, Willow spotted the trunk in a dark corner, wedged in by stacks of luggage on either side. It felt warm and cramped within the aperture, and smelled faintly of perfume and moth balls. Someone had obviously meant to hide the trunk.

Willow wondered if the owner was missing Tildey ... if they were worried who might have taken the doll and seen their things. A bubble of emotion rose within her chest—almost ticklish. Her dearest hope would be that she'd imagined all the circus paraphernalia due to being ill. That instead, the trunk belonged to her friend of years gone by, and they would soon be reunited.

She had just set aside the lantern and crouched down to open the lid when a hand clenched her shoulder from behind. The grip wasn't tight, but insistent. She knew his touch without even looking.

"I should have known you'd beat me to it." Julian's baritone washed over her, prompting every nerve in her body to stand at attention with learned anticipation of the pleasure he could bring them.

She cast an upward glance over her shoulder to take in his expression in the soft light, studying him for signs of anger, yet finding only concern. "I had to see inside the trunk with my own eyes and a clear mind. I'm looking for something specific." Before she could elaborate, someone rustled behind them in the shadows.

Newton's head appeared in the dome of light.

Willow sighed in relief. "I thought you were with Berta," she scolded.

Newton ignored her and looked up at Julian, pointing wildly to his shoes.

Julian patted the child's hat. "Sorry, mouse. I haven't found the shoes yet. Looks as if we'll have to find some way to raid the women's quarters."

The disappointment on Newton's face pinched Willow's heart. She had wanted so much to get the shoes back for him before they left this ship. How would he react, should he never see his ghostly sister again?

Her hands stalled on the trunk's lid, remembering the old man in her dream, and how he was holding Nadia's shoes. Was it possible? Could they have found their way back to steerage and ended up in here? Maybe Nadia's spirit had tried to reach her through the dreams, and all the answers were just at her fingertips...

"Well, hurry up then," Julian prompted, "before we're caught. The judge is standing guard."

Biting her lip, Willow threw open the lid with a creaking snap. They all leaned over to look within. Emptiness stared back from the satin-lined depths. Everything was gone. The harnesses, the ballet shoes, the ropes and cylinders of maps. *Everything.* As if the items had drifted out of reality and secured themselves firmly into Willow's feverish, sea-sickened dreamscape, never to be corporeal again.

"What exactly were you hoping to find?" Julian asked, gently sculpting her wrist to help her stand.

"Tools of a sort," she mumbled, handing the lantern off to Newton.

"Tools? You saw tools in here when you found your doll?"

Willow sighed and shut the lid. Julian's arm went around her waist as he ushered Newton through the passage in front of them to light the way.

"I dreamt about them earlier ... remembering what I saw when I lifted out Tildey." Her throat felt itchy. "Spin ropes and anchor shoes. The sorts of things used in a circus. The sorts of things I used as a child when I trained. It's been so many years; it just took me a while to remember what they were used for."

"Could you describe these anchor shoes?" Julian guided her toward the entrance where the children and Judge Arlington waited.

"Well, they look rather like ballet slippers, with tiny metal spikes on the sole. Good for gripping."

Julian turned away, but even in the darkness she could see tension stiffening his shoulders. "Perhaps you were dreaming of your childhood, and imprinted it onto your experience with the trunk while you slept. Tildey could have evoked the nightmare and caused the association. Could it be that your imaginings misconstrued what you saw?"

Willow didn't answer, her throat burning and thick. She knew she hadn't imagined those things. For what she hadn't yet told Julian was that a distinctive smell had hit her nostrils when she opened the trunk this time. Chocolate and brandy, a foreign tobacco. The same tobacco she'd smelled in her dream—as indelible to her as her mother's perfume.

Even without seeing the contents again, she knew what they had been, and that the person who owned them was the man from her past. For she could never forget the scent tied to her mama and papa's murders.

EIGHTEEN

"Are you absolutely sure it was the right trunk?" Julian raised his voice so the query reached Willow from the opposite side of the closed door.

"Oh, it was the right one," she answered loud enough to be heard from inside the bedchamber. "No doubting it." She slipped into the beautiful dress Julian had bought for her. He'd finally given her the package he'd brought back from the tailor three days ago. While she was sick, he kept it tucked away. Now after seeing it, knowing how much thought he'd put into the gift, she couldn't help but smile, in spite of how uneasy she felt discussing the trunk.

Willow flattened her ear to the door's frame in an effort to visualize what he might be doing in the parlor. There was a muffled thump and scraping, a rattle of paper, then a sweet, tinkling song which only played a few chords before screeching to a stop.

"You know, the fact that it had no manifest number"—she resumed the discussion—"only proves whoever owns it is hiding something."

"Well, we'll find out tomorrow who it belongs to." Julian's response drifted back, riding the screech of chairs being scooted along the floor. "For now, it's pointless to conjecture."

"Agreed." Willow propped her left side against the door. Julian had conferred with Captain Everett after lunch. The captain gave Julian permission to wait in steerage beside the trunk once they reached port in the morning, so he might solve the mystery when its owner came to pick it up.

Willow repositioned her shoulder seams and held the dress's back seam with clamped fingers. She had no corset with her and her pantalets bunched beneath the dress' supple fabric in an awkward manner. She wanted to look like a courtly maiden, not a frumpy toffer from the rookery. So she'd left everything off underneath to allow the gown to hang as it should. The fabric slid—slick and cool—against places vulnerable and overtly responsive to the foreign sensations.

"So, does it fit?" Julian asked from amid his racket.

She cleared her throat. "Hard to tell, without buttoning it. But I believe it will. Julian?"

"Yes?"

"Thank you. It is above lovely. Your taste is impeccable."

"In ladies as well as dresses." Willow could hear a smile in his masculine voice.

Grinning, she pressed her cheek against the chilled door. Her fingers curled around the knob. "Might I come out and thank you properly?"

A loud shuffle then the clanging of metal erupted. Julian muttered an oath, followed by a swift apology for her benefit. After she heard the rearranging of silver, he spoke again. "I will be very disappointed if you come out and haven't the mitts on."

Willow rolled her eyes. How had he known she'd forgotten those? She borrowed Julian's oath, but kept it under her breath, determined to be a proper lady tonight.

Newton was off to eat with Judge Arlington in the first-class dining room and they intended to stay for the orchestra program. Mr. Sala was still closed up in his room, so there was no chance of him seeing the child. Otherwise Willow would never have allowed it, despite that it would buy her and Julian two hours of uninterrupted solitude.

This evening could be all she'd ever dreamed of, if she could just get past this morning's experience. To think that the devil who was responsible for all of the misery in her childhood shared this seafaring vessel with her—it left her soul ravaged and clamoring for revenge. He was old now. She intended to use that to her full advantage. She meant to see him suffer the way her parents had ... the way she had.

Julian wouldn't approve—at least of her plans for revenge. If for no other reason than he would worry for her safety. That's why she had yet to tell him about the tobacco smell or the *significance* of the training tools which had been in that trunk. Although she had confessed most of her past to Julian, she had yet to tell him of her strange daily routines at the orphan workhouse. Even now, she couldn't understand why she had been encouraged to continue her acrobatic training all those years. But apparently, it was under her abductor's advisement.

Over the last few days, it had been easy enough to avoid discussing her past due to her seasickness. This afternoon had flown by with the judge and Julian mostly gone, seeking the shoes and the owner of the trunk. But tonight she would have to keep him distracted enough not to ask any more questions. Keep his thoughts in the present. Darts of guilt pricked at her chest, but she hardened her heart against them. She had every right to seek vengeance.

Willow strolled over to the bed where she'd laid the mitts and eased into them, smoothing the gossamer ruffles up to her wrists. She wriggled her fingers so they would plunge through the holes. The gloves covered the back of her hands and her palms by catching at the bends of her third knuckles while leaving her fingertips exposed.

Turning to the cheval mirror—her back facing the door—

she studied her image, almost giddy with delight at the reflection. Never in her wildest imaginings would she have thought she'd be pleased to be wearing such elegant attire.

The last residue of sunset flashed in pink ripples along the walls, reflecting off of the waves outside. In less than a half hour, it would be necessary to burn the lamps. But for now, Willow rather liked the dimming glow ... the way the rosy tones graced her olive skin with a shimmering affect.

She reached up and stroked a glossy curl at her temple, admiring how her hair had taken the pin curls she'd earlier coaxed into place to feminize the cropped hairstyle. And the jeweled hair pins Julian had bought added just the right amount of sparkle to the finished coif.

She posed, moving her arms like a dancer, to watch the black elbow length sleeves wind and twist. The gown boasted a coppery color as deep and lustrous as the pheasant feathers Mistress Juliet used on her millinery masterpieces at home. The satin bodice clung to her curves, wrinkles spreading like eager fingers across her breasts as the hem fanned out at her ankles. Her toes peeked from underneath the hem. She grinned, thinking upon what Aunt Enya's reaction would be to see her feet and ankles bared in such a way.

When Julian's reflection appeared behind her, her breath hitched. She hadn't even heard the door open.

A savory scent wafted in from the parlor. "Dinner?" she asked, unable to think of anything more appropriate.

"Roast duck in mushroom sauce. And a special dessert." He had taken off his spectacles so they hung hapless in his hand, baring the direction of his gaze to her naked back. A pink flash from the window danced over his face, lighting it to brilliant bewilderment. The same look he wore days ago, when he helped her out of the union suit.

Julian dropped his spectacles to the chair beside the door.

"You forgot," he mumbled. "*I* forgot. Under things."

The observation reminded her that her dress gaped all the way past the bend of her lower back, leaving her tattoo on full display. Feeling the hummingbird's fluttering echo beneath her skin, she reached behind to pull the panels together, unable to look away from Julian's lovely, entranced face—acutely aware that he had closed the door, cutting off the parlor's lamplight.

He came up behind her and caught her hands. Breaking their hold on the dress, he coaxed the fabric to separate. "No more hiding from me." The demand ended on a growl that sent shivers of submission up her spine. Her hands fell to her sides, immobile. Julian's rough fingertips and velvet palms eased between the panels of fabric to follow the curve of the tattoo, memorizing every line. The hummingbird busted loose, buzzing up her spine where its feathers fanned every nerve ending within her, making each one ache for want of his touch.

Burrowing his hands deeper within the satin dress, Julian laced his fingers at her naval to draw her close. "That marking is a part of you. And I wish to know everything ... *every part of you.*"

"The sinful parts as well?" She craved validation that he would want her, despite her evolving penchant for thievery.

"Most especially the sinful ones." He nuzzled her nape, oblivious to her inference. His fingernails lightly raked her abdomen and a delectation of tremors skittered through her body. "The day I saw your head pop up from that trunk in Aunt Bitti's wagon, I knew you were the epitome of sin."

Willow settled her palms over her gown, the satiny fabric sliding between his hands and hers. "Perhaps that's why you tried to resist me for so long," she chided, becoming breathless as he massaged her stomach. Her abdomen twitched, the muscles flexing as if they already knew him, as if they reached for him. *Il signore la aiuta.* How could a man who'd never seduced a woman have such a knowing touch? She arched into him, her arm reaching up to enfold his neck from behind, coaxing his warm lips to sweep the corner of her mouth.

"A fool's effort." His amber scent tickled her nose as his breath tufted around her. "For I dreamed of you. Every night." He kissed her then, a tender, hot pulse before his lips trailed to her nape again, leaving her mouth hungry.

His hands slid in a slow descent beneath the gown as she struggled to control her erratic heartbeat. "What sorts of dreams, Julian?"

His palms stopped inches above her pelvic bone. He held the tension between them taut like a tightrope and lifted his head so their eyes met in the mirror. He looked so elegant and princely, dressed as the gentleman yet acting evermore the rogue beneath the hushed purpling light. His loose hair waved around his shoulders like a halo of golden mist, his eyes too dark to discern. "The sorts of dreams a gentleman should never admit to; most especially to a lady."

"Even if said gentleman is about to bed said lady?" Willow baited, her voice trembling.

"Oh, I'm not to bed you."

"*What?* I thought tonight was for—"

"Tonight is for romance and passion. But I'm leaving your maidenhood intact."

Fighting a surge of frustration, Willow tried to turn to him, but he tightened his arms around her, holding her shoulder blades against his chest as he kissed the vertebra of her neck. Tiny shocks of heat followed each press of his mouth.

Aflame with need, she opted to take charge of the seduction.

"Wicked and earthy dreams. Dreams that taste of salty dew and longing ... dreams of us writhing naked in the leaves, our bodies sweaty and pocked with dirt. My legs twined in impossible poses around you, holding you inside of me."

Julian's gaze met hers in the mirror, shifting to primal in an instant. His teeth bit down on her neck—a show of dominance, just like Willow had seen the stallions do to their mares at the manor—hard enough to make her gasp. Unexpected pleasure mounted alongside the sharp, lingering pain. "I am the seducer tonight, and I will draw the necessary lines." His hand sunk lower then, as if to curb any further deliberation on the subject.

Willow's legs almost gave beneath her. The hummingbird's phantom wings swept along her inner thighs, a surge of feathered sensations spurred by his long, fine fingers—almost touching her where she burned for him—but not. Her fingers clamped over his, urging him to find her, but the slick fabric between them thwarted her efforts.

She whimpered a plea.

"Shhh," he soothed. His hands withdrew from beneath the dress and settled on her shoulders.

"No..." She hadn't the strength to voice her intense dismay any louder than a fierce whisper. "Julian, please..."

"Patience." He studied her sullen reflection with rapt intensity, as if she were an equation he was determined to solve. Coaxing the dress sleeves from her shoulders so they glided down her arms, he left behind chill bumps, revealing her breasts as the fabric slid along her torso. The sleeves caught on the ruffled mitts at her wrists.

"Tonight we're going to dance on the fringe of those dreams ... just a sampling of heaven." From behind, he caressed every inch of exposed skin, no hesitation now. A cry garbled in her throat and she tried unsuccessfully to reach for him, her arms held useless by the sleeves binding her hands.

Responding to her frustrated moan, he worked her hands free, leaving the gloves in place. She stilled then, compliant as he bared her flesh in increments. He knelt behind her to follow the fabric's descent with his mouth, his breath intruding on her tattoo, lips trailing the marks. Gripping her waist, he kissed every line scored by angry needles, every curve of fiery ink left behind, dousing the poisonous flames, taming the torturous memories. By the time he finished, she was vulnerable, shaken, and lax—but she was no longer a victim. She was empowered: a woman and a willing participant.

When he stood again, a pool of satin hugged her ankles on the floor. She had the wicked thought that her unshod feet were no longer an issue, being the only thing now covered in fabric, until Julian lifted her against his chest and swept away the discarded gown with his shoe, coaxing her feet free before setting her down again.

Instead of trying to cover herself, as modesty dictated, she forced her arms to stay against her sides. Julian's reflection fluctuated between reverence and awe, and she refused to compromise her naked body's hold over him.

"You are every inch a masterpiece." He tilted her head upward to kiss her from behind, not allowing her to turn full around. His fingers trailed her jaw, neck, and breasts, stoking her nerves to a tingling titillation. He wrapped her tongue with his, demanding more until she gasped for breath. Only then did his mouth move away to graze upon her shoulder.

Twilight shaded their surroundings with deep purple brushstrokes. A full moon appeared outside the portal, gracing everything with a silvery haze. Willow's naked body seemed to absorb the moonbeams—making her glimmer with the pearlized distinction of a statue. She watched Julian's powerful arms, dark inside his brown chambray sleeves, encircle her pale form, his breath hot upon her nape.

"Now show me ... show me how to please a woman. How to please *you*." His husky voice broke upon that final syllable, as if it hurt to speak, and Willow knew he was just as astonished and daunted as her. Trembling, she guided his hand to that place where her awareness centered and sensation ebbed like a swirling fever.

With every touch, he kissed her jaw, her ears, her neck, his silky hair following in the wake of his mouth. Liquid heat simmered within her blood, sending it in a blinding rush to her head, blotting out all other thoughts. There was no one else on the ship ... no monster from her past ... no vengeance to appease; only two silhouettes in a mirror learning the ways of love.

A dark, searing ecstasy coiled deep within her, wound tighter and tighter beneath Julian's patient ministrations. Only when he demanded she open her eyes and watch, did she at last find release. A slash of moonlight shone on his face, his chin propped upon her shoulder. His irises reflected the light in waves—as if a tide of passion and pain swirled around them. She understood what made him hurt. His desire, hard and unrelenting, pressed against her lower back ... while in front, his fingers played her like an instrument, locking her in a vise between his unfulfilled passion and her escalating pleasure.

She gripped his wrist as the hummingbird sensations burst to a pulsation of smoldering feathers within her blood, her bones, the very center of her. Crying out, Willow became weightless and heavy at once. Her legs went limp as jelly. Julian eased their descent as they sunk together to the floor, both of them on their knees. He guided her to her back, the carpet between her shoulder blades an itchy counterpoise to his fingers—now a comforting anchor, motionless and soothing where earlier there had been a misery of friction.

"How do you feel?" he whispered.

How did she feel? If only she could describe it. *I love you,* each pump of blood said. *I loved you as the boy whose fingertips were smudged and inky from hours of calculations, as the youth who preferred repairing carousel ponies over riding in a fox hunt ... I love you as the man who protects and pleasures me with the hands of an inventor and an engineer. I love you, I love you, I love you ... with every beat of my enraptured heart.*

She smiled secretly at her unspoken confession; she'd been spending far too much time reading Emilia's romantic ponderings. She was beginning to wax poetic herself.

Julian settled beside her, propped on his side. Cued by her contented sigh, he glided his warm palm to her abdomen. "So ... I did it correctly then?"

Adrift on sleepy currents of serenity and bliss, Willow hadn't the strength to hold back a giggle. She lifted her hand from its relaxed stasis to touch his cheek. "You're such a flummox."

He grinned and leaned in so their noses touched. "And you are exquisite. You're glowing."

Her face and neck grew hotter at his observation. "Because of you." She clasped his temples, her gossamer mitts catching stray stubble along his hairline. "Never, never doubt your ability to pleasure a lady."

"Mmm. I believe I need more practice still, just to be sure." He caught her hands and banked them over her head against the carpet. Utilizing the moonlight, his gaze roved the length of her. His scrutiny made her squirm in senseless embarrassment. After what he'd just done to her body, she was surprised she had any modesty left. As though sensing her shyness, he let the top half of his torso cover hers, his elbows supporting his weight. His clothes rubbed her breasts as he kissed her deeply, working his hands through her hair and leaving her lips slick with his flavor. "And to think, that was only the beginning."

Willow's eyes fluttered half-closed. Feeling lazy and satiate as a sunning cat, she nuzzled his neck and pressed her mouth along his skin, delighting in the tremor she provoked. "Who would've thought there were so many facets to the naughty rumpus?"

It was Julian's turn to laugh. "The naughty rumpus?"

She grinned against his collar bone. "Or we could call it the electron-spin. Is that better?"

His lips smoothed her hair. "Either way it sounds like an amusement park ride."

"Ah ... then there's no doubting you'll be magnificent at it, right?"

"We both will. When the time comes."

A wanton impulse roused Willow from her state of drowsy elation. Her eyes snapped fully open. Why could tonight not be the time? Before Julian knew what she was about, she ran her palm along the hard length at the front of his trousers. "Amazing. You're the mathematician ... surely you've noted the disproportion in sizes. How is this *ever* to fit?"

Julian's breath caught, as if between a chuckle and a strangled gasp. He shoved her hands away and rolled to the right, but Willow used her nimble acrobatic skills to straddle him and pin his back to the floor. In a matter of seconds, she had her gloves off and his vest and shirt unbuttoned. Eager fingers skated through the fine, soft hairs of his chest where they glistened in the moonlight.

"Willow, ah, Willow ... wait. *Damnit*."

"Just one peek." Her hands were at his trouser fastenings again, though he refused to allow her to open the plackets. She covered his face with kisses. "Please..."

"I'm trying to do the right thing here," he growled, reluctantly kissing her as her lips passed over his.

"For once in your life, could you just give in? Enjoy yourself."

"What do you think I was doing earlier? Surely you know I enjoyed that as much as you. Can't you tell?"

She leaned over him, nuzzling his chin. "There's no question. But you selflessly gave in to my passions and suffered your crisis. Now it's time to surrender to your emission."

"Oh for heaven's sake," Julian retorted. "You're spouting medical terminology ... words you know nothing about."

Her desire to look upon him, to feel him, made her dizzy and daring. "Then teach me. Let me do for you what you did for me. Show me how to please you."

"I would never be able to stop there." A gruff edge broke his voice. "And I won't risk leaving you alone and with child."

The gravity of his statement crashed over her like an arctic wave, knocking the air from her lungs. *"Alone?"* Willow pushed away and crossed her arms over her breasts, her heart stripped naked and vulnerable like her body. "After all that's happened between us, that we've admitted to one another, you still refuse to commit to me?"

Wearing a pained expression, he scooped up her dress and draped the fabric over her nakedness then stood to straighten his clothes—looping fasteners and buttons into place. His hair fell in a thick, golden spray around his shoulders. "I can't be dishonest with you any longer."

Standing shakily, Willow stepped into the gown and

yanked it all the way up to her shoulders. The satin felt chilly to her skin, but couldn't compare to the ice his rejection had sheathed around her heart. She concentrated on smoothing out the wrinkled fabric to keep herself from crying. "So you've been lying, all along? About wanting a future together."

"No!" Julian stared at her, somber and resolved. "I've been lying about the World's Fair. You aren't going. You never were. You're going back to London the moment we dock in the morning. I'll be traveling to St. Louis by myself. Your journey ends here."

NINETEEN

Julian's statement nailed Willow's gaze to his. "My journey ends ... going back—" Her jaw dropped. "You've been in contact with Uncle Owen!"

The muscle in Julian's neck throbbed, making it appear to drizzle like a stream of water in the silvery light. "That first morning after I discovered you here, when I went to the captain to apprise him of my stowaway 'brothers', I wired a telegraph home. In it, I told Uncle to have Leander take the next available ship. He'll be waiting at the Queensbury Hotel in New York. He reaches port tomorrow evening. Another ship leaves for London two days after. You are to board it with your brother and accompany him back to the manor."

Willow's stomach clenched. No wonder the judge had acted so strange when she'd mentioned they could keep her identity a secret all the way to St. Louis and back. It seemed everyone knew but her. All this time that Julian had been kissing and pleasuring her, he had known ... and all the while he'd led her to think she would attend the fair with him. "They're sending me back to Ridley's." She cursed, not even caring a whit about looking like less of a lady. What did it matter? She was soon to have the transformation pounded into her.

"I said nothing of the academy," Julian answered.

"As if you had to. You know that's where Uncle will send me, you duplicitous snake-skinned milksop." Her cheeks flamed. "Oh, this is as fine as frog's hair, this is." She pinched together the open seam behind her, purposely grappling skin along with it in hopes the bite of her fingernails might curb her rage. Her eyes darted around the room in search of something hard and sharp to throw at Julian's ever swelling cranium. "You were perfectly happy to play this charade, so long as we are to be locked within this stateroom. You wished to learn the ways of seduction and I was your willing lab rat."

His gray eyes flared as if they were windows reflecting the moonlight. "This was *never* a game to me."

"Oh, it was. But you came to an ante your conscience would not let you play. A violation of my innocence would be intractable, unmanageable. You would be forced to commit to me then. Since you're not willing to do so, you're sending me back to nullify the temptation."

"I'm sending you back to protect you from circumstances out of my control. There are ghosts everywhere on this blasted ship. From your past. Even a real one connected to a pair of latchet shoes. I don't want you in danger." He moved toward her, cautiously, no doubt anticipating her wrath.

Willow side-stepped him, attempting to fasten the buttons along the gown's back seam. She hissed with the effort. "You don't want yourself in danger of being seen with me. You made this arrangement before we knew about Tildey."

He gave her some space and backed toward the bed. "Yes. When I first made it, I was thinking more upon your reputation. Of how it would look for you to travel with a man. You may have managed to play the part of a boy while in the poor lighting of steerage. But you are far too beautiful a lady to fool thousands of people at a fair in broad daylight. Someone will know."

Refusing to let the compliment soften her, Willow lifted her chin. "If you were willing, if you truly wanted me there, we could pretend to be sister and brother in St. Louis. My not being enough of a proper lady for you ... that is why you won't take me. Why you're sending me back home. So I can finish my training and become someone worthy of your public attention."

Hand shoved in his pockets, Julian butted the back of his head against a bedpost, having the gall to look flustered. "Have you not heard a word I've said?"

Willow yearned to strangle him. "Yes. You want to protect my saintly reputation. It's simply an added coupe that in the process I will recommence my training at Ridley's."

"If that is what I wanted," he answered with forced composure, "then why did I write a note for you to give to Uncle Owen ... a note that specifies under no circumstances are you to be sent back to the finishing school?"

This unexpected twist jumbled Willow's reasoning ... but only for an instant. She looped four buttons in place over her tattoo. "Because the manor is isolated like the ship's cabin. You can keep your hoydenish circus urchin hidden away and take her out only when she's become the elegant debutant. No doubt you plan to have Aunt Enya tutor me while I'm in seclusion."

His neck and face appeared to redden in the dimness. He raked a hand through his hair, mumbling an oath. "You've flipped your noddle."

"Have I?" She slipped five more buttons into place, allowing her to move without the back seam flopping open. "Have I truly? Or am I finally seeing you for the *bugiardo viscoso* you are?" Turning on her heel, she strode to the bedchamber door and opened it, squinting in the bright flood of lamplight from the parlor.

Before her eyes could focus, Julian twirled her around, thrusting her against the door frame with his body. He held her arms to her sides. The wood pinched the buttons between her shoulder blades. "I never intended to lie to you. I was afraid, if you knew, you would slip away again."

She struggled to ignore his scent, his rough warmth, his sensual proximity. "So you let me humiliate myself. You let me prattle on and on about the exhibits at the fair ... all the while knowing I was never to experience it. All the while leading me to believe that we might have a future together, when you cannot even bear to be seen in public with me." She tangled her fingers with his in her effort to break free of his grasp. "I should just accept it. After eleven years of nurturing a half-starved dream. You will never love me ... never want to marry me like I do you." The moment the confession tripped off her tongue, her body drained of all blood.

She tried to turn away.

Julian pressed harder against her and released one wrist so he could catch her jaw. He tilted her face up, his expression no longer exasperated but arrested, as if he had stumbled upon something precious, unexpected, and rare. "What did you just say?"

"Nothing." She shoved him back with her free arm and broke away, but the moment she felt the slick wood of the parlor floor beneath her feet, she froze in place, her surroundings holding her captive.

Yellow lamplight illuminated Julian's mysterious preparations of earlier. A borrowed phonograph sat in one corner of the parlor—the origin of the music she'd heard through the door. Sketches hung from strings tacked to the ceiling with straight pins. Willow recognized them as the designs Julian had kept hidden from her on the trip. They were now painted; reds, greens, oranges, and purples filled the lines, bringing the pictures to life.

Julian thumped the doorway's frame with a knuckle. "Newton helped me color them," he answered as if reading her mind. "Kept us busy while you were ill. I was hoping to sweep you off your feet tonight, to waltz you through the plans for my newest ride."

He came up behind her. Her skin remembered him ... welcomed him with tiny twitches as he buttoned up the rest of her gown. Upon finishing, he pressed a kiss to her shoulder and stepped around her without a word. He leaned over to crank the phonograph's handle, and the *Doctrinen*—the very same Eduard Strauss masterpiece she and Julian had danced to at their first gala—burst forth in a tinkly melody of notes, slow and evocative.

Willow wanted to ask him how he'd found that particular song ... she wanted to ask him how he'd remembered ... but astonishment and shame simultaneously clenched her throat.

"That one there," Julian spoke over the music and pointed to a dangling picture of a plump queen holding a flamingo mallet, "is the Queen's Croquet Court. And this one," his finger reached overhead to sway a sketch of farcical characters around a table filled with cakes and kettles, "is the Hatter's Tea Party. The ride will be called: *Journey into the Looking Glass*. I intend to have a gala when I'm ready to present the finished attraction. I'll invite all of London's most prestigious guests. And I hope to be the proud escort of my muse's inspiration." The short winding of music had played itself out. Julian turned to her.

Dumbstruck, she regarded the sketches. Could it be true? That she had been Julian's motivation for such a grand undertaking? He'd been so pleased with her when she'd read the second Lewis Carroll novel without any help. The fact that he still remembered and wished to honor her made her earlier indignation seem petty and trite. This terrified her ... as anger was her only defense against the undertow of emotion threatening to drag down the walls of her heart.

He'd heard her admission of love ... even marriage ... and had yet to say anything in response, other than having her be his escort to a gala. Despite this lofty gesture and his careful preparations, was his silence not proof that her feelings, her devotion and commitment, were unreciprocated?

She blinked to fight the confused tears burning behind her lashes. Her gaze slanted to the other corner of the room where silver utensils glinted on a lavishly decorated table as if winking. A domed lid covered the main course. Steam seeped from the edges in a succulent fog and swirled around a vase of fresh peonies. The special dessert he'd mentioned had melted to slush in glass goblets.

"Raspberry ice," she whispered.

"Not as fine as the ones back home." Julian strode to the table. His half-buttoned shirt gaped to reveal his chest as he picked up a goblet and held it to the light. A reddish glow reflected off his face. "They don't serve ices on the ship. I had to shave the block myself. And the raspberry syrup, well, it is just the water they boiled the berries in for the compote they were serving tonight. I added some sugar to it. Bristles would like the concoction, no doubt. But a lady's refined taste might not be as forgiving as a squirrel's. So ... should I pour it over my head, or allow you the honor?"

Willow stared at him, disoriented. "Whatever do you mean?"

He set the goblet down. "The look in your eyes when you found out I'd sent the wire to Uncle ... you were seeking something to throw at me. Some way to lash out at me." His focus on her sharpened. "Is that what made you say those extraordinary words? Were you trying to topple my defenses? Or was the sentiment sincere?"

Willow's body tensed. What did he expect of her? That she should say them again? Lay out her affections on the chopping block and give him the ax? She couldn't bid such courage. Instead, she dropped her gaze to the floor.

The thump of Julian's shoes metered out irreversible increments of time and distance as he came to stand over her. His palms cupped her shoulders and their eyes met.

"That was cowardly of me," he offered. "A man should be a man. A man should have the backbone to speak his heart, regardless of the outcome." He leaned in so his forehead pressed to hers, his thick blonde lashes closing. Weaving trembling fingers through her hair, he nuzzled her nose. "I am a mechanist. A designer of frivolous rides and amusements. I'm not one who can easily conjure pretty words." He huffed, his breath a warm and ambrosial veil across her face. His eyes opened to hold hers once more. "I tried to show you the depth of my feelings through my actions tonight. But now ... well, now I understand that a lady needs to see and *hear* it." He jaw twitched nervously. "Another layer falls away from the mystery of the fairer sex. I fear I'm to be buried beneath a mountain of them before it's all said and done."

Willow watched the tension in his throbbing throat, sensed it in the way his hands shook as he knelt to the floor in front of her and clasped her fingers in his. All of her vulnerabilities resurfaced—raw and exposed—as the man became the boy again ... the boy with inky hands and moonlit eyes working out some intricate universal mystery as her own world stalled on its orbit around him ... waiting for even one breath ushered over her skin, one look in her direction, so life could recommence.

Her cheeks flushed and the pulse throbbed in her neck like a runaway metronome. A hopeful smile tugged at her lips, but she held it in check, a practiced patience she had learned over years of unmet expectations.

Julian looked up at her and opened his mouth to speak then closed it on a gulp before trying again. "I-I—" Another gulp. "I ... oh, blast it." His face paled. Clearing his throat, he tried once more, blurting out the Italian equivalent: "*Ti amo*." Color rushed back into his face, as if that small step had unleashed his courage. "Yes. *Ti amo*. I ... *love* you. From the first moment I saw you adjust the pistons and cylinders on a compressed air engine, I was yours. Now I can't remember a time when I didn't belong to you. And ... and even should you not return my feelings ... well, that will never change. Not for the rest of my life."

Willow's smile broke free then, along with a rush of tears down her cheeks. She dropped to her knees, throwing her arms around his neck. "And you said you had no pretty words. Was that so difficult?"

He clutched her to him. "Wretchedly so," he answered, lips smiling against her cheek. He drew back and held out quivering hands. "See? I'm shaking like a scarecrow in a windstorm."

Willow sniffled. "I find it most endearing."

His grin deepened and he wiped tears from her jaw with his thumbs. "And here I was hoping for virile."

Running the back of her fingers along his jaw, Willow nodded. "Oh, that too. Always that." She sobered. "I love you, Julian Anston Thornton. So very much. For so very long."

"Quite so." With a relieved smirk, he helped her stand. "I rather suspected such. Otherwise, I mightn't have been so forthcoming."

"Forthcoming? Ha!" Willow giggled and shoved at his shoulders. "I'll expect you to say it thrice each day from this moment forward ... so you might learn to recite it without stammering."

His amused expression flickered to desire as he pulled her closer. "*I love you, Willomena Antoniette.* I intend to prove it as soon as the opportunity allots itself, by making you my bride, and bedding you right and proper."

The words washed over her like rain from heaven. She closed her eyes and opened her mouth to drink of them ... to make them hers forever.

"How's that for not stammering?" he asked, his breath hot on her ear.

"*Perfetto,*" she said, lifting on tiptoes to loop her arms around his nape. She smiled against his shoulder, scraping a tear from her chin onto his shirt. "But you've still one more recitation left for today."

His lips followed the curve of her lobe and sent delicious tremors throughout her neck and spine. "Hmm. I believe I'll save it for just before I tuck you in tonight, so you can have something other than a pillow to rest that pretty head upon." He gave her a lingering kiss on her temple—gentle and sweet. "I suppose I'll have to try to squeeze in a few extra dozen tomorrow before we part ways, to last you until I return home."

Willow snuggled her head beneath his chin, not wanting to think of them being apart. She fought the self-righteous ebb of anger rising again.

As if feeling her muscles tense, Julian murmured, "I'm not commanding you to go home. I'd be a fool to assume I can tell you what to do in any instance. You're going to follow me if you wish, no matter what I say. Should I even attempt to force you, you'll outwit me at every turn. So I am *pleading,*

Willomena. There are no longer any doubts. You're in danger here. Possibly more than we even imagined. At home, you will be safe."

Willow sighed. Even though she knew without a doubt that his precluding her from the fair came from a place of love, she still considered stowing away on the train.

"Wait." She pulled back, not even trying to hide the horror she felt chilling her cheeks. "You said you couldn't risk leaving me alone and with child. You're afraid something will happen to you. That *you* won't return." Her heart chilled like her face—drained of blood.

His gaze slanted to the left, not quite meeting hers. "No, no. That's not it. I'm just ... it's a precaution."

His evasion tactics left her even more rattled. "You have Judge Arlington as an investor. There's no need for you to go the fair now. Come back home with me."

Eyes trailing back to hers, Julian traced her trembling lower lip with his thumb and shook his head. "It's not so simple. I should get at least one more investor. I've learned from my dealings with Lord Desmond that I should have a secondary means of income. I also need to find an artist who will carve figurines for the displays, now that Nick's away. And there are challenges in maintaining the temperature within the ride during the summer season; if I talk to other inventors, scientists even, I can find a solution." His chin set to granite. "Most importantly ... I plan to find Sala. To confront him."

Willow balked at the thought of him pursuing the mysterious Italian alone. "Why? I don't care if he stole the shoes! I care only for your safety."

Julian frowned. "There's a puzzle yet to solve before we can close the door on your past. Ends to wrap up. I can't be sure how the shoes fit. Perhaps Sala bought them from the real thief, or hired the thief himself. He fancies himself a collector of antique oddities with unusual stories attached to them. Those shoes definitely fall into that category. But he seems to be genuinely terrified of them ... of Nadia's ghost. Perhaps he had something to do with her death. If he did, I suspect it was accidental. He feels remorse for it. I've seen it on his face." Julian led her to the table and eased her into a chair. "What say we talk about this over dinner? I've already lost my chance to dance with you before the little mouse returns."

At the mention of their orphaned cabin mate, Willow leapt out of her chair, causing it to topple with a clunk. "Newton! Is that why you're confronting Sala? You can't still mean to return him to—"

"No." Repositioning the chair and coaxing Willow back into place, Julian took the seat across from her. He draped a napkin over his lap and spooned out some fragrant roast duck onto Willow's plate. "I discovered something most disconcerting while searching Mr. Sala's room this morn. I only got a glimpse before he started to stir from his dozing, but I distinctly remember some studded shoes within his wardrobe, just like the ones you described. The ones used by acrobats and aerialists. I also recognized a scent emitting from the trunk today before you closed the lid. Sala smokes cigars from Italy that share the very same aroma."

Willow had a bite of duck balanced on her fork, but couldn't bring herself to taste it. Her hand dropped, the silverware clanging against the porcelain plate. "You mean to say—"

"That trunk is his. *He* had your doll." Julian's ears flashed to red. He paused, as if to measure Willow's expression, then pulled apart a loaf of bread, dropped some on her plate, and continued. "There was a rumor being tossed about ... that

Sala has a ring of harlots ... that he kidnaps girls at a young age and raises them to serve in his 'troupe'. In which case, being actresses is merely their front."

A faint palpitation rippled Willow's lower back—ugly feathers of ink, hate, and terror breaking loose. The room seemed to spin around her, as if she were high upon a trapeze, unable to contain the momentum of the ropes.

Her parents were murdered because they wished to protect her from being preened as a specialty whore? What mother and father wouldn't try to prevent such a fate for their daughter? How could something so natural as protecting your offspring merit death?

The senselessness of the revelation left her empty and shattered. A queasy throb festered within her stomach, reminiscent of seasickness, and she spun again on her dangling ropes.

"Willow." Julian grasped her hand. "I am so sorry to have to tell you this, tonight of all nights. Are you all right to hear it?"

She nodded, letting his concern anchor her until she swayed to a stop and could focus. She sucked in a threaded breath. "Why? Why would he have wanted me?"

Julian leaned closer, pressing her knuckles to his lips before continuing. "He was enthralled with your hair that afternoon I dined with him. Said something about such color being rare ... people paying a high price for it. At the time, I assumed he meant for a wig. But now—"

"The old man," Willow interrupted, unwilling to let him finish his speculation. "The moth-eaten cripple that Berta and Christoff spoke of?"

"A decoy? Most likely one of his girls in full costume. I intend to find out tomorrow. I have yet to understand how the acrobatics and contortionism could possibly fit into this scenario. Unless..." His lips fought a tremor, either of disgust or disbelief. "Unless it's to explicate a higher price for their services."

Willow's nausea resurfaced. All of those years of training at the orphanage, she had always felt so safe and at ease soaring upon the heights. Now the memory deteriorated to filth beneath such lascivious motives. If Julian was right, if it was Sala who had murdered her parents, then she couldn't use his frailties against him like she had planned. From her memory of bumping into him in the corridor, he was robust and healthy. A faceless shadow-giant ... like the man of her memory, standing in the tent's opening, smelling of expensive tobacco. A full body shiver shook her.

She no longer cared to go to St. Louis. She no longer cared to tour the fair. She wanted only to go home. "I-I don't want to see him when we disembark tomorrow."

"Of course. You will stay here in the stateroom until everyone else is ashore. I'll have the judge and Newton wait with you while I scope out steerage."

Willow nodded, shutting her eyes to retain her precarious balance. Her cowardice shamed her. It proved she wasn't the plucky wanderer she'd always prided herself to be. In light of this new wrinkle, her childhood fears trumped all earlier thoughts of revenge. Evasion came into focus with suffocating clarity. All she could think of was escape. For her ... for Newton.

For Julian.

She opened her eyes to find him kneeling on the floor next to her, one hand on her quivering knee to steady it.

"You know I will protect you." He lifted the other hand to stroke her hair.

She grasped his wrist and pressed her temple to his palm. "But who will protect *you*? And what of Newton?" She could only whisper against the nerves bundled in her throat. "We cannot let him find the little widget—ever."

"I agree. I aim to keep you and Newton both as far from that man as possible. And don't you worry for me. Judge Arlington will be accompanying me to St. Louis, in the same as our mouse will accompany you and Leander back to London where he'll live at the manor ... where he'll be safe. He's in our care now, Willow. Dependent upon us to keep him out of the clutches of his corrupt father." Julian squeezed her knee. "His safety matters most. So please, no more tricks, no more stowing away or furtive escapes. He needs you for stability. Go home with him; help him adjust to his sister's absence."

"I will," Willow said. And she meant it. Now that she knew her future was irrevocably bound to Julian's and Newton's, her wandering flyaway-days were behind her, forever. All she wanted was to be home. Safe at home with the family she loved. But that family would be incomplete unless she could convince Julian to give up this crusade and follow *her* this time.

Diurnal assignments for Sunday, April 27, 1904:
1. Capture and detain Sala's decoy until she talks; 2. See Newton and Willow safely to the hotel; 3. Find the bastard Sala and cut his throat for hurting Willomena...

Julian waited with a pasty-faced steward inside the putrid, sweltering depths of steerage, wrestling the rage that had been rocking his stomach all morning. There was only the infamous trunk and a portmanteau left. Upon reaching port earlier, the marked parcels of luggage had been dragged up to the promenade so they could go ashore with their rightful owners.

"What happens to these if they go unclaimed?" Julian asked, readjusting his vest. His voice echoed in the absence of the roaring motors. Without all of the immigrants milling about, the dimly lit belly of the ship seemed fathomless.

The steward shrugged bony shoulders and looked up at Julian, who was a head taller than the young man. "They'll be auctioned off to the crew," his nasal reply came. "The luggage and their contents. Hope it comes to that. I'd give up half a week's pay for that box you're guarding. It's a beauty."

Julian took a seat atop Willow's mystery trunk. The bumps and scrollwork on the lid made for an uncomfortable perch. He imagined it would seem well-crafted and intricate to the innocent eye. Although he himself wished to bust it into splinters with an ax. He wished it had never been brought aboard this ship. Hell, he wished he had never boarded himself.

If he had simply confessed his feelings to Willow at the school—the true scope of his feelings instead of choking out a half-hearted attempt that left her hanging between hope and turmoil—she might have felt secure enough in their future not to follow him. In truth, he might have decided to stay and not attend the fair because having admitted his love, he wouldn't have been able to leave her at that school at all.

As of now, the thought of parting ways rendered him crippled and imbalanced. She'd become a part of him on this ship ... actually long before that. The difference was, now he realized it, and his days and nights would be miserable and pointless without her—even in a didactic environ such as the World's Fair.

Upon seeing Willow nurture a child, upon becoming

enamored of said child himself, Julian was ready to raise Newton, to take him as their own. In fact, Julian was finding himself prey to a windfall of domestic fantasies: Willow, wearing his name; Willow, bearing his seed; Willow, aging hand in hand alongside him, watching their grandchildren grow big enough to enjoy their amusement park—the rides they would build together throughout their lifetime.

That's if Willow would ever forgive him enough to wed him one day. She'd been furious when he'd left the cabin a half hour earlier, but instead of throwing breakfast in his face, she had begged him not to go; to leave it alone; to stay in the stateroom until everyone disembarked, then come back to London with them.

It had unnerved him, to see her crying the tears of a woman-child, so soft and fragile in his arms as she whimpered. This change in her—this uncharacteristic passive apprehension—was a complete turnaround from the night before.

After their dinner, she'd tried once more to reason with him. To convince him to come home. Things had escalated into an argument by the time the judge and Newton returned. Willow calmed down then, preoccupied with getting the mouse to bed, and was so exhausted she fell asleep while telling the child a nursery rhyme.

However, her subconscious wasn't so easily subdued. Late in the night, she'd had another ill dream, so disturbing she'd moaned in her sleep and awakened Newton. The mouse stumbled into the parlor in the dark, grabbed Julian's hand, and tugged him into the bedchamber just in time for Julian to witness her thrashing in her sleep with her eyeballs rolling beneath shut lids. Julian slipped beneath the covers and held her in his arms until morning, with little Newton balled up on the other side of her. Not the way he'd envisioned their first night together in the same bed, but he wouldn't have traded those hours for anything. To hold her ... to be her security. He wanted nothing more than to help heal those scars. Her sleep had been fitful even in his embrace, until Julian finally convinced her they should turn out the lamp. Strangely, that's when she relaxed, snuggled against his chest, and slept peacefully.

She had seemed resigned to Julian's plan at breakfast until they made another disturbing discovery, unhinging her once again. She had pulled Tildey out from the drawer while packing and studied the bird etched on the doll's back. Newton settled beside her and pointed to the marking then to his shoes ... a sure sign he referred to Nadia. Stunned, Willow untucked the shirt she wore and eased down her pant waist just enough to show her tattoo to Newton. His eyes grew wide as he pointed to his shoes again and nodded. An inconceivable notion came to light—that there was a skin-deep connection between Willow and the dead girl.

After recovering from the shock, Julian busied Newton with some paper and pens so he and Willow could have privacy. Together, they surmised that the tattoos must be etched into every girl's skin upon her induction into Sala's ring. The fact that the Italian used a hummingbird for the mark was apparently coincidental—not brought about by Willow's chanting cries as she had once assumed.

Most unnerving of all, it appeared even Sala's own daughter had not been exempt from his depraved enterprise, assuming Nadia truly was Newton's sister. Newton maintained that she was, but his word was all they had to go on. The word of a mute.

"Five more minutes," the steward's announcement tapped into Julian's thoughts, blotting away the memory of Willow's pleading tears. "After that, we assume them abandoned. By now the passengers will have all cleared out and gone ashore."

Julian's breath hung in his lungs, a sharp, angry scrape. He tried not to think of it ... not to imagine what would've become of Willow had she not escaped the orphanage. Those bastard caretakers were working for Sala ... training Willow to bend and move in graceful, aerial poses only to exploit her amazing talent by turning her into a victimized whore. Just the thought of those words in the same sentence as Willow's name, and fury seared through him. To think he might not get the chance to make Sala choke on his due rewards almost burned a hole through his chest.

He had no intention of bringing Willow into it. He had to protect her anonymity above all else. But he wanted to acquire some solid proof so he could take the matter to the proper authorities. Thus Willow would receive vindication, if only from afar, and he could rescue any other innocent girls from that monster.

As it stood, no justice would come to Sala unless Julian proved the women in the troupe had been kidnapped. Each one seemed to hold an impervious loyalty to the Italian devil. He must have taken them from poverty stricken homes and offered possessions and wealth in exchange for their silence.

Standing, Julian stretched his legs and smoothed the wrinkles from his trousers at the bend of his legs. Loyalty notwithstanding, Sala's decoy was going to sing like a rabbit being primed for stew. Julian would never manhandle a woman, but he wasn't above frightening one. At the very least, he planned to expose her lower back and see if she had a hummingbird tattoo like he suspected. His plan would fall to rot, however, should she not show up at all.

"Well ... that's it then." The pasty-faced steward slapped his hands together and started toward the stairwell. He paused, noticing Julian still leaned on the trunk. "I can't leave you here, sir. Now that we've docked, steerage is off limits lessen you're accompanied by a crewmember."

Julian nodded, taking one last look at the lid. His palm skimmed the cool, carved surface, resigned to hopeless frustration. They'd been waiting for well over forty-five minutes. He was sure the young man had tasks to attend before he could go ashore. He'd mentioned to Julian earlier that his crewmates often indulged in drolleries at a local tavern on the eve of their docking. Julian had no right to detain him any longer.

Julian had just started to follow the steward up the first step when they heard a shuffling sound from above. Within moments, an old man appeared midway, inching down the stairs; the bulbous bump between his shoulder blades set him off kilter and made him take each step with premeditated hesitation. Or so it appeared...

Julian caught the steward's elbow and tugged him back down to floor level into the shadows, shushing him as they awaited the elderly man's arrival. His mind raced ... he wasn't sure how to handle this. Every part him—bones, blood, and soul—wanted to jump the decoy, pin him to the ground, and throttle out some answers. But most likely, it was a woman under there ... one who had been forced into this life as a child, as Willow almost was.

Once the old man had taken the final step, Julian emerged from the darkness and offered his hand. "Sir, might we help you? We were just on our way up. Steerage is now closed to the public, as this young steward has informed me."

When the decoy's eyes met Julian's, he saw a spark of shocked recognition. That was all he needed. In the same moment the suddenly spry old man turned on his heel to leap back up the stairs, the hosiery-encased-birdseed-hump fell from his jacket. Julian caught him by the scruff of his neck and spun him around.

As the decoy tried to wriggle free, Julian lifted off the wig and hat and peeled away part of the flesh colored mask. He and the crewman both gasped at the result. It was the owl-faced steward Julian had met upon his first morning aboard the *Christine Victoria*—the very one he'd saved from losing his job by taking Mr. Sala's room—staring back at them.

"*You?*" Julian asked as the-red haired decoy stripped off the remaining mask to reveal his freckles.

"Orville?" The other pasty-faced steward came out of the shadows, addressing his crewmate.

"One of Mr. Sala's actresses hired me," Orville answered. "I saw her in the corridor just afore we docked. She offered me a sterlin' pound to don this costume and come down to steerage to get her trunk." He shrugged. "It seemed harmless enough. And I wanted the lucre so I could buy some company at the tavern tonight ... can you blame me?"

Julian clenched Orville's lapels, lifting him so the owlish youth's boot soles slid on the floor. "Is this the first time you've helped her like this? Answer me!"

Orville winced and clutched his borrowed hat. "Aye. And I'll not be doin' it ever again, judgin' by this reception."

Julian released the jacket, giving his captive some balance. "So where is she now?"

Before Orville could answer, another rush of footsteps pounded down the stairs. Julian looked up to see Newton taking the steps two at a time, holding onto the rail, knuckles deathly white as though his fear of heights was at war with his desire to get to the bottom swiftly.

"Newton?" Julian took a step forward, balking when he saw the judge following close behind the boy. "What in hell?

Who's with ...?" Julian remembered the two stewards and stopped himself just short of blurting out Willow's name.

Newton lighted the last step and pushed past Julian, rushing toward the trunk. He flung open the lid. It was apparent by his desperation that he sought Nadia's shoes. But Julian knew he'd find nothing within. He himself had looked with the steward when they'd first arrived.

The judge tottered down, his feet meeting the floor none too gracefully. "Sala's girl," he bent at the waist and panted, "introduced herself as Louisa. She came by to retrieve the fair's ground plans." Judge Arlington drew out a handkerchief and swiped his brow. "She waited at the door while I went to the desk to get them." He swallowed more air. "Newton stood there, staring up at her as if he knew her." Leaned against the wall, he tucked his hanky away. "She bent down and whispered something to him, then he bolted out of the room."

A dark premonition folded over Julian's soul, chilling him. "Where was *Wilson* all this time?"

"In the water closet. I thought it best to chase the boy down before your ... other brother ... could fret over his absence."

The chill skittered up Julian's body, lifting his hairs so they pricked and snagged his clothes like the twines of a comb. "You mean you left Wilson with that woman?"

Judge Arlington's moustache waffled. "I locked the door behind me, left Louisa in the corridor—"

"*Distractions.*" A buzzing heat niggled through Julian's earlobes. "She told Newton the shoes were in the trunk. You were sent down here as distractions." He shoved Orville out of his path. "*The whole lot of you.*"

Julian was already halfway up the stairs—leg muscles quaking beneath the strain of taking three steps at a time—

when the judge started the climb behind him, huffing and puffing like a mule put to plow on a mountain. "There's no way Louisa could've got in ... aside from picking the lock. Surely she can't pick a lock?"

"Considering one of her playmates broke into my room and stole the shoes the night of the masquerade"—Julian shouted over his shoulder—"I'd venture she bloody well can!"

PART IV

When you see, however distant, the goal of your wandering...
It matters not how many ranges, rivers or parching dusty ways
May lie between you; it is yours now for ever.
~Freya Stark

TWENTY

Julian crouched on the parlor floor in his stateroom, chest sore after a battery of unconstrained raging wails. His eyes clenched ... his spine ate into the wall ... his chin wedged on his knees. The past half hour's events pounded his forehead like iron fists. He had scoured the ship's hull—staying ahead of Newton and the judge, never allowing them to catch up. Not one cabin, galley, or pantry had been unturned in his wake.

Willow was nowhere.

He'd even brokered a glimpse into the captain's quarters, feigning concern for his missing "brother." After allowing him to look, the captain suggested *Wilson* had simply run off again ... pulled another adolescent trick; to whit Julian had an inexplicable urge to tromp the man upside his head, but instead turned away and left to question the crew.

In the end, it all proved futile. Somehow, Sala and his girls had managed to get Willow off this ship without anyone seeing her. Even searching the dock had proved useless. Now he was back where he'd last held her ... seeking something he might've missed. But he found nothing which would point him in the right direction.

He still smelled her on his clothes from their embrace this morning, still tasted her skin—fresh from her bath. She'd told him how much she loved him, begged him not to leave her.

He lifted his face just enough to squint at the overcast light streaming through the portal. A fine mist had started outside and fogged the glass, a benign companion to the mania which rose like steam from the backs of his eyes.

Willow had once told him he had no idea how terrifying it was for a child to be held captive ... to feel helpless. *Powerless*. Well, he damn well knew such futility now.

He had lost her to that bastard. After his pretty promises of protection, he'd let her be captured. Her mother and father's noble sacrifices were for rot. In one careless, unthinking moment, he'd robbed Willow of the chance they'd died to give her, and landed her back within the grimy paws of Carmelo Sala.

She must be so terrified.

A spasm tore through Julian's gut. He yelled and kicked the chair beside him. The wooden leg refused to bend, sending a shooting pain through his ankle. Fury engulfed him—a tide of disdain triggered by his own uselessness. He leapt up and grabbed the chair, ripping it from its screws and thrusting it across the room. It crashed into the wall with a satisfying scrape as the offending leg snapped.

Something took over then ... something primal that paid no mind to logic ... that wouldn't give him pause to assess the situation and reason out the next step. Something that begged immediate release.

He jerked the drawer from the desk and chunked it hard into the air, garnering a long splinter in his finger which drew blood. The drawer's contents rained across the parlor as it went sailing. It hit the opposite side of the room with a sharp crack, denting the wall and clunking to the floor.

Newton and the judge stumbled in from the bedchamber. Julian didn't look up. He continued his rampage, tossing more drawers and curios around until he had a pile in the midst of the parlor tall enough to cast a bird-shaped shadow on the carpet. The image reminded Julian of Willow's tattoo, and fed the inferno in his chest until it burned all the way down into the soles of his feet. He stood staring at the shadow with his back turned to his companions and panted, his clothes sweaty and disheveled, his mind fuzzy, and his thoughts dark.

"Master Thornton. Contain yourself! You have an audience." Judge Arlington's command fringed the edges of Julian's consciousness. He'd heard him call out during the tirade—a drone as benign as a horsefly's buzz. Only now did the words break through. Julian shoved his finger in his mouth and sucked out the blood-slicked splinter, refusing to respond.

"This is so unlike you."

Julian whipped around and glared at the judge. "Beg pardon, but how would you know what I'm like? You've been acquainted with me all of a week, *sir*."

Judge Arlington stared back, his white moustache drooping, almost touching the tip of his chin where his neck bubbled out over his collar. Julian's own neck throbbed. The man couldn't possibly know him. For Julian no longer knew himself ...

"Use your sense, lad." The judge tried again. "We know where Sala and the girls are going. To the fair, to the competition."

Julian narrowed his eyes, observing Newton's sudden preoccupation with the pile of broken furniture and the drawer's contents littering the floor. "Their being actresses, it was all a front. Just like the rumors said. Sala is the proprietor of their bodies. He employs women who have ... special talents. Contortionists, aerialists. And this man has in mind to put Willow to work for him. Lord only knows if they're actually going to St. Louis. And we've already missed the first train. We'll be over three hours behind them even if we catch the next one. A hell of a lot can happen in three hours. So don't dare tell me to get a hold of myself."

The judge's mouth gaped. "We'll put in a word to the authorities. We'll start with the captain."

"What ... tell him my brother who stowed away on the ship is actually my lady, and I'm worried that an Italian prostitute ring has solicited her against her will? Of course he'll believe in her maidenly innocence. After all, she's been bunked up with me day and night. And I'm sure, once I confess how I've been lying to him all this time, that he'll trust such an outrageous accusation against one of his highest paying patrons. We're on our own here. Even the authorities won't get involved without proof. Everyone will simply think Willow has taken off again, just like she always does."

"And you're sure she didn't?"

The suggestion struck Julian with the force of a slap. His deaf mother was the fortunate one ... being protected from the bite of such well-intentioned, tactless sentiments.

Of course Willow hadn't left him. He relived last night—just as he had a thousand times over—relearning the secrets of her glorious body in his mind. He was the first man to ever give her pleasure. The first man to experience her afterglow ... to give her his love. That poignant interlude had strengthened their resolve to be together; they spoke of marriage, the ultimate commitment. She wouldn't try to escape—not after all of the intimacies they'd shared on this ship. Not after all of the years they'd grown up alongside one another, sharing the same goals and hopes. Anytime she'd ever run off was to be *with* him ... not to leave him. And she would never have abandoned Newton.

No. This had not been her decision.

Her face flashed in front of his eyes—just as she'd looked

last night lying naked on the floor, flushed and glistening beneath the moonlight—sweat lining her forehead like a halo of stars. So willing to give him her innocence ... so trusting. Yet she had never even touched a man.

To think of someone violating her forcefully, hurting her...

Julian's eyelids squeezed shut to subdue the rage rising again. He'd be no good to her if he exploded into a thousand pieces. He kneaded his temples to chase away the agonizing speculations.

"Perhaps she followed them of her own accord, to steal back the shoes." Judge Arlington's observation brought Julian back to the present. "She did admit to rather enjoying pilfering the costume from the tailor. The lady has a bit of a packrat in her. There's thievery in her blood, I believe."

Julian's eyes snapped open. "Thievery," he repeated with a whisper, something in the word calling to him. Before he could reason it out, Newton's little fingers curled inside his. The child's wide, black eyes locked his attention. He held up a pin-watch he'd found within the rubble then pointed to his shoes, tying it in some way to his sister.

"What did you find, mouse?" Kneeling, Julian took the watch and rubbed the boy's silky hair, trying to understand the reference to Nadia. The only thing this proved was that Willow had indeed been taken by force. She'd been wearing her watch this morning when he left. She must have fought back when they tried to take her and lost it in the struggle; she would never have taken it off intentionally.

Julian's jaw muscles tightened. *That's my fiery little acrobat. You just keep fighting until I find you...*

He froze then, noting the swatch of torn fabric twisted around the fastening. It was tulle in the glossy hue of an egg yolk. Willow had been wearing a linen men's shirt this morning ... a soft celery shade. In fact, this wasn't Willow's watch at all. It was more of a brooch than a pin. By turning it to the back to seek the familiar engraving of Willow's name, he only found one word: *Fontianna*.

He recognized it. But from where?

When Newton pointed to his shoes again, an epiphany hit Julian like a blinding burst of lightning. The stolen shoes ... the stolen gown. They were *Fontianna* creations. That was the name of the designer. The tailor had said as much ... along with his description of this very brooch. And this brooch belonged to Louisa ... *Medusa*. Julian remembered her glancing at it for the time that night while she preoccupied him so her accomplices could steal the phantom shoes. She wanted those shoes to go with the dress ... they needed the costume complete for it to be worth the fortune it once was.

Julian couldn't believe he had overlooked the obvious for so long. He slapped his forehead. "Of course!"

Newton bounced up and down, feeding off of Julian's excitement.

The judge plopped himself onto the lone chair left standing and mopped his face with his handkerchief. "Have you both gone mad?"

Julian patted Newton's shoulder then stood and held up the brooch watch. "Those ladies are no more prostitutes than I am a wet nurse. But I can see why their special talents appeal to our Italian friend ... so much so he would abduct the girls in their youth and continue to train them."

Still baffled, the judge sighed. "I've no inkling to what you refer."

"Remember how the article about the stolen shoes and dress mentioned that all of the locks and window panes were undisturbed at the museum? There were speculations that the shoes and dress walked out on their own, right past the night guards posted at each door."

The judge shrugged, still not following.

"I'm unsure how the thieves got out," Julian continued, "but I think I know how they got in. What if they visited during the day, when the museum had been opened to the public? What if they found a way to hide in the ceiling or in small spaces, waiting for the doors to close, for the lights to go out? Like bats bide in the rafters or mice in their dens, until darkness comes to cloak their scavenging."

Judge Arlington perked up. "Circus talents."

"Precisely. Louisa, when I met her in Sala's cabin yesterday ... she mentioned that I had something that belonged to Sala. Something far more personal and consequential than a pair of shoes."

The judge nodded, loosening his tie. "The ground plans."

Julian tucked in his shirt and headed over to the mess he'd made, searching for his most recent *Threshold*—the special edition highlighting the World's Fair. "What about those plans made them so consequential, other than the location he'd marked with pinholes?" Having found the magazine, Julian flipped through several pages until he landed on an article Newton had dog-eared days earlier after trying unsuccessfully to tell Julian something about it.

Julian held up the feature about a priceless set of silk screens being displayed in the Japanese Pavilion. The prints were rumored to come to life beneath the light of a full moon, the screens having been made from the hair of a Japanese majo—or witch.

"You've known all along, haven't you little mouse? You know who originally stole the latchet shoes, the entire *Fontianna* costume for that matter. I'm guessing they also stole that enchanted knife Sala used to cut meat the day we lunched together. And you know what they're planning to steal next. This is why they want to be at the rehearsal the night before opening. The grounds will be all but abandoned. Those girls aren't actresses or anything untoward, other than thieves. *Specialty* thieves."

Newton nodded, then pointed to his feet.

"Nadia was one, too?"

Newton nodded again, a cloud darkening his tiny face.

Relief slowed Julian's pounding heart. He no longer had to worry that Willow would be prostituted; but she was still in danger. Why would Sala want her now, after all this time? The only thing he could figure was that Louisa must've seen Willow's tattoo that night he exposed it on the promenade deck. She must have told Sala about the mark, and he instructed Willow be abducted, realizing it was the child that escaped him so many years ago. Perhaps he simply wanted his property back.

Fresh panic detonated the pulse in Julian's neck. After helping Newton into his coat and hat then putting on his own, he took the mouse's hand, grabbed their luggage, and started for the door. He glanced at the befuddled judge then at the mangled room. "If you could pay for the damages and loan me enough funding for an extra train fare ... I will see you get a twenty percent increase on your intake of the profits from the park this summer."

The judge struggled to stand, rolling from one hip to the other until his belly was centered between his knees to give him leverage. He grunted upon rising. "What of Willow's brother? You said he was meeting her in London."

"I'll send a missive to the hotel; apprise him of Willow's fate, of our destination. I saw some Hansom cabs waiting to carry passengers from the docks to the city. We'll hire one to take us to the depot."

The judge's forehead furrowed. He still had questions.

"I'll explain more on the way. We have to catch the next train. We've two days to get to the fair in time for that rehearsal. We'll go to the fairgrounds the moment we disembark."

The judge waved for Julian to exit the room in front of him.

Julian squeezed Newton's hand as they stepped into the corridor, guilt burrowing deep into the marrow of his bones. Willow would despise him for what he was about to do. But he didn't have a choice. She meant more to him than anything in this world. To rescue her, he would have to bargain with the one thing which could stop Sala in his tracks: his only son, resurrected from the dead.

Willow awoke to the rumble of a train shuddering through her legs and thighs. She wriggled on the cushioned bench beneath her, her buttocks stiff from being in the same position for too long. Even with her eyes open, blackness swallowed her. She blinked, and the satin tugged at her lashes where a blindfold grated against her soul like the knotted ropes chafing the tender skin of her wrists and ankles.

She stretched her interwoven fingers out on her lap, and began to recount the events which had landed her here. When she'd stepped out of the water closet in the stateroom, she found the judge and Newton gone. In their place was Louisa, accusing Willow of withholding Newton from his father. The woman said she had Newton in her cabin in the ladies' quarters, and threatened to go to Mr. Sala unless Willow accompanied her.

Willow had sensed foul play. She knew it was a one-way trip, and if she went, she might not see Julian again. He wouldn't know where she was ... might even assume she had left on her own so he couldn't send her back to London. As much as it pained her to think of him feeling hurt and betrayed, she couldn't bring herself to risk the chance that Louisa's threats were real. So she'd left with the woman without too much fuss, although she did manage to feign tripping and discreetly ripped off her captor's brooch. She'd tucked it in the desk drawer in the hopes Julian would find it and realize who had her.

When they'd stepped into Louisa's stateroom, two other women came at her with a gag and bound her in ropes. Forced into the dark depths of a trunk, she folded her body to the most comfortable position and sought out Julian's scent on her clothes. Immersed in him, she wove a placid net of memories ... tempering her impulse to panic. Her captors had warned her not to make a peep or Newton would be handed over to his father. Though she hadn't seen any sign of the little widget, she had no choice but to bide their rules. So she endured being dragged up a bumpy staircase and loaded onto a hackney stage in silence.

She became a child again in that trunk, a child equipped with the cruel wisdom of a woman. For this time, she no longer had a doll to hold, or a bag over her head, and her mind's eye could see with vivid clarity the horror awaiting her. Throughout the ride, her tattoo flitted along her back— a taunting reminder of what she had been marked to become.

But somehow, during that painful interim, she remembered the wandering song from her youth. She drew courage from the melody, from the words, determined not be powerless. She would not allow the beautiful intimacies she'd shared with Julian to be tainted by a forced tryst with a stranger ... or lose her innocence to some *bastardo stupratore*—for any man who used women so thoughtlessly was a rapist whether he paid or not. She was an aerialist, a contortionist, and a master of escape. She would find some way out of this, away from Sala, just as she had when she was a broken little girl whose parents were murdered before her eyes.

Now, freed from the trunk and seated inside this private couchette compartment, she was no longer hidden away. Just thinking upon her Italian nemesis—the giant faceless shadow she had yet to meet face to face—a nervous tremor rushed through her body, as if she were sliced open beneath the train instead of riding in it. As if her veins formed the rails on which the razor-like wheels ground and spun.

Sucking on her lower lip, she tugged at her bindings to find them even tighter than before she'd slept. She fought the urge to writhe upon the bench and demand her freedom. Earlier, when the girls first pulled her from the trunk, her rebellion had won her nothing but a blindfold and a dose of bitter tea that promptly cast her into a world of dreams—dark and disturbing. She'd awakened from time to time, yet never fully until this moment.

From the scent of breakfast seeping beneath the door, she surmised she'd missed an entire day and night. She hadn't eaten for hours, but her nerves squelched any hunger pangs. By tomorrow morning, the train would reach St. Louis and whatever depraved plans her captors had for her would be realized. Shoving aside her anxieties, Willow turned her senses to the cues around her, trying to assess who guarded her now.

She'd made mental notes of each of the four girls when they first captured her on the ship and when they'd taken her out of the trunk here in their car. She tied their names to their mannerisms and scents much like Julian's blind grandfather used to categorize the different parts of a watch by their shape and the metal which formed them. She decided, if he could build a watch in utter darkness, she could piece together a person's identity.

Louisa was the oldest and the leader, without question. Willow had immediately recognized her voice as the dominant woman outside the door of Julian's stateroom when she and Newton had first taken Nadia's shoes—the brazen Medusa Julian had almost kissed on the deck of the ship before Willow intervened. Louisa moved with such confidence that her skirt rustled harshly with each step as if it murmured aspersions against her. She radiated seduction when she spoke, a provocative cushion of words, and Willow imagined the woman could charm a famished snake not to strike at an overweight rat. Her scent brought to mind gardenia blossoms planted in the midst of a strawberry field.

Gwenaviere moved like a sparrow, nervous and flitting—which led Willow to deduce she was the thinnest one. Her shoes patted the floor like bared palms smacking flat stones. She cleared her throat constantly—an allergic affliction which inflamed and annoyed both Josephine and Louisa. Each time Gwenaviere was in proximity, a flourish of damp oak and molding moss put Willow in mind of a stroll through a rain-slogged forest.

Josephine was the voluptuousness one, judging by how her petticoats slapped her hips when she moved, sounding much like the flapping parapets high atop the poles within Julian's amusement park. The woman loved coffee, indicated by the drink's pungent scent upon her skin, so strong Willow wondered if she bathed in it. Her speech had a jolly slant, and she laughed most of anyone in the group, though to Willow she had been nothing but indifferent.

Now, Willow measured the traits of her present company. Her warden's breathing—rhythmic and whistling—along with the delicate scent of citrus and cinnamon, told Willow all she needed to know. It was the youngest of the girls, Katherine—the second woman Willow had heard speaking outside of Julian's stateroom door days ago.

Willow's heart gave a small leap. She'd been waiting for this opportunity, praying the others would leave them alone together. Katherine had a sweet nature, gentle and curious. She had stood back in the corner of Louisa's stateroom on the ship as the others bound Willow. Her frown grew longer with each knot her companions tied. It was also Katherine's soft voice Willow had heard demanding the men be careful when they were unloading Willow's trunk from the stage to place it on the train.

Willow supposed such compassion was considered a weakness by Louisa, judging by how she constantly reprimanded the girl. Willow was surprised the others would risk leaving her with Katherine unsupervised. She imagined they'd gone to eat and assumed their captive would sleep until they returned.

They had assumed wrong.

Willow forced a gasp, as if she'd just awakened. "Hello?" Another drag of air through her lips. "Is someone there ... please ... I'm afraid of the dark. Please ... I ... I need light."

"Shhh ... shhh. I'm here with you." The delicate swish of a hem crossed the floor toward her. No footsteps echoed the movements, validating Willow's theory. It was indeed Katherine, for she was the only one who liked to lounge about with her feet unshod—a preference that bore holes in her stockings and won scalding admonishments from Louisa. Of all the girls, Willow had the most in common with

Katherine, rendering her an easy read. She planned to use this to her full advantage.

"I suppose it shan't hurt to unveil you," Katherine soothed. "If you promise to behave."

"I do ... please..." Willow felt Katherine nudge the knot on the back of her head. Now all she'd need was to figure a way out of the ropes. "Please tell me," Willow said as the fabric started to loosen from her eyes. "Do they have Newton?"

Katherine paused, her hands stalled on the ties, keeping Willow's eyes covered. "They never had him. You are the one Louisa wanted all along. Ever since she saw the mark on your back."

"The mark that we all share?" Willow braved the question as the fabric slipped from her face.

"No, none of us have it." Katherine stepped sideways, the silk scarf dangling from her delicate fingers in a flash of deep purple.

Willow squinted against the daylight. That wasn't the answer she expected. "Then why does my having the tattoo matter?"

Katherine wound the silk scarf around her hand nervously. "Because another person we once knew had an identical one. And she's—"

"She's what?" Willow ignored the whispering sensation of her tattoo. Not receiving an answer, she changed her tactic. "What am I doing here? I demand to know what you all want of me."

Katherine turned her back, lifted a biscuit from a tray, and curled Willow's fingers around it. "We must avoid speaking of this ... or I'll have to give you more of that special tea." She bent down to tuck the scarf into a portmanteau. "Let us talk of simple things. Things that can't get us into trouble."

Willow bit back a groan. She could do this. She could be pleasant long enough to gain Katherine's trust. She lifted her bound hands as one, and considered taking a bite of the bread, but hesitated. She felt a bit like Alice in the rabbit hole after the experience with the tea earlier. Perhaps this bread would shrink her to bird size and they would lock her in a cage.

"You can eat it. It shan't harm you. See?" Louisa took a piece off the biscuit and ate it.

Willow touched it with her tongue then, savoring the buttery flavor. After sinking her teeth in for a bite, she absorbed her surroundings. Just as she remembered from her brief glimpse before they blindfolded her, the private compartment was luxurious. Crimson velvet encased the three bench style seats which could convert into triple-level bunk-beds with an iron ladder secured between the ceiling and floor to aid in climbing to the top beds. A matching red velvet runner ran the length of the aisle floor, leaving it bared on either side to reveal white tiles beneath. The walls shimmered white as well, reflecting the passing scenery from the long rectangular windows as if one watched a silent film.

An ache unfurled in Willow's chest as trees and shrubbery passed on either side. She wondered how many miles were between her and Julian now. She wondered how he'd ever find her. If only they could talk to one another mentally, as Nadia and Newton could.

Taking another bite, Willow searched for her one chance at freedom ... Nadia's shoebox. Her heart skipped a hopeful beat to find it right where she'd remembered, in the far corner, sticking out from beneath an extravagant gown and lace-up stomacher bejeweled and beaded to match the color and design of the shoes. She didn't have time to question the similarities; instead, she concentrated on her plan. If she could somehow get the shoes out of the box and on her feet, Nadia could see and tell Newton where she was. Since the little widget had learned to communicate with Julian, he could pass on the information. Perhaps Nadia would even be willing to help Willow escape.

"They call it Blood and Pudding."

Katherine's observation startled Willow from her machinations. "The food?" She glanced at her dark-haired warden who had taken up residence on the bench across from her and turned up her nose at the half-eaten biscuit she held, her stomach lurching.

"No. Not your food. The décor. It is of European inspiration." Katherine smiled, an effort which propelled her otherwise pretty features to the level of stunning. Her upper lip, much fuller than the lower one, nearly touched the tip of her nose. As if it tickled, she reached up and rubbed it, then moved her fingertip to tap the tiny bump of cartilage at the bridge of her nose which seemed to be the root of her whistling breath. "It is the theme of the train. I heard some of the passengers talking earlier. It has the nickname because of its color scheme. Only two shades are used, even on the outside. Though you missed seeing that." Her smile faded to an apologetic frown. "Scarlet and white. Blood and pudding. You see?"

Willow nodded, setting aside the remaining biscuit then repositioning her hands on her lap to alleviate the pinch of the ropes at her wrist. Allowing silence to wreath them, Willow considered her companion's lifestyle ... how tragic to be so young and already corrupted by immoral, insatiable men.

She couldn't help but wonder what the poor girl's first time with a man had been like. Certainly not a gift of awe and immaculate sensation, as it should be. She remembered Julian's selfless indulgence of her needs, his tenderness as he learned how to please her. This poor girl had probably never experienced gentle arms, or the warmth of passion in a touch motivated by love. And it was possible Willow would never again, herself. A sick roil tugged at her stomach— empathy for Katherine or terror for her own precarious situation, she couldn't be sure.

Katherine chewed her lower lip and picked up a large oak shadowbox. It slanted slightly in her grasp, and Willow regarded its contents: vivid butterflies displayed on a cork background. Katherine had the glass lid set aside already on the bench, and proceeded to ease a new specimen into place, piercing its lifeless thorax with a silver pin as she pouted in concentration.

Willow watched, intrigued by the girl's meticulous handling of the dead creature, as if she feared to hurt it. Julian's sister would be sickened to see this display of corpses. Emilia believed in letting the insects live so the wind held up their wings ... in letting foliage and flora be their shadowbox. This thought made Willow even more homesick, and she wrestled a wave of panic, worried she might never see the manor again.

"They are New Guinea Bird-Wing Butterflies." Katherine's long dark lashes fluttered up, showcasing sad eyes—glistening and gold, like autumn leaves wet with rain. "I know it seems a cruel sport." She frowned again. "But I simply adore butterflies. And as I'm never where I can admire them in their natural habitat ... we travel so much you see ... I must settle for this substitute, to enjoy their beauty at all." She slipped the glass lid back into place, setting the display aside. "I should one day like to have enough money saved up, so I might buy some land and have a … well … a butterfly zoo, or whatever they are called." With that, she smoothed her lilac-colored dressing gown, looking no older or any less innocent than Emilia herself.

Her confidence in any future surprised Willow. Even in such a demoralizing situation, chained to a man who made her perform illicit favors for money, she still had aspirations for an honorable life. She hadn't lost her spirit, her hope. Willow respected that. And liked Katherine all the more for it. "Conservatory," she offered, licking some crumbs from her lips.

Katherine looked up from running her fingers along the shadowbox's polished sides. "Pardon?"

"Butterfly conservatory. That is what they're called. My dear friend back home … her father is building her one."

Katherine beamed and clapped her hands together, leaning forward. "Oh, do tell! What a wonderful father!"

"He is."

"So … does she have any butterflies yet?"

Willow paused. It felt odd to be having this cordial conversation with her hands and feet tied. But she bit back her rising anxiety and attempted to play along. "Not yet. She's been corresponding with a duchess. A caterpillar breeder. She sends my friend information about what foliage appeals to what species of butterfly."

Katherine studied her collection. "Huh. Here I thought they all liked the same things. I've much to learn." She curled her legs up on the bench, thrusting her small feet out from beneath her lacy hem. The littlest toe on her right foot poked through a hole in her knitted wool stockings. "So each species likes to eat different flowers. They have their own unique tastes. Like people. I shall have to tell Carmelo this. We've always given him such a tuzzle over eating desserts for breakfast." She smiled again, but the dazzling result couldn't distract Willow from the shock of the words.

Katherine spoke fondly of Sala. How could she harbor anything but hatred for that monster? And the fact that he had anything in common with Willow, even something so trivial as breakfast preferences, made Willow's tongue too brittle for a response.

"Your friend," Katherine continued. "She must like the insects as much as me."

Willow refocused, remembering her objective. She had to make nice with this poor deluded girl, if she had any chance of getting free of the ropes. Her goal was to get those shoes out of the box and on her feet before any of the others returned.

"Yes," Willow said, "she does like them. So much so she's writing a novel about swallowtail butterflies. Oh, and a ghost." She awaited Katherine's response, thrilled when she saw excitement flush her companion's skin. Just the reaction Willow had hoped for.

"A ghost! How delightful! I've always been very intrigued by the ... *inexplicable*." Katherine's gaze slid to the corner of the room where Nadia's shoes waited, hidden and secure.

Willow took her cue. "You know, we had the shoes for a time. And I saw some things, experienced some things ... well, I don't wish you to think me daft."

Katherine stood. "No, no. Do tell ... oh please. I've not even been allowed a glimpse of them since—" She stopped herself short.

Shrugging off the unfinished statement, Willow squirmed on her bench. "I would rather *show* you than tell you. It is much more exciting that way. Just slip them on my feet for a moment. You won't believe your eyes."

Katherine's head tilted in consideration, her fear of retribution so palpable and binding Willow could almost picture rope burns on the girl's neck.

Rope. Willow suppressed a grin as she realized her own bindings could be the key to her freedom.

"What could happen?" she asked her warden. "I'm tied up. It isn't as if I can escape. I simply want to show you what I saw. I need someone else to experience it with me. Otherwise, how am I to know I'm *not* daft?"

Katherine gazed at Willow. The passing scenery danced in shadows across her ivory skin. Curiosity overcame her reservations, and Katherine strolled to the other corner of the room to get the box. She returned and crouched next to Willow's feet, working the lid off. Within moments, Willow's boots had been replaced by the latchet shoes, and Nadia appeared, hovering silent and cautious behind Katherine.

Hearing the water drip from Nadia's hem, Katherine spun on her heels and saw the puddle in the floor. "Oh!" She threw a glance over her shoulder at Willow then dragged a fingertip through the puddle, gasping when it disappeared like a mirage. "I smell something. Perfume." She held a finger to her nose and turned around to glance at Willow again. "I know this perfume ... she's truly here!"

Stunned, Willow locked gazes with the ghost floating behind the girl's head.

Footsteps sounded on the other side of the compartment door and the knob began to rattle.

"Oh!" Growing pale, Katherine began to try to take off the shoes. "You must tell no one we did this. If Louisa were to find out—"

"She would stick your head with a pin and hang you in the box alongside your butterflies." Louisa stood in the now-open doorway, shaking the glassy green beads which fringed her orchid day-dress like a swirl of glistening ivy. "Go have some breakfast, little fool. I'll deal with you later."

Willow's hope plummeted as Louisa slid the door shut behind Katherine's swift retreat.

Skirt rustling angrily, Louisa knelt beside Willow and tried to take off the shoes, grinding her fingernails into Willow's skin with the effort. Nadia hovered in one corner of the room, hands on her hips and mouth in a tight line. Willow smirked. Just as she'd hoped, Nadia held the shoes in place by sheer force of will. Since Newton wasn't here to remove them, no one would get them off now.

Glowering, Louisa sat upon the bench across from Willow. "I don't know how you're doing that, or what you are hoping to accomplish, but you've just cost your new friend her most valued possession." Her blue eyes pierced into Willow's as she raked the butterfly display to the floor. The glass shattered and sliced several wings and bodies, crumbling them.

Willow's stomach clenched in sympathy for poor Katherine.

Louisa leaned forward, elbows on knees, the sun gleaming off of her blonde hair in blinding flashes. "First, you lost my pin brooch and cost me the completion of my most prized possession." She indicated the expensive yellow gown that matched Nadia's shoes. "Now you've ruined Katherine's collection as well. You will compensate for our losses."

Willow snorted. "As if I have the means."

"Oh, you will. By doing this job for us, you will."

Willow spat at her.

Louisa wiped the spittle from her brow. "How charming. I suppose a lesson in etiquette will be our first order of business today."

Willow struggled against the ropes, tugging until they ground into her flesh. She only stopped when she felt warm wetness seep from the edges and saw driblets of blood. "I'll not sell my body for you. Not for anyone."

Louisa laughed and caught Willow's chin, holding her still. "Surely you don't believe those rumors. Do you truly think we'd lower ourselves to servicing men, the lesser of the sexes?"

"But—"

"You have been misled." She stroked Willow's bangs from her face. "Now, before you meet Carmelo for dinner tonight ... we need to get our story straight. And you should be preened and made presentable, *Nadia*."

The ghost stiffened at the mention of her name, appearing as confused as Willow felt.

"You can see her?" Willow asked Louisa, feeling the train jostle through her veins again.

"See who?" Louisa slanted a puzzled gaze around the room before settling her attention on Willow again.

"Nadia," Willow answered.

Louisa smiled, the curl of her lips as venomous as a nightshade opening its deadly blooms. "Of course I see her. She's sitting right in front of me. *You* are Nadia. Your father will be so pleased to know, after all these years, that you finally found your way back home."

TWENTY-ONE

Father ... *father*.

No. Her father had been murdered years ago. Killed by the beast she was being prepped to meet. "My father is dead."

Louisa's lips tightened. "No. The man who stole you from Carmelo and renamed you is dead."

Willow's world tilted. Her captor's words frayed into syllables as fine as gossamer threads, each one spinning around Willow's mind; she felt drained of her very existence ... snagged inside the filaments and captured within a web of anonymity.

"You were too young to remember," Louisa continued matter-of-factly, unconcerned as to how life-altering her confession was. "Carmelo loved his wife; so much so that when she left him for another man, taking their two-year-old daughter with her, he searched for them for three years; sent people to find them. Things went wrong; got out of control. Carmelo never intended for anyone to die. His motives were sincere ... he simply wanted his family back." She stood and ran a comb through Willow's tangles, pinching her scalp.

"Lies!" Tears searing her cheeks, Willow lifted her bound legs in one sharp motion, kicking Louisa's shin. "He abducted you, just as he did me! Why are you lying for him? Why do you all defend him so?"

Wincing, Louisa shoved Willow's ankles back into place with her foot then crammed the comb's metal prongs against Willow's windpipe. "He never abducted any of us. We were orphans. Gwenaviere, Josephine, and myself were adolescents living in Rotten Row. The sewer rats had a brighter future than us. And Katherine ... he found her in the Indies, about to be sold at a slave auction. If not for his intervention, she indeed would've been servicing men ...by the age of seven. He saved all of us, taught us unique talents which have amassed us great wealth. Why would we *not* defend him?"

Willow swallowed against the press of the comb's twines. "I don't believe you."

"Believe what you will. I cannot imagine how you and Newton found one another. Perhaps there is something to fate after all. You obviously don't want Carmelo to know that the boy is still alive. That, my sweet, is kidnapping. Whether you are the boy's half-sister or no."

Sister ...

Willow's logic struggled to stay afloat as she drowned in the memory of her talks with Nadia. Was it possible that the little widget was Willow's brother, her blood relative?

The comb dug deeper into Willow's throat, distracting from this one shimmering pin-light of beauty buried in the depths of Louisa's dark and ugly revelations.

"You are fortunate I have been aiding you all this time." Louisa's rant continued. "Did you truly think Carmelo hadn't seen the lad? He even saw you. I had to convince him he was seeing ghosts, play upon his grief. But I never thought he would believe it to the point he'd imagine his hair floating across the room."

"If you care so much for him"—Willow asked on a wisp of air—"why did you lie about his son?"

Louisa shrugged. "That is none of your concern. From this moment on, you shall do as I say. No questions. Or I *will* go to Carmelo about Newton's livelihood, and he will stop at nothing to get his son back, including killing the man who's helping you hide him. You choose. Will you sacrifice the child's freedom for your own? Sacrifice your lover's life?"

Willow gulped. The puncturing sensation at her windpipe eased away as Louisa dropped the comb to rummage through a trunk.

Desperately clinging to her identity, Willow sought out Nadia only to find her in the corner—a trace of astonishment dawning within her glowing gaze.

"*Willomena*?" Nadia asked the question on a frequency only Willow could hear. She had never told the ghost her full name. None of these girls knew it. Even Newton only knew her as Willow. So how did Nadia know the name of that little orphaned circus girl?

"Let us see." Louisa dug through the trunk's contents, pushing aside laces, chintz, crepes, and Damasks. "You appear to be closest to Katherine's size." She fished out an extraordinary gown of delicate silver lace overlaid on black crepe. A black braided trim accented the waistline and bodice seams. Ruffled French lace of the same black shade embellished the dipped neckline. "Here is our story. I met you on this train. You were dressed as an adolescent boy trying to steal from our car last evening while we were out at supper. I caught you, wrestled with you ... accidentally exposing the mark on your back. When I realized who you were, I took you under my wing. We got to know one another over the long hours of the night and I arranged for you to meet your father. I have already told him I've a surprise for him."

Willow listened, too stunned to respond. This wasn't true. It couldn't be. She remembered her father. Bedtime rhymes and dancing on his feet. The mosaics he used to help her craft out of the treasures she would find beneath the circus benches. The day he bought Tildey ... bargaining with a man who wanted the same doll by giving him free circus tickets. Then her most vivid memory: watching the life drain from his hazel eyes as a club dented the back of his head and toppled him to the ground—her gentle and steadfast hero as empty and used up as a crushed cigar. How could such tenderness, such self-sacrificing love, have been a lie?

"Concentrate, Nadia." Louisa squeezed Willow's chin, bringing her back to the present. "You must make Carmelo believe there is nothing in this world you want more than to get to know him. That you've been seeking him all your life." A smug quirk turned her lips. "You look so much like your mother, you shall have him eating from your hands from the moment he sees you. You are to ask him to teach you the family business because you wish to follow in your parents' footsteps." She laid the dress on the bench behind her and turned back to Willow with comb in hand. "That business would be *stealing*, my little vagabond. Something you already have an innate knack for. It is in your blood from both sides, simple as that."

The tugs on Willow's scalp from the comb barely registered this time, overshadowed by her inner turbulence. Could this be real? Had her mother been a thief, married to a thief? Could that be why Willow had a tendency to sweep her morals beneath the carpet?

In a daze, Willow stared across the compartment at Nadia's ghostly form. If this was all true, if Willow was *Nadia*, who was the dead girl drizzling water on the floor across from her?

Louisa coaxed Willow to stand so she could slip off Julian's shirt. When the sleeves stuck on Willow's bound wrists, Louisa took a piece of glass from the butterfly box and ripped the seams so the shirt fell away. Even in her vulnerable state, even with goosebumps lifted along her arms and torso from being exposed to the air, Willow didn't attempt to cover herself. She didn't even question her captor when she rolled up Julian's shirt with Uncle Owen's precious pin-watch still attached. Willow let Louisa continue her ministrations, numb and oblivious to anything but the ghost. She tamped the inner fires scalding her chest—saving the burning questions for Nadia. For this dead girl knew the answers to each and every one.

As if reading her thoughts, Nadia came to her side in a rush of cool air, the scent of perfume potent enough to sting Willow's tongue.

"Get rid of Louisa," the ghost said. "We must talk."

Louisa looked up from working Willow's legs free of her trousers, her nostrils quivering as if she smelled the perfume, too. Her face paled and she glanced at the shoes on Willow's feet. She shook her head, whispered something about erratic imaginings, and continued to rip the seams of the trousers until Willow stood with nothing on but her pantalets and the shoes.

Willow waited for Louisa to conceal her bared breasts in a strapless corset. Her small curves formed an hourglass as Louisa fastened the loops and posts of the busk in front then laced up the back. Satisfied with her modest covering, Willow cleared her throat. "There is a way to take off the shoes."

Louisa set aside the torn trousers. Her blonde lashes curved downward as she regarded Willow's feet.

"I know Sala fears them," Willow continued. "I suspect he is not even aware that they are in your possession. How are you to explain why I am wearing them? They certainly don't compliment the dress."

An amused smirk flitted across Louisa's face. "What do you suggest? I cut off your feet at the ankles?"

Willow ground her teeth to hold back a nasty retort. "You will need a spoon, and some lard. Try the dining compartment. Surely they have such articles in the kitchen car."

"I suppose I'm to grease up your skin and pry them off at the heel? The lard will ruin the fabric."

"What does it matter? The diamond latchets will be left untouched."

Louisa's gaze fell to the shards of glass on the floor. "Such a clever girl. Trying to get rid of me so you can cut away your ropes." She looked up, smiling. "Just like a thief, ever resourceful. You are going to fit in beautifully with our troupe." She bent down to pick up the glass. "But for now, 'tis best if I just remove temptation, aye?" After wrapping the glass inside the scarf that had earlier served as Willow's blindfold, she took Willow's hands and secured her wrist and ankle ropes to the rungs of the iron ladder. Willow was forced to stand between the bench seats with her arms over her head, unable to move in any direction.

Louisa gathered up the glass and strode to the door. "I shall return with a spoon and some lard. Should it fail to work, it can suffice as your lunch."

Then she was gone.

Willow jerked against the ladder, but it didn't budge. Her shoulder muscles stretched and burned at the awkward positioning. She met Nadia's bewildered gaze. "Could you get these ropes loose for me?"

"It shan't do us any good. Newton is in danger now. You have to do as Louisa says."

Ever since Willow had first met the ghost, something had always seemed familiar about her. Only now, having at last put all the pieces together, did she understand why. "You're Vadette."

Her childhood companion sighed and flopped onto a bench, wringing water from her sleeve cuffs. "Yes. I always wondered what became of you after you left the children's home."

The air in Willow's lungs grew heavy and cold. "Oh Lord. You took my place."

Vadette said nothing, every bit as good as a confirmation.

"Is Sala who Louisa says he is?"

This time, Vadette's wet lips framed an answer. "He is your father, by blood."

Even without the answer, Willow already knew it to be true. Why else would her abductors have been so careful with her? Why else was she sent a gift on each birthday at the orphanage? Her captor was intimately familiar with that date, for he had been present at her birth.

Newton's image drifted into her mental periphery. His dark, bottomless eyes ... his round face ... his black hair. Nothing registered as similar to the ghost's. Though in truth, he looked little like Willow, either. But there was one thing which had tied her to him from the very beginning. An intense connection, an instantaneous bond which had surprised her. Something had always drawn her to him. She thought it was their similar situations—the fact that they had both been orphans or perhaps even his inability to speak— that had roused the intense maternal instincts. But there was more to it. He was her brother. The sibling she'd always longed for. Her heart would have brimmed over with happiness if not for her present predicament.

"How did it happen?" Willow asked.

"You remember our caregivers? The farmer and his wife, their in-laws?"

Willow nodded numbly.

"They were terrified after they lost you that day in

Manchester. Not only for their lives, but for their funding. Sala had been paying them highly for keeping you. He wanted you safe and hidden away until he finished some thefts in the Orient. He was coming for you the very week of your escape, and upon your transfer into his hands, had promised the farmer enough sterling to make his family wealthy for the rest of their lives. Sala had not seen you since you were two. Being as you had trained me in acrobatics and taught me a fair share of Italian, I was the perfect doppelganger. They rinsed my hair with henna so it would be closer to the color of yours. They had a tattoo etched into my back to match Tildey's. They forced the other children to call me Nadia, and pawned me off as you. And I was happy to comply. Remember all of those presents you received for your birthdays and threw away unopened?"

Willow nodded, numb with shock.

"I dug them out of the rubbish bin each time and kept them as my own. They were splendid. Cashmere shawls, velvet mantelets with French lace, jeweled hairpins, silk petticoats and stockings in bright colors. I knew the man coming for you was wealthy beyond imagining; and I embraced the opportunity to better my station in life. I pretended for eleven years to be his *Nadia*."

Tears banked behind Willow's eyelids. "So you had a good life. You were loved."

"I was."

"But the way you spoke of him in steerage … as if you hate him. You said he would corrupt Newton. I thought perhaps he took your life."

Vadette scoffed. "No. He would never have harmed—" She turned her eyes to her dripping, bared feet. "I was angry with him. At times, I still am. You must admit, this lifestyle is not ideal for a child. It is why your mother left Sala all those years ago. And the man you thought was your father, he was a detective who had fallen in love with your mother while tracking Sala's thefts. He was the only one who had ever found any proof. But before he turned in the evidence, your mother went to him and asked him to run away with her instead. They had to go into hiding since you were with them. Your mother's choice won Sala his freedom, but cost him his family. And it nigh broke him. So, no. I do not hate him. I love him. Too much so."

Pressing her spine against the ladder to ease the pressure on her wrists and shoulders, Willow studied the ghost, trying to read her expression in spite of the white wall showing through her. "You said Newton is in danger. Yet you vow your love for Sala. It makes no sense..."

"Newton is not in danger from his father. It's ... a complicated tale." Nadia's image shuddered. Whether caused by the shadow of the passing trees which had thickened to a forest outside, or the dead girl's nerves, Willow couldn't be sure.

"You have to understand." Vadette's ghostly complexion appeared to pale, if that was possible for a ghost. "Sala thought from the beginning that I was his daughter. I knew from the first day we met that I was not. Over the years, as I spent time with him, saw his gentleness with me and the other girls ... saw his devotion and protectiveness ... his generosity and cunning. I-I grew into feelings for him beyond a daughter's love." She sniffed. "I knew it was wrong, but yet it wasn't." Her eyes met Willow's, a plea for understanding. "It truly wasn't. For he was a man, and I was a woman, and there was nothing standing between us but a lie. A lie, that even should I have confessed, Sala would never have been able to look beyond. It was hopeless."

Moisture gathered in the corners of Willow's eyes.

Vadette slumped on the bench. "I took comfort in Sala's pride. I was turning out to be a natural thief. He told me I was just like my mother. *Your* mother..." Vadette sniffled. "But Sala became overprotective after Newton's precarious birth. He started leaving me with Newton and a governess in London while he went away with the other girls to do the jobs. When Newton turned five, Sala gave up thieving completely to spend more time with us. But I had always wanted to perform one more job, and to perform it alone, to convince Sala that I was better than your mother. Better than the other girls. So when he took me and Newt to Spain for a holiday, I arranged the Fontianna theft—dress, shoes and all—behind Sala's back. I chose that particular prize because of the folklore tied to it. The illegitimate daughter that never truly belonged to the Spanish prince. I thought it fitting."

Vadette stood, leaving the velvet seat wet from her clothes. "I hid in the rafters when the museum closed. Then I slipped to the floor, found the display, put the costume on beneath my clothes, and hid again until morning when I joined a tour group and walked out the door wearing the stolen costume, including the shoes concealed beneath my long skirts. I kept it from Sala as we travelled back to London a day later. Within a week, news had leaked of the theft. One night, I donned the costume and walked into his room, prepared to show him my prize, to win his accolades." She buried her face in her hands. "He was in bed with Louisa. At some point, they had fallen in love. Sala tried to explain that it was all right because she was so much older than me and they weren't related." When Vadette looked up, the agony in her gaze was palpable. "He was embarrassed, scolded me like any father would his child. I screamed at him; told him that I wasn't his daughter either. I told him my true name, everything about the switch, everything about my feelings, then ran out to escape the unbearable shame."

Tears slipped down Willow's cheeks—a hot race to her jaw where they clung for an instant before falling to the floor. "You threw yourself from a bridge. You drowned, didn't you?"

"It was late at night ... and no one was about. I stripped out of the stolen dress and left it on the street as I ran. I kept the shoes on ... couldn't bear for Sala to reap the spoils of my hard work. But I wanted him to be left with a reminder. A reminder as incomplete and empty as I felt in that moment." She sobbed. "I would never have jumped had I known Newton was behind me ... had I felt him grab my petticoat. He had been so attached to me his whole life ... magnified by the blood transfusion. He had the *Fontianna* brooch in his hand. Had taken it from the dress. I suppose trying to return it to me."

The thought of Newton's tiny body plunging into gushing water from dizzying heights made Willow so cold her tongue stiffened like ice.

"Sala chased us," Vadette continued, looking at the scenery now. "But he is terrified of heights and can't swim. He saw us both fall and disappear into the dark waters. He cried out for help. Louisa came up behind him on the bridge in the same moment the heaviness of my petticoat dragged me beneath the churning currents. When I came to, I was hovering above Newton who was sitting on the river bank in dry clothes, holding the shoes in his hands. It was a full day after the event. Somehow, the shoes had drifted onto the banks—undamaged by the water. He looked up and saw me, and grabbed me in a hug. I realized I was dead when I could hear him forming words. He had been unable to speak his entire life. For me to hear him without his mouth even moving, I knew. Somehow my spirit had been entwined with the shoes, and my body remained at the bottom of the lake."

"You were your own murderer." Shock, pity and astonishment thawed Willow's tongue. "How did Newton survive?"

"Louisa. She dove in after us. It was too late for me, but she rescued him. So I cannot completely despise her for what she did thereafter. She'd never approved of Sala leaving the business. It was easy for her to convince him that she couldn't find his son in the blackness ... that she couldn't save him. That way, she could go back to the lifestyle she craved. She took the *Fontianna* brooch Newton held clamped to his chest in his unconsciousness. Took it as proof of his death, and so she could reunite it with the dress. She also sought the shoes, but didn't find them. Perhaps they were still upon my feet beneath the water, or perhaps somehow they hid from her purposely. I cannot say. She carried Newton to a church, leaving him on the doorstep. She pinned a note to his wet clothes, claiming his mother was a widow giving up her child for adoption, knowing that without him being able to write well or speak, he could never tell anyone otherwise. The next day Newton awoke on a hospital cot. He escaped his room and went back to the river to search for me. That's when he found the shoes on the banks ... when we were reunited. Once he told me what Louisa had done, I took care of him from then on."

"You've been chasing Sala for a year."

Vadette shook her head, as if angry with herself. "Not me. Newton. Even in death, I cannot be away from Carmelo. Newt won't let me."

"Yet you won't let Newton reunite with him."

Vadette's jaw clenched. She rubbed away a stream of water from her forehead. "I fear what Louisa would do were

Newton to come back into their lives. Now that she knows he's here, you will have to do as she says, or endanger him. Having the entire *Fontianna* costume united, all but the pin, has only made her greedier. She'll not let him ruin her way of life again. She is the one who's a threat to our brother."

Willow's hands had started to tingle, falling asleep from their unnatural pose. "Not anymore." A smirk started to curl her lips. "Newton is safe. Soon he'll be well on his way to our manor in London with my brother, Leander."

"You are mistaken." Vadette glanced toward a window and the scenery flashing by outside it. "Newton's on a train right behind us. He'll be in St. Louis come tomorrow. Your lover is planning to trade him for you."

"So, you're to hand the boy over?" Judge Arlington barked. "Just like that."

"Of course not. And would you shut your bonebox? He mightn't be able to speak, but his ears work just fine." Julian folded a napkin in his lap and glared at the judge before looking over his lenses at Newton's back turned to them. The sleeping mouse stirred beneath a blanket on a bench seat in their private first-class car.

"You know, you've been an unbearable ass ever since Miss Willow has gone missing." Judge Arlington took a bite of the thick, soft gingerbread Julian had brought back from the dining car for a pre-dinner snack, dribbling crumbs across his bulging belly. "I would think you'd be more beholden to the one who kept you out of the brig for destroying a stateroom on a passenger liner. If it weren't for that tiny lad, there, I would've already absolved our partnership."

Julian felt a pang of contrition. The judge was right. He

had been cross and difficult to everyone. Well, everyone other than Newton. Pushing up his spectacles, Julian plucked off a corner of bread and nibbled it—though he couldn't taste the sweetness or the spice. He'd hardly eaten anything over the past day and a half. His appetite suffered the same slow demise as his spirit. Life without Willow had no flavor, and he no longer hungered for it.

"I apologize," Julian managed in a half-hearted effort to salvage his business venture, though at this point he wasn't sure he even cared about that anymore. "I don't wish Newt to hear you and assume the wrong thing." Julian leaned toward the opposing bench where the judge sat. "I'm not going to *hand* him over to Sala," he whispered. "I would never endanger him in such a way."

Aside from the fact that Willow would never forgive him if he did, the little mouse had managed to gnaw his way into Julian's heart. He would rather take a knife to the gut than see harm come to the child.

"I'm planning to use the Italian's superstitious nature to make him think Newton is haunting him," Julian continued his explanation. "To cause confusion until I can rescue Willow. I'll leave St. Louis with the both of them."

Judge Arlington raked crumbs from his moustache. "I'm still not convinced this will work."

"What other option do I have?" Julian's gaze snagged on the trees breaking up the late afternoon sun where it streamed through the windows behind the judge's head. The train was passing through a forest. The thought of Willow riding through these very trees hours earlier—alone and frightened—made his chest ache. "We know that Sala and his troupe are planning to use the actress's dress rehearsal as a distraction somehow, so they can steal the silk screens."

"And how do you propose getting onto the grounds at

all?" the judge asked. "It's closed off to the public until Saturday. They're only allowing the performers and their chaperones to enter tomorrow night."

Julian sighed, catching a whiff of the steaming peppermint chocolate he'd brought for Newton. The kettle sat on a tray beside the judge's seat. "I've been talking to the other passengers. There is one troupe onboard made up solely of pantomimes. They perform a silent mummer's play in black gowns with large, bubble-like contraptions beneath their skirts. They wear thick makeup and wigs and have veils over their faces; it is their tradition never to speak until after the performance, even at rehearsals. I saw one of them in the dining car earlier when I retrieved our food. She's stout for a woman ... I could easily fit into her costume. Newton can hide underneath the skirt's hoop crinoline. I've seen clowns pull off the trick in circus acts. It will work for us."

Judge Arlington shoved his food aside, his elbow grazing the kettle and rattling its silver lid. "Please tell me you're not planning to steal her costume. To don a dress and take her place while she stands there naked?"

Julian wiped his mouth with his napkin. "She won't be standing. I aim to get her drunk. She won't miss the disguise if she's dozing off the sauce."

The judge scoffed. "Scandalous. How do you propose to get her alone to do that?"

Julian hardened his lips to a wry smile. "Why, I'm to charm her, of course."

"Right. The state you've been in of late, you couldn't charm feathers off a molting goose."

"Never underestimate the muscles and carriage of youth." Julian took another bite of gingerbread, relishing the flavor almost as much as flinging the judge's words from the night of the masquerade back his way.

Judge Arlington rolled his eyes. "So ... what of her chaperone?"

"He's ancient and sleeps even when he's walking."

"This is a fool's errand. You've lost all perspective."

"No. My perspective is crystal clear. There's no black and white obscuring it anymore. There is simply what must be done. I'm not to hurt the actress; just tuck her away for a bit. A stranger's discomfort, a borrowed costume. These are but minor inconveniences ... slashes of gray in the broad spectrum of it all."

"Justify it any way you like. It's still breaking the law. Go to the authorities, tell them of your suspicions."

Julian ground his teeth. "For all I know, Sala has coerced Willow in some way to help them with the theft. If I were to bring the bluecoats into this, Willow might very well be arrested with the rest of that troupe. She is the woman I *love*. I will do whatever it takes to protect her ... to get her back. Lawful or no. Would you not do the same for your wife, the mother of your children?"

"But you have no children."

Judge Arlington's comment sliced into Julian's dwindling hope, leaving such a deep gash he no longer cared about the amusement park, his blasted rides, or the funding it would take to maintain them.

He caught his investor by his lapels, dropping his gingerbread to the floor. "Every time I look into Willow's eyes, I can see my children inhabiting her. She is my past, present, and future. This plan will work. The question is ... can you, a judge, turn a blind eye? Dissolve our partnership if you feel so inclined. Just let me do what I must." He tightened his grip on the judge's clothes. "Either that, or I bind you in rope right now, and you can keep our drunken mime company."

TWENTY-TWO

Willow stood by the window in the private car. Dazed and disoriented, she watched the scenery pass in flashes of moonlit white and hazy shadows. Dusk had fallen hours ago. The scene was set.

She had been gilded and glazed like a painted lily. Louisa had given her a sponge bath so she even smelled like a flower. Louisa had also managed to take off the latchet shoes, thinking all along it was the spoon's contribution. Only Willow knew the truth. That Vadette had allowed them to slip free because she couldn't bear to be present when Sala met his daughter—the real Nadia.

After Louisa took off Willow's wrist binds, she helped her into the silver-laced dress and motioned to a bench. Willow sat as her captor worked the ankle ties free.

"So we have an accord," Louisa said. "You'll not try to escape. You will bide my plan, else Newton will be brought into the equation."

Willow rubbed her wrists and nodded. The press of her fingers stung where her earlier efforts at escape had left raw burns and bloodied chafing. Louisa quickly covered up the evidence of her struggle with long, black gloves.

Willow no longer feared for her brother's physical safety by way of Sala, but how could she allow the widget to be raised by the man who had killed her mother? Also, seeing the bitter flares behind Louisa's eyes upon each mention of Newton's name convinced Willow he was indeed in danger if he fell into Louisa's hands. The nasty woman had as much as said that she regretted saving him from drowning.

"If I help, you must uphold your end of the bargain." Willow paced to the window again while Louisa tidied the room. "I take Newton away with me. We'll never tell Sala of his existence."

Brushing splinters of glass beneath the rug, Louisa glanced up. "Agreed. If it is a success, I will not ask anything of you again. But if you fail, I will take Newton to Sala myself. And I will have the rest of my life to make the child rue the day he ever returned."

Willow chewed her inner cheek to keep from lunging into Louisa and pinning her to the floor. "I have your word you'll allow me to leave?"

"Lose yourself in the chaos after the theft. We only need you this once. Your acrobatic prowess far surpasses any of ours. None of us have the stomach or ability to dangle from two-hundred feet above ground. Only Nadia..." She stopped herself, as if trying to retrace her words. "Only your *impersonator* could have managed that feat."

Willow pressed her shoulders against the cold window pane, letting the chill douse the apprehension igniting like grassfires in her blood. The fairgrounds—spanning over one hundred and twenty acres—would be poorly lit tomorrow night to preserve energy for opening day and the following week of activities. Her duty during the theft would be to provide a distraction by disabling the Ferris wheel's motor in the darkness and climbing to the very top car. There she was to dangle haplessly and play a convincing damsel in distress to stir the other thespians into a frenzy of panic and attract the attention of the guards.

Due to the late hour of the rehearsal, the fair workers would be retired to their assigned sleeping quarters on the opposite side of the grounds a good one hundred acres away.

Security would be sparse; guards posted at each main entrance and exit, then two guards limited to each of the exhibitions containing priceless displays. The closest valuable exhibition to the Ferris wheel was in the Japanese Pavilion—the very reason they chose that particular ride.

To ease the jittery tingle in her legs, Willow went back to her seat. Louisa unfolded a small round table and wheeled it between Willow's seat and the one across from her.

"My pin-watch?" Willow asked her. "I need to wear it, for luck."

Louisa's chin stiffened. "You don't need luck. All you need is your pretty face and your skills. I will leave your precious watch at our getaway point once all of my companions are safe. It will be tucked within your lover's shirt. 'Tis more incentive to insure your distraction is successful."

Willow sucked on her lower lip. Louisa was in charge of arranging her troupe's escape. Since each exit would be guarded, they planned to leave the fair via the River Des Peres. After the theft, the troupe was to rendezvous at the point where the river flowed in from Forest Park. Louisa would be waiting within the covered watercourse on a row boat to carry them all into the forest and out of danger.

"I'll get your father." Louisa turned and slid the door closed behind her.

Spine stiff against the bench cushions, Willow took a long breath. From beneath a serving tray's lid, a fragrant steam rose, tangy with a hint of bacon and nutmeg. She had eaten enough sausage-meat cakes at the manor to know the scent, and normally would've welcomed the hearty meal. But even the promise of creamed turnip greens couldn't tease her appetite from its hiatus.

She still struggled to accept that Sala was her father. A part of her wondered what he would look like; how he would react upon seeing her. Another part of her wanted to run and never look back. If Newton had been on a ship on his way to London, she would have taken the latter option.

What was Julian thinking? How could he possibly believe throwing Newton to the wolves would solve this mess?

Shame sliced through her—sharp as a razor. He loved her. He'd admitted it in an endearing display of vulnerability— his tongue tangled and his forehead trailed with fretful wrinkles. He thought she was to be exploited as a prostitute; of course he would go to extremes to ransom her innocence, to draw her back into his arms where he could keep her safe.

So she shouldn't be angry with him.

Yet she was.

She smoothed her gloves, glancing at the floor where Louisa had missed a spattering of broken butterfly wings. The vivid blues and oranges shimmered beneath the lamplight, the colors reminiscent of the painted sketches Julian had hung upon the ceiling in the ship's stateroom. She'd seen the incredible rides he'd designed throughout this life. He was a master of computations and problem solving. She needed to have faith in him, that he'd actually thought this through and had a brilliant plan in mind.

But the not-knowing left her in a quandary.

As it stood, she would have to stop Julian before he managed to enact any trade. That would mean finding a way to search for him while trying to uphold her bargain with Louisa. Of course, everything was contingent on if Julian could get into the Fairgrounds with Newton to begin with.

She considered how far of a leap Julian's personality had taken since they'd first left London. He once was so reserved and premeditative. He would never have done anything so spontaneous or reckless in the past. But now?

This was her fault. All of it. She chose to board that ship

and bring his emotions to the surface. Now they ruled his every decision ... clouded his judgment.

Still, she could never regret stowing away. She would not have met Newton otherwise. What she regretted was her cowardice. If she had just been brave enough to go with Julian to steerage the morning they docked, no one would be in this situation now. She and Newton would be headed back to London on another ship, and she would have convinced Julian to go back with them. She might never have known Newton was her brother, but she would have raised him with the love of a guardian, nonetheless.

Her thoughts flitted back to her father. According to Vadette, Sala was a good man, aside from his shady vocation. He was a loving parent and a compassionate ward. Loyal and protective to those who depended upon him. To listen to Louisa, he was a victim—abandoned by his wife and tricked into thinking an orphan child was his.

Willow had the power to mend Sala's broken heart. Yet deep inside, her gutted spirit cried for vengeance, and she could think of no sweeter requite than to keep Newton from him forever. Rubbing her temples, she nudged the jeweled pins Louisa had secured in her hair.

No. She would never trust the man who gave her life, for he had taken away her mother's.

She heard the door slide open. Heart pounding, Willow forced a glance upward, her body nailed to the bench. There he stood—tall, broad, and refined. Ruggedly handsome with olive skin. Thick dark hair and eyebrows offset his eyes— black and bottomless like his son's. He could have been anyone in that moment, even a friend, as finely dressed as Julian and as unassuming as Newton. But he was a stranger ... and her father.

As much as she wanted to look elsewhere, she couldn't stop

staring, seeking some likeness other than their complexions, some indication that she was his. Then she saw it, the dimple in his chin. Deeper and more prominent than her own—more of a cleft actually—but an echo of hers, just the same. Sliding the door closed, he leaned against it. The vein in his right temple throbbed an erratic rhythm. He raked his left palm across his forehead, as if trying to scrub away the residue of a dream. His rings glistened on the movement, and Willow caught sight of the one worn upon his pinky, its stone shaped like a hummingbird. Her stomach twisted.

Minutes stretched long like the shadows outside. Steam from the food drifted between them, as cursory and elusive as the childhood that had been snatched away at his hand.

"I saw you on the ship," he broke the silence on a rich current of flawless Italian. His deep voice was soothing, like a distantly familiar lullaby. "I thought you were your mother's ghost. By God, you have her hair and eyes." Judging from his expression, the observation pained him.

She tamped the impulse to rush at him, to scratch his perfect face until he bled like her papa when the glass had gouged his skin. Instead, she loosened the accusation that curdled within her, setting it free on an answering purl of Italian. "And you have her blood upon your hands."

His face fell, a visible slide of features from hopeful to despondent. Tears raced down his sculpted cheekbones before dribbling from his jaw to land on his brocade jacket. He stumbled to the seat across from her, bumping the table between them and causing the silver to rattle. He slid onto the bench and captured her palm, his grip hot through her gloves, his eyes damp and pleading. The scent of cigars caught Willow by the windpipe and choked her.

"It was never my intention," he said. "The men I hired, they took things too far."

"Men you hired? I remember the tobacco on the murderer's clothes. You reek of it now."

His eyes grew round with shock. "I shared my cigars with them ... before they left to retrieve you. Oh, God. I'm so sorry for the reminder." His free hand scraped his face and mouth, as if trying to wipe away the smell. "I will never smoke them again."

Willow frowned. She liked him better as the monster without a face, couldn't bear for him to be human like this ... to pretend to care. "It doesn't matter if you bathe in rosewater and roll in lilies, you'll still bear the stench of guilt. You hated her for leaving you."

"No. I simply wanted you back. My darling child ... my tiny Nadia. So much like your mother. You must know I never wanted Mariette harmed. She was my hummingbird." He sniffed and glanced at their joined fingers.

Willow's hand stiffened in his. She studied the ring on his pinky, her tongue rigid and heavy. "I want you to tell me of her. Tell me everything."

Sala's fingers fidgeted. "She grew up in a circus. Her troupe came into my town on my nineteenth birthday, and I saw her on the posters. So brave, bold, and beautiful. I snuck into the big top one night to see her perform. I got dizzy just watching her in those heights. Only sixteen years old, yet she moved like a bird ... all feathers and glitter and grace." A dreamy smile slanted his lips. "I fell in love with her in that very moment. We met in the shadows outside the tent every night for a week. We were both from broken families; both seeking a place to belong. We found it in one another. She ran away with me."

"She was a thief, like you?"

"No. Not like me. It was in my blood. For Mariette, it was learned. But she was a natural study. With her physical talents and my gift for strategizing, we were unstoppable. We were careful what we stole—only taking treasures rumored to be cursed or haunted. People are more inclined to fall prey to superstitions when such items go missing. And we always performed the jobs without leaving any evidence that could be tied to a human, although we never tried to hide the theft by using counterfeits or replacements. We liked having attention drawn to our daring feats. When she gave birth to you, Mariette changed ... wanted stability. But that lifestyle was my opium; the rush of sensation when I escaped with prize in hand was indescribable. She left with another man, because he promised her and you the security I could not."

A warming empathy threatened to melt the edges of Willow's frozen heart. She had tasted that sensation, that rush of stealing. The allure of it terrified her. Setting her chin, she tugged her hand free. "So, you ensured he couldn't keep her safe, by chasing us."

"I chased you because you belonged with me. Both of you." His gaze lifted—a tortured appeal within the inky depths. "Even as a babe, you loved to fly." He touched the ring on his pinky. "You loved for the wind to ruffle your beautiful hair. When I would hold you up high, your arms would spread and you would laugh. You were born to soar, just like Mariette. *My hummingbird.* It is what I called her. And you remembered ... you remembered somehow. The men told me that you said it over and again that night."

Willow's insides cinched to an excruciating heaviness, as if someone had sewn all of her organs together and tightened the seams. "Did they also tell you that I watched Mama die? That her neck cracked when she hit the ground? Did they tell you of the sound, how it snapped the air like lightning ... how it torched my heart to ash?"

A garbled sob shook Sala's throat. "They both paid with their lives for what they did to her. I wept for her, Nadia. For so many years ..."

"And what of my papa? Did you mourn him? He was good to me. Kind and devoted. He didn't deserve to die."

Sala's jaw twitched as a lamp overhead flickered with the train's motion. "He stole your mother from me. For that he merited a flogging. But the moment he took you, he merited death." An agonized turn to his chin, Sala held out the hummingbird ring. "This was Mariette's wedding ring, discarded in our room when she left me. I put it on my finger. A vow to find you ... a vow that when I did, I would take you back and care for you—the one perfect product of our union." He slipped the ring onto Willow's finger over her glove.

In spite of the flood of emotions radiating from her finger to her heart, she scowled and tugged it off, returning it to him. "Subjecting a child's tender flesh to the needling fire of a tattoo; sending her to a rundown orphanage where no one knew or loved her. Is that your idea of caring, *Sala?*"

His dark-lashed gaze fell to the floor and snagged upon the crumbled butterfly wings. He leaned over to rake the fragile fragments onto his palm before sitting up again, forehead wrinkled. "I could not lose you a second time. I had to ensure you would be safe while I was away. Had to have some means to keep you separate from the other children, so there wouldn't be any mix-ups." His brows furrowed further as he rubbed the wing particles against his hand with a fingertip then shook them into the air. They drifted to the ground once more, leaving an imprint of their tinted dust on his skin. "I marked you to protect you." He held up his colorful palm, as if to underline his point.

"Ah. And your plan was flawless." Willow caught his wrist

and forced his palm to swipe a cloth napkin on the table, transferring the residue. "Did you ever consider how easy that mark would be to emulate?" She shoved his hand away.

Another sob caught in his throat. "Louisa said you wished to forgive me ... to know me."

I will never forgive you, voi bastardi. Willow bit back the response. For one, she couldn't say it aloud because a small part of her somewhere wanted to learn to forgive. To get past this obstacle that had always stood in the path of her future. According to Louisa, this was the part where Willow was supposed to fold to tears and mold Sala like putty in her hands so he would agree to her participation in the theft.

But she had no tears to give. She'd cried most of them alone throughout her childhood then shared the remainder with Julian on the ship. Her well had run dry. Without tears, forgiveness was out of reach. So far out of reach.

"I am here because of my blood," she retorted, stamping her Italian words with proficiency, as if she'd never traded them for English. "It drives me, just as it does you. I've glutted myself on petty thievery my entire life, never feeling fulfilled. I suspect I need the danger of something bigger—the thrill of possible capture—to appease me. Louisa informs me that you need an aerialist for this job, since you lost the one you had. I want to become part of the troupe."

Sala frowned and lifted his hand; he looked as if he might reach out to touch her hair, her face. Instead, he removed the lid from the tray of food and began to dish out round cakes of meat smothered in gravy. "No, the climb is too high."

Willow huffed. "*Too high*? Is that not the very reason you had me keep to my trapeze training in the orphan house? So I could steal for you one day ... take on capers such as this that no one else could manage?"

His face darkened to sternness. "No. I had you keep to

your aerial stunts because you loved to fly. It made you happy. This job. It is too big a risk. I am not willing to let you take it. Your mother wouldn't have wanted you to."

The joy in his voice when he spoke of Willow's love for flying, the worry upon his face at the thought of her in danger—his duel reactions were as conflicted as her own feelings. The train's shuddering movements rocked through her limbs but she kept her gaze steady on him, unwilling to fall prey to his counterfeit sentiments ... too little too late.

"Mama is dead. She has little say in my choices. And as you're the one who took her from me, you have no say at all." The words tasted of vinegar and bile. She noted the glimmer in her peripheral where the hummingbird ring he'd placed back on his pinky caught a snatch of light.

Wincing as if she'd struck him, he pushed a plate of steaming food toward her. "Where have you been all these years?"

"What bearing does that have on our present situation?"

"It is just ... I never expected you to be so calculating. So cold."

Willow took a fork in her hand and stirred the gravy, hardening her heart against a nauseating desire to act the part of a gentlelady for the sole purpose of experiencing his paternal pride. "Would you rather I be like you? A murderer, haunted by ghosts. A daring thief so fearful of heights he stood helpless as his son drowned ... a doting father who broke the heart of a girl he thought was his daughter and drove her to take her own life. You are tormented by thoughtless mistakes and choices. I'd much rather be calculating and detached if it means freedom from guilt."

Her cutting remarks had the desired effect. She watched his spirit crumble, affecting a deep slouch of his broad shoulders. Her own shoulders drooped in sympathy but she stiffened them back to a straight line. She couldn't allow remorse to seep in, or she'd lose all of the control she had gained.

"Louisa has told you far more than she should have," Sala mumbled.

"Why do you think it was Louisa? Perhaps it was one of your ghosts."

A sickened tinge tainted his complexion, mirroring the hue of the turnip greens on his plate. He nudged his food aside. Elbow propped on the table, he massaged his temple. "If I let you do this, will you stay with me? Give me time to make everything up to you?"

An eternity would not be long enough to make such losses up to me.

"Yes, I will stay." Willow choked out the lie then plunged a savory bite of meat cake into her mouth to quell the bitterness. For the first time since she'd boarded this blasted train, she had the upper hand. And in spite of the uncountable, incomprehensible emotions at war within her, her appetite had returned.

TWENTY-THREE

Diurnal assignments for Tuesday, April 29, 1904:
1. Detain the big-boned actress before the train reaches the
depot; 2. Accompany the mime troupe to the fairgrounds;
3. Send Newton to find Sala and lure him to me; 4. Rescue
Willomena.

A wrought iron fence ran along the middle of Forest Park, enclosing the fairgrounds. Weaving through the gates, Julian's carriage rolled across Skinker Road behind a caravan of actresses. Horse hooves clopped in procession, overplaying cricket songs and the trickling water from the Fountain Angel which greeted the group one by one as they came through.

His own troupe had split up, each taking a separate hackney cab from the depot as opposed to the hansoms the other two thespian troupes and their chaperones had shared. The open four-wheeled hackneys were often used for patrons with inordinate amounts of luggage, as the back seat was roomy—three times the size of a hansom. In the case of the mimes, they needed the extra space and open ceiling for the huge hoop-skirts that nearly bubbled up to their chins when they sat.

Julian propped his arms over the balloon-like contraption, feeling like he'd swallowed a parasol that sprouted open within him. He had worn trousers, a vest, and shirt beneath the disguise in hopes that once he and Newton found a place to hide, he could lose the cumbersome outer-trappings.

Exerting pressure on the skirt with his gloved palms, Julian assured the hem grazed the carriage floor, keeping Newton hidden within the tent-like space. By Newton's stillness, Julian surmised the mouse had fallen asleep. It gave him an unexpected comfort to feel the warm breath against his trousers and a tiny pair of arms wrapped around his shin and calf. A coil of protectiveness unwound within him. The boy had shown his adroitness, bobbing in and out of crowds on the ship's deck to pickpocket, and he knew the fairground map, inside and out. Otherwise, Julian would've forfeited this plan hours ago. He was relying on the hope that Newton was as adept at subterfuge as he seemed.

The chill, damp breeze picked up and the thick netted veil attached to Julian's velvet toque swayed and clung to his lashes. He thanked the stars that his brother wasn't here to witness this humility. Nick would never let him live down wearing a wig, theatrical white-face, and fancies, especially now that the driver was nursing an ill-born infatuation. The rat-nosed lout had been enamored ever since Julian first climbed into the cab.

In order to keep anyone from seeing Newton, Julian told the lad to hold on for dear life to Julian's waist beneath the steel-framed hoop upon the climb into the carriage—to keep Newton hidden beneath the billowing black skirts. When Julian had tried to scale the step, he'd almost fallen backward due to the misbalanced weight. The driver caught him from behind. He proceeded to push Julian into the rear passenger seat, but not without first giving his bust two firm squeezes.

The birdseed bosoms must have been convincing, for ever since the incident, the driver kept looking over his shoulder at Julian from the raised seat in front, a depraved glint in his eyes.

As if hearing Julian's thoughts, the driver swiveled and glanced down at him. "I know yer not to speak and all that ... but what say"—he leaned over the seat's edge to spit a wad of brownish saliva onto the passing road—"once yer practicing gets done, you meet me behind the boiler house there." He motioned to a big square building coming up on their right. "Don't need words to be hospitable with one another." The sickly sweet scent of tobacco drifted back to Julian as the man laughed.

Julian narrowed his eyes, tempted to pound the weasel into a greasy puddle. Instead, he drew out a black fan tucked within the sash at his waist and opened it in front of his veiled face. A grunt then a creaking sound announced that the driver turned back around in his seat.

Rainclouds had rolled in. They couldn't be seen, but the smell was unmistakable. Julian was glad the mimes had anticipated this weather. Their costumes were made of a water-proof wool fabric called Auquascuturn, and though heavy and rather warm, would protect his clothes and Newton underneath. St. Louis had been excessively wet over the past month, affecting the rivers and watercourses. In fact, the River Des Peres had been temporarily placed underground in a wooden channel for the fair, to allow people to walk over it where the river flooded parts of Forest Park.

The carriage lurched as they took a right turn on a skinny road between the boiler house and the Machinery Pavilion. From behind the fan, Julian scanned the scenery. The sounds and smells of animals grew more prominent on the breeze. Elephants, cattle, and even giraffes were to be exhibited on different parts of the grounds. The fifteen main fair attractions were separated into temporary 'palaces,' immensely intricate buildings made of a disposable fiber-based plaster.

Shadows draped the ornate domed columns. Spired towers pierced the night sky and blocked what little moonlight filtered through the clouds, leaving only the lamps from the carriages to light up the extraordinary sights Julian had once been so anxious to see and learn from. Now he didn't give a whit. All he wanted was to be on his way home with Willow and Newton safe in his arms.

He wondered how much longer it would be until they reached the Japanese Pavilion. Even in the dark, the vastness of the grounds was awe-inspiring. It would be impossible to take in an exposition of such size in less than a week. One would have to stay for an entire month. That's why many families, including Judge Arlington's, had rented rooms at the Inside Inn, which was said to have space enough for two thousand people.

Julian could've shared one of those rooms with Willow had he not been such an overbearing prude. She could've been awaiting opening day with him right at this moment, had he bought her a ticket from the very beginning instead of dropping her at the school. She never would have been in steerage, never would have found that blasted doll. He could have shared his stateroom, pretended they were husband and wife. Now he might never have the chance to make that fantasy a reality.

The edge of Julian's skirt lifted. Newton ventured a peek out over the cab's low hanging boot. Julian let the boy have his curiosity, being it on the side opposite to the driver. No doubt, Newton was disappointed by what he saw tonight, having heard the descriptions Julian read aloud from the magazine's articles. Enthusiastic writers wove scenes of the tantalizing scents: hot dogs, sauerkraut, gumbo; of the sights: a giant flight cage filled with birds, the Festive Hall and water Cascades illuminated with thousands of glimmering lights, stands brimming with vividly colored spun-sugar delights called fairy floss; and of the sounds: the buzz of foreign languages, music on every corner, and the hum of commerce in full swing.

Tonight, the only sound was a horse's occasional nicker, hushed voices in the hansom cabs speaking of the upcoming rehearsal, and the roll of thunder.

Newton jerked back into his hiding place just as lightning streaked the sky, illuminating the Ferris wheel looming ahead like the skeletal web of some mythological spider-god. Even from this short distance, the cars were enormous. Julian had read they were the size of a train's caboose, each one able to hold up to sixty passengers. He wished Willow could be sitting next to him to share the magnificent sight. He loved the way her eyes sparkled upon seeing one of his rides come to life. Thinking of how she would react to this masterpiece made the ache within his chest excruciating.

Some movement caught his attention, as if the giant wheel were rotating; but it was little more than a distorted shadow from behind his veil now that the sky had darkened again. It must have been a trick of light, as the ride would not be running tonight.

They reached the Japanese Pavilion and the carriage pulled up alongside the others in the caravan. Julian scrambled up in his awkward attire, managing to descend from the carriage before his rodent-faced suitor could put on the brakes and climb down himself. Newton did a tremendous job of hanging on for life beneath the hoop, then tottering along in sync with Julian as they took up walking.

Julian disregarded the driver's parting lewd comments and caught up with the mimes. The patter of rain eddied beneath the voices of the other troupes walking in front of them. Julian took up the rear. He moved slower than anyone, partly due to the boy hidden beneath his vast skirt, and also to facilitate his search for a hiding place in the Japanese Imperial Garden.

The actresses crossed a footbridge over a small, gurgling stream, their path lit by the soft amber glow of ground lanterns carved in stone. Julian found the perfect secluded spot just on the other side of some Bonsai trees. He ventured a step to the right behind some unknown foliage—aromatic as cherries—and felt his way along the lightless trail which led around a small hill. Little Newton scrambled next to his legs beneath the skirt. As soon as he was out of sight, Julian lifted his crinoline to allow the mouse an outlet.

With Newton's help, Julian peeled off the costume and the corseted birdseed bosoms. He drew off the veil and took a deep breath of rain-scented air while setting aside the bubbling cage and petticoat. Then he slid the blousy water proof shirt over Newton to help keep him dry. The hem came to just below the boy's knees.

After Julian pulled the waterproof basque and hoop-less skirt over himself again to protect his own clothes, he tried to glimpse the Ferris wheel once more. The drizzle had grown harder, almost biting on the exposed flesh of his nape beneath his wig, and it was difficult to see through the downpour. Julian coaxed Newton to slip with him under the dress hoop where it bubbled on the ground like a giant mushroom. The petticoat that stretched atop the crinoline was similar enough to a tent to provide sanctuary from the rain.

Crouched inside with the mouse, Julian listened as a million droplets pelted their sanctuary. His wig—weighted down with water—slipped sideways on his head. He cast it to the ground and rubbed the wetness from his neck. Thunder shook all around and lightning torched the darkness again.

Newton knelt beside him, his black eyes eerie, vapid holes in the bright flash. His curly hair stood up on his head—a mess of static from rubbing against the fabric on the walk over. Julian had used some of his white makeup to smear along the boy's face for a ghostly effect. He presented a haunting image; one that would surely disturb and beguile his father enough to follow him. Julian wrestled another bout of guilt for endangering him. "So, you know what to do then?"

In way of an answer, Newton pointed to his feet as lightning struck once more.

"Yes." Julian ruffled the boy's damp hair, magnifying his disheveled appearance to a ghoulish level. "Yes, we will search for Nadia later. But first, you bring Sala to me. He'll know where your sister is. Let him see you, but do not let him catch you. Keep looking behind to see that he's following. Then make your way back here."

Their surroundings grew darker. Julian felt the movements in the small space as Newton pointed to his shoes again. "The only way to get Nadia back is to bring your father to me. Understand?"

Julian cupped the boy's nape to feel him nod. Noticing the wetness on Newton's neck, Julian buttoned the waterproof shirt all the way to Newton's collarbone. "This will keep you warm and dry, alright?"

Newton nodded again.

Taken off guard by his own emotions, Julian tugged the child forward and gave him a hug. A pair of tiny arms closed around his shoulders. He blinked away a burning sensation from his eyes.

"Godspeed, little mouse." Julian nuzzled his warm forehead, tasting the basil-honey soap he'd washed the boy's face with last night. As soon as the rain let up, Julian sent

Newton down the trail, biting his tongue to the point of cutting just to keep from calling him back. Then Julian settled beneath the caged contraption to wait.

The soggy petticoat sagged and touched his head. Reaching beneath the skirt he wore, he nudged the *Fontianna* brooch within his trouser's pocket. It was his backup plan. If anything went wrong and he had to bargain for both Willow and Newton, he hoped Sala would be greedy enough to give them over in exchange for the brooch. He doubted the stolen costume would be worth anything to the man unless it were complete. Why else would Sala have gone to such measures to steal back the shoes despite his fear of them?

Julian's mind muddled. He hadn't slept any over the past two nights, tortured by images of Willow and where she was, what she was being exposed to. Now the dripping sounds mesmerized him, and he fought against the heavy pull of his eyelids, trying to stay awake.

A cacophony of nervous voices and screams startled him from nearly falling into a doze. Shoving the crinoline off, Julian leapt to his feet. He hesitated, unable to see anything for the hill. He wound the skirt's long train around his left arm and followed the muddy path around to get a glimpse of what caused the uproar.

He leapt behind a cluster of tall plants with fernlike leaves as a crowd of over thirty actresses in outrageous costumes—poke bonnets with tall feathers pinned in place over bouncing curls, absurdly buoyant bustles and long trains being dragged through the mud, leg-o'-mutton sleeves flapping on the breeze—shuffled across the footbridge. They were all jabbering, even the mimes, some to the point of hysteria as they headed in one universal direction: toward the Ferris wheel.

Lightning flashed to highlight the form of a woman in a pelisse coat and large brimmed hat hanging on the uppermost tension spokes of the wheel, as if she had slipped from the top car. She was at least a good two-hundred feet in the air; one arm flailed—waving for help. Her face couldn't be seen for the hat, but one thing Julian did see ... Nadia's shoes peeking out just beneath the coat's hem. The latchets sparkled with each erratic crackle of light across the angry sky.

Two guards rushed by Julian's leafy hiding place. He stepped out after they cleared the path and glanced numbly over his shoulder at the abandoned Observation Cottage they'd just exited.

A sharp breath pierced his chest upon a dire realization. That was Willow on the wheel—causing a distraction to lure all the guards and guests to the spectacle, so Sala's troupe could perform their theft. That was why Sala had wanted her, for her acrobatic abilities. Julian tried to contain his terror and rage. Under the best of circumstances, Willow could do this without batting an eye. But there was the weather to contend with. And the lightning...

The rain started up again, cold and pelting on his hair, neck, and the exposed sleeves of his shirt. Forgetting Sala and the theft about to take place at the Japanese Pavilion, Julian sprinted over the bridge, tripping twice on the tangled skirt before he finally tucked the skirt's hem into its waist to free his feet. At last, he plunged into the midst of the panicked crowd.

Looking up to the heights, he felt as if he'd swallowed a knife. The screams of the surrounding actresses escalated as a smaller form was revealed by lightning: A child had clambered up the spokes toward the trapped woman— progressing slowly but already past the axle's halfway point, at least one hundred-and-twenty feet high.

"*Newton* ..." Julian choked on the mumbled name.

The mouse's devotion for both Willow and Nadia's shoes was so strong he was battling his fear of heights just to get to them. Now both of the people Julian loved and had sworn to protect were in danger. Just behind the boy, another climber moved upward. The sky darkened again and Julian couldn't make out the third party's identity through the curtain of rain. But he'd seen enough.

He shouldered his way through the perfume-scented throng.

One of the mimes caught him by his sleeve and regarded his costume. "Wait there! That dress belongs to Iris!"

"And she'll bloody get it back when I'm done." Julian broke the woman's hold, then rushed up the boarding ramp where the guards held one of their cloaks over the engine case to protect it from the rain. They tinkered with the gears, both obviously befuddled.

"Know anything about these?" the skinny one asked Julian before looking up from poking at the mechanism. The man did a double take upon noticing Julian's effeminate attire and makeup.

Julian brushed him aside. "I do."

The stocky guard raised his lantern, giving Julian's appearance a disconcerted once over. "Um ... someone's tampered with it. We can't get those people down unless—"

Trying to steel his nerves, Julian forced himself to look away from Willow and Newton and squinted in the soft light provided by the lantern. He swept strands of dripping hair off his forehead and leaned over the motor. The end of a wrench stuck out from the interlocked gears—wedged in place. Whoever had arranged this knew what they were doing.

Before Julian could even assess the damage, he caught

movement in his peripheral. Several actresses wrestled to detain a scantily-clad woman in pantalets and a corset trying to climb onto the car closest to them. Her gown and stockings lay at her feet in a puddle of silver lace to facilitate her ascent. Julian couldn't see her face for all of the gaudy hats and plumes blocking his view.

"I must get up there!" she screamed. "This is my fault!"

Recognizing the voice, Julian caught the man's wrist beside him and directed the light toward the parting actresses. A guard lurched forward to grab the half-naked woman's bared elbow. "Oh no, there's already enough people in dire straits. You stay put."

Julian balked at the sight of her rain-streaked face—beautiful yet frenzied like some wild, caged animal.

"Willomena!" Relief hedged within him. It wasn't her at the top of the Ferris wheel. He glanced up into the murky sky, baffled now as to who the trapped woman was. "Willow, what in hell is going on?"

TWENTY-FOUR

"Julian?" Willow gasped, honing in on the familiar baritone. She craned her neck to see over the guard wrenching her arm. "Julian!"

She'd finally found him. But too late. It had all went to rot so quickly. "Step off, you codswallop!" She tugged her elbow free from the guard and flung herself into Julian's embrace as he wove his way through the crowd, burying her face in his clothes. His wet shirt sleeves pleated in her fists. "Why are you here?"

The crowd around them stared, their petty eavesdropping taking precedence over the life and death situation unraveling overhead.

"Where else would I be?" His fingers wove into her hair, holding her against his heartbeat, his touch both rough and tender in the same stroke. "Lord, Willow ... I thought that was you up there! We have to get Newton—" His voice broke.

Willow sobbed then pushed away. "You should never have brought him here!" She wiped the blur of rain and tears from her eyes, noticing Julian's appearance for the first time. "Is - is that makeup on your face?"

His expression cleared, as if he'd been in a daze and had water splashed in his face. Embarrassment reddened his ears as he smoothed the skirt at his waist. His gaze met hers, then their eyes simultaneously lifted again to the dangers overhead. "I never meant for this to happen. Any of it ..."

Willow had forgotten she'd taken off her gown to ease her climb until Julian slipped off his basque and covered her drenched corset, lacing the ties in place over her breasts. Next, he took off his trousers from beneath his skirt and helped her into them, one foot at a time, cinching the waist with a long scarf offered by one of the actresses. His body heat transferred with the clothes and warmed her.

"I was just trying to get to you," he said, an apology grating his voice as he knelt to roll the trousers' hems into tight cuffs at Willow's ankles while she tightened the scarf at her waist. "It was the only way I knew to do it. I haven't eaten or slept for days. I've not been thinking straight. I even lost the judge's investment to come here." Upon standing, his expression was bewildered; his hair hung in dripping waves around his shoulders making him favor a repentant puppy. The dark circles under his lower lashes went deeper than the makeup painted there, picking up the color of the black skirt around his waist and exacerbating his forlorn image.

In spite of a surge of tenderness, Willow's temper flared. She pressed toward the Ferris Wheel, intent on finding a way past the guards to Newton's tiny silhouette. "It was too risky, Julian. If anything happens to him—"

A collective gasp from the actresses joined her own as Newton's small, dark shadow clung by one hand to the upper middle spokes, only a few dozen feet from Vadette's shoes.

Willow's breath coiled like a frightened snake in her lungs, wrapping her screams within it.

"Newton!" Sala yelled from just beneath his son, managing to slide across his spoke to grapple the child around the waist and ease him back into place.

"The third climber is Sala?" Julian delivered the revelation in awed disbelief.

Willow couldn't answer. Newton had broken away from Sala. Swinging to the next spoke like a practiced monkey, her brother started toward Vadette's shoes again. Sala followed, robotic and cautious, crying out a prayer in Italian.

"Newton, stop!" Willow screamed—triggering a soul-deep chill that rattled her bones. Sprinkles of rain coated her lips and face. "Stay where you are! I'll get the shoes and help you down!" Her brother paused. She thrust against the guard closest to her and managed to clasp the car's cold metal frame and lift herself. The metal chilled her bared feet as she started her climb up the spokes.

The guard tried to force her to the ground but Julian shoved him aside.

"Willow..."

She licked raindrops from her quivering lips, unwilling to lose this family the same way she'd lost the one of her childhood. "I have to save them. That's my father and brother up there."

"Your ... your *what*?" Julian's face grew pale as lighting cracked the sky.

The bolt came close to striking the giant metal wheel and terror burbled up within Willow's chest. Julian was going to try to stop her. She could feel it. "I have to get to them before the storm does. This is my chance ... my one chance to right the mistakes of my past."

Julian now knew how she'd always felt responsible for her parents' deaths. But what he didn't know is how responsible she felt for Newton's present situation, for *she* had snuck Vadette's shoes into the fair. *She* had tied the pelisse overcoat and hat in place on the spokes along with the *Fontianna* shoes and dress so the ghostly girl could animate the costume and wave her arm to attract attention once Willow raised the wheel into position. All so Willow could be free to find Newton. She had never, in her wildest imaginings, expected the widget to find Vadette first. Or for Sala to abandon his theft and fear of heights in an effort to save his resurrected son.

Both guards came up behind Julian wielding pistols now. "No you don't, little miss. You're staying here. Bad enough if we have three corpses to explain to the boss."

Willow tightened her grip on the car. Though her teeth chattered from the wet chill of her underclothes and her knees grew weak at the sight of the pistols, she stayed on her perch.

Julian stared up at her; protectiveness, confusion, and sympathy battled within in the depths of his gaze. "Let me go with you."

Willow shook her head. "You'll make no headway in that skirt."

His face fell.

"I go alone," she murmured. "Don't worry. I was born to do this."

Lips tightening, Julian turned to the guards, holding up his hands in submission. "Let her go, damnit. She's an aerialist. The engine can't be fixed quickly enough ... the chains have come loose due to the wrench in the gears. They weigh a ton. We are the only three able-bodied men here."

Both men swept their gazes across Julian's effeminate attire and makeup.

"Able-bodied, you say?" The skinny one asked.

Growling, Julian gestured to the shivering and hunched group of elderly chaperones accompanying the troupes. "More so than them. It would take at least seven stalwart men to heft those chains into place."

The guards conferred in whispers. The one with the lantern turned and hung it on a post, then aimed his pistol at Julian. "We will send someone to gather horses from the carriages. They can pull the chains into place."

Willow's stomach clenched as two chaperones volunteered and slipped from the crowd. She glared upward at Sala and Newton, blinking back tears.

Julian's hands fisted. "Time is of the essence," he ground out between gritted teeth. Willow climbed another two spokes, taking advantage of the distraction. "It will take them a half hour to get the horses unhitched and brought here. Then another fifteen minutes to harness them to the chains. Not to mention it takes a full ten minutes for a wheel of that size to make a revolution once the motor is fixed. The lightning is getting worse. Those people are in immediate danger. She"— he glanced at Willow over his shoulder and to his credit, didn't even bat an eye when he saw her marked progress—"is their only hope."

The stocky guard stepped forward. "No. It's our job at stake." He jerked his wrist, gesturing with the pistol's barrel for Willow to get down.

Julian's shoulders tensed, the wet fabric of his shirt showcasing every agitated ripple of muscle. "And here I thought your *job* was guarding the priceless silk screens that have now been left completely unattended."

As if just remembering their post, the two men lowered their pistols. Their mouths gaped. They turned tail and sprinted off the ramp toward the Japanese exhibit. The actresses parted for them and the two men vanished into the cove of foliage surrounding the Observation Tower.

Julian turned back to Willow. "Go on." The worried creases on his forehead filled with rain and reflected the lantern light. Her heart swelled with gratitude.

She glanced to the top of the wheel, dreading the utter blackness of the heights, only able to make out her father and brother in dangerous flashes of lightning. What she wouldn't give for the gentle, consistent night skies of her childhood spent atop the manor's starlit tower. Judging by their stiff silhouettes, both Sala and Newton were frozen in place on the bars. Neither one would make it down without her—not with their shared fear of heights. For the first time, she felt a pang of fear for herself. "I-I don't have my pin-watch. I don't have my luck."

A rustle of skirts stirred beneath her as Julian climbed enough spokes to ease his hand into the right pocket of her trousers, fingers scraping across her thigh. Their eyes met, and she thought upon their stolen moments on the ship, hoping they wouldn't be the final expressions of their love.

"Take this." He offered what he'd dragged from her pocket: a brooch with a watch's face.

She recognized it as Louisa's. Turning it over to the back, she read the etching: *Fontianna*. It was the final piece to the stolen outfit—the one she ripped off of Louisa.

"Perhaps," Julian said, "since it's meant to be with the dress and shoes, it will guide you safely there."

With a slight nod, Willow pinned it in place above her left breast.

"I love you," Julian said—voice husky but no hesitation. He caught her lowered hand and kissed it. "I owe you two more recitations today, and three from yesterday. Come back for them."

She sniffled and nodded.

Red rimmed his eyes, irritated by either the rain or an effort to contain his emotions. He reluctantly released her hand before easing down the spokes.

Taking a deep breath, Willow looked upward, squinting as the rain pelted her face. Then she started her ascent.

She used the flexible cross-spokes of the Ferris wheel like the rungs of a rope ladder. Years of mastering heights while holding balance came into play, her honed abilities as natural as her lungs' metered respirations. The muscles in her arms and legs contracted and expanded without strain, a remembered rhythm from a lifetime ago.

Making it past the midpoint's axle, she heard the dead silence below as her audience stalled their breaths in morbid fascination. Their hushed awe carried her back to her childhood, when Mama would glide through the firmament of the big top—a glittering, glorious bird skimming the sky of an elliptical world—above a crowd of spectators as silent and un-breathing as leafless trees.

Mama had always had a net. Until the one time she didn't ...

Surrounded by the darkness, bleak fear crept up from Willow's hummingbird tattoo, a flutter of emotion that burned on its journey to her chest. She felt tiny again—no more than a child—climbing head first into a dark bag where terror and confusion waited to shatter her identity.

But she wasn't a child. She knew who she was, now more than ever before. So, casting the sensation aside, she honed in on the prize: her family—still living, here and now.

The rain started to soften to mist and she could better make out their silhouettes. Newton was perched close to the shoes, and Sala perched several spokes beneath, stalled in his effort to get to his son. His fear of heights had taken over. How Newton had kept going despite his own could be attributed to nothing more than his sheer obsession to get to Vadette ... his Nadia. He had no idea that his true sister was below him, trying to make her way up in time. Trying to save his life, just as Vadette once had. Willow prayed for the chance to tell him one day.

She held one hand in place while swiping away the droplets from her lashes with the back of the other, then resumed her climb. Lightning streaked the sky, sending shivers through her spine.

A cold, wet glaze coated the spokes and caused her hands and bared feet to slip in intervals. Each time she grappled to steady herself, the steel cords sliced her skin—already tenderized by over-exposure to the wetness. She had a passing wish that she would've had time to wrap her palms with something. Her body continued its advance, gripping one line and then another as if she were a piano-playing automaton moving robotic fingers to the flowing pattern of a pre-programmed melody.

She could no longer hear the silence below. For the higher she climbed, the louder the wind howled in her ears and whipped at the ties on the basque covering her chest. The cloth smelled of Julian, and it grounded her ... gave her courage to continue. He was waiting at the bottom. Were she to fall, he would never forgive himself for letting her go.

Another gust of wind shook the spokes, this time hard enough that Willow had to grip with the entire length of her bared arms, the cord eating into the tender skin underneath them. Upon her first opportunity, she resumed. Once she came within reach of Sala, she tapped his ankle. Though she couldn't see his face with clarity, she could sense the terror radiating off of him.

"I knew ... you would ... rescue him ..."

She barely heard his raspy Italian over the gusts. Clasping tight to the steel cords, she forced herself up several more spokes, pausing to balance beside him against the wind's resistance.

"I never dreamed you would have the courage to try," came her answer.

A roll of thunder and a snap of blinding light sent a buzzing hum through the Ferris wheel's frame. Sala's profile intensified, and only now, on the same level as him, could Willow see the whiteness of his knuckles.

"I ... I was all right, until the lights."

"Just hold on," she said.

Another flash shattered the sky, and she noticed his gaze

had locked on the menacing depths below them.

"Dare not look down," she said. "That's a mistake. Do you hear me?"

He tensed his muscles—she felt the reverberations in the spoke they shared. She slid her hand along the length of the steel so the edge of her palm touched his. "Just hold on and look up. I'll see to Newton. Do not move, whatever happens. Once he's safe, I'll return for you."

Sala still looked down, rigid and un-answering.

"*Father*. Look at me." The sky blinked again as he met her gaze. "I *will* come back for you."

"Thank you—" A sob choked his words.

"Just focus on the *Fontianna* costume above. Look only at it."

He lifted his pinky enough to curl it around hers on their spoke. Her mother's hummingbird ring pressed into her skin. "I knew you were like her. I knew you were forgiving and wise ... just like Mariette."

Willow saw his hand, marred by the blood oozing from gashes where the spokes had sliced into them. Feeling warmth seep from her own mutilated palms, she mused that they would have matching scars one day. Then her attention caught on the ring again, and she realized they already did.

A garbled whimper came from overhead, nailing all of her focus on Newton's silhouette. Willow pulled her hand from Sala's to recommence her climb, but paused two spokes up as she noticed the outline of Newton's movements—black against a flashing sky. He had one arm looped around a cross-spoke to hold on; with his free hand, he yanked one of Vadette's shoes loose from the rope cinched through the latchet. He proceeded to lift it, then slid it in place in midair. Willow sucked in a sharp breath of rain and wind.

He was putting the shoe on Nadia's ghostly foot. It

levitated there, as if hanging by invisible threads. Newton did the same with the second shoe. Willow gasped and Sala sobbed as Vadette's glowing, ghostly form materialized— visible and hovering in place inches away from the spokes, at last wearing her full *Fontianna* costume. All but the brooch.

"My God, Vadette!" Sala shouted—his voice teetering between disbelief and the razor's edge of pain.

The startled screams of their audience rose above the wind and thunder. Willow knew they couldn't make out a clear image in the darkness from such a distance, but no doubt they saw the glow. Still ... her mind raced on an epiphany that overplayed any other concerns. Nadia had told Willow that only Newton could free her from her earthly binds. It must be because only he could touch her to return the shoes to her feet and the brooch to the dress, when he deemed the time appropriate. Perhaps, once in full costume again, her spirit could be released. In which case, Willow had the final key to unlock her childhood friend's prison.

Touching the brooch to assure it still hung in place, Willow climbed the rest of the way until she shared Newton's spoke. She lifted an arm around him. After securing her hold, she followed with her leg, anchoring him between the steel cords and her. Taking a deep breath, she buried her nose in his damp, dust-scented hair, cherishing the feel of his warmth snuggled against her. "Little widget. Do not ever scare me like that again. Never."

He tilted his head back and pressed his cheek against her sternum so their gazes could meet. Utilizing Vadette's otherworldly glow, Willow could see recognition in his eyes. A bone deep recognition. *He knew.*

"Nadia told you." Through the wetness of her lashes, coated in rain and tears, Willow watched her brother's heart-shaped mouth tremble. A lump fisted in her throat and she resituated her grip on the slippery upper spoke and tightened the bend of her legs around the lower, holding him secure. "Then you know that we're family and I love you. You will never be alone again. So it's time to let Nadia rest. She's tired."

Vadette looked down from them to Sala, her expression shifting between anger and anticipation. The wind whipped her ghostly hair in knots beneath the hat tied to the spokes above her head. Newton sniffled and nodded against Willow, the movement causing the brooch on her basque to pendulate. The trinket caught his attention and he wiggled, trying to reach for it. Willow's heart ached at his valiant effort, knowing how hard this goodbye was going to be. "Wait, let me get it for you; I understand what you need to do."

She borrowed Newton's earlier tactic, looping her elbow around a cross-spoke so she could unfasten the brooch without compromising her hold on her brother. She handed off the watch to Newton and together, her body acting as a cradle to his, they inched closer to Vadette's hovering form so he could pin it in place. The ghost made no move toward them. Instead, she drifted further out of reach, shoes and clothes no longer touching the spokes. She wasn't yet ready to leave. Her ethereal gaze met Willow's for an instant before she turned it downward, again meeting Sala's. He was weeping so hard his body shuddered with the strain of his sobs.

"Sweet Vadette," he wailed. "Forgive me! I never knew ... how could I have? My precious, precious child. I never meant to break your heart."

It seemed to happen in slow motion: Sala lifting his hand to move up to the next spoke in an effort to get closer; his rain-slicked fingers failing to grasp the steel just as a gale of wind ripped through the wheel's framework.

"Father!" Willow screeched.

It was too late. Sala lost balance and fell backward, his face frozen in a silent scream of horror as he dropped to the depths below.

TWENTY-FIVE

Willow's cries burst in her chest as she held Newton close to shield him from witnessing the tragedy.

In a blur of soft light, Vadette skimmed from the heights, swooping in beneath Sala to act as a cushion moments before he hit the ground hundreds of feet below.

Shaking and numb, Willow descended the Ferris wheel with Newton holding tight to her. She barely felt the rain pelting them. Barely noticed that the lightning and thunder grew further apart and farther away. She was a dreamer trapped within a nightmare, only able to focus on the faint ghostly glimmer that moved around her fallen father and lit up Julian's form where he knelt beside Sala, trying to rouse him.

Finally, Willow's feet touched the car where she'd first started her ascent. Julian hurried over to help her down. She let Newton slip safely to the ground beside her. Her brother still clasped the brooch in his plump little hand. He took one look at Sala—lying in a lifeless heap—and his arms wrapped around Willow's waist, his face buried in her abdomen to muffle his sobs.

She bit her tongue to hold back her own shuddering sobs.

Julian embraced both of them. He kissed Willow's forehead. "I'm so sorry."

Willow leaned into his warmth, but only for a moment. She drew back to find their entire audience gone, short of Josephine, Katherine, and Gwenaviere—who knelt at Sala's side, staring up at Vadette with mouths agape. Willow looked questioningly at Julian.

"The girls came seeking Sala when he didn't show up at the Japanese exhibit," he explained, stroking Newton's hair. "When I told them the situation, they cleared the audience, claimed no one was truly in danger, it was all part of their rehearsal. That the Ferris wheel incident had been their elaborate plan to win the contest the next day with the most shocking debut. But now that they had damaged the fair's equipment, they were being forced to forfeit the contest. The other troupes—realizing they'd lost almost an entire night's worth of practice on the farce—grumbled and left before Sala fell."

"The theft?" Willow asked.

"Never took place."

Willow had a passing thought of Louisa's part in the plan. She was the one holding the rowboat docked at their rendezvous point in the water tunnel. Now she would have a long wait ahead of her.

Willow met Vadette's gaze. The ghost hovered over Sala's awkwardly posed body, tears streaking her phantom cheeks. "Newton wanted those he loved to find peace." Willow watched everyone's reaction to the ghost's voice. Just as she could now be seen by all, she could also be heard. "'Tis why Newton kept me here. He refused to let me leave until I had forgiven his father. So he revealed me tonight with us both trapped in place, unable to avoid one another."

Katherine, Gwenaviere, and Josephine moved aside to stand, silent and wary as Vadette knelt down beside Sala. Her shimmering hand caressed his cheek, leaving behind a residue of glittering water droplets that Willow suspected would vanish before she could blink.

"I understand," Vadette whispered to Sala. "I only hope you can. All is forgiven. You were a wonderful father to me.

Never doubt that. No more regrets, for either of us."

Sala's lashes fluttered as though trying to open.

Seeing the movement, Willow gasped. She came forward with Newton still leeched to her side. Julian picked up her brother so she could take her place next to Sala. On her knees, she clasped his cold, bloody hand and found a pulse, though very weak. She leaned in, stroking his dark hair off his forehead, unable to find any wounds. There was no blood on the back of his head or on the ground, only puddles of water and mud. By the position he'd landed in, it was obvious he had broken his back.

If not for Vadette's intervention, he'd most surely have cracked his skull open. He would be dead instead of clinging to life.

Willow cast a grateful glance to Vadette and the ghost tilted her head in acknowledgement. Then her attention shifted to Sala's mumbling troupe. Her translucent image shuddered. "See that he retires from the profession forever, like he tried to when Newton was born. Make Louisa understand."

The three girls nodded, their bewildered faces a pale green in Vadette's preternatural glow. The ghost turned to Newton. "I am ready now, Newt. Please."

Julian stepped up, still cradling Newton. Vadette caught the sniffling child's hand and kissed the back of it. "I will always be a part of you. We share blood like any brother and sister. But you have a new sister now. You've a family and a lifetime to love them."

Julian settled Newton on the ground and stepped back. Newton reached up to pin the brooch in place on Vadette's gown. Her arms enfolded him, hugging him as he cried. A thick fog clotted the air—slithering into place as suddenly as the storm had lifted. Through the clouded veil, Willow saw

Vadette release Newton and drift toward a soft light—a rift in the firmament where a man beckoned her to join him. Still holding Sala's hand, Willow waved her free palm, trying to clear the fog to see the face of Nadia's ethereal companion. But what she saw made no sense. It couldn't have been him...

Before she could make sense of it, the fog lifted and the rift had closed. It was as if Vadette and the man had never been there at all. Hearing swift footfalls splash through puddles, Willow jerked a glance toward the entrance to the Japanese gardens. Several actresses bustled down the path in their direction.

"They've found one of your troupe," a woman with a neck like an ostrich spouted to Josephine. "Found her drowned inside the water channel. The currents..." She caught a breath. "The flooding was too strong. It filled the channel. She was floating face down in the River Des Peres."

"Louisa!" Josephine screeched.

Looking back only once, Katherine jumped to action, following her troupe as they faded into the darkness. The ostrich-necked actress left to get help for Sala.

Silence again wreathed Willow and her small crew, all but the patter of mist falling around them.

Julian had picked up Newton to ease the boy's whimpering.

Willow studied them, the lantern glazing their disheveled appearances. Her friend, her lover ... the man she'd always dreamed would one day be her husband. And her tiny brother. So young. So damaged.

Then she turned to her father. An inanimate, shattered hull. His eyes were still shut, no longer even trying to open. Willow could see so much of herself in him now ... so much she hadn't allowed herself to see before. She traced the cleft in his chin, squeezing his hand in hers. His rings cut into her fingers. An impulse led her to slide off the hummingbird ring from his pinky and place it upon her finger, as he'd tried to on the train. All the years she'd envisioned the man responsible for her parents' deaths dying in the same excruciating way her mama had, but now here it was laid out before her, and all she wanted was to get back all the time lost with him. Did that make her a traitor to Mama's and Papa's memories?

"If he survives, he will need a personal physician," Julian finally spoke, interrupting the unsettling battle between her mind and emotions. "And many months—possibly years—of care. He might never be the same. Dependent upon others for even the smallest things. There are institutions in Italy .... they will be able to relate to him better there. Speak his language. You can visit him..."

Hot tears edged Willow's lashes, blending with the cool mist to a lukewarm stream of grief. She'd heard Sala's choppy attempts at English. She agreed, he would be more comfortable in such surroundings, especially during the grueling months of recuperation. But he would need hope to heal, and his children were the only things he loved enough to give him that will to fight.

She could not leave him there alone.

"Families belong together, Julian." She looked over her shoulder, humbled by Julian's beautiful compassion as he nuzzled her brother's hair with tears in his eyes. She swallowed back a sob. "My family will stay together. From this day forward..." She paused, for the bitter irony didn't escape her. Those were the very words she had once rehearsed as a young girl and saved in her heart for Julian. She nudged the ring on her finger. "From this day forward, we will never be parted."

"Then I go with you." Julian's voice was strong and

resolved where hers trembled. He held Newton closer to him. "You and Newton are my family now."

Willow's heart felt as if it were ripping in half. She clutched at the place over her sternum where she earlier wore the *Fontianna* brooch ... the place where Uncle Owen's pin-watch belonged. She'd lost that heirloom forever. Lost the one remaining piece of her past with her parents. She couldn't take that away from Julian. He'd never planned to live anywhere but The Manor of Diversions. For his entire life he'd wanted nothing more than to tend the grounds and the amusement park, to be there with his parents always and see it thrive.

"Your family *and* mine," Willow said, eyes burning. "Uncle Owen, Aunt Enya, Leander ... they need at least one of us there. You must go back to London. Emilia and your parents, they're struggling already with Nick gone. You've the park to maintain and build. The summer session starts soon. Your father is unable to run such things alone. Only you and I understand the mechanics behind it all. We can't both be gone for that long. Everything will fall apart."

Julian groaned in acknowledgement, a guttural sound that came from so deep within his chest it hurt Willow just to hear it. "But, Willomena ... without you *I'll* fall apart."

Diurnal assignments for Thursday, June 6, 1905:
1. ~~*Test the Looking Glass ride one last time before its premier;*~~ *2.* ~~*Assure the decorations are in place;*~~ *3. Breathe...*

Julian laid his pen upon the journal opened in his lap, leaning his nape against the oak's rough bark. He positioned himself so the sun dappling through the canopy overhead could warm his face. His eyes closed and he smelled the spice of magnolias on the morning breeze, letting it carry him back to a year ago, when things had been so different.

He grinned, a smile turned inward, remembering how Willow used to follow him here to this very spot. How much simpler things were then. His father once told him that simpler wasn't always sweeter.

Julian pondered that now, wrestling an uncomfortable jitter in his gut. He'd never told his father of the man he and Willow saw escorting Newton's phantom sister into heaven. He wondered how Father would feel about complexity, were he to know it had been his twin brother's ghost—Julian's dead Uncle Nicolas—helping the woman's spirit cross over.

Hearing a rustle in the shrubbery wall surrounding the tree, Julian glanced up and squinted, letting his lashes filter the bright sunlight. A lady's figure appeared in the opening ... a silhouette of grace and loveliness against the blue sky. Julian set aside his journal and stood, wiping grass from his linen trousers.

He held out his palm. "Miss Katherine. I had hoped you would come."

She allowed him to kiss the back of her gloved hand then laced her fingers over her gown, a lavishly tiered ensemble of alternating lace and hand-beaded embroidery. Her upswept hair sported fresh flowers the apricot hue of sunrise.

"Lovely dress," Julian said, trying to be cordial.

"Thank you. I bought it at the Ladies' Mile in New York. And do not worry. The other girls and I don't intend to spend all of the money from the latchets on apparel." She grinned. "In fact, we have found an apartment to let in London, until we can acquire some acreage whereupon to build a home."

"Congratulations." He tried to frame his next words carefully. "Did you not read the invitation? It is to be a casual affair today."

"Oh, I intend to change." She blushed, the tiny bump of cartilage on her nose darkening to a deeper red than her cheeks. "I just returned from seeing your sister's butterfly conservatory. She insisted we dress thus, in the case we were to meet any of your eligible guests on our tour."

"Ah." Julian smoothed his braided hair and dropped his hat on his head. "Always thinking ahead, that one."

Katherine's breath whistled in the resulting uncomfortable silence, and her gaze swept Julian's hiding place. "Do you come here often?"

The jitters in Julian's stomach renewed with all the force of a hornet's nest. "What say we cut to the chase, aye?"

Her gold eyes glistened. Smirking, she delved into the pocket-bag tied about her waist. She handed him a satiny handkerchief. "I hope it meets your expectations."

Eagerly, Julian unwrapped the slick fabric, revealing the mother-of-pearl pin-watch Uncle Owen had given Willow upon her first trip to Ridley's—her good luck charm. "Hello, old friend." His smile deepened as he turned it over to see the inscription on the back. He met Katherine's gaze. "Perfect. When I received your missive telling me you'd found this..." He lifted it, watching the metal cast flashes of light on a cluster of magnolias behind Katherine. "I couldn't believe it. After all these months. I thought it was lost forever."

"I apologize that it took so long to find. When we'd checked into our hotel, before the theft was to take place, Louisa had taken a box of things to have sent back home, with instructions for our maid to put them in storage." Katherine's countenance darkened. "When we took Louisa's body to Italy to be buried, the maid gave me the box. It took me months before I was ready to look through her things. But when I did"— her face brightened with a smile—"there was the pin-watch, wrapped within a handkerchief. Louisa lied when she told Willow it would be waiting by the riverbank. For once, her deceit proved a blessing. Otherwise, it would have been washed away in that storm."

Julian nodded, still mesmerized by the reflections of light dancing from the silver metal to the white flowers in the background. He rewrapped the watch within the handkerchief and tucked it in his trouser pocket. "What you did for Willow ... helping her steal the shoes ... helping her smuggle them onto the fairgrounds that night. I never had the chance to thank you properly. You've proven yourself a true friend. I only hope you have no regrets."

Katherine glanced down, nudging a fallen magnolia with her shoe. A butterfly came to light on her toe and she stilled, letting it flap its wings in time with her whistling nose. "I believe everything happens for a reason, Master Thornton. If this was the only way for Willow to be reunited with her family ... well, then it was all for the best."

The butterfly took to the air, fluttering like the nerves in Julian's stomach. "Have you visited Willow and Sala?" he asked, his throat drying on the question.

Katherine's lips curved up on one side. "I have."

"And ... how is she?"

"Have you not seen her yet?"

Julian shrugged, his linen shirt gaping open at the neck in the absence of a cravat. "I can't face her. One look at her and ... well, I fear I would ruin everything. I wrote her a note."

"Hmm." Katherine glanced over her shoulder. "That in mind, I shouldn't be here with you too long without a chaperone. Just think of the gossip your guests could contrive."

"Good point." Julian escorted her through the opening. "I'll see you soon."

"Very soon." As she strolled away, her voice had a teasing lilt which exacerbated Julian's emotional unease.

He settled once more beneath the tree, lowering his hat's brim over his eyes to attempt a short nap before time to make his debut, knowing all along his mind would not allow it. Of late, his thoughts often spun out of control, fraught with worry, mainly for his brother. They had received a letter from Nick in January, announcing that his infant son had died during birth. Nick had never sounded so devastated and despondent. Since then, they'd lost all contact with him, with no word as to where he and his wife were living. This news had cast a dark cloud over all of the Thorntons. Julian hoped that within the next few weeks, he could offer something to help ameliorate some of that pain.

His eyelids snapped open as a cold droplet plopped on his nose. He reached up, transferring it to his fingertip. The sticky, red goop brought a smile to his face. *Raspberry ice.*

"Sharing your breakfast again?" He turned his gaze upward where Newton hung in the branches like a drowsing sloth and nibbled the icy treat—a habit his sister had wasted little time passing on to him.

Upon slurping the last bite, Newton tossed down the metal cup and dropped to the ground with all the grace and confidence of an aerial virtuoso. His stained lips and teeth turned up in a goading sneer. He gestured in the direction of the amusement park.

"They sent you to fetch me did they?" Julian grinned. "Perhaps they thought I was to make a run for it?"

Newton snorted then shaped his fingers and hands into

words. Julian's mother had been teaching the boy to sign. At this point, everyone in the townhouse, even the servants, knew the basic signs so they could accommodate Newton's needs. The only problem was, the boy tended to get ahead of himself in conversations, talking too fast.

Julian reached out to stall Newton's hands. "Say again?"

The mouse formed the statement once more, his cherubic face stiff with concentration.

"Oh-ho! You think *she* would catch me, do you? Ha! Surely you don't think her faster."

Newton crossed his arms, smug.

Julian laughed. "True enough. We both know she is. But she has been a bit slower of late. Perhaps I might beat her this once?"

Newton's eyes rolled.

Julian sighed. "Right again. It's emasculating, to say the least." When he didn't stand, Newton grunted and caught his sleeve's cuff, tugging him. "Fine, fine." Battling an erratic heartbeat, Julian stood and dusted himself off one last time, bending to retrieve his journal and pen. "Lead the way, Sir Importunate."

Julian and Newton strolled toward the trellised archway beneath the familiar swinging sign. He held Newton's hand, more for his own comfort than the child's. By now, Newton knew the grounds inside and out. The parapets flapped overhead in a honeysuckle breeze, a mere wash of sound beneath the myriad of conversations taking place amongst his guests: the elite of London, here at the opening of the summer season to partake in the special ceremony.

Everything glistened with morning dew, contributing to the magical allure Julian had hoped to portray with the runners of gold crape and silver sarcenet he'd draped along the wrought iron fence. His father had contributed strands of lights from the star tower, and his mother added her own hat-maker's touch: flower swags made of dried blossoms. The petals were tipped with silver paint and glitter. She brushed glue along the stems and leaves which, when coated with iridescent seed beads, looked as if they were kissed with frost. The final result was a glistening spectacle—winter captured within a setting of summer.

Upon walking past the entrance, Newton broke free and ran toward *The Looking Glass* ride at the park's farthest end. Julian wanted to run with him, but didn't have the benefit of unbridled youth. Winding through the crowd to shake hands with the attendees, he wrestled another bout of nerves. It wasn't so much about being the center of attention. It was about wanting to please *her* ... to bring her even a fraction of the happiness she'd always given him so effortlessly and without reserve. Only when he'd succeeded in that feat could he breathe again.

All those months, while Willow had been at the hospital in Italy with Sala, Julian had nigh lost his mind missing her. The one thing that kept him grounded was planning and building her ride. Each time she came home with Newton for a visit, he would take her hand and lead them both to the site, allowing Willow a chance to view the newest advancements before requesting her input. Without fail, she offered suggestions that always trumped any of the workers' decisions, and ultimately improved the final product.

Julian had been determined for the undertaking to be their brainchild, something he and Willow shared in giving birth to. Practice, he hypothesized, for one day when they shared a real child of flesh and blood.

The scent of grass and greenery piqued his senses, and Julian glanced about. He had made the required rounds, sufficiently milling through all of his guests. Looking past the Ferris wheel and the other rides, he winced from the glare in the mirrored façade of his premier ride. The gigantic pocket watch pendulated and a wooden white rabbit's face winked atop the entrance tunnel where boats awaited boarding on the glistening water. Julian was to take the maiden voyage today. Pending any unforeseen bugs in the gearing, rides for all of the guests would commence thereafter.

Newton stood in front of the mirrors, surrounded by family. He and Bristles were entertaining the others, using Sala's and Uncle Owen's wheelchairs as platforms for the squirrel to jump from one whicker handlebar to the other. Newton held out a twig and the white ball of fur turned flips over it between landings.

Sala—paralyzed from the waist down due to spinal damage—had come to stay three months ago. It had been a fairly easy transition, since the manor already accommodated Uncle Owen's wheelchair. They renovated the ramps and hired a personal nurse for Sala. True to his generous nature, Uncle Owen had accepted Willow's newfound family into his own with open arms.

Julian watched the men now—Willow's two fathers— enjoying one another's company as if they were old friends who had travelled all of the same paths. Perhaps they had to some extent; for both of them had loved and lived for the same little girl throughout different stages of her life.

Emilia and Mother stood to one side with Father. On the other, Aunt Enya fussed over Leander's newborn daughter snuggled in a blanket within her mother's arms. They all looked up to see Bristles land expertly atop Newton's head. Willow appeared from behind Leander's tall frame and borrowed Newton's stick, coaxing the squirrel to clamber up to her shoulder. She tapped his fuzzy head gently with the twig and he leaned as if bowing, winning a piece of apple from Newton's fingertips. Everyone laughed and applauded.

It looked as if Emilia had a hand in all of the women's hairstyles today, for Willow wore the same flowers woven through her shoulder length locks as Miss Katherine had in hers. Only on Willow, the apricot petals paled to her radiant complexion.

As though feeling Julian's gaze, Willow glanced up to match his stare. Skittish tremors scattered in his gut. A sensual light shimmered behind her eyes, and he knew she'd read the note he'd left on her pillow after they'd made love just before dawn.

Even now, after all this time, Julian's heart still gave a tumble when he saw her. She'd given in to Aunt Enya and started wearing dresses of late: flowing, feminine, empire waist gowns in soft colors with hems of lace that came just to her ankle, though they had no crinolines or hoops to bind her. And she still refused to wear shoes on the manor during the warmer months, even on social occasions, much to Enya's constant annoyance.

Only a few feet from reaching his family, Julian came to a halt as Judge Arlington snagged his arm. "It is splendid lad!" His moustache wiggled in excitement. "In the pink of the mode, to be sure."

Julian patted his investor's shoulder, smiling at the American's attempt at the British slang. "I am glad you approve."

"And my family, they also approve."

Julian nodded to the judge's elegant wife and strapping adolescent sons waiting beside the newly painted carousel. "Well, without yours and Sala's contributions, it would never have come to fruition. Same for my sister's butterfly conservatory. Thank you for forgiving my impertinence in St. Louis."

The judge chortled. "Couldn't very well stay angry with you. After all, even that pantomime saw fit to forgive you after hearing yours and Miss Willow's story."

Julian smiled at the memory. He was fortunate the actress had been such a romantic at heart, or he would no doubt be imprisoned in the states today.

Once Sala had been rushed by buggy to the nearest hospital in St. Louis on that fateful night, Julian had been so worried Willow would leave with Newton and her father and stay forever in Italy, he'd asked her to marry him on the spot. She'd said yes—much to his relief—and since they could only manage an "exchange of consent" ceremony in such haste, he had sought out the judge at the Inside Inn to ask him to pull some strings and arrange a common license. The judge agreed, on the grounds he was allowed to officiate. Three days later, Judge Arlington accompanied Julian to the hospital and married them in the chapel. A chaplain, two nurses, Newton, and Leander—who had arrived in St. Louis to a letter informing him of where to find his family—had all stood as witnesses.

Willow and Julian honeymooned for two weeks at the Inside Inn as Sala healed enough to travel. She didn't comment on why a honeymoon should last so long, since solitude was rare between visits to the hospital, taking care of Newton, and Julian's appointments with artists, inventors, and scientists that the judge had met at the World's Fair, intriguing them with stories of Julian's amusement park.

Thankfully, Judge Arlington and Leander stepped in from time to time when Newton would allow them to take him from his sister's side. In those cherished moments, Julian did just as he'd once promised: learned every precept and secret of his new bride's beautiful body—until, with just a glance, a word, or a touch he could make her eyes shimmer, her voice plead, and her skin glow. Until they were no longer unmoored, but deeply anchored, two souls once lost at sea becoming one complete being, secure upon their own island paradise.

Once Sala was strong enough to be transferred, Willow and Newton left with him for Italy alongside Sala's girls. A few days later, Julian and Leander took another ship to London where Julian had been ever since, waiting like a man starving for each visit his new bride could spare.

"Are you ready then?" Judge Arlington asked, shaking Julian back to the present.

Julian nodded, wrestling the quivery twist in his chest. "Ready as I'll ever be. Do you remember your lines?"

"Of course." The judge patted his rotund belly. "I'm not all gluttony and boon. I have a brain, you know."

"Right-ho." Julian grinned and tipped his hat's brim. "Round up our guests."

While the judge circulated the crowd, hedging everyone in the direction of the ride's entrance, Julian returned his parents' proud smiles. He saw Nick's absence in the marked shadows behind their expressions, and relived that knife-slash to his heart ... the phantom reminder of the amputated portion of his soul that he prayed would one day find its way back home.

The sadness faded as Willow stepped up, drawing him aside.

"It's not the same without him, is it?" As always, she knew Julian's thoughts. She placed his palm upon her burgeoning abdomen—a reminder of all the hope life had to offer. "But your brother will find us again. After he finds himself." Her hand covered Julian's, her hummingbird ring nudging the gold band upon his left hand. She stole his breath with a maternal smile. "Now, onto other matters. You have been avoiding me today," she scolded, changing the subject with all the deftness of a politician.

"Never." Julian grinned. "Just ... had a list of things to accomplish."

"Did you finish?"

He gulped a knot from his throat. "I've one more left."

"Huh. I am astounded you made such progress with your spectacles missing as they are." Her nose twitched, holding her lips from curling upward.

"Ah. As to that..." His free hand lifted out his wired frames from his trouser pocket and he blew several blackish-brown crumbs off the lenses. "Fine hiding place—the coffee tin."

"Thank you. I thought it rather fitting. What with your fondness for wearing food."

Grinning, he settled the aromatic spectacles in place on his nose and pulled her closer for a hug, his left hand growing warm on her belly.

Willow and he had been indulging in a new game of late, stealing things from one another and hiding them. Julian had suggested it, to appease Willow's innate penchant for thievery while keeping her out of trouble. Not to mention, it kept their relationship exciting and fresh.

"I must wonder ... have *you* anything gone missing today?" he asked against her bared neck, pleased that she'd worn her shoulder-length hair in a chignon for him.

She leaned back and narrowed her eyes at him. "My cameo choker, in fact."

"Intriguing. Wonder where that might've walked off to." Before Willow could respond, a rolling shove from within her womb bubbled beneath his hand. "Ha! Did you feel that?"

She laughed. "Of course I felt it, pollywompus. From both

sides." Her hand squeezed his and her face beamed. "I believe it to be his head."

Julian grinned back. "Or her posterior. Seems rather big for a babe's cranium."

"Oh posh. Not if *he's* to be a brilliant mechanist like his father."

"I rather imagine *she* will be a gifted acrobat like her mother and Uncle Newt. In which case, the plump posterior will help soften her falls."

Willow snorted. "Is *that* what this is for?" She gestured to her buttocks which, much like other parts or her body, had developed a more womanly cushion over the past few months.

"I already showed you what that is for." Julian leaned close so only her ears could hear. "This morning? The electron-spin."

"Oh, right," she purred. "I remember."

He pulled her arms up around his neck. Her protruding abdomen rubbed his groin and he had to temper his body's overzealous reaction. He leaned in to nuzzle the flora of her hair, winding his fingers through the silken strands, careful not to loosen her flowers. He pressed his lips to her forehead. "I love you."

She snuggled against him. "Mmm. And I you. By the by, you have far superseded your quota today by at least a dozen recitations. And this is only the first time I've seen you since dawn."

"You don't say? I was keenly unaware hand-written proclamations of how I plan to show my love later tonight counted. Wouldn't wish to supersede my tally. I'll have to bear that in mind hence and make allowances."

"Do. Not. Dare." Her finger poked his chest upon each word.

Sporting a side-long smirk, he fished the handkerchief from his pocket. "For you." He studied the dimple in her chin as she unwrapped the cloth.

She gasped, holding up the pin. Her eyes lit to that luminous glassy-green which always waited for him in his best fantasies.

"You found it?" She held the watch's face to her cheek, as though warming it with her skin.

"Look on the back." He brought it down and flipped it over.

"Willomena Antoniette *Thornton*." She shook her head, beaming. "How did you ever make time to have it engraved again?"

Julian helped her pin the watch on her bodice. "I begged some assistance from a mutual friend."

Tears sparkled behind her gaze. Julian savored the vision. In the past, Willow would've despised falling prey to such a sissified display of emotion. But during these last few months of her pregnancy, she'd surrendered the fight and simply let herself weep at the drop of a hat. Julian found her new vulnerability very alluring, and had told her so countless times.

"Thank you," she whispered, lifting to her bare toes so she could kiss him, uncaring as to the startled gasps and clucking tongues of their spectators.

"This is highly improper behavior," came Aunt Enya's muttered reproach from over his shoulder. Willow's lips curved to an impish smirk beneath his as they finished the kiss—taking their time about it.

Once they'd parted, Willow punched his ribs playfully. "Auntie is right, you insatiable rogue. Your audience awaits." With a flick of her chin, she gestured to the gathering crowd who had softened their conversations to a low murmur.

Julian traced her full lower lip with his thumb. "That would be *our* audience."

Her eyebrows arched curiously. "No. You alone deserve the acclaim, Julian. You designed the ride."

"They are not here to celebrate some petty ride. They're here to witness a wedding. Or so said their invitations."

"A wedding? Whose?"

Judge Arlington took his place as Julian and Willow's family blended into the audience, knowing smiles on all of their faces. It had grown so quiet that even the birds and wind seemed to hush in the lull.

Julian knelt to one knee, reaching for Willow's hand. His lungs tightened, contracting to the point he could hardly catch a breath. His tongue stuck to the roof of his mouth and sweat beaded his brow. He felt every bit as anxious as the first time he confessed his love. "Willomena Antoniette Thornton." He swallowed. "Will you marry me again ... here before the cream of society?" Another swallow. "To prove once and for all that I am proud to have you by my side for life, in the off chance you still have any doubts."

Her bottom lip disappeared beneath her top teeth, an obvious attempt to hold back tears. "You planned this, for me?" She glanced over his head at their family. "And all of you knew?"

"They helped with the planning, in fact." Julian nodded toward the mirrored façade and the boats drifting behind her. "All the way down to our sailing into Wonderland. We are to take the maiden cruise together." He kissed her knuckles.

Her eyes settled on him again and she patted her belly. "It's rather obvious I'm no longer a maiden, *il mio piccolo cavolo*."

Hearty chuckles from several of the men in the audience

stirred Julian to smile. Responding to Willow's tug on his hand, he stood. She threw her arms around him.

He held her close. "Are you happy then ... happy enough to never need wander any further than our rides will take us?"

"I am."

"Then I'll see you stay that way." He stretched her to arm's length. Holding her gaze, he positioned her to face him in front of Judge Arlington.

The judge opened his Bible. Before he spoke, Julian held up his hand. "Wait." He drew out his journal from his pocket and flipped through the pages. Finding this morning's entry, he marked out the final task then tucked the book away.

His fingers laced through Willow's as they faced each other once more, and at last, he inhaled.

End

Now that you've finished *The Hummingbird Heart*, please help support the author by writing an honest review on Amazon, Goodreads, and other online sales sites of your choice. Authors make their living off of sales, and reviews are the most effective way for new readers to discover their books. Many thanks! Also, be sure to watch for the next installment in the Haunted Hearts Legacy, *The Glass Butterfly*, coming your way August 15, 2018!